Every home has a story to tell

60 Suntides Boulevard

Derek Wachter

"Every house has a story to tell…."

-Riley Sager

Table of Contents

Chapter 1	Pg. 4
Chapter 2	16
Chapter 3	34
Chapter 4	46
Chapter 5	55
Chapter 6	64
Chapter 7	77
Chapter 8	83
Chapter 9	97
Chapter 10	112
Chapter 11	118
Chapter 12	126
Chapter 13	134
Chapter 14	145
Chapter 15	155
Chapter 16	163
Chapter 17	171
Chapter 18	179
Chapter 19	189
Chapter 20	200
Chapter 21	210
Chapter 22	221
Chapter 23	238
Epilogue	249

CHAPTER 1

The second hand slowly ticked by on a small gold clock on a desktop that read 4:45 p.m. It was a special clock, a Christmas gift from 5, maybe 6 years ago. It was Friday, March 14th, and the day seemingly had gone well for Angela Kennedy, one of two secretaries for Marshall and Stone Family Law Firm of Portland, Oregon - a very busy law firm specializing in family and divorce law located on the fourth floor of the Ed Hock Business Center. A law firm service Angela would soon use for herself, as her husband Todd of fourteen years had grown fond of a younger woman ten years his junior, whom he had met at his company's Christmas party a few months prior.

The phone rang on the glossy walnut desktop, and the time on the gold chrome Christmas gift read 4:56 p.m.

"Oh great," Angela said to herself. "One more client and four minutes before I get to leave for the day."

Although Angela didn't seem to care about leaving work. This would be the first weekend she had spent alone. Her soon-to-be ex had already moved out of their home, the one they had been living in for the fourteen years they were together. Her ex now lived in his new, younger girlfriend's home in an area called Camas, a suburb just outside of Portland. It seemed fitting, as they appeared happy together, even if it came at Angela's own expense.

Angela's best friend, Miss Jennifer Rose, who was the second secretary and Angela's "left-hand woman" (as she was positioned on the left side of Angela at work), instinctively had a feeling that something was wrong with Angela, starting from a few months back when things went bad in her life. Really, Jennifer knew more about Angela than Angela's own mother, simply because the two confided in each other all the time.

"Okay ma'am, I've set an appointment for you to meet with Mr. Stone on Wednesday the 19th, at 9 a.m. Will that work for you?" Angela briefly paused and listened to the client over the phone.

Jennifer could overhear the client on the other end talking loudly to Angela. Hopefully, she wouldn't give Angela a headache from the excessive volume of her voice. Angela listened intently to the client and then replied, "Thank you Ms. Gladstone, excuse me, Ms. Gladstone, we will see you then. Okay, bye-bye."

"Angela, it's time to leave work for the day. Meaning that it's time to enjoy your weekend," Jennifer said.

"There is no enjoying this weekend, Jennifer, nor any other weekend," Angela replied. "This is the first spring that Todd hasn't been in the house. This spring marks the first time Todd hasn't been around the house. We used to spend our weekends cooking breakfast together, tackling yard work and household chores side by side, and then winding down the day with an evening out or simply cozying up on the couch to watch a movie. Going home doesn't feel right, Jennifer. I'm tired of returning to an empty house."

Jennifer knew that she may have just opened a conversation that could last a few minutes, or even a few hours. As much as she loved Angela, sitting and listening to her share what was going on in her life at the time was depressing.

"What do you mean, you don't want to go home?" Jennifer asked.

"I've been thinking about something since I knew Todd and I were going to divorce, and that being…I don't want to live in that home anymore. I've put it up for sale just this last week and I need to sell it and move on with my life. I need to."

Jennifer breathed a sigh of relief, realizing the conversation shouldn't last too long.

"That is admirable, Angela. I know things are difficult for you right now. I'm happy to be there as your friend. Whenever you need me. Have you told your family yet?"

"No, just you. And well, Mr. Marshall, obviously since he is handling the divorce paperwork for me and thank God at a reasonable price, too," Angela said. "I've thought about telling my parents, but I know my mom will launch into one of her lengthy lectures about how she and Dad have been together for nearly 40 years. She'll say things like, 'If you truly love him, work it out,' and then give me a laundry list of solutions for my problems. I don't need to hear that right now. They won't be supportive."

"What are you doing tonight?" Jennifer asked.

"Nothing. Just going home to that damn empty house."

"Let's go out for dinner. We'll look at some new places for you to move into and tonight, we will start your new life. No more sad and depressed feelings." Jennifer got up, grabbed her coat and purse, and asked, "Where do you want to go tonight for dinner?"

"I really don't know, Jenn. I'm not even sure if I'm really that hungry. I can't stop thinking about how bad things went so fast," Angela said.

"Great! I know a place near downtown. You like Mexican food?"

"I don't like spicy foods."

"How about Chinese food?"

"I don't care for Chinese food. The last time I had Chinese food I got as sick as I've ever been in my life."

"There's a new burger place down by the Columbia River. Nice, quiet, great food and they have salads! I went here for my birthday last year. Let's go there."

"Oh Jennifer, your enthusiasm cheers me up. Okay, let's go."

Deep down inside, Angela knew what Jennifer was trying to do. Angela slowly pulled herself up, put a fake smile on her face, logged out of her computer, and grabbed her coat and purse. Along the way out of the office, Mr. Marshall wished the girls a good weekend and asked them to turn off the lights on their way out.

Jennifer walked out the double glass doors of the office with the writing of Marshall and Stone Family Law sprawled in gold lettering, followed closely behind by Angela. Pausing for a moment, Angela grabbed the door handle, flipped the light switches off and shut the door, leaving the only light in the office on in Mr. Marshall's office. Even Mr. Stone's light was out as he had left earlier in the day to begin his vacation with his family in a coastal town in Oregon called Waldport. When Mr. Stone had told the girls about his vacation trip 3 weeks ago, it had brought back a flood of emotion in Angela. It was the same beach where Todd had proposed to her years ago. Angela simply pretended to have an allergy attack to explain why she cried that day, especially since she hadn't told Mr. Stone what was going on in her life just yet.

Angela and Jennifer walked down a long corridor hallway filled with doors to other offices. One office was a local candle shipping business, while another was a mortgage lending company. The elevators were conveniently located at the end of the hallway and to the right of the elevators was a janitor's maintenance closet that the janitorial staff used as their own office. The small room contained a little 13" flat screen television with pirated cable channels.

Angela never figured out how they managed to run stolen cable channels to the TV in that room. Most days, she just continued on her merry way to the elevator, sometimes opting to take the stairs.

Tonight, Jennifer beat Angela to the elevator and pushed the red downward facing arrow. Jennifer turned to Angela and said, "Downstairs in the coffee shop, there is a rental and home sale magazine. We can grab it and take it with us to the restaurant to look through. That mortgage lending company compiles a list of different realtors in the area. We could pick that up and look through it over dinner."

"To be honest, Jenn, what would I do with that?" Angela asked.

"Okay. This may sound like a crazy idea, but I totally think you should get your own place! Sell that depressed, empty house and start fresh! Start new Angie!"

"Jenn, I can't afford that."

"Why not? You said yourself that you've had people drive by that house and comment about how nice it is. I bet if you put it on the open market, it would sell fast!"

"Well, okay. We'll grab the magazine before we leave."

Angela felt a mix of emotions at the thought of selling her home. It was a home that she had worked hard for, but had still relied on her husband's support. The more Angela thought about it, the more she realized that the house she was living in represented the fact that she couldn't do it by herself. She always needed the support of her husband to pay the bills, the mortgage and to stock the house with furniture, goods and even groceries. Without her husband's financial support, it never would've worked.

Maybe Jennifer's idea wasn't such a bad idea after all. The idea of a fresh start lit a fire inside Angela that she hadn't felt in a long time.

Jennifer had grown accustomed to seeing Angela sad every Friday afternoon for the past few months, but now even Jennifer saw a different type of gleam in Angela's eyes. She could see the wheels turning in Angela's mind, her thoughts racing.

The elevator door dinged loudly. Slowly, its doors creaked open, and the girls rushed in just before the doors slammed shut. The doors were too temperamental. If maintenance wasn't so busy watching their stolen cable television in their room, then maybe they could fix the doors so that a girl didn't have to rush into the elevator. Luckily, the doors never caught Angela or Jennifer, but they both imagined the devastating fate that awaited the poor soul that didn't know the doors closed so fast.

The elevator carried them downward until it dinged when they arrived on the first floor. As true to how it worked, the doors slowly opened and both Angela and Jennifer raced out before the elevator acted as a guillotine and chopped one of them in half.

On the first floor was a carpeted lobby, in need of being shampooed and cleaned. A coffee stand called "The Coffee John" was operating its small stand near the entrance to the building. They did great business there, as many workers of the building stopped for their world-famous caramel macchiato coffee drinks. Well, at least they were famous in the building. Outside of the building, maybe not so much.

Jennifer stopped by the coffee shop and grabbed the home rentals and sales magazine. Jennifer blushed as she waved at her favorite barista, a young man named Jeff.

It was no secret to Angela that Jennifer had a crush on the barista. Jennifer stopped by the stand for her caramel macchiato coffee on her way to work every day. Angela knew that she only did this to see and talk to Jeff. Angela quickly caught on to Jennifer's feelings towards Jeff as one day a few months back she remarked, "You seem to like coffee a lot now all the sudden. You've had it every working day for the last month."

Jennifer's face turned red that day and she ignored Angela's comment, although the two mutually knew why Jennifer was suddenly an everyday coffee drinker.

The two girls exited the building through the glass doors and walked towards the parking garage together.

"Where are we going, Jenn?" Angela asked.

"To Bob's Burgers," Jennifer replied.

"Should I follow you to Bob's Burgers?"

"No, we'll just take my car and I'll bring you back here. It's easier that way rather than fighting through Portland's five o'clock traffic and trying to follow one another," Jennifer said.

Angela was very nervous about riding with Jennifer. She knew Jennifer was not the greatest driver in the world. In fact, the last time they were in the car together, Jennifer nearly crashed into a parked car along the side of Sherwood Lane, near Angela's soon-to-be previously owned home. That was three months ago, at her office Christmas party. Just the thought of her Christmas party alone brought back the feeling of Todd leaving her again. For the past two months Angela cried herself to sleep at night, but now crying wasn't an option for her anymore. There were no more tears to cry out.

Another day of rain in the great Pacific Northwest. Jennifer and Angela forgot their umbrellas upstairs in the office. They elected not to go back for them and instead dashed to Jennifer's car. Jennifer unlocked the door and jumped in while Angela opened her door and was met with the smell of strawberries, Jenn's favorite car scent. If she opened the glove box to her car, she would've found at least 6 packs of strawberry car fresheners ready to replace the one that would eventually lose its potency.

Angela jumped into Jenn's car and quickly shut the door. Jennifer started her car and fidgeted with the defogger.

"So earlier today, around noon, I got a phone call from a husband who wanted to make an appointment to speak with either Mr. Marshall or Mr. Stone. After I had made an appointment for him, he told me he caught his wife messing around with his neighbor's wife! Apparently, after she had given birth to their firstborn, she got chummy with their neighbors. I guess the wife of the neighbor will be calling us soon now, too. Can you believe that?" Jennifer asked.

"I'm sorry Jenn. I don't really care. Everyone cheats on everyone. It's basically only a matter of time."

"That's not true Angela. Some couples have been faithful to each other for years. Sometimes things happen and mistakes are made."

The mood in the car turned awkward. To pass time through the 5 o'clock traffic, Angela began thumbing through the magazine that Jennifer had picked up in the coffee shop. Angela was also trying to avoid watching Jennifer's driving skills. How she didn't get into more accidents amazed her.

While looking through the magazine, Angela noticed that a lot of homes were near a million dollars and located in high priced communities. Some gated, no less. Angela knew that her price range, now that she was living on her own, was going to be much lower than a million dollars. That revelation disheartened Angela. Maybe she needed to move back in with her parents. Even though she didn't want that. Perhaps she could ask Jennifer to be her roommate?

Angela didn't like this idea. She loved Jennifer to death. However, the two would kill each other if they had to live together in less than a week's time. Some people are amazing friends, but they're just not meant to live together, she thought. Angela rolled up the magazine and placed it in her purse.

True to her driving ways, Jennifer nearly side swiped a nearby garbage truck, drove above the speed limit and ran two red lights on their way down to the river. In Jennifer's defense, one of the two lights was changing from yellow to red. While Angela disagreed with her friend's driving, at least they arrived safely at Bob's Burgers as the car came to a halt, brakes squeaking as Jennifer swerved into the parking lot.

"You are going to love this place, Angela!" Jennifer said. "They really have the best burgers in Portland! I would say all of Oregon! Maybe even the Pacific Northwest!"

Angela knew this place already. For their 10-year Anniversary Todd had taken Angela here. Todd always liked the view of the Columbia River from the back-patio seating area and Angela didn't really care, she just loved spending time with Todd.

Jennifer parked the car, two spots away from the front entrance, right next to the handicap stalls. It was as close as they could get without having special state handicap plates. Together, they rushed out of the car and into the restaurant, doing their best to avoid the evening downpour.

"Good evening, ladies," the host said. "Can I interest you in a table at our lounge and bar? Or would you like to be seated near a window table overlooking the river?"

Before Angela could say anything, Jennifer immediately spoke up and said, "The window table, please! I love the view of the river from the patio. You will too, Angie."

Angela smirked as if she agreed with Jenn, but she didn't really care about the view anymore.

The host led them through the crowded restaurant and past the bustling bar area, where Angela was certain that some drunk bystander had "inadvertently" touched her side, but Angela didn't care to listen to an excuse me or an apology. Angela was grateful for the rain now as she desperately wanted to sit inside instead of conjuring up old feelings by sitting at the same patio where her and Todd shared their 10th anniversary.

The host sat them at a table overlooking the river across from another couple sitting behind them. They looked happy. Angela figured they were celebrating their own anniversary.

Angela stared through a glass window at the table she and Todd had previously sat at for their own anniversary dinner. Waves of blurry memories laced in melancholy flooded through her mind. Angela remembered what her soon to be ex-husband said that day that, "he would always love her to the end of his life and do anything for her."

That lying son of a bitch.

The girls glanced through the drink menu as they looked across the river to Washington State. It surprised both Angela and Jennifer that the table was even open, and on a Friday evening, no less. Jennifer ordered her favorite drink, a white Russian and Angela ordered her drink, a Smith & Kearns.

"Very good," the host said. "Your server will be here shortly with your drinks and to take your order."

The host scurried away, leaving Angela to stew in quiet turmoil as she watched the rain patter down into the river.

"Can I say something?" Jennifer asked.

"Sure."

"I know things for you are rough right now. You've been living in that house for a couple of months by yourself, and I think it would be good for you to take what you have and sell it for a fresh start."

"Jenn, I haven't been completely honest about something. I think your idea is good. In fact, I thought it was a good idea a couple of weeks ago because I already put the house up for sale. I just haven't told you yet. I guess I'm still coming to terms with everything that has happened to me over the course of the last three months when I found out Todd was cheating on me. Him moving out of the house made things even more surreal, and I just didn't want to believe that this would happen to me."

"Why didn't you tell me?"

"I was scared. I didn't know if I was doing the right thing or not, but when you mentioned it too, I guess I felt reassured that maybe it was. And well, I haven't told you this yet, or anyone else, but a buyer is already interested in the home. And in all honesty…"

The waitress interrupted Angela's train of thought as she appeared with their drinks in tow.

"Are you ladies ready to order?" asked the waitress.

"Oh, no. Not yet. We haven't even looked at the menu yet. Could you give us like 10 minutes?" Jennifer asked.

"Of course," she said and placed two napkins down on the table and gave a slight nod before she walked away.

"So, you were saying, Angie?"

"Oh. Well, I really want to sell the house and move out."

"So...do you want to leave Portland?" Jennifer asked hesitantly.

Angela knew that Jennifer didn't want to ask that question. She was nervous about the answer she could get. The thought of Angela moving out of Portland to a different city was sure to upset her.

"No, I don't want to leave Portland. I want to stay in a nearby suburb. I have friends here, you're here, my church is here, my grocery store. I'm just not sure where I want to move around here yet, is all."

Jennifer smiled. "Well, okay then! Where is the magazine, we picked up at the coffee shop? Let's look through it."

Angela pulled the crumpled, rolled-up magazine from her purse, feeling discouraged as she looked at the high prices of the homes advertised on the front page, which were listed for millions of dollars. The cheapest home available was a nice 3-bedroom, 2-bathroom property near a vineyard of Cabernet Sauvignon grape vines, listed at $900,000. Shoot, that was disheartening. "The dream dies on the first page," Angie thought.

"Never mind those houses. Not everything around here is a million dollars. Keep looking," Jennifer said.

The two flipped through the magazine, looking for anything that would be a starter home. Sure enough, Jenn was right. Home prices seemed to be a bit more manageable for Angie. This was encouraging and brought hope to Angie's heart that the possibility of making it on her own could happen after all.

Angela wanted something with a fenced backyard. She always wanted to get a dog for home protection, as well as having another living creature to share her time with so that she wasn't so alone. Preferably a border collie. Something that would be a true and loyal companion, who wouldn't abandon her like Todd had.

"Hey how about this one?" Jennifer asked.

"Jenn, this says Astoria."

"Yeah, that's like a suburb of Portland, isn't it?"

"No, it's on the northern corner of the Oregon Coast. I'm not commuting from Astoria to Portland. What other homes are there for sale?"

The two continued to flip through the magazine, randomly finding a home or two that fell within in the price range Angela could afford on her own. However, each of these homes appeared to be in the neighborhoods of Portland, where you'd would need more than just a dog to sleep safely and soundly at night—perhaps an armed police officer to watch the house 24 hours a day. Finally, three pages towards the end of the magazine, Jennifer spotted it first.

"What about this one?" Jenn asked.

"Ladies, would you like to order now?" the returning waitress asked.

"Oh," Jennifer said, startled. "Has it been 10 minutes already? Yes, we can. Can we just get a couple of cheeseburgers, please?"

"Can you put mushrooms on mine, please?" Angela asked.

"Hold the onions on mine," said Jennifer.

"Of course. Would you guys like fries, salad, or chips as your side?"

"Fries please!" the girls said simultaneously.

"Sounds good. I'll have those out right away. Are your drinks, okay?" the waitress asked.

"Yes, they're great," Angela said.

With that, the waitress turned and left the table. Angie and Jennifer looked back over the magazine where Jenn had pointed out the house before being interrupted by the waitress.

On page 17 of the Portland Suburbs Real Estate magazine was a nice 3-bedroom, 1.5-bathroom home for sale. Remarkably, it was being sold dirt cheap, well within Angela's price range. It even had a fenced-in backyard and was in one of the better Portland communities called Suntides.

Angela looked for something in the property's description, anything really. Water well problems? Problems with the roof? Was the foundation caving in? Plumbing issues? Was the ceiling falling apart? Was this some sort of fixer upper requiring thousands of more dollars to make the home even livable, let alone comfortable? However, she couldn't find anything wrong with it in the magazine's advertisement. For all these reasons, this home was meant for her, given her current situation.

"Call the realtor! Let's see it. It'll give us both something to do tomorrow," Jennifer said.

Angela was hesitant at first. She wasn't really expecting to find a home so fast, but what could it hurt? She wasn't signing a contract by simply asking to see the home. And for the asking price of the home, it would be a terrible decision to not at least look.

"Okay, I'll call. Do you think they're open on a Saturday?" Angela asked.

"Sure. They're realtors, Angie. They will be open whenever you want them to sell you a house." Jennifer said with a smile on her face.

"Alright, I'm going to call right now."

Angela pulled out her cell phone from her purse, flipped open the phone and punched in the numbers to the realtor who was showing the house. She hadn't been this excited about something for a long time now. Angela was finally doing something for herself, albeit with a little encouragement from her friend, but she was doing things for herself. Good for you, she thought to herself.

The phone rang once before she heard a deep, old voice answered with a homely tone and a slight southern drawl. "McGuire Realtor Service, Jack McGuire speaking. How can I help you?"

"Yes hi, I'm calling about a property that is listed through your realty service. I would like to see it tomorrow, if that is at all possible?" Angela asked.

"Of course it is, sweetheart. I would be happy to show you any of our listed properties. Which one are you looking to see?" Mr. McGuire asked.

"Well, I don't have my information about me on file with your realty service. I've never done business with you or any other realtor around here by myself. I would like to come see property number 166682 if I can. It's listed in the March edition of the Portland Suburbs Real Estate magazine," Angela said.

She heard the rustling of papers in the background on the other end of the phone, followed by a momentary pause of silence. A silence deep enough that Angela could hear the distant tick of a clock in Mr. McGuire's office.

"Oh, yes. Over there in the Suntides area. Okay, okay. I can show you that property tomorrow. What time will work for you best, my dear?"

Angela detected a small bit of hesitation in Mr. McGuire's voice. However, she didn't think much about it.

"What time works best for you tomorrow? 10:00 AM?" Angela asked Jennifer.

"10:00 AM? It's my morning to sleep in. How about noon? Then afterwards we can go get lunch," Jennifer replied.

"That's sounds fine to me, how about noon Mr. McGuire?"

"Noon will work fine, just as long as it's not in the later evening. I uh, I have some plans later in the evening. My son is coming to visit from out of town and I need to be home with my family. He's bringing his new daughter that he and his wife just recently had. So, I can't miss that. I hope you understand, Angela."

"That sounds fine, Mr. McGuire, my friend and I will see you at noon. Would you like for us to meet you at your realty office downtown?"

"No, that's alright. I will meet you both at the property. The address is 60 Suntides Blvd. I'll see you guys there at noon. It's been wonderful talking to you sweetheart, I'll see you tomorrow. Call me if anything changes," Mr. McGuire said.

"I will, thank you."

With a flip of the phone, Angela hung up and the device back into her purse, just in time for the food to arrive.

Even on a diet of cheeseburgers and caramel macchiatos, Jennifer kept herself in perfect shape. Oh well, Angela thought to herself, I can splurge on some fries once in a while, too.

Angela enjoyed her burger, and the mushrooms were a nice touch. Still, she wasn't that hungry. She left behind half of her burger and most of her fries untouched, while Jennifer finished her burger and mopped up the rest of her fries.

"This is so exciting, Angela. Today really is the beginning of a new life for you and it's going to be great!"

"I don't know. I still have a lot on my mind. But maybe this will help push me to where I need to be. I need to learn to be independent all over again. It's been so long since I've been by myself. Since our college days really and even then, I was in a dorm with other friends who were all my age too. I'm glad I have you in my life, Jennifer. I need a friend like you so badly right now," Angela said.

"I'm glad to have you in my life too, Angie," Jennifer said. "So, what kind of dog do you want to get?"

"I'm thinking about a Border Collie."

"A Border Collie? Sure, if you want it to lick an intruder to death. You need to get a German Shepard or something."

"Well, I'll figure that out when the time comes," Angela said.

Hesitantly, Jennifer asked, "So, do you want to talk about it more?"

"Talk about what?"

"About Todd. And what's going on?"

Angela sighed and deeply inhaled, swallowing tears as she was still hurt by what Todd had done to her. The waitress returned to the table to ask if everything was alright.

"I'm so sorry. I forgot to bring you your water earlier," the waitress apologized.

Angela quickly grabbed her glass, took a drink, and relaxed.

It's alright. Our drinks were very good, thank you," Angela said.

Relieved, the waitress left the table. All the wiser now to make sure that her guests get glasses of water before they even order next time. Quietly, for the first time, Angela explained to Jennifer what had happened between her and Todd.

"Back in December, Todd had a Christmas party he attended with his company up in Vancouver, Washington. I couldn't go because I had to work. One of his friends from the office introduced him to their sister. And I guess the two of them hit it off. From what I heard, they talked for about ten minutes and then went back to his office. He ended up pursuing her and threw away everything that we had made together for the last 14 years."

"I'm sorry," Jennifer said. "I know things hurt now, but time will heal your heart."

"I know. I've surrounded myself with friends here to help get through these tough times, but I always end up going home alone, to an empty house. I may get through the day, but at night it's a lot harder."

The waitress returned with their bill. Jennifer offered to pay for Angela's meal, but Angela wouldn't have any of it. What a good meal it was, too. After not eating a complete meal after a few days, maybe Angela's appetite was coming back. Maybe she was finally coming to terms with what had happened and started letting go.

The two paid for their meal and both left a generous tip for the waitress, even though she forgot their waters until the end of the meal. She was young, and probably new. Angela could tell she didn't do it on purpose. The two left the restaurant and on the way back to the car, Jennifer asked her another question.

"Angie, do you want to go to a movie tonight?"

Angela thought about the question, but in all honesty, all that she wanted to do was go home and relax. Tomorrow was a big day in her life. A big change was going to happen. It was the first day in the life of Angela Kennedy. No, no, Angela Brown. She was changing her last name back to her maiden name prior to marrying Todd soon, so she may as well get used to being a Brown again.

"No, thank you for the offer though, Jenn. I think I just want to go home and get some rest this evening."

"Want me to come over and watch a movie with you? We can rent a movie and just stay in, make some popcorn, have a movie night."

"You know what? That sounds good, Jenn. Thanks."

"It sounds fun to me!"

However, as Angela left the restaurant, she realized she might never see tomorrow or make it home tonight, considering that Jennifer was driving her back to her car, which was parked back in the office's garage. The two got into Jennifer's car and drove out of the parking lot. True to her nature of driving, Jennifer started the car and slammed her foot on the gas pedal. The engine roared to life.

"Oops, I forgot to put the car in gear," Jennifer said.

"Maybe I should drive us back," Angie suggested.

"Don't be silly, we both know between the two of us I'm the better driver!"

Angie wasn't so sure about that. Jennifer put her foot on the brake, slipped the car into the rear gear, removed her foot, and slammed her foot back down on the gas. Angela's head whipped back against the headrest of her car seat. She had sworn she had just broken her neck, but she could still move her hands and feet, so she guessed she must be okay.

Jennifer somehow made it back to their work safely. This time stopping at all the red lights. A vast improvement compared to earlier. This must have been an omen of good things to come for Angie. Tomorrow was going to be a new day and a new beginning in Angela's life. Whether it's a good or bad beginning, however, that remains to be seen...

CHAPTER 2

Angela slowly turned down Sherwood Drive on her way back to her house. She had decided on the way home in the car that she just wouldn't be up for company tonight. All she wanted to do was crawl into bed and go to sleep. So, when Jennifer brought her back to her car, she told Jenn that she changed her mind and just wanted to go to bed.

Jenn sighed and said, "Alright Angie."

It was 8:15 p.m. and Angela spent an extra hour after Jennifer took her back to her car at the office, simply just driving around some of Portland's neighborhoods. At all costs, they avoided the Happy Valley area. Angie wished that area of Portland's suburbs would just sink into a hole in the ground. But the evening cruise was just an excuse to keep her from returning to an empty home.

Finally, Angela pulled into her empty driveway and up to the garage connected to a spacious two-story home at 1487 Evans Dr. The home was painted white with green trim. It encompassed everything a modern-day American family could ever desire: a white picket fence, a front porch with a deck that overlooked the perfectly manicured front yard. On the deck sat two rocking chairs where Angie and Todd would sit during warm August evenings, sipping lemonade together.

When the garage door opened, Angela pulled her cherry red Toyota Camry into her usual parking spot in the very empty three-car garage. Now that Todd's bulky black Ford Expedition wasn't parked there, it seemed that there was much more room to park now. If Angie wanted, she could park sideways in the garage and still have room to park the riding lawnmower in there.

Angela shifted her car into park, killed the ignition, and closed the garage door with the remote. She watched the garage door snuff out the remaining daylight while she sat in her car. Opening the car door, Angela sat still for a minute with her eyes downcast towards her lap, lost in thought as she observed the silence, and listened to the low hum of the fluorescent tube lights overhead that lit up the garage.

Slowly Angela lifted her head, brushed the hair from her face and exited her car. She shut the door to her car, which caused an echo throughout the garage, which reminded her hollow the space was now. On the way into the house, Angela switched off the fluorescent lights in the garage that were causing the eerie hum that filled the still, dark house.

Angela flipped the lights on as she walked into the kitchen and grabbed a bottle of pink Moscato wine from the fridge, and a wineglass from the cupboard. She poured herself a glass of wine and considered putting the bottle back. "Who am I kidding? I'm probably going to have more than just one glass of wine," Angie thought.

She shut the door to the refrigerator and walked into the living room with her glass of wine in one hand and a bottle of chilled pink Moscato in the other. In the living room area, Angela sat down in her favorite chair to relax. She had owned it since her college years and it had held up remarkably well from all the wear and tear it had been through over the years. It was a fine leather recliner, a bright tan color, with a leg rest that opened and allowed her to kick back and recline. Angela could have fallen asleep in it every time she got into the chair. In fact, she has before in the past and tonight might be no different.

Angela hated to go into her bedroom now that her husband was no longer in the house. The empty bedroom imposed an overwhelming feeling of failure she felt as a wife. What did she do wrong? And what did she not do for her husband after 14 years of marriage that her soon to be ex's new homewrecker could do?

When Angie sat in her chair now, so many questions swarmed through her mind. What went wrong in her relationship? And why did she always feel the worst at night, when she was alone, trapped with her own thoughts? Even on a couple of occasions, she cursed God for allowing things to happen the way they did. She questioned the motives of God himself for why things happened the way that they did.

Angela slowly sipped her wine, thinking about all these reasons why things happened the way they did and how it was out of her control, when her phone rang loudly. The surprise phone alarm caused Angela to choke slightly on her drink. Angela had set the alarm on her phone to remind her of her appointment with the realtor at noon tomorrow, however she forgot to set the alarm to p.m. It was now midnight, and the loud ring of the alarm indicated Angela's failure to set her alarm right.

Angela swallowed the last of her pink Moscato and poured a second glass. She sat in silence for what seemed like hours, listening to nothing, staring into the darkness. Finally, Angela got up, walked into the kitchen, and put the glass in the sink, filling it with water and leaving it to soak. She corked the bottle of wine and placed it back into the fridge.

"Just enough for one more drink tomorrow night," she thought.

Angela turned the lights off in the kitchen and walked down the long hallway leading towards the master bedroom when she stopped halfway, 10 feet from the bedroom door. Angela's heart sank as she remembered times that her husband would wait for her in bed. Angela paused briefly, turned around and walked back down the hallway and back to the living room. Finding her leather recliner in the dark, Angela sat down and opened the leg rest. Laying back she reached over to the ground where she kept a hand knit blanket she had kept since her high school years that her long-time deceased grandmother had made her for her birthday when she was 13.

Angela felt at peace when she wrapped herself up in the blanket. Like her grandmother was still there and comforting her during the tough times in life like she used to do when she was a kid. It offered her a sense of security from what was going on in the real world around her. She pulled the blanket close to her chest, buried her face in the soft cotton texture and remembered how soft her grandmother's hands were. Angela rolled over into the soft leather chair and glanced at the time on her phone. It was now 1:30 a.m. Angela shut her eyes and eventually slipped into a deep sleep.

The sound of silence was heavy through the house. Angela lay sleeping in her recliner, barely moved from the position she fell asleep in earlier in the morning. The sun shone bright through a crack in the blinds, illuminating the once dark living room, hitting the headrest of the recliner chair Angela lay resting back in. Angela pulled the covers of her grandmother's home-made quilt over her head to keep the light away from her eyes.

The sound of a ringing phone broke the dead silence in the house at 9:30 a.m. Angela thought she had heard her cell phone ringing, however thought it was just a dream at first as she stirred and drifted from her deep sleep into reality. Leaning up and grabbing at her phone, Angela looked at the phone's screen and saw that Jennifer was calling her. Why was she calling so early? Perhaps she didn't have a long night like Angela thought she would have. Angela tapped the small green button on her screen and answered.

"Hi Jenn, how was your night?" Angela asked.

"Eh, not all that great. After I got home, I invited Jeff over from the coffee shop and he came over but left earlier than I had hoped he would and didn't stay the night. So, oh well. Maybe next Friday."

"Well, maybe that's a good thing, Jenn. It's good to take things like this at a slow pace."

"Yeah, I suppose. So, are you ready to go see the realtor?"

Angela had forgotten all about it. Sleeping in on Saturday mornings had become a routine for her. For the past couple months, Angela would make it all the way to noon without so much as moving a limb.

"I guess I am."

Deep down inside, Angela was still somewhat apprehensive about going to see the house out at 60 Suntides Blvd. She knew it was going to really be the beginning of the end of the life that she had grown accustomed to over the years. Perhaps she needed this, though, so she had to go through with it for herself.

Weeks prior, Angela received the news from her lender that they approved her for a mortgage of $200,000 dollars. With the sale of the house being finalized soon, Angela had told the lender she was certain that she was going to be putting a nice sized down payment onto the loan too. Angela knew it was simply just a matter of taking that next step to see the home of her choosing.

"Do you want me to come pick you up this morning?" Jennifer asked.

"No! I mean, no thank you. You drove us to dinner last night. It's only fair that I pick you up. After we're done looking at the house, we'll go out to lunch at that sandwich shop that's over in the West Linn," Angela said.

"Oh, you mean 1st St. Subs and Deli. I've heard they have amazing roast beef sandwiches. That sounds great. Okay, I'll be ready to go by 11 a.m. We'll stop for coffee on the way to the house, too," Jenn said.

"Sounds great. I'll get out of bed here shortly and I'll meet you at your place by 11," Angela said.

"Okay, I'll see you in a bit."

Angela touched the end call on her phone screen, ending the call. The time now was 9:45 a.m. Angela needed to be up by 10, in the shower and ready to leave her place by 10:30 a.m. depending on how bad traffic was in the greater Portland area.

Sometimes on Saturday mornings around the bigger city, a lot of couples and families went out shopping together, and depending on the time of the year, it depended on what they were shopping for. During the spring and the summer months, many families shopped for gardening supplies and bags of fertilizer to plant their favorite vegetables in their gardens. In the winter months around the northwest, a lot of families shopped for snow shovels, bags of salt to salt the sidewalks of their homes, and sleds and such.

After having lived in the area for as long as she had, Angela figured out exactly when it was best to leave her place, both to get her friends, and to get to work or church on time. She even knew how to avoid all the weekend traffic to the home improvement stores. Her awareness of alternative routes and back roads was valuable, especially if the main route became overcrowded with those who are less fortunate or didn't know any better about alternative ways to get to their own destinations.

Angela slowly got up and out of her recliner and dropped her knit blanket on the floor in front of the footrest. Bending over and picking up her grandmother's precious heirloom, Angela folded her knit blanket up neatly and placed it on the headrest of her recliner. Angela stood straight up, raising her arms over her head. She stretched and yawned simultaneously.

She then walked to the kitchen, feeling like she didn't get much sleep at all last night. She grabbed a glass from the kitchen cabinet next to the sink and filled it with cold water from the faucet. It always took Angela's sink a long time to pump out the coldest of water, so she waited while looking out the kitchen window to the backyard. Testing the temperature of the water with the back of her hand, she finally deemed the water to be cold enough to fill her glass with and drink. Angela filled her water to the brim of the glass and took a large drink.

Angela paused momentarily from her drink as she gazed out of the kitchen window, her eyes fixed on the neighbor's backyard beyond her wire fence line. There, she watched Mr. Harrison pulling the lawnmower out from his tool shed. Poor Mr. Harrison and his lawn mower. Many times, she had witnessed Mr. Harrison fight with the old motor, attempting to start it. One day, Angela counted Mr. Harrison yanking the cord to start the engine a total of 28 times before he finally strung together a series of obscenities that would have made a sailor blush on his first night of shore leave from the naval boat.

The mower yet again was giving Mr. Harrison problems. Angela could hear distinct words that seemed to start with the letter F, followed by some words that started with the letters S and D. A smile crossed her face, accompanied by a chuckle, as she watched Mr. Harrison kick the side of the old mower. The poor man spends nearly all his time at work during the week, then on the weekends had even more work to do at home around the house. It was commendable. Angela thought Todd was never really like that.

As she thought about it, while watching Mr. Harrison go from kicking to punching the engine of the mower, Angela hadn't seen his wife in nearly a month now. Not that it mattered anymore, however. Angela was moving out soon and needed to find her own place to rent, but preferably to purchase. It was time to establish herself as a strong-willed and independent person. Renting to Angela felt more like being under the control of a landlord. At least with buying, she was building her credit and was working to own something by herself.

Angela finished her glass of water, put it in the sink and finally walked away from the back window just as Mr. Harrison overturned the mower and walked away. Perhaps this was the last straw for the battle between Mr. Harrison and his old bastard of a lawn mower.

Angela and made her way to the bathroom upstairs, slowly making her way up the stairs. Angela spent almost a full hour showering, combing her hair, and finally brushing her teeth clean. She applied a small amount of makeup to cover a small scar on her right cheek she acquired in a bicycle accident when she was a 10-year-old girl. It was a long story involving her neighborhood friends, riding down a hill and crashing face first into some gravel at the bottom of the hill. The only scar that was left rested on her right cheek, just under her eye. Thank God she had her helmet on that day, too.

On the way out of the house, Angela quickly grabbed a banana from the kitchen, peeled it and ate it while walking through the house. She rushed out the door at 10:40 a.m. Ten minutes late! She'd have to use the alternative route around the bigger city in order to make it to Jennifer's place in time to pick her up by 11.

At 11:05 a.m. Angela finally pulled into Jennifer's driveway. She would have made it on time if it weren't for an older couple that managed to consistently stay in front of her for nearly the entire drive to her place. Angela shut off her car, got out and walked to the front door, only to be greeted at the door by Jennifer, who was patiently waiting and ready to go. She looked like she had been waiting for nearly half an hour, too.

"Hi Angie, are you ready to go?" Jennifer asked.

"Yes, I'm sorry for being late. I got stuck in traffic this morning. Even on the back road," Angela replied.

"It's no problem. Did you figure out where you want to get coffee at this morning?"

"There's a stand down by the corner called Cruiser's Coffee Stand. They have an Irish Cream flavored espresso drink that I've wanted to try for a while now."

Jennifer turned the knob, double checking to make sure the front door was locked. Sometimes it acted like it was locked but turned out it wasn't. Jennifer lived in a duplex in a nice neighborhood of Portland City. Not completely crime free, but better than most around the greater area. Walking to the car, Jennifer stooped down to pick up a rolled-up newspaper at the end of her driveway. It was the neighbor's paper from the duplex next door.

"Jennifer, why are you taking your neighbor's newspaper? Do you really read it that much?" Angela asked.

"I like to read the comics," Jennifer replied.

"Then go online and read comics there."

"I do. I get on their wireless internet too. They don't have a passcode on their wireless service."

"How naïve could these people be?" Angela thought. For the better part of two months, Jennifer had been leeching off them, using their internet service and taking their paper and they had yet to figure it out.

The two entered Angela's cherry red Toyota Camry and backed out of the driveway. Putting the car in drive, Angela pulled out onto the road and drove to the coffee stand.

"See this?" Jennifer asked, pointing to one of the comic strips in the newspaper.

"Jenn, I'm trying to drive."

Jennifer read nearly every comic strip from the newspaper out loud to Angela. Angela let her voice go in one ear and out the other, occasionally giving a small smile and a courtesy laugh to commend Jennifer's efforts.

They arrived at the coffee stand at 11:30 a.m. and ordered their drinks inside the small building. Inside were two small chairs with one table, not nearly enough space to allow a couple of people to sit comfortably. Angela thought that the table and chairs must have been for looks and nothing more. She ordered her Irish Cream Espresso, which wasn't as good as she thought it would be. Jennifer ordered a wild cherry and lime spritzer which at first didn't sound good at all, but Jennifer let Angela try it and Angela soon regretted ordering her Irish Cream Espresso.

"I thought you wanted to try the Irish Cream coffee, Jenn?" Angela asked.

"I did, but I changed my mind. The cherry and lime spritzers they make here are incredible!" Jennifer replied.

It was true. Angela thought about dumping the Irish cream coffee and going back for the spritzer, but for one, what was the point of wasting good coffee? Second, they needed to hurry to the property to meet with Mr. McGuire.

Both Jennifer and Angela raced out of the building and back to Angela's car. Getting in, Angela put her coffee down in the cup holder and put her keys in the ignition. While Jennifer was getting into the car, she spilled a splash of spritzer in her lap.

"Damn," Jennifer said.

"What happened?" Angela asked.

"Oh, I spilled some spritzer on my jeans."

"Oh, well," Angela thought. There are more important things to deal with right now than a small stain on Jenn's jeans.

Not willing to waste another minute, Angela sped out of the parking lot. Finally, they were on their way to 60 Suntides Blvd.

"So, I investigated the neighborhood that the house is in, and I gotta tell you, it's nice. It's out in the Camas area, so you don't need to worry about city pollutants like sound or lights or anything. It's quiet, with a white picket-fenced backyard and a hill behind it that slopes down to a cool old creek. I think it even flows into a bigger creek outside the neighborhood. There are a lot of trees behind the fence line too, so it'll be a great yard to get that dog you were talking about. Wait till the leaves change colors. I mean, besides having to rake a bunch of leaves out of your backyard that's going to be pretty in the fall," Jennifer said.

"I hope so. I get a feeling just by looking at the pictures from the magazine that there's something special about this place. It's unique. Perhaps I have a good chance of starting a new life here. If the house is clean and has a good foundation and no major problems, then it'd be safe to say I'm making this house the place for me," Angela replied.

"Well, that might be a little too soon. Don't you want to look at a couple more places before you decide?"

"I don't really know if I have the time to. I need a new place to live. Most of all, I'm tired of living in that home, Jenn. I'm tired of going back to all the memories of what once was, and I need to move on. I need to just do me right now."

Angela arrived in the Happy Valley suburbs. A lush area, with an abundance of pine trees and the leaf trees Angela loves to watch change colors in autumn. It wasn't a long drive to the Suntides area of Happy Valley. Angela arrived at the house at 11:55 a.m. She grew increasingly excited for the first time in a long time as she parked her red Camry in front of 60 Suntides Blvd., next to a green sign that read McGuire Realtor Service. McGuire utilized an image of a dancing leprechaun on his sign to make the business more inviting, but in turn Angela thought it looked cartoonish.

Angela turned her car off and stepped out. The front yard was fenced with white pickets as well, but in the backyard there was a newer wood fence line installed. Angela walked to the back of her car and gazed at the two-level, 2200-square-foot house. It was painted white with forest green trim around the doors and windows. Angela also saw a chimney along the side of the roof, where she imagined the living room must be.

Looking up and down the silent street of Suntides Boulevard, a sudden feeling of allure came to her. She was uncertain why she felt this way about a house. Almost like the home was interacting with her in some way, but Angela attributed the feeling to starting over in life and thought nothing more of it.

At exactly noon, a black Buick sedan drove up and parked directly behind Angela's red Camry. Out of the driver's side of the sedan stepped out a short and stocky man, clean shaven with white hair and glasses. Angela recognized Mr. McGuire from his portrait in the realtor magazine yesterday evening.

Mr. McGuire closed the door to his car with a loud thud, cleared his throat, walked up to Angela and Jennifer, stretched out his hand and introduced himself.

"Hello ladies, I am Greg McGuire. You sweethearts can call me Greg for short if you like. It's a pleasure to meet the both of you. Would you ladies like a donut or a maple bar I bought from Alvin's Donut Shop? They were made fresh this morning."

"Hello," Angela and Jennifer said in tandem.

"No thank you, we're going to go out for lunch after this, but thank you anyway, Mr. McGuire," Angela said and shook his hand. "My name is Angela, and this is my friend Jennifer."

"Hi, pleased to meet you," Jennifer said and extended her hand to shake with Mr. McGuire.

After their introduction, Mr. McGuire guided them on a tour outside of the home.

"Here around the corner of the house you ladies will see this spacious, fully fenced-in backyard. Over in the corner is a small shed to keep your bicycles, lawn mower, tools or whatever else you want to keep covered and that can fit into such a standing fixture. I think the owner's before you used it as a tool shed for yard tools and stored building material in it."

"Mr. McGuire, there is no garage, is there? For cars or storage?" Angela asked.

"Well, no. There is not," Mr. McGuire replied. "But there is room around the corner between the neighbor's fence line and your home to build a decent sized one in the future if you would like to. Honestly Angela, if it were me, I would invest in doing just that. Someday, if you choose to sell the home yourself, it will do nothing but help raise the value of the home. And make it heated, too."

Angela knew a little about building in neighborhoods like this and knew that it would require a lot of different city, county and buildings permits and she'd have to adhere to building codes. God almighty all the building codes that must be taken into consideration, but she wasn't going to argue with Mr. McGuire about it.

"Now, beyond that fence," Mr. McGuire said, introducing it with a wave of his arm, "Is a small creek. It can be accessed through that gate in the middle of your fence line, but I'm not too sure why you would need to access the creek. There really is nothing more down there than just trees and weeds and a small trail that leads to the creek. The creek isn't even big enough to cast a small fishing line in, let alone hook anything living."

Mr. McGuire pointed to a decently sized wooden gate. Large enough for a normal sized person to walk through, with the latch to the gate on the house side of the fence. Mr. McGuire took Angela and Jennifer right to the fence line and opened the gate with his chubby fingers.

Angela and Jennifer walked through the gate and followed a small dirt trail that weaved in and out of the trees and sloped down towards the creek. Angela marveled at how dense the trees and grass were covering the creek from her vision. Mr. McGuire, however, would not walk through the gate to the other side of the fence. He stood, fidgeting with his hands and fingers, while looking around himself as if he was expecting someone else.

After taking a moment to look around and not going any further down the trail, Angela and Jennifer turned around and walked back through the gate. Once through, Mr. McGuire shut the gate and locked its latch.

Mr. McGuire then paused briefly for a minute. Taking a breath and gathering his thoughts, Mr. McGuire then said, "Well then, Ladies. Would you like to see the inside of the home?"

"Finally," Angela thought. I get to see the inside of this beautiful home. "Yes Greg, can we go through the back-sliding door?" she asked.

"Well, unfortunately, darling, we cannot. That sliding door locks from the inside of the home, but we can get inside using the laundry room door right over there."

Mr. McGuire pointed at a small door with a small green stained-glass window in it that was along the same side of the house, just right of the sliding glass doors. Mr. McGuire walked Angela and Jessica to the door and took a pair of keys out of his pocket. He tried the first key; however, it turned out to be the key to the front door, and it didn't work for him. Mr. McGuire tried the second key and this time, the door unlocked. The door creaked open, revealing the laundry room.

It surprised Angela to be greeted by a set of washer and dryer machines. Oddly, the machines looked to be nearly brand new without ever being used! Not a scratch on them. Angela thought it was odd to find two nearly brand-new appliances left behind by the previous owners. But she thought it was more of a blessing in disguise considering she didn't need to purchase a new washer and dryer set. Mr. McGuire led them through the washroom and through another door, into a long hallway.

"And through this door is the hallway. To your left is a small ½ bathroom. Now down the end of the hallway and to the right leads to the living room area. And to the left of the end of the hall is the dining room and kitchen. This room to your right is a spare bedroom for guests or whomever." Mr. McGuire opened the door, revealing a ten-foot by ten-foot square room with a single windowpane along one wall, looking out towards the driveway and street.

Angela and Jennifer walked into the room and looked around.

"Decent sized closet," Jennifer said.

Angela nodded along. After looking around the room, they walked out and Mr. McGuire shut the door behind them.

"Okay, so let's head upstairs, and I'll tell you more about the second level," Mr. McGuire said.

For a home that was 2000-square-feet, the hallway was oddly long. It led from the side of the stairs to the back of the house, where the laundry room was located. Angela supposed that to support the bedroom on one side and the bathroom and laundry room on the other that the hallway would have to be long enough. Walking up the stairs, Angela looked up and noticed an attic door at the top of the staircase in the ceiling, and without hesitation asked, "Mr. McGuire, is that the access to the attic area?"

Mr. McGuire stopped presenting the house for a moment, and without looking up to see what Angela was asking about, said, "Yes. It is. But you need not concern yourself with anything in there. It's more of a storage area for electrical wires and extra insulation. There's nothing more than that up there. Barely enough room for an electrician to crawl in and check a problem out. I wouldn't worry about storing anything up there, my dear."

Angela found it odd how Mr. McGuire had presented the attic area. Up to that point, everything on the property had brought a smile to Mr. McGuire's face, and he had talked about it cheerfully. However, when it came to the attic, his demeanor had changed. He appeared very nervous, almost as if he was afraid to speak about it and trying to avoid the subject altogether.

Angela hadn't noticed before, but it was the same demeanor that Mr. McGuire had exhibited when he was presenting what lay behind the fence line in the backyard. Nevertheless, Angela didn't think much of it, and Mr. McGuire continued showing them to the master bedroom on the second floor, down another long hallway.

Down the hallway were small storage closets that appeared to be used for towels and storage for small items such as blankets, towels, and spare pillows. The master bedroom was a decent sized room, with a walk-in closet and an ensuite bathroom equipped with a shower. Adjacent to the master bedroom door and one of the three-bedroom doors on the opposite side of the hallway, was a railed opening that offered a view overlooking both the main living room area and the front door of the house.

After the master bedroom was shown, Mr. McGuire showed the remainder of the upstairs portion of the home. Jennifer liked the bedroom next to Angela's room and made a joke about moving into it. Angela laughed it off, hoping that Jennifer was only joking.

The third bedroom door, however, was locked shut with a padlock. Mr. McGuire attempted to unlock and open the room for viewing. However, among the six different keys he had, none of them opened the padlock. The crack under the bottom of the door was lit up, which indicated to Angela that the room had a window, and no blinds or shades were covering this unknown window that must have overlooked the backyard.

"Ladies, I'm sure we have a key back at my office for this room. When the home inspector inspected this house, he must have accidentally locked this door. So when I get back there, I will look for it and if I can't find it, we'll break this lock and replace the whole door for you, Angela. I'm not too worried about the padlock either. We can get a set of bolt cutters and get rid of that easy too," Mr. McGuire said.

"That's fine, Mr. McGuire, no problem," Angela said.

Mr. McGuire paused for a moment. "You know Angela, this is an older house. Not too old, but not too young by any means either. I'm betting that the third bedroom is nearly identical to the second bedroom that you saw next to the master bedroom. I mean, right down to the color of paint on the walls and the color of the carpet. Nearly identical. Either way, though, the room is fine. Before we can sell the home, each room, and every wall, including plumbing, electrical and all the components that go along with it are inspected by the county house inspector, so there's nothing to worry about at all."

Angela was fine with it. So far, she liked what she had seen. She was beginning to trust Mr. McGuire and feel that he was an honest guy. He wasn't afraid to admit when he made a mistake and forgot something. That was refreshing. Angela always thought all guys were going to lie to her at some point. With the second-floor tour concluded, Mr. McGuire took Angela and Jennifer back downstairs to the kitchen and small dining room area that sat parallel to the living room. He showed them the kitchen, which was outfitted with a refrigerator and a stove the previous owners left behind as well. The stove itself didn't appear to be older than a couple of years at most, and it was a glass top too.

Angela thought, "Why would the prior owners leave the refrigerator and nearly a brand-new kitchen stove behind too?"

They also left behind a toaster oven, a toaster, microwave, and dinner plates with utensils and glasses. The kitchen sink sat side by side with the sliding screen door, with a window above the sink that overlooked the backyard and the fence line. From here you could see the gate that Angela and Jennifer had walked through earlier, swinging open.

"Mr. McGuire," Angela said, "The latch must have come undone at the gate because it's open."

Hesitantly looking out the sliding door window, Mr. McGuire said, "Well, look at that. I must not have latched it as good as I thought I did. Well, no bother."

The sliding screen doors that led from the kitchen to the backyard were now accessible and Angela opened the door and stepped back out onto the covered patio area, admiring the back yard. Angela turned around and came back in and closed the sliding door behind her.

Jennifer was looking through cleaned-out refrigerator, but she still felt awkward about using a refrigerator that was used by the prior owners, whom she didn't know very well.

Angela looked through the cupboards at the sets of glasses, dining plates, and bowls that had been left behind. In one cupboard, she even found a blender that looked like it had never been used.

"Mr. McGuire, what about these plates, glasses, utensils, and such?" Angela asked. "There's just so much left behind. Are the original owners going to come back for them?"

"Well, if they do, they do. But for now, Angela, everything that you see would be yours if you purchased the home. We would consider it abandoned property and we would document that in the contract and once you sign for it honestly, you can do whatever you would like with it all. It would be yours," Mr. McGuire said.

Angela nodded as Mr. McGuire led Angela and Jennifer from the kitchen across the hall to the living room now.

"Ladies, here is the living room area. It's a nice sized living room. The front door is located over in that corner there, with a closet for you and guests to hang coats up in. The vaulted ceilings have fans with lights attached to them as your main source of lighting in the living room here, and they are controlled by that switch on the wall over there. Or you could always get lamps to put around on tables here," Mr. McGuire said as he pointed out the different areas of the living room.

Mr. McGuire then pointed at the front door in the corner of the room. Next to the front door was the large closet for storing coats and shoes or anything else Angie would want to store in it. Angela opened the closet door and sure enough, it was quite a large closet for lots of clothing and shoes to be stored if she wanted. Around the corner of the living room closet there was a smaller hallway that led to an extra bathroom for guests that had both a toilet and a walk-in shower. Sitting across the hallway was a small office that looked out into the backyard.

Angela walked into the small office area and very much liked the space. The small room was about eight feet by eightfeet, however Angela noticed something out of place. A small sheet of plywood covered an opening in the wall that barely reached about a foot off the wooden floor.

Angela pointed at the covering and asked, "Mr. McGuire, why is this sheet of plywood here?"

Mr. McGuire paused again, swallowing deeply, as if he knew exactly why the hole in the wall and piece of plywood covering it up was there. However, she could tell that Mr. McGuire didn't want to elaborate on it, and instead he replied, "Angela, that was at one time…an air vent. An air vent that the previous owners were going to place into this room. I can't go into too much detail about it because that would breach my client's confidentiality. However, I'll tell ya what happened here without going into too many details."

The realtor cleared his throat and continued, "The previous owners ran out of money during their renovations, and the husband left the wife. From what I understood, he didn't want to be financially liable for the home anymore. Also, these air vents were a part of the renovation. The ductwork is about one foot wide and one foot high, and leads to every room of the house. Unfortunately, they ran out of funds before they could hook it up to a unit. So, our realtor agency installed a standard heat and air unit to pump air conditioning and heat throughout the home, with the vents and duct work finished, it's fully functional."

Angela thought it was another odd occurrence that the previous owners wanted to install air units into an eight by eight-foot room, when they could have just as easily opened the window or installed an in-window air conditioning unit or even simply just plugged in a desk fan. However, hearing the story about the previous owners, Angela's curiosity about the hole in the wall was overcome by her thoughts of the asshole husband that abandoned his wife in their unfinished home. Angela felt a connection to the wife because of it, likening the story to her own circumstance. Just another story of relationship abandonment, just like all the rest. Just like her own.

Jennifer poked her head in through the door and examined the room. She felt that the room seemed colder than the rest of the house, but didn't bother to say anything.

Angela looked closer at the plywood on the wall that covered the hole and noticed at least a dozen nails pounded into each corner of the plywood. "These people really must not have wanted that plywood to accidentally fall off the wall or something," she thought.

Angela walked out of the room and back into the hallway as Mr. McGuire shut the door behind them and continued showing the rest of the house.

Mr. McGuire took Angela and Jennifer through the front door of the home and into the front yard. It was a small yard but boasted a couple newly planted maple tree saplings along with some rose bushes that lined up against the front of the house that were in full bloom of red and pink. Rose buds in Portland during the spring were the best anywhere in the northwest, maybe even the world.

"Well, that's it. Is there anything else I can talk to you about the house, ladies?" Mr. McGuire asked.

"All in all, it's a beautiful home," Angela said. "I would like to talk more about the asking price."

"That is very negotiable," Mr. McGuire said. "The original sellers, as I stated before, abandoned the home, so it went into foreclosure with Columbia Bank of the West. They officially own the property now and they would like to unload it off their books as soon as possible. Right now, they are asking $150,000 for the home and property."

"I will offer $140,000," Angela countered.

Mr. McGuire turned his back to Angela and Jennifer, scratched the back of his head as he thought for a minute, and replied, "Okay, I am fine with that offer, my dear. Let me get a hold of the lender at the bank and we'll see what they say. How's about I give you ladies a call later today and I'll let you know what he says?"

"Thank you, Mr. McGuire. I would appreciate that. I know you're busy and it's Saturday and all and you have family coming into town, too. I really appreciate that you'd do that for me," Angela replied.

"It's my pleasure, darling. And it was my pleasure meeting both of you girls. You have a wonderful time at lunch, and I'll be talking to you real soon, Angela."

"Thank you, Greg."

Mr. McGuire shook the girl's hands and walked back to his car, taking an extra moment to position himself correctly so he could slide his large body into the driver's seat. Starting the black Buick, Mr. McGuire shifted into gear and pulled away.

Angela turned around and looked at the house one more time and thought that even if the bank didn't take $140,000 for it, she wouldn't have any problem paying the asking price. Both Angela and Jennifer walked to Angela's car and got in, but before Angela could close the driver's side door, a voice from across the road spoke up.

"You gone done be looking to buy that their house there, eh?" a voice asked in a southern accent.

Angela looked up and saw an elderly gentleman crossing the road. He was a smaller fellow, with thick glasses that magnified his blue eyes. A man who appeared to be years well past his prime who gingerly crossed the road towards her car with a limp in his right leg. It appeared he was favoring his hip as he walked with a cane. Angela bet the elderly man had hundreds of stories to tell about life through his years of living in the neighborhood.

"That house done been around this area for quite some time there, it sure has," the old man said.

"Has it?" Angela asked. "I am looking into buying it."

"It sure has been. I been livin' in the house cross the street from this one for…oh, some odd 30 years now. Since the early 80's I have. My wife and I moved here on the account of our kids gone movin out our home, but she done been with the Lord since the turn of the year 2008 she had. I'm sorry, I forgot to introduce myself to ya'll there. My name is Tom Butler. My deceased wife was Esther. We were married for 52 years. Our kids long gone moved out of the area a couple years ago, but I love the area so much here I decide to go on and stay behind."

"I'm sorry to hear about your wife, Mr. Butler. It's a pleasure to meet you. I'm Angela Kennedy. Well, I mean Angela Brown. I'm, well, basically looking to start my life over and I'm hoping this house helps propel me in the right direction."

"That house there been around for a long time it has! Lotta people gone lived in it, they all come and gone," Mr Butler said. "It'd be an interestin house, lotsa stuff happened there it did, lotsa stuff."

"Stuff? So, what kind of things happened there, Mr. Butler?" Angela inquired.

"Nuttin too serious there, nuttin too serious. Just a house been round for a long time it has," he said. "I'd avoid the well out back I would, I'd avoid it. Especially if ya gots some kids, don't want them playin round that well. It's a deeper one it is, goes down a long way! Right downs to the core of the earth!" Mr. Butler laughed.

Angela thought the well behind her fence in the backyard was a bit odd. Mr. McGuire didn't mention anything about a well beyond the fence line, but only a small creek and a small trail leading down to it. Not a creek even large enough to cast a fishing line into is what Angela thought Mr. McGuire's exact words were. In fact, without looking, Angela could hear the running water from the creek behind her property. She remembered that when she was on the other side of the fence, neither she nor Jennifer ever went down the trail because of the thick brush and trees that overtook the trail. If there was a well back there, then why wouldn't Mr. McGuire mention it? Maybe this old fellow was a little off. Maybe he was thinking of a well somewhere else where he lived before living in the Suntides area.

"Alright, well, my friend and I are going to head to lunch, Mr. Butler. Maybe you and I will be neighbors soon," Angela said and turned back to her car.

"This house likes ya it does," said Mr. Butler, "this house likes ya and it picked you for a reason. It likes ya it does. You can tell when a person is made for a house, or a car, or even a boat. It's like there is a special bond between the two. A special bond indeed. Like a marriage. Lots of interestin things happened here, you'll see when y'all here with us. Y'all will see."

Angela didn't hear what Mr. Butler said as she got in the car and shut the door. Jennifer was anxiously waiting for Angela to come back to the car. Angela was a bit intimidated by Mr. Butler and didn't feel like sticking around talking anymore.

Mr. Butler watched from the street as they drove away.

"So, you like the place, huh? How about that neighbor? Kinda a strange old man, huh?" Jennifer asked.

"Oh, he seems harmless. A nice old man who wasn't afraid to approach a potential new neighbor. He might be a little off, but he seems to be okay. He lives alone and trust me, being alone does that to a person, anyway. I do like the place a lot. I like the backyard the most. It's clean. And the neighborhood is friendly. Why they're only asking $150,000 for a two-level home with that many bedrooms in it is beyond me. It seems underpriced to me," Angela said.

"But you asked $140,000 for it."

"You always ask lower than the asking price. It can't hurt Jenn. And if they accept it, then great. It's less than seventy-five percent of what I was approved for from the lender a couple of weeks ago. I can put a good-sized down payment on that $140,000, with maybe a little left over for some renovation projects. I could finish up on what the original owners tried to do before that asshole left her. Mr. McGuire said that the home had already been appraised along with the inspection. I really think this will be a great opportunity for me to do what I want and start over fresh. Establish myself as an individual."

"So, where do you want to go for lunch today? It's almost 1 p.m." Jennifer said.

"How about we go to an Italian place called Rigatoni's, down by Blossom Way? They have some amazing Caesar salads."

"That sounds great. I haven't gone to an Italian restaurant in a while."

Angela continued her drive to the restaurant. By taking the highway, it was only ten minutes away from where they were, making it an easy commute. It was right off the highway exit, too. Saturday afternoon traffic was no bother to Angela, either. Her driving was safer than Jennifer's had been the previous evening. However, Angela knew that Jennifer's patience was being tried. She could sense that Jennifer felt that if she were driving, they would have arrived at the restaurant by now.

After a short drive, Angela pulled into Rigatoni's parking lot. It was a nice Italian restaurant with affordable prices that offered a never-ending salad and pasta bowl special. Angela thought It seemed as if they'd offered the special for a long time too.

In the early afternoon, business was very slow at Rigatoni's. Which was fine. Angela enjoyed the silent company with Jennifer. They found a parking place close to the front of the restaurant and parked the Camry. Together, they got out and walked in through the front doors of the restaurant. Low lighting and the dark paint on the walls in the lobby made it difficult to see the details inside of the building.

A nice young female hostess greeted them with a smile. She looked like she was home from college for spring break and trying to make a little extra money to take back with her to school. God knew Angela had been there before. Good for her, putting her effort into her work instead of going out and partying or relaxing on a nice tropical beach somewhere.

The young hostess sat both Angela and Jennifer at a table by the window, overlooking a large parking lot to a nearby outlet shopping center. The hostess asked if they would like anything to drink and both Angela and Jennifer replied, "A glass of water with lemon wedges, please."

The hostess acknowledged their request for water and went to get their drinks and notify the waitress of their pending orders.

Angela took her phone out of her purse and set it down on the table. She was getting eager for her phone to ring, so she could hear what the portly Mr. McGuire would say about her offer. However, Angela could sense that something was different about this home. It seemed like some sort of energy drew her to that property and welcomed her and her fresh start.

She thought about how weird it was that she never had a desire to look for any other homes through the realtor magazine. She saw some others that she thought would be super cute, including a nice duplex in a great neighborhood and a single level rambler home that overlooked a small pond. But 60 Suntides Blvd. attracted her to it. She didn't care about the little renovations that still needed to be done. She had free appliances, a nice sized backyard, and free dishes if she wanted. She would probably get rid of those though and use her own dishes.

But why was so much left behind in the house? Why would a two-level home nearly done with its renovations only cost her $150,000? Either way, though, maybe she was getting her hopes up for nothing. What if the bank refused the offer? Or found something wrong with the property and they pulled the home off the market? Angela tried not to think about that as she opened her menu.

Jennifer had already opened hers. They flipped through the menu, however, they each already knew what they had come for. It was all about the salad and pasta.

"So, Angela, how do you feel about this place?"

The hostess returned with the girl's water and set them down on the table. "Is there anything else that I can get for you ladies?" she asked.

"No, thank you," Jenn said.

"Your waitress will come back to take your order in a moment," the hostess said.

Angela grabbed the glass of water after the hostess turned and left. Taking a small sip of water, she swallowed a gulp. Inhaling for a moment, Angela said, "Yes Jenn, I do. I feel like that home is the place where I can start my life over again. I know that there are some things that still need to be done to make the home perfect for what I want, but I'm willing to work on that and make it happen."

Angela took another drink of water, this time a little bigger than the first initial sip.

Jennifer took a drink of water, set her glass down and said, "I like that there's a fenced-in backyard. And the covered back patio would be great for summer barbecues. You could get a small table to put back there and have lunches and dinners on the back patio if you wanted. You could even buy and install a hot tub. A covered hot tub would be awesome, Angie! The kitchen seems a little out of date, but that's alright. We can re-paint in there, maybe add some new cabinets and it'll be fine."

"Yeah, with the price of the house, I might be able to afford a small remodel in that kitchen too," Angela said.

"Angie, wasn't it weird that Mr. McGuire seemed nervous about the attic? I mean, it's just an attic, ya know?"

Angela really didn't give the attic too much thought until Jennifer mentioned it. "Perhaps he's just apprehensive about small spaces, Jennifer. Some people don't like small and tight spaces. Or maybe he had a bad experience in the attic of his house when he was a young boy? I'm sure it's nothing. Maybe he was just gathering his thoughts about presenting parts of the house, too. It's hard to be a realtor. Give'em a break Jenn."

The conversation between Angela and Jennifer was interrupted by a young 20-year-old girl who said, "Hi I'm Nancy, your waitress for this afternoon. Have you guys had enough time to decide on what you want to order?"

Angela replied, "Yes, we have. We both want to get the never-ending salad bowl and bread sticks. And to drink, I think we'll get a couple glasses of the St. Peter's Vineyards Moscato, please."

The waitress wrote everything down and informed them she would be back with their drinks shortly. As the waitress left, Angela's phone rang.

Angela quickly rifled through her purse, unable to find her phone until Jennifer finally pointed to the tabletop to where Angela had placed her phone earlier. While Angela answered the phone, Jennifer giggled to herself. On the fifth ring, Angela answered, "Hello?"

"Hi Angela," the portly all too familiar voice on the other end replied, "I hope I'm not interrupting your mealtime," Mr. McGuire said.

"Absolutely not!" Angela replied with glee. "What's the word on the house?"

Jennifer hadn't seen Angela this excited in a long time. Jenn was happy for her friend and hoped that the realtor had good news for her. What would it be like if the realtor had bad news? She didn't want to even think about it.

"Well, it's great news. The bank lowered their asking price about a week ago without telling me about it and the house is for sale for $140,000."

Now Angela really thought that there must be something wrong with the home. However, it had been appraised and checked over by the county auditors. There were no plumbing issues, nor were there foundation issues, or electrical wiring issues mentioned. There weren't even issues with the neighbors. The only problem was that the central heating and air conditioning unit was not really hooked up properly, but even that wasn't an easy fix.

"They're only asking for $140,000 dollars?" Angela asked.

Jennifer's ears perked up and her eyes opened wide at the sound of that.

"That is correct," Mr. McGuire replied. "Do you want to think more about it and get back with me, sweetheart? I know that buying a house is a big investment and I've handled plenty of these deals over the years. So, I'll give you the weekend to decide if you want it and if you're serious about it. You can either call me or swing by my office on Monday morning and we can talk more about it then, okay?"

"Alright Mr. McGuire. Thank you so much for everything you're doing for me."

"It's Greg, Angela. And you're welcome, my dear. Enjoy your lunch."

Angela thanked Mr. McGuire and hung up the phone. There was a moment of silence before Jennifer asked, "What did he say? The house is for sale for $140,000?"

"Yes," Angela replied. "Isn't that odd?"

"Umm, for the location you would be in, Angela, that is very weird. Especially if the bank accepted that offer. Some houses around that neighborhood retail at twice as much as that. Maybe even three times as much."

"No, they didn't accept my offer. That's just the selling price. It's been appraised and inspected by the lenders and the only problem is that the house doesn't have an air conditioning or heating unit hooked up. Jenn, I can afford to hook that up myself. And this is Oregon. I won't need air conditioning until at least July."

"You want this home, don't you?" Jenn asked.

A pause between the two ensued. Without thinking twice about what Jennifer said, Angela picked up her cell phone from the tabletop, dialed Mr. McGuire back. The realtor answered the phone on the first ring and said, "I figured you would call back soon, my dear. What have you decided?"

"Mr. McGuire, I want the house. I will come in on Monday morning to talk more about it and start signing papers."

"That's wonderful, sweetheart! I'll have some paperwork ready to go for you Monday morning and we'll run all the background and credit checks to get you all set up. You've already got approval for your home loan and with your down payment, this could go easy. And one more thing, it's Greg."

Angela finished her call with Mr. McGuire. Placing the phone back in her purse and taking a sip of her wine, she looked across the table at her best friend Jennifer and said with a sudden surge of joy, "I just bought my own house!"

The two ladies took their drinks and clanked their glasses together in a toast over the new opportunity that presented itself to Angela. She was finally writing new chapters in her life. A life that would help to establish her independence. A sense of self-worth and the strength to prove to her family, friends, and everyone that she did not need anyone to help her get through life. She need not rely on the finances of a partner. She didn't need to rely on another person to help operate a home. Very soon, Angela would embark on a new life and new opportunity for herself. But what the future had in store for her, Angela nor Jennifer or anyone else for that matter could predict what would happen.

CHAPTER 3

Monday morning came about as a typical day in the great Pacific Northwest. Dark clouds blanketed the sky, and the rain seemed to match the biblical floods of the days of Noah. There was enough harsh wind that Angela wondered why the city hadn't built windmills to harvest some of the energy from the brutal gusts that came in over the Columbia River.

May always presented the strangest weather in Portland. In a week, one could experience shorts and t-shirt weather. The very next day, the rain and storms could roll in. And the next day one could get a little bit of snow mixed in with that rain, getting one to break back into their winter clothes again, only for the weather to transition to clear and sunny skies the following day.

Traffic was rough, as it always was on Monday mornings in the Portland metro area. Mr. McGuire's office was in the downtown area of the north side of Portland, so there were no alternative routes to reach the realtor's office from where Angela was coming from. Especially with the Vancouver traffic flooding into town from Washington state across the river.

Angela left her home at approximately 7:00 a.m., giving herself an extra half-hour to reach her McGuire Realty, which was about half an hour away from Angela's current but soon-to-be ex-residence. Even leaving so early, Angela arrived at the office nearly fifteen minutes late. At least she survived the drive. Someone nearly sideswipe another car on the freeway, which would have caused a serious accident and really made her later than she already was.

Angela took exit 15B off the freeway, which left her mixed in with more city traffic.

"I really wish they would make the roads easier to traverse around downtown," she said to herself.

While at the traffic light, waiting to get onto a city street from the exit, Angela heard her phone ring in her purse. Quickly rummaging through her purse while the traffic light was still red, she found her cell phone just in time to look at the caller ID and see who was calling. It was Jennifer. Angela had just answered her phone when a car honked behind her. Angela looked up, and the light had turned green while she was looking at her phone.

"Hello?" she quickly answered and took off through the light, turning onto the city street.

"Angie, I told Mr. Marshall that you wouldn't be in at your usual time this morning. He said he's okay with that, so long as you get all your paperwork filed today before you leave work."

"Thanks for letting me know, Jenn. I'm almost at the realtor agency, so I'm not sure how long it will take to fill out all the paperwork, but as soon as I'm finished, I'll be on my way in. I'll call you when I'm leaving the realtor," Angela said.

"Okay, sounds good. I'm so excited for you! Okay, okay, I'll let you go. You're probably trying to drive, huh?"

"Yes Angie, right now I am trying to drive."

"Okay, call me when you're done. See you in a while."

With that, Angela was nearing the realtor's office. She slipped her phone back into her black Coach brand purse and pulled into the parking lot of McGuire's Realtor Service. She spotted Mr. McGuire's black car parked in the front. Angela parked nearby, got out of the car, and walked up to the front door of the building. An electric bell chimed as she entered. Something that sounded almost British, really. Angela wondered if that's what Big Ben in London sounded like.

From the back corner cubical of the office emerged the small, round, balding man named Mr. McGuire. Angela heard the hollow thumps of his footsteps as he walked down the long hallway towards her.

"Angela, my darling! How are you doing, sweetheart? Was your drive here this morning, okay?" he asked.

"Hi Greg, yes, I am fine. The drive was, well, a typical drive on a Monday morning in downtown Portland," Angela said, laughing.

"Well, I went ahead and got all the paperwork ready to go here in your file." Mr. McGuire held a manila-colored folder with papers in it and tapped it against his empty hand. "I know you're on a time crunch. You must be at work just like the rest of us, too. Are you ready to go through the paperwork?" Mr. McGuire asked as he gave Angela a hug.

"How long will it take? I need to be out of here by 10. Any later than that, I need to call my office and let them know."

"Well, because I've taken the liberty of coming to the office a little earlier this morning to try to help you out with some paperwork. I have everything organized. This shouldn't take too long at all. Maybe looking at half an hour tops."

Mr. McGuire led Angela back to his cubical. "What's awful about this is all the papers you need to put your John Hancock on. I tell ya your wrist may hurt after you finish signing your name to all the papers, but that's the way it goes when you buy a house, Angie. I can call and verify employment with your office, which shouldn't take too long because you told me you've been there for a few years now. They can fax me your recent paystub and tax report so we can include that in your file. I already picked up the paperwork from the title company next door before I got here, so that should save you an extra trip, too."

"Okay," Angela said. "As long as I'm out of here by 10 this morning, then it should be fine."

Mr. McGuire laid out the paperwork for her to sign on his desk. Angela noticed that his office was adorned in the black and orange colors of Oregon State University.

"Did you go to Oregon State in Corvallis?"

"I did! Proud alum of the Beavers, way back in 1978. Their football team is less impressive these days, but at least their baseball and softball teams put up a good fight in the springtime," he said with a grin.

Corvallis. Angela remembered the last time that she was in the area. It was when she and her ex-husband were on their way for a trip to Newport, on the Oregon Coast. She always liked the gel candles that the Newport Bay Candle company made. Her favorite was the marionberry candles.

While reminiscing about their trips together, Mr. McGuire continued to lay out the paperwork on his desk, as he explained what each sheet meant. Angela was focused enough to hear about the 20 years fixed percentage rate, and how flood taxes weren't necessary for the property. "Good," she thought.

Angela signed her name on the lines Mr. McGuire pointed to while he conducted the employment background check. Thankfully, Jennifer faxed over the paystubs and Angela's employment history. Finally, Greg collected one final signature on the last piece of paper that agreed to the title company's conditions, and they were finished.

Mr. McGuire placed a phone call to double check on Angela's credit and pre-approved home mortgage, which of course came back excellent and ready to go. Angela budgeted her money and finances very well. In fact, she had taught Jennifer how to budget and helped get her back on track with her own finances three years ago.

After the background check came back, and all the paperwork was signed and finalized, Mr. McGuire shook her hand and thanked her. He reached into his desk and pulled out a small white security envelope. Using his pen, he tore open the envelope and dumped out a pair of keys into his chubby hand. He dropped the keys to 60 Suntides Blvd. and into Angela's palm.

When the keys fell into Angela's hands, she felt a new sense of independent pride from being a homeowner. For the first time since her husband left her, Angela felt empowered to be writing a new chapter in her life. A chapter that would read to others as being a strong, independent woman. One that didn't have to rely on someone else to make it in this world as she had since her college days.

"Angela sweetheart, it has been a great pleasure to get to know you and I know you will enjoy this home. If there is anything else that I can do for you, please don't hesitate to call me. Or stop by and talk to me. You know where I work, and you've got my number."

With tears welling up in her eyes, Angela said, "Thank you, Mr. McGuire. Thank you for all your help."

She looked down at her hands and noticed that there were three keys, to her surprise. Angela thought to herself that one key must be the front door, one key the back door leading out of the laundry room, but what was the third key for?

"What is the third key for?" she asked.

"It is for the third bedroom in the home that was locked," Mr. McGuire said. "It's supposed to be the padlock key. If it doesn't work for you, then let me know and we can cut that lock with some bolt cutters, so that way you can use that room. Also, Angie, would you like the number to a moving company? They come highly recommended and have great reviews on their website. They will help come and haul your things to your new home. And they'll even unload and move things into your house like your bed set upstairs for you, too. I remember when I purchased a new mattress for my wife and I, I moved our new bed into our home a few years back just by myself, and trust me, if I could do that all over again I would. I'd just rather call these boys and have them move the heavier things into our home from now on."

As Mr. McGuire spoke, he stroked his chubby hand along his lower back, showing that he must have hurt it hauling the bed upstairs in his own home. However, Angela thought hiring a moving company was a great idea. After all, she was taking her king-sized bed, along with the frame and headboard, with her. She would need a lot of help to haul that upstairs, so she wouldn't have to stroke her back with her own hand explaining why it hurts so much all the time now too, along with moving the rest of her property into her new home.

"Thank you, Mr. McGuire. I would very much like the help if it's not too much of a hassle."

"It's my pleasure, sweetheart. I won't even charge you for it. It's on the house, courtesy of McGuire Realty."

Mr. McGuire rummaged through a cabinet drawer in his desk and pulled out a small black binder. He flipped through a few pages of business cards in this binder, Mr. McGuire found the card to the moving company named VanGuard's Professional Moving Company.

"Here you are. These are good people and will treat you and your belongings well," Mr. McGuire said. "I recommend them to everyone who does business with us here at McGuire Realty. They will get you taken care of in a day's time."

"Thank you, Mr. McGuire. I will call them when I get to work. Is there anything else that you need from me?" Angela asked.

"Not at all, darling," he said. "If something comes up, then I'll give you a call, however from this point forward, you're good to go. I'll submit this paperwork to the bank. If there's something else, then I have your number. Other than that, your home is yours. Just remember the conditions of our contract. The mortgage payment is due on the 28th of each month and you'll be fine."

"Okay, thank you, Mr. McGuire," Angela said with a smile.

Angela stood up and turned to leave when Mr. McGuire said, "Angela, remember, it's Greg. And congratulations on owning your new home."

With a smile and turn to walk down the hallway, Angela could swear the sun was shining brightly on this rainy day in Oregon.

* * * *

Angela pulled into her parking stall in the garage at Marshall and Stone Law Firm at 10:45 a.m. Traffic yet again was still terrible, as it usually is on Monday mornings in Portland.

Angela got out of her Camry and shut the door, locking it with the remote key chain as she walked towards the law firm's building. Unfortunately for Angela, on the way to work, the rain didn't seem to let up one bit, but the wind was a little calmer now than it had been earlier. Once she was out from the covering of the garage, Angela sprinted to the building's front door. Running in heels was a challenging task that few women can truly master, unless you live in Oregon and even then she nearly rolled her ankle a couple times before she reached the front door, swung it open and stepped inside.

Jennifer was downstairs on the first floor talking to Jeff the barista while ordering a coffee. Angela walked over to the coffee shop and placed an order with Jeff as well.

"Angela," Jennifer said. "Where's your umbrella? It's raining out."

"I'm not worried about that," she said as she rummaged through her purse, pulling out the set of keys and dangled them in front of Jennifer.

"I got my keys to the house!" Angela proclaimed.

Jennifer hugged Angela out of sheer excitement for her, then said, "Angela, that's wonderful! When are you going to move in?"

"I can move in whenever I want. I finished all the paperwork a little bit ago with Greg, and I need to see if I have time to move out of my place this week. The sooner the better and all the things that I'm taking with me are packed up in the garage and ready to be moved."

"One nonfat chai tea pumpkin flavor," Jeff said.

"Oh, that's mine," Jennifer said.

Jeff kept his hand on the cup while Jenn caressed his hand as he grabbed her coffee. Angela simply rolled her eyes.

"Anyway, Jenn, I don't have much to move, and Greg gave me the phone number to this moving agency to call and have them help me make the move," Angela said.

"One nonfat caramel macchiato," Jeff said.

Jeff held onto the cup just how he did with Jennifer, however Angela didn't show any interest, grabbed her coffee and walked towards the elevator with Jennifer. Both girls darted into the lift just in time before the doors slammed shut, nearly taking off Jennifer's leg. Angela hit the button for the fourth floor. When the elevator dinged, both Angela and Jennifer dashed out into the hallway and spotted Mr. Marshall who was sitting at the front desk, helping with the incoming phone calls.

Mr. Marshall looked up and saw his two secretaries walking in and said, "Thank Christ, you girls are here. I know why I pay you so handsomely to be my secretaries. And I thought my job was difficult. Angela, did you get everything squared away with that realtor this morning?"

"I did Mr. Marshall; I have my keys to the home," Angela said.

"That's wonderful, Angie, congratulations," Mr. Marshall said as he walked over and gave Angela a hug. "Now you ladies get to work. I'm going to take some ibuprofen, and maybe lay down on the couch in my office. Somehow, this secretarial work for twenty brief minutes brought on this throbbing headache. It's right here behind my left eye."

Angela and Jennifer quietly snickered after Mr. Marshall had walked back into his office. They knew of the head pain that Mr. Marshall was talking about, as they had both felt it before. How could someone not, when they consistently heard some of the reasons why people called to speak to a divorce lawyer?

Angela's favorite client, since she started working at the office 12 years ago, was a woman who wanted to divorce her husband because he was in love with his motorcycle. "Motorcycle? What's the problem with that?" Angie thought. It wasn't until a minute later that the wife had explained to her that this relationship with his motorcycle was sexual in nature too. Angie had nearly dropped the phone that day.

Angela and Jennifer turned the corner of the secretary's desk and took their seats. Angela rummaged through her purse and found the professional mover's business card that Mr. McGuire gave to her. She called the number on the card as she tucked her purse underneath her desk. The phone rang four times until an elderly woman on the other end of the line answered.

"VanGuard's Professional Moving Service, this is Margaret," the voice said.

"Hello," Angela said. "I recently purchased a home through McGuire's Realty Service, and they told me you would help to move my property from my previous residence."

"Oh yes, yes, we can help you with that," Margaret said. "I can set up a time for you to meet with our senior mover, Brian, and see how much you'll need moved and then we can give you an estimate. Are you moving into town? Intra state? Or out of state?"

"I am just moving across town. Not very far at all. It's from 822 Sherwood Dr. to 60 Suntides Blvd. and Mr. McGuire said that he would pick up the bill for the move for me too."

"Oh, what a dear he is. He's been like that for a long time. Okay. Are you available today to help show Brian what all you need moved?"

"Of course. Would you be able to come out later this afternoon?" Angela asked.

"How does 4 p.m. sound?"

"4 p.m. will work just fine for me. I'll make it work," Angela said.

"Okay, Brian will be at your residence of 822 Sherwood Dr. at 4 p.m. today to give you an estimate of moving expenses and we can go from there, okay?" Margaret asked.

"That sounds good. Thank you, Margaret. Tell Brian I will see him at 4. Goodbye," Angela said and hung up her phone.

"Are you going to leave early today?" Jennifer asked.

"Yes," Angela said. "I've got to tell Mr. Marshall, too. I'll be right back."

"Angela, it's fine. Do what you need to do today. I have extra ibuprofen, so I can answer the phones if it gets too hectic until we close at 5," Mr. Marshall yelled from the desk in his office.

"Thank you, Mr. Marshall," Angela yelled back.

Mr. Marshall was a very easy-going man and very understanding. Trying to get Mr. Stone to be the same was a different story. However, Mr. Stone was still on his family vacation to the Oregon Coast, so for now, Mr. Marshall was in charge. Which worked in Angela's favor today because Mr. Stone wouldn't have been as receptive to Angela doing this during her workday.

"Jennifer, I'm sorry for having such a mixed-up day. But the sooner I get all this done, the sooner I can get out of that house and start being on my own," Angela said.

Jennifer replied, "It's okay, Angie. I get it. You're never usually this erratic. And it's a hectic time since you're, well, going through so much. It's okay. Leave early and get your business taken care of."

3:15 p.m. rolled around and Angela packed her things up to leave. Her last phone call of the day came shortly after 3 p.m. and was a really good one. A woman called the office to speak with Mr. Marshall about setting up an appointment to discuss divorcing her husband of 2 years.

It turned out she had just discovered that he was running a sex club in their basement for the past year with friends from work and even some of their fellow neighbors. Before taking the transferred call from Angela, Mr. Marshall opened his bottle of ibuprofen, took six pills out, swallowed them dry, and picked up the receiver and answer the call.

Angela got up and gave Jennifer a hug goodbye for the day and grabbed her purse and walked toward the exit.

"Let me know how everything goes, Angie," Jennifer said.

Angela walked down the long hallway, past the janitors who were watching a pre-season Mariner's baseball game on their pirated cable television in their closet, pressed the button to summon the old elevator. She could hear the elevator slowly meandering up to her level. The doors slowly opened, and Angela quickly darted in as the doors slammed closed behind her.

Angela hit the ground level floor button. The elevator slowly went down and announced with a loud ding that it had reached the first floor. Once the doors opened, Angela ran out of the elevator and into the lobby.

Jeff was still at the coffee stand. He waved and smiled at Angela as she walked by, however Angela didn't stop to chat. She just smiled and waved back. Angela didn't feel the same way towards Jeff as Jennifer did.

Sunshine and a cold breeze greeted Angela as she stepped outside. It was very nice weather indeed for this time of year in Oregon, especially when compared to earlier this morning. Angela walked to the parking garage and got into her car. She started her car, pulled out and drove back to her old residence of 822 Sherwood Dr.

She regretted having to step foot back there. What if she saw Todd? What would she say? Todd would never be there anyway, but Angela always thought, "What if he was? What would she say to Todd?"

Angela knew one thing, however, and that was she didn't want Todd knowing where she lived at all. If she did happen to see him, she had already concocted a lie that she was just moving in with her friend Jennifer for now.

Angela pulled down Sherwood Dr. at approximately 4:10 p.m. She was concerned that with her tardiness that the mover would already have left. However, at a distance she saw a large white truck was already parked in the driveway with a man sitting in the front driver's seat.

Thank God he hadn't left yet. She looked around the neighborhood and at her driveway. Apart from the large white truck, there were no other vehicles around. Good. Todd wasn't there.

Angela opened the garage door and didn't see Todd's vehicle anywhere either, so she determined she was in the clear. A man in his mid to late 40's hopped out of the driver's seat. She could tell he was a working man, from his rugged in appearance. His hair was cut short, with a reddish-brown goatee. Angela pulled into the driveway and exited her car.

The man approached her and said, "Hello Ms. Kennedy, my name is Brian from VanGuard's Moving Company."

"Hi, Brian,," she said. "You can call me Angela. Or Ms. Brown would be fine, too. Would you like to see the things I need moved to my new place?"

"Yes ma'am," Brian replied.

"Great, thank you for waiting for me, too. Traffic this time of day is, well, you understand."

Brian replied, "Yes ma'am I do understand. No need to explain. Now, do you have everything packed into boxes? All the little things like kitchen appliances? Blankets and bedspreads? Or anything else you feel needs to be packed in a box?"

Angela replied, "Yes Brian, I do. Everything is in a box and if it's not in a box, it means it's just too big to put into a box."

"Uh huh, uh huh," Brian said. So, what all needs to be moved to, is it...60 Suntides Blvd? That's a nice area, ma'am. I had a friend who lived out there a long time ago. I had lots of good times as a kid out there. Nice and quiet area indeed."

"Thank you. I just signed the papers this morning. So preferably the sooner I can move out there, the better. It's hard to explain, but I need to be out of this house," Angela said. "What I need moved out is the TV and the stand that goes with it, the boxes in the kitchen and the garage are all mine. The reclining chair in the living room, along with the stand next to it. The couch by that wall, along with all the pictures hanging on the wall in the living room. In the bedroom, I need the bed, along with the frame and headboard as well. Oh, and the computer desk in the den, too."

"I understand ma'am. Well, that doesn't seem like too much to be moving out of here. Let me call over one of my guys. If they say we could do this tonight, would you be interested?" Brian asked.

"Yes! Absolutely. I didn't think you guys could do it all today."

"Oh, it's no problem. I have a couple guys that I can bring over and we can get this all done in a couple hours, and you could be sleeping in your new home tonight," Brian said. "I'm going to say, oh, about $300. I'll write up an invoice and have it sent to Mr. McGuire tomorrow morning."

"Sounds good," Angela said.

"$300 should cover all the moving expenses. There's not much to move, and you're only moving about half an hour away, and that's simply an estimate on traffic alone. We can get this haul done in one load, and you should be ready to move in tonight to your new place."

"That's great Brian, thank you!"

Brian pulled out an old-style flip phone, dialed a number and waited for a moment while Angie gazed at the house she once called home. She looked at the front window where the brightly lit Christmas tree would be during the holiday season. On Thanksgiving weekend, she, Todd, and a couple of other friends used to go north into Washington state and cut down their own trees from the mountains. It had been a tradition they carried out for years. Sadly, Angela wasn't going to be going into the mountains anymore for her Christmas trees. She wasn't going to re-visit anything that she had done in the past with her ex. From here on out, she would probably just get a fake tree.

Angela overheard Brian talking on the phone with someone named Nick, who he asked to come help with the move. Nick must have agreed to the work late in the evening because Brian closed his phone and said he was going to get started before Nick could beat the Portland traffic and come out. Approximately twenty minutes went by, and a blue car pulled into the driveway. A man in his mid-30's exited the vehicle and walked to the front door, knocking three times before Angela answered it.

"Hello ma'am. I'm Nick. Brian called me from VanGuard's and said you're looking to move this evening into your new house. Said that between the two of us, we could get the job done in just a couple of hours."

That was depressing, thought Angela. She only had enough stuff to put two movers to work for only a couple hours. Either way, Angela shook Nick's hand and introduced herself to him.

Nick was an attractive, middle-aged man, and if Angela wasn't recently divorced and was ready to date again, this would be the kind of man she would go for. He was slightly taller than Angela, with a well-trimmed beard, blue eyes, and a decent body, too.

Angela welcomed Nick in and told him that Brian was in her bedroom, preparing to unbolt the bed frame. Nick met up with Brian in the bedroom as the two began hauling the heavier pieces of property out of the home. While Nick was on his way to the house, Brian had already moved all the boxes from the kitchen into the moving truck, leaving only the bulky items and some of the boxes in the garage. Over an hour later, the two men had all of Angela's property moved from the house and safely packed into the moving truck. It impressed Angela how quickly they worked.

"Okay, Angela," Brian said. "We're going to take off here shortly. Nick is going to follow me, but please lead the way to your new home and I'll just follow you. That way, I don't have to program my GPS unit."

"Sounds good, Brian. Follow behind me. The address is 60 Suntides Blvd., just in case we get split up," Angela said.

Angela took one last look inside the living room. She saw an empty room where she and Todd shared their late evenings on the couch watching sitcoms together or talking about their days, or even making plans to take a weekend trip away together. Over by the window was an empty spot where the Christmas tree would shine brightly for the entire neighborhood to see. She saw where she had spilled red wine on the carpet and remembered how they shared a laugh about it.

Angela sighed deeply to herself and closed the front door behind her, ultimately closing the door to a past life that didn't exist for her anymore. Angela got into her car, started it, and pulled in front of the truck. Brian and Nick followed behind her as she pulled out of 822 Sherwood Lane, leaving her past behind in the rearview window.

Surprisingly, the traffic subsided by the time they hit the freeway. "Most everyone must already be home and enjoying dinner and TV night with their families," Angela thought.

Without getting separated on the drive, the three of them reached Suntides Blvd. shortly after 7 p.m. The white truck backed into the driveway and stopped. Nick parked along the street behind Angela. Angela got out of her car and walked into the driveway to where the driver's side door of the moving truck was.

Upon stopping the truck, Brian got out and looked a little surprised. He said, "I didn't know this was a two-story home."

"Is that going to be a problem?" Angela asked.

"No. No, no way it's not. We've got this ma'am," Brian said.

Angela walked up to the front door, while the two men opened the moving truck and prepared to unstrap her belongings and to move them in. Angela opened the front door to her new home for the first time and looked inside at the living room area. The home seemed cleaner than it was when she had viewed the home on Saturday. It was as if someone had cleaned it from floor to ceiling. The kitchen appeared to be cleaned as well. Angela stood in the living room and examined her new living arrangement.

"We're ready to start movin ma'am," Brian said as he and Nick carried the bed into her home.

"Oh! Jeez, you startled me. Sorry, want me to show you where things will go? The master bedroom is upstairs, and it's the room down that hall and to the right. Last room at the end of the hall," Angela said and pointed.

Brian and Nick took the bed upstairs and Angela followed behind. While the two men went to the master bedroom, Angela stopped momentarily by the third bedroom door and flipped through her set of keys that Mr. McGuire had given to her. She found the key that was supposed to be the one that would unlock the padlocked door. Angela put the key into the padlock's keyhole, however it would not unlock it. She would have to call Mr. McGuire tomorrow and see if he could call someone to cut the padlock off after all.

Damn it. What a silly thing to call Mr. McGuire to ask for help for. Angela felt like she was already starting off on the wrong foot. She was out on her own but couldn't even break the padlock to a master lock, because she didn't own a simple set of bolt cutters. She was annoyed to once again depend on someone else.

Meanwhile, Brian and Nick continued to unload the truck and move boxes into the home. They quickly moved the bedroom set upstairs where Angela wanted it. They even took the time to set the frame up and lay the box spring and mattress on it. The smaller boxes got moved into the kitchen, and they put the computer desk into the office space that was barely large enough to fit the desk. But being the professionals they were, it was no problem at all. They brought the reclining chair and the table stand into the living room, along with the sectional couch that fit perfectly into place against the wall by the front door.

"It must be an omen of good luck," Angela thought.

Nick even took some extra time to hang up some of Angela's pictures along the living room's walls too.

The last piece that Nick and Brian had brought into the home was an old grandfather clock. Angela had forgotten that she even had it. It was a nice antique grandfather clock that didn't belong to her. It belonged to Todd. However, she considered he had abandoned it when he abandoned her and the home, so to hell with it. She would set the clock up in her living room. Brian took a cloth rag out of his back pocket and wiped the dust from the face of the clock and along the sides of its frame.

"What a beautiful grandfather clock," Brian said.

"Thanks. It's been in our family for a couple of decades now," Angela replied. A boldfaced lie, since she knew she had purchased it just a few years ago to add to the living room. Todd didn't care for it much, so its main residency was out in the garage where it gathered dust. Brian wound the clock with a special key and pushed the second arm to get it swinging. Tick, tock, tick, tock, tick, tock the clock repeated its sound. The second hand repeating its back-and-forth motion.

"Where would you like the clock, Angela?" Brian asked.

"Against the corner of the wall, leading to the kitchen. Over there," Angela said, as she pointed towards the wall just before it turned the corner of the staircase.

Brian and Nick moved the clock to where Angela was pointing. Brian moved the clock's arms while checking the time on his phone.

"Oh wow, 10 p.m. already. It's late," Brian said.

"I'm sorry," Angela said. "Thank you both so much for doing this for me. It's nice to be home. In my own home."

Brian finished setting the time to 10 p.m. The clock chimed ten times to indicate that it was 10 o'clock at night.

"Well Angela, it was a pleasure to meet with you this evening. Nick and I are going to call it a night. If you need anything more from us, just give us a call and ask for me."

Brian took out a business card from his breast pocket and handed it to Angela. Angela thanked him and escorted the men to the front door. Before they left, Angela tipped Brian and Nick an extra fifty dollars each for their efforts and staying late. Brian and Nick thanked Angela once more before she closed the door behind them.

It was finally done.

Angela was officially moved into her new home. Her own home. Though it felt a little empty on her first night, so she grabbed her phone and called Jenn.

"Hi, Angie," Jennifer said.

"Hey, so I just got completely moved into my new home."

"Angie, that's great! How's the place?"

"It's wonderful, but I'm kind of lonely. Would you like to come over and spend the night? We can go to work together tomorrow morning."

"Sure. Sounds good to me," Jennifer said.

"Great. I'll see you in a bit, then."

"Sounds good. I'm leaving right now."

Angie hung up the phone and set it back down on the kitchen counter, taking a moment to pause and look at the kitchen table with the set of chairs the original owners had left behind. She walked to the table and lifted one corner of it. It was a heavy, old table and very difficult to move. She looked around the table to see if there was a company name of who made it, but there was none. She did, however, see some scratch marks along the inside and outside of the table's legs.

She figured the owners before her must have owned a dog or a cat. The claw marks were carved deep and narrowly spaced together into the wooden table legs. Probably the work of a cat, no less. Angie grabbed a drinking glass from the cupboard and filled it with water from the sink and pausing for a moment to look out the window into her backyard.

"Damn," she muttered to herself as she peered out at the gate in the fence line. It was swung wide open, revealing the tall grass behind the fence line. Angela thought she would have to get a new latch for the gate. Especially if she wanted to get a dog for herself. Angela refilled her glass with water, walked into the living room, and took a seat in her recliner.

Jennifer came over to the house at around 10:30 p.m. and the two of them stayed up all night talking. They talked about work, the coffee shop, the new house, and what kind of dog Angie wanted to get for herself. Finally, Angela looked at her phone and saw that it was 2 a.m. They both admitted it was time for bed.

Angela and Jennifer got up off the couch and walked upstairs together. They crawled into Angela's large king-sized bed and continued to talk until nearly 3 a.m. when Jenn finally fell asleep. Angela fell asleep shortly after, resting comfortably, knowing that she was now officially on her way to starting a new life.

The gate remained open all night in the backyard.

CHAPTER 4

Tuesday morning came too soon for both Jennifer and Angela. Angela's alarm on her phone went off with a loud chime at 6 a.m. Jennifer's phone followed suit at 6:10 a.m., playing Beethoven's Ode to Joy. Getting only a couple hours of sleep last night made Angela wish she had already unpacked her coffee maker from the moving boxes.

Angela packed a suitcase with personal effects for a couple nights such as clothing, underwear, bathroom accessories. Angela dug through her suitcase, gathering clothes for work and cosmetic accessories, soaps, and shampoos for her bathroom. Before walking out of the bedroom, Angela opened the blinds to the windows, forcing Jennifer to wake up to a wonderful sunny Pacific Northwest morning.

"Angela, shut the blinds, please."

"Jennifer, it's Tuesday. You can't sleep in. Wake up," Angela said.

Jennifer moaned in displeasure and turned over in the bed to keep her eyes out of the sunlight. Angela glanced out the window and investigated the backyard. She noticed something that she had forgotten all about. The door in the wood fence line was still swung wide open. Or it had been previously open since she was there on Saturday and just didn't notice it during the move yesterday evening. Either way, before work, she reminded herself to close the gate and lock it shut.

Angela entered the bathroom and got ready for work, while Jennifer sluggishly made her way out of bed. Jenn had never been a morning person, which is why she craved Saturday mornings during the weekdays. There was a time Jenn slept past nearly noon on the weekend. Angela got after her about that. After getting ready for work, Jennifer went into the bathroom while Angela finished getting herself dressed.

Angela went downstairs and walked out into the backyard towards the opened gate. Angela pushed the gate closed and double checked the latch to ensure it remained locked. Angela walked back to the house and entered through the sliding door next to the kitchen. By this time, Jennifer had finished in the bathroom and was dressed and ready to go to work.

"Are you ready to go?" Angela asked.

Groggily, Jennifer replied, "Yes, let me just grab my purse. Can we go get a coffee before work?"

"If we leave now, we can stop by the coffee stand downstairs at work. You can see your man at the shop. That'll wake you up."

Jennifer smiled and turned around to grab her purse from the coffee table in the living room where she had left it, but the purse wasn't there anymore.

"Angela, I thought I left my purse here on the coffee table?" Jennifer asked.

"Jenn, I can't remember where you left it. It must be around here somewhere. You didn't leave it in the kitchen, did you?"

"I was never in the kitchen last night."

"What about the dining room table?"

"No, I was just in the living room. Maybe I left it in my car? I was sure that I had brought it in the house, though," Jenn said, slightly confused.

The two searched the home for Jenn's purse, ultimately finding it on the computer desk in the office.

"I don't remember being in this room at all, let alone putting my purse here, Angela."

"I don't either, but we both were tired last night, Jenn. Maybe you did and just don't remember. Come on, we must get going to work."

Jennifer left the house, followed closely by Angela. Angela shut the door and locked it behind her. They both drove separate cars to work as Jennifer wasn't planning on coming back to Angela's house afterwards.

Angela noticed that the commute to work was cut short by about five minutes compared to her old drive from Sherwood Dr. This would be great, meaning she could get an extra five minutes of rest, or take five minutes to make coffee or make a quick breakfast. Jennifer arrived at work first, beating Angela by a couple minutes and waited for Angela in the parking garage. Angela parked next to Jenn's car.

"How do I always beat you to work, Angela?" Jenn asked.

Angela knew exactly why. Angela has always wanted to tell her it was because she drives so fast and recklessly that she would have made a good taxicab driver in the Portland metro market.

They walked to the office building from the parking garage and entered. Jeff wasn't at the coffee stand today, so Jennifer didn't feel the need to stop and get a coffee anymore. Both Jennifer and Angela made their way to the elevator. Jennifer punched the button on the elevator to go up. The elevator roared to life and rumbled down from the top floor of the building; the doors opened and released a couple of employees from the neighboring business on the fifth floor. Both Jennifer and Angela darted into the elevator as it slammed shut, nearly cutting Jennifer's purse clean in two.

"Someday this elevator is going to kill someone. Cut them clean in half!" Jennifer said, as she hit the button to go up to the fourth floor.

"You have a great house, Angie," Jennifer said. "I can't believe how quiet it was last night. I haven't slept in such a peaceful environment since I lived back in my parent's house in Packwood."

"Packwood. Where is that?"

"It's in Washington state. Really small town, but they like the small-town atmosphere," Jenn replied.

"So, it was quiet last night, wasn't it? Just needed a little more time for rest."

The elevator came to a stop on the fourth floor, and the doors slowly opened. The girls forced their way into the hallway as the doors were still opening. As soon as Jennifer stepped out, the doors slammed shut. Then they both walked towards the front door of their office building.

Today was the day that Mr. Stone was coming back to work from his family vacation to the Oregon Coast, so they needed to ensure that they made it to the office on time. Mr. Stone was a bit more demanding than Mr. Marshall was. In fact, both the girls loathed the fact that Mr. Stone was coming back to work, and wished he extended his vacation for a few more days.

"Where do you want to go for lunch today?" Jennifer asked.

"I'm not sure yet," Angela replied. "I may head to the store and get some supplies for the house. I need to do a little cleaning in the kitchen. Would you like to come over tonight and help?"

"No, I can't. Jeff and I are supposed to be going out for drinks this evening to this new place in Gresham. He said it just opened last weekend," Jennifer replied.

"Well, that should be fun," Angela said. "What time will you be leaving for Gresham?"

"At 6 p.m."

"Okay. So right after work, then?"

"Yup."

The work morning was going fast. Both Angela and Jennifer received a couple of calls a piece, but their clients were asking more questions than they were making appointments with Mr. Stone and Mr. Marshall. Jennifer received a call from a potential client that asked her if it would be appropriate to divorce her husband after he had gambled away his paychecks over the past two months. As Mr. Stone and Mr. Marshall had suggested to both Angela and Jennifer, it was wise never to recommend anything themselves and to leave it to Mr. Marshall and Mr. Stone. So, Jennifer did her job and left the decision up to them and scheduled her client for an appointment later in the week.

Angela wasn't as lucky. She received a phone call during the latter part of the morning from a male client. This surprised her, as most of the clients she worked with were disgruntled women. However, the man claimed his wife was having an affair with their neighbor's son out of all the people.

"17 years old! That's statutory rape, isn't it?" the caller asked.

Again, Angela did what Mr. Stone and Mr. Marshall wanted her to do during the duration of her employment and made an appointment for Mr. Stone on Thursday. And thank God too, because that seemed like a call she didn't want to go into detail about. 12 o'clock came around fast for both Jennifer and Angela. They ordered a sandwich from the local sub shop down the street.

"Angie, it's time to go to lunch," Jenn said at noon sharp.

"Okay, let me grab my purse. Are you ready to go?"

"All ready."

"Okay, let me tell Mr. Stone and Mr. Marshall."

Angela walked over to Mr. Stone's office. Mr. Stone was typing on his computer at the desk. Angela knocked on the door and said that she and Jennifer were going to lunch, which to Mr. Stone replied with a grunt. Angela turned to walk away and Mr. Marshall, who was next door on the phone, placed his hand over the receiver and told Angela to have a good lunch. Angela thanked Mr. Marshall and continued to walk to the front door where Jennifer was waiting for Angela. The girls proceeded to walk to the elevator together.

"While we're out, I need to stop by the store and get some cleaning supplies for the kitchen," Angela said.

"That's fine. They're usually quick at making subs at the shop, anyway."

They approached the elevator, and Angela hit the button to go down. The elevator came roaring up to the fourth floor and opened slowly to allow them access. Jennifer and Angela jumped in, while Jennifer hit the button to go down.

"I think I'm going to look for a dog after work today."

"Really?" Jennifer asked. "What kind of dog?"

"I'm thinking a lab, or maybe a border collie."

"A border collie would be a fun dog to own. What about a German shepherd? They're tough dogs and for a single woman living alone, you want a tough dog."

"I could see myself owning a German shepherd too. Just any kind of dog, really. It would be nice to have something else living around the house."

The elevator door slowly opened and Angela and Jennifer both jumped out of the elevator before nearly being killed by the doors again as they quickly slammed shut. The girls then walked to the front door of the building. Jeff still wasn't at the coffee stand, which prompted Jennifer to ask Angela where she wondered Jeff was. Angela really didn't care as the two walked out of the building.

The sub shop was about a block away. Angela really enjoyed the sandwiches they made. Jennifer enjoyed them very much as well. Angela would always get her favorite turkey and ham, while Jennifer would get the Italian style sub sandwich. The girls opened the door and saw Ray, the sub shop owner. He was always working hard at making the orders of every customer who came into his store. Amazingly, he knew the names of all his regular customers. He knew the girls as they had been to his restaurant time and time again for lunches. The girls never had to say a word, other than visit and chit chat with Ray. True to his form, Ray whipped up a couple of sandwiches in under 5 minutes.

"Looks great as always Ray, you're the best sub sandwich maker in all of Portland!" Jennifer said.

Ray blushed, and the girls thanked him at the register for their food and they turned to sit at a nearby table together while Ray went back to work.

"So, Jenn, did you notice that the door in the fence was opened this morning?" Angela asked.

"Was that why you were in the backyard this morning?"

"Yeah, I was closing it. I guess the latch was unlocked or something and the wind blew it open, or even the neighborhood kids may have pushed it open, I guess."

"I wouldn't worry about its Angie, it probably just wasn't latched properly and opened from the wind or something."

"Yeah, that's true. When I was out there closing the gate, I looked behind the fence and saw a small trail that must lead down to the creek that Mr. McGuire was talking about."

"Well, this weekend you'll have to go down there and check it out. See how small this creek is and what's down there. Wouldn't that be cool if you could go fishing back there?"

"I really don't think going fishing in a creek is for me, but maybe I'll walk down there this weekend and have a look around."

Angela never thought about walking down the trail to go look at the creek and see what was behind her fence line, but now that Jennifer had said something she was curious about it. Perhaps she would check out the creek and see what was down there. She remembered that Mr. McGuire didn't really talk much about it, nor did he go past the fence line.

"There is a store around the corner here that sells household supplies, we can walk there and get some cleaning supplies after we're done with our sandwiches," Angela said.

"That's fine by me," Jenn replied.

"I'm thinking this afternoon I'll look for a dog on the internet. You want to help me out?"

"Yes! I would love to find a dog with you!"

Jennifer loved dogs, however the dogs she liked weren't the kind that Angela wanted. Jennifer loved the kind of dogs you could carry in a bag with you wherever you went. Jennifer never owned a dog before, but she always talked about owning a teacup chihuahua. A breed not nearly as intimidating as the German Shepard. Both Angela and Jennifer finished their sandwiches and left the sub shop.

"Have a nice day girls!" Ray said.

"Thanks Ray!" the girls said together. "We'll see you tomorrow!"

As they walked to the store to get the cleaning supplies, Jennifer asked, "Have you decided what kind of dog you want to get?"

"It's going to be a bigger dog. At least a border collie, but I like the German Shepherd you talked about."

"I just think it would be a good dog to get. It would keep like strays and the neighbor kids out of the backyard, ya know?"

"That's true. That reminds me, I should get a lock for the gate in the backyard. Put a new one on there."

"Angela, it still bothers me that my purse wasn't where I had left it from last night. I don't ever remember going into your office room. I've been thinking about it on and off this morning."

"Jenn, it was late last night and maybe you just put it in there and don't remember doing it."

"Yeah, I guess."

Angela and Jennifer reached the store, walked inside and greeted the shop owner. The shop owner waved at them as they walked over to the household cleaning supplies section. Angela quickly sifted through the cleaning chemicals and found the lemon based organic one that she wanted and quickly paid for the product. After paying, both Angela and Jennifer left and walked back to work. They still had a bit of time, so they didn't have to rush at all.

Angela and Jennifer made it back to their office about five minutes before their lunch break was over, but that was okay. It only meant they could leave five minutes earlier at the end of their day. Setting their purses under the desk, Angela logged back onto her computer and browsed the internet, looking for the dog she had in mind. Jennifer watched as she clicked through various websites.

"What about that one, Angela? It's golden brown."

"I don't really care about the color too much, Jenn. I just want a dog," Angela said.

"Well, what about that one?"

Jenn pointed at an ad for a nice looking one-year-old Labrador that needed a home. The ad said that the original owners were moving out of state to Maryland and that they could not take their dog with them to their new residence.

"That looks like the perfect dog," Angela said as she wrote down their contact information.

Angela called the owners later in the afternoon. It sounded as if it was the wife who had answered the phone. Angela asked if she could come over and see the dog, which the woman agreed to. At five o'clock Angela grabbed her purse and wished Jenn a good time in Gresham that evening. She quickly made her way to her car, hoping to beat the five o'clock traffic in Portland, however she was unable to. As usual.

The dog she was interested in was on the other side of town from her office, so it took nearly an hour for her to arrive. Angela parked her Toyota Camry in front of the residence and walked up to the front door and rang the doorbell. No answer. She rang the doorbell a second time and heard footsteps on the other side. The door unlocked and opened, revealing a woman who introduced herself as Mrs. Mackie.

"Hi, you must be Angela," Mrs. Mackie said.

"I am. Thank you for having me over," Angela replied.

"Well, thank you for coming to look at Lilly. Come on in."

Angela walked into the spacious living room with very little furniture.

"I appreciate you coming over. I don't mean to push you into taking Lilly, but if you don't take her today, she is going to the pound. We're moving in two days, and what you see here is going to be gone by tomorrow afternoon," Mrs. Mackie said.

Mrs. Mackie walked Angela through the back of the house to the backyard and called for Lilly. The black Labrador came running from the furthest part of a large backyard.

"I hope you have a backyard that has room for her to run. She's a very energetic dog and loves to run and play. She doesn't really bark much unless someone is around that she doesn't know. So anytime she barks, you'll know someone is around that doesn't need to be," Mrs. Mackie said.

"That sounds great. She seems like a very nice dog. Full of energy," Angela said.

Lilly ran up to Angela as if she had been her master for the last year of her young life. She sat at her feet and raised her head to Angela, waiting to be stroked along the throat and pet on the head. The two seemed like they belonged together.

"I think she likes you," said Mrs. Mackie. "Would you like to take her?"

Angela thought for a few seconds, then said, "I would. She's the perfect dog for my place. I have a large backyard, so she won't miss her space either. Plus, I'd hate to see a beautiful animal like this go to a pound."

"That's great! We were hoping you would take her. I'll get her leash, food and water dishes for you and you can take her this evening if you'd like."

Mrs. Mackie took Angela and Lilly into the house, retrieved Lilly's leash, food and water dishes, as well as a half a bag of dog food.

"You seem like a good person, Angela; I know you'll take good care of her. She's great with kids, too."

"Oh, I don't have any children. It's just me. Well, there are some neighborhood kids. But I don't associate with them."

"I know you'll provide a wonderful home for her."

"Thank you so much, Mrs. Mackie. She will have a good place to call home."

Angela walked to the front door with Lilly tied to the leash. Lilly walked willingly with Angela, as if Angela had owned her since she was a puppy. Lilly jumped right into the passenger seat of Angela's Toyota Camry. Mrs. Mackie stood at the front door, about to cry, watching Lilly leave.

Angela started her car and drove off with Lilly, heading back home. Of course, Angela ran into traffic again on her way home from the Mackie residence. Lilly proved to be a good dog to travel with in cars, too. It was an attribute that few dogs had. Angela finally made it home to 60 Suntides Blvd. an hour after picking up her new pet. Both Lilly and Angela got out of the car and walked to the front door.

Angela held Lilly's leash in hand as she fumbled for her keys in her purse. Finally, finding them, she fit the key into the doorknob and opened the door. Lilly ran in, in front of Angela. It was still sunny outside, so Angela took Lilly and put her in the backyard. After a few laps around the backyard and sniffing her new environment out, Lilly looked as if she fit in just nicely. Angela called Lilly over and took her leash off her collar. While she was rolling up her leash, Angela noticed Lilly ran over to the gate in the fence line and sniffed around it. Watching for a minute, Lilly barked at the gate.

Angela thought this was odd, remembering what Mrs. Mackie had told her that Lilly didn't bark very much at all, unless someone was snooping around that didn't belong there. Angela instantly thought of the neighborhood kids that must have been playing around in the creek. After scolding Lilly for barking, Angela went back inside the house to make a quick dinner. Angela put her new cleaning supplies under the sink in the kitchen. She planned to do a thorough cleaning later this weekend, but not tonight.

Glancing out the window, she noticed Lilly was still barking at the gate. Not thinking much about it, Angela cooked a package of noodles along with some fried vegetables. After preparing her food, Angela sat down on the couch in the living room and watched a few television shows.

Angela waited for a phone call from Jennifer that evening to see how her time with Jeff was going in Gresham, however, Jennifer never called. She must have been having a good time, thought Angela. There was no need for Jennifer to call her. As the time grew late into the night, she grew more and more sleepy. Finally, Angela turned the TV off and walked upstairs to her bedroom. As she passed the locked room on her way to bed and she made a mental note to call Mr. McGuire to see if he found the key to that locked room. Otherwise, he would need to call someone out to replace the doorknob.

Angela walked into her bedroom, shut the door behind her, and locked it. She walked into the bathroom, brushed her teeth and applied a nighttime wrinkle reducer facial cream. Before getting into bed, Angela stood by the window. She opened it to get some fresh air, as well as closed the curtains. Looking out back, she noticed Lilly was still sitting at the gate in the fence line. She stopped barking and tilted her head as if she was trying to listen to something on the other side.

Angela didn't think too much about Lilly staying outside for the night, if that's what she wanted. The weather was supposed to be clear, and the temperature was going to be warm enough that it wouldn't be a big deal. Angela finally shut the curtain to the window and crawled into bed. After laying down, Angela closed her eyes and before she fell asleep, Lilly began barking again. Aggressively.

CHAPTER 5

Two weeks passed since Angela moved into her new residence at Suntides Blvd. Angela and Lilly had been enjoying one another's company and bonding. Lilly even got along with Jennifer when she would come over to visit.

Angela spent her free time on the weekend going out for walks around the neighborhood with Lilly. She even found a nice small park nearby where Lilly could play. The park had a couple basketball hoops where neighboring kids would come and play games of Pig, Bump, and 3 on 3 basketball. All in all, Angela was really beginning to enjoy Lilly's company in her new home. The one strange thing about Lilly, though, was her bizarre fascination with the gate in the backyard, and how she excessively barked at it.

Occasionally, Angela still found the gate open, which frustrated her. She always worried that one day the kids that played back there were going to open the gate again and Lilly was going to take off. Nearly every day, the gate was open, but Lilly stayed in the backyard. Angela would catch her sitting by the open gate, barking at the tall blades of grass behind the fence when she would get home from work in the evenings.

On Saturday morning, Angela slept in after a long week of listening to husbands and wives call her office to not only make appointments but vent their frustrations to her. Sometimes her job made her feel more like a psychologist than a secretary.

Lilly was in the backyard, but for once, she wasn't making a sound, which was nice. Angela needed the rest. The night prior, she and Jennifer had gone out to a nice Mexican restaurant called El Rincon. They had just opened in the downtown Portland area, and it was ladies' night with two-dollar happy hour drinks until the bar area of the restaurant closed at 2 a.m. Angela spent twenty dollars on herself, as well as twenty dollars for the taxi ride home. Jennifer came home with Angela, since Jeff had left them earlier in the night to go take one of his guy friends back to their home. Angela was skeptical about Jeff's reason for leaving early that night and then not coming back to hang out with Jennifer, but who knew? Maybe Jeff was tired and was ready to call it an evening himself.

It was nearly nine in the morning when the doorbell to the house rang. Angela stirred around in bed, thinking she was dreaming of the doorbell. However, the doorbell chimed again, and Lilly started barking in the backyard and she realized it wasn't a dream. Who would ring the doorbell at nine in the morning?

Angela sat up and got out of bed, noticing that Jennifer was still fast asleep on the other side of the bed. Angela threw her robe on over her pajamas and walked downstairs. On the way downstairs, the doorbell rang two more times.

"I'm coming, just a minute!" Angela said as she answered the door and noticed that it was her elderly neighbor from across the street, Mr. Butler, with a newspaper in his hand.

"Hi there Angela, how do ya do this fine mornin?"

"Hello, Mr. Butler. How are you this morning?"

"I'm mighty fine, mighty fine indeed. I didn't wake ya up now, did I?"

"No, no. I've been up for a little bit."

"That's mighty fine now. I just wanted to bring you over your newspaper this mornin. I ain't been by since ya moved in now. How's the house treatin ya?"

"That's very nice of you, Mr. Butler."

"Please Angela, call me Tom now. We be neighbors."

"Okay Tom, thank you. The house is great. I just recently got a dog, and her name is Lilly. She isn't keeping you awake with her barking at night, is she? Her previous owner told me she doesn't bark much at night, but for whatever reason, she's barking a lot here."

"Not one bit Angela, she ain't keepin me up one bit. I can tell you like this house now. The previous owners gone liked it a lot too."

"Did you know them, Tom?"

"Nope, I didn't know dem personally, but they gone seemed like nice people."

"What happened to them, Tom? Would you like to come in for a minute?"

"No, Angela, no not now. I just stopped by to say hi, is all. You know I don't really know what gone happened to them. One-minute dem folks were here, and the next minute, whoosh! They gone done be gone."

"Well, thank you for stopping by. I'll see you around. Come over any time you feel like it and thank you for the newspaper, too."

"You be mighty welcome, Angela, mighty welcome indeed. I'll be seein ya around the neighborhood. You done call me whenever you need somethin too, ya hear?"

"I will. Thank you very much Tom."

As Mr. Butler turned to walk away, he turned around and said, "This house gone done likes you Angela, it likes you a lot too!"

However, Angela didn't hear Mr. Butler. She had already shut the door and walked away, back towards the kitchen. She set the newspaper down on the kitchen table, opened the refrigerator, and grabbed a bottle of orange juice. Remembering however that one of her drinks the night before was a mixture of orange juice and vodka though, Angela put it back and made coffee instead.

After starting the coffeemaker, Angela went outside to feed Lilly and noticed that the gate to the fence line was ajar again. It surprised and frustrated Angela because she always locked the gate and somehow it still opened. Stepping outside from the sliding glass door, Angela looked around and noticed that Lilly wasn't in the backyard anymore.

"Oh, shit," Angela said. It was her worst dream come true.

Angela panicked as she quickly put her shoes on and rushed outside. The closer Angela got to the fence line, she noticed something strange next to the gate along the fence. Blood. Not very much blood at all. In fact, it looked like a smear from a cut on someone's hand when they went to grab the latch to the gate.

It would be the first time Angela walked back behind the fence as she hurried through the gate and into the tall grass, looking for any sign of her dog. Angela noticed a small dirt path leading down the hill to what she assumed would lead to the small creek that Mr. McGuire had told her about. The path was worn and overgrown, slightly covered by leaning blades of grass.

"Lilly!" Angela called as she continued to follow the small trail.

Angela noticed a small trail of blood leading down the path, speckled on the blades of grass. She wondered if a wild animal had attacked Lilly and carried her off. Angela also noticed strange small footprints along the trail as well. She thought it must have been some sort of small wild animal, a squirrel or a muskrat? The small footprints appeared to have three claws in the front, but nothing in the back. Weird, she thought, as she continued to walk down the path.

The path eventually leveled out, and Angela heard the babbling creek water drawing closer. The dirt path narrowed further and further as the grass swallowed the clear path until it seemed as if the trail never existed in the first place. Angela then came to a set of bushes.

It must've been the end of this trail, she thought. Peering through the bushes, she saw what appeared to be an old well. Angela looked closer at the bushes and noticed some shrubs were bent as if something heavy was dragged into the clearing towards the well.

"Oh my God, if the neighbor's kids have done anything to my dog, it's going to be their ass!" Angela said.

Upset and fearing the worst for her dog, Angela walked up to the well, slowly leaned over the round stone border and looked in.

The well was deep. Very deep. Freezing. Very dark.

Angela felt a frigid breeze coming from inside the well. How was that possible? And what was the source of such an icy blast of air? As hard as she peered into the darkness, though, she could see no light. Maybe the well connected to a cave system somewhere in the area, but even then, it wasn't windy in the morning.

Angela looked around the well and found a small bright white rock lying nearby the creek. She picked the rock up and dropped it into the well. The pebble disappeared into the mass of darkness within the well. She waited to hear the rock hit the bottom of the well or ricochet off something. Angela continued to hold her breath and listen. Incredibly, the rock never made a sound. No sound of it hitting water. No sound of it hitting other rocks or stones. No sound of it hitting the bottom.

"The well went on infinitely!" Angela thought, who took a couple of steps back from the well and yelled for Lilly one more time. There was no response. Only the sounds of the nearby babbling creek. Angela turned and walked back up the trail and back to the house. Walking through the tall blades of grass, she thought she had seen something small in the corner of her eye in the brush line scurrying along the side of the creek.

"Too small to be my dog. Probably just a squirrel," Angela said.

Either way, she yelled for Lilly one more time, but never received a response. Once she got back into her backyard, Angela left the gate open, hoping Lilly might come back in that way. Angela looked at the spots of blood on the inside of the fence line and noticed that they were dry. She didn't remember seeing those spots the last time she closed the gate, so if something happened to Lilly, then it must have happened overnight.

Angela walked back into the house and poured a cup of coffee as Jennifer made her way downstairs.

"I thought I heard you yelling for Lilly?" Jenn asked.

"I was. Lilly isn't in the backyard."

"Oh my gosh, do you want to go looking for her?"

"Yeah, we can walk around the neighborhood before we go back to the restaurant to get our cars. I hope she's okay. I made some coffee, and there are some cups in the cupboard. Grab a mug with a lid from the cabinet and let's see if we can find her."

Jennifer poured herself a cup of coffee and the two of them got dressed and went out looking for Lilly in the neighborhood. Angela knocked on some doors and asked if any of the neighbors had seen Lilly, however everyone replied they hadn't. Angela became discouraged. They went back to Angela's home and called Jeff. Jeff arrived about an hour after Jennifer had called him to take them back to the restaurant to get their cars. Having to work that day, Jeff dropped the girls off at the restaurant and went to work.

"Angela, you want to keep looking for Lilly?"

"No, I'll just drive around the neighborhood and see if I can find her. I know you have things you need to get done, too," Angela said.

"Are you sure, Angela? I don't mind going with you. I can help you make some fliers too. You have a picture of her."

"Yeah, I have a couple of pictures, but no, it's fine. I'm sure she'll come back home eventually, anyway. When I get home, I'll make up some fliers and post them around the neighborhood."

"Okay, call me if you need help."

Jennifer turned and got into her car, started it, and drove out of the parking lot. Angela did the same. Going to the store to get some groceries was the only thing Angela had to do today. On the way to the grocery store Angela thought maybe she could call the humane society, some vet offices, as well as make some fliers to hang up around the neighborhood when she got home. She also remembered that she still needed to call the locksmith that Mr. McGuire had scheduled to come out today as well.

Angela's trip to the store was short and quick. Having a lot weighing on her mind, Angela called the number to the locksmith. The phone rang twice and was answered by a coarse and heavy voice.

"Hello," the heavy voice said.

"Hi, my name is Angela. Mr. McGuire scheduled the appointment for you to come out today to break the lock on the third bedroom door upstairs in my home."

"Yes, of course Angela. Greg told me you'd be calling today. My name is Edgar. Can I come out to the house today still and work on that door for you?"

"Yes please, I'll be home by this afternoon."

"Perfect, I'll come by, say, around two this afternoon. Will that be alright?"

"Yes, it'll be fine. Thank you. I will see you then."

"Yes, see you then."

Angela hung up the phone and drove home. She tried to remember if she saw Lilly outside last night when she had gotten home from the restaurant, but she couldn't recall much other than waking up to the sound of the doorbell in the morning. She figured she was probably lucky enough to make it home with her purse. Angela made her way back home, carrying her groceries in tow. She walked up to the front door. Fumbling for the keys in her purse, Angela unlocked the door and walked in when her phone rang again.

"Not now," Angle said as she hustled towards the kitchen with an armful of bagged groceries. She set them down on the countertop and answered her phone on the sixth ring.

"Angela, are you home yet? Did Lilly come back?" Jennifer asked.

"I just got home, but I don't see her in the backyard. I'm going to make some fliers and a poster to take down to the humane society and to hang up around the neighborhood. If someone sees her, then they can call me, but I don't know what else to do, Jenn."

"I'm sorry Angie, if I can help in any way let me know."

"Thanks Jenn, you've always been a good friend to me. I appreciate you."

They said their goodbyes to each other and Angela set the phone down. Sighing and looking up out the window, Angela saw the gate swinging open from a small breeze, but no sign of Lilly. Angela put her groceries away. Shortly after putting the groceries away, Angela began placing phone calls to the nearby vet offices, as well as calling the humane society. The doorbell rang as Angela was making a poster to take to the local humane society and fliers to post around the neighborhood.

For God's sake, who can this be now? Angela answered the door and noticed a gentleman standing there with a tool bag and an outstretched hand. Angela reached out and shook this man'' hand.

"Hello Angela, I'm Edgar. I'm sorry for being a little earlier than I stated before, but I finished my last job and thought I'd see if you were okay with me starting on your bedroom door job?"

"Oh, yes, Edgar. I'm sorry, I completely forgot you were coming; it's been a long day today. My dog ran away from home this morning so I'm hoping she comes back, but in the meantime, I'm just working on making fliers for her. It's nice to meet you. Yes, you are welcome to work on the door. I'll be home for a while," Angela said.

"Are you sure, ma'am? If you need me to, I can always come back another day?" Edgar asked.

"No, no. It's perfectly fine. Come on in."

"Very good," Edgar said. "If you want, I can take some fliers and I'll post them around the neighborhood for you."

"That's sweet of you. Thank you, Edgar."

"It's my pleasure," Edgar said and glanced up to the second floor at the white door behind the banister. He pointed and asked, "Is that the door you're wanting unlocked, Angela?"

"Yes, yes, it is. I haven't been able to get it open since I've moved in and Mr. McGuire said he had a key, but I guess he couldn't find it. It's weird because it's locked from inside the room. I've had no way of getting in there so honestly, I don't even know what it looks like or if it needs repainted or what."

Edgar laughed. "Nothing like being surprised then, huh? Okay. It'll be no problem. I can have that door opened for you in five minutes. And Greg said he was going to pay to have the doorknob replaced, so if you want, I can do that too. I've got just a standard knob, dark brass color, but it would work."

"That'll be great, thank you Edgar."

Edgar went up the stairs and began working on the door. Angela could hear Edgar upstairs fidgeting with his tools and could hear picking noises on the door's lock, then eventually a drill.

"This is a pretty old doorknob," Edgar said as he peered over the banister to the lower level of the home.

"Well, it's an old house. I haven't been able to get into that room since I moved in. Mr. McGuire told me the room basically looks the same as the other spare bedroom," Angela said.

"They do. Older houses in this area weren't built with much character in terms of how the bedrooms looked. They really focused on the design of the kitchens and living rooms. Something about family values back then. They thought families spent their time in the dining and living rooms. So that's where they needed to focus their effort in making the better-looking rooms," Edgar said. "So, all the homes around this neighborhood have immaculate looking living rooms, beautiful kitchens, but when it comes to their bedrooms and bathrooms, they're pretty basic."

Angela went back to working on her poster for the humane society and her fliers to hang up around the neighborhood when she heard the bedroom door's knob being broken, followed by a slow creaking noise as the door opened.

"Oh, my God!" Edgar said.

"Edgar, are you okay?" Angela asked.

"Angela, can you come up here?"

By the tone of Edgar's voice, Angela thought something was wrong, so she left the office and walked up the stairs, noticing the temperature decreasing with each step. It was getting colder, nearly to where Angela could almost see her breath as she moved closer to the room. She turned the corner of the door and walked into the room to find Edgar staring down at the floor.

"What is it?" Angela asked.

But Edgar was shocked and speechless.

She saw what remained of her dog, Lilly. The poor animal was torn into five pieces and, remarkably, there was no blood on the floor. Each leg, along with the torso, appeared carefully placed to form a circle around the room.

Inside the room there was an old area rug that looked as if it had been there from when the house was built, Angela had guessed, but more importantly she had found her dog which raised the question, what happened to her? And most of all, how was she placed in a room that Angela didn't have access to?

Seeing the body of her dog torn into pieces, Angela gasped and covered her hands over her mouth. Edgar remained stunned, looking at the pieces of the body scattered on the old carpet.

"Edgar, that's my dog," Angela said.

"How did she get into this room when it was locked? And what happened to her?" Edgar asked.

"I don't know. I haven't been able to open this room since I moved in."

"Where is her head?"

Edgar and Angela checked the window, which was securely locked from the inside by an old metal latch. The window's frame was painted over as well, showing that the window hadn't been opened for years.

Edgar inspected the closet to see if an animal had come through that way and dragged the body into the room, however it was just an ordinary closet. There was nothing special anymore about it and no holes, no entry points, no way for Lilly to be in this room.

Angela looked in the room's corner and noticed an old dresser. It was the only thing in the room besides the old area rug. Its wood was worn, dry, and in need of cleaning and color staining. She pulled the dresser out from against the wall and found a small opening, much like the opening in her office downstairs. She remembered that Mr. McGuire had told her that the previous owners of the home wanted to put in the air conditioning unit. So, was this the way Lilly was brought into the room? And even if that was the case, how could she travel up the air duct and through this hole in the wall? And that still didn't explain what happened to her in this room.

Angela got down on her hands and knees and investigated the opening.

Edgar grabbed a flashlight from his tool bag, turned it on, and passed it to Angela. She examined the opening in the wall and noticed a small white object that would gleam bright when hit by the light. She stuck her hand into the hole, but could barely reach far enough to grab the object. It was hard.

"My God," thought Angela. She hoped it wasn't a piece of bone from Lilly.

Pulling her hand back out with the hard object, she discovered it was a small bright rock laying in the ductwork system.

"Why is there a white rock lying in the ductwork so close to the opening?" Angela asked.

Then she remembered earlier in the morning when she was out looking for Lilly behind the fence. Was this the same small white rock that she had dropped into the well earlier? Angela stood up with the white rock in her hand. She was dumbfounded as she fondled the rock in her hands. Tears streamed down her cheeks.

"Angela, I'm sorry. I'll take care of this for you if you want," Edgar said.

"No," Angela replied as she wiped the tears from her face. "I'll take care of it. Thank you, Edgar. Can you replace the doorknob for me and that'll be all?"

Edgar slowly went back to working on the doorknob again, while Angela left the room with the rock in hand. Walking downstairs, Angela headed to the kitchen and grabbed a handful of garbage bags from underneath the sink. She set the rock down on the kitchen table and sat down in a dining chair. She needed a moment to process what was going on. Gathering her emotions, Angela walked back upstairs with the garbage bags.

Edgar was replacing the doorknob with a new dark brass colored knob and, most importantly, one that didn't lock, when Angela walked back into the room with garbage bags and gloves. Placing each piece of Lilly's body into the garbage bags, Angela bobbed her shoulders and cried again. Edgar stopped working on the door, set his tools down, and walked over to console her.

"I'll help you, Angela. Let me see the bags."

Through tears, Angela said, "I just don't know how this happened. This room has always been locked. How could she have gotten in here, and who would have done something like this?"

Edgar began picking up the pieces of Lilly's body and placing them into the garbage bags. He noticed that each piece of the body was drained of its blood, which he thought was the weirdest part of the situation.

Together they walked back down the stairs, to the backyard where Edgar retrieved a shovel from Angela's small tool shed in the back and dug a grave for Lilly, behind the fence line. Once the hole was deep enough, he helped Angela lower the body into the hole and filled in the grave.

"A at least you have closure now," Edgar said.

"I don't feel like I do. Sure, I found her, but how she ended up where she was and in that state, I will never know."

Edgar patted Angela on her back and turned to walk back through the gate into the backyard. Angela walked back into the yard and closed the gate in the fence line, and locked it. They walked back into the house, which seemed to be colder than usual.

Angela turned the furnace heat on in the house while Edgar walked back upstairs to continue working on the bedroom door. A short time later, Edgar finished the job. Walking back downstairs with tools in hand, Edgar stopped by Angela.

"Angela, are you going to be alright?"

"Yes, I will be. I called my friend. She's going to come over."

"Alright. If that door gives you any more trouble, you have my number and Greg's. Just give us a call and I'll come back out and make sure it works for you."

"Thank you. And Edgar, thank you for helping me with, umm…"

"It's alright Angela, I'm sorry for your dog."

"You're right. At least I know that she's not lost out there somewhere."

But Lilly's death and how she ended back in that room were still unexplained. Angela still couldn't get those questions out of her mind. Edgar left and shut the front door behind him.

Angela headed back into the kitchen. She stopped in front of the table, noticing the small white rock that she had dropped in the well.

"That has to be the same damn rock I dropped down that well!" she said. "But how in the hell did it end up in that hole up there in that wall?

As she looked up from the rock and out the glass sliding door, Angela noticed something odd. The gate that she had locked a short time ago while burying Lilly outback was wide open again.

That night Angela went to bed early. She wasn't feeling very social after finding the remains of her pet dog. She slowly cried herself to sleep that evening, all the while thinking about how that rock had found its resting point in the hole in the wall.

CHAPTER 6

Angela slept through the night soundly, only waking up around 3 a.m. because she had thought she heard something in the backyard. She woke up and dragged herself out of bed and into the shower, still feeling upset about the death of her dog, but more confused how it happened.

Animals don't just die the way her dog did. Angela grew concerned at the different ways her dog could've got into a previously locked room. She turned the shower off. Steam coated the mirrors in a fine mist. Angela dried her body off and threw on some clothes to do some yard work. She had the day off, so it was a good day to do some gardening out front. Planting some primroses and pansies out in the garden seemed like a good way to get her mind off what had happened to Lilly.

Angela spent the whole day planting flowers in the flower bed out front. One by one, she dug small holes and planted primroses, then carnations, and pansies, followed by marigolds. She planted until she was out of flowers and needed to go to the store to buy more. It was late in the afternoon, close to dinnertime, when she stepped back to admire her work in the garden. After setting up the sprinkler in the middle of the garden, Angela turned the spigot on at the house and the water rushed through the hoses, raining down onto her flowers. She then went back into the house to make a small dinner for herself.

"Hmm...I think I'm going to make a beef and vegetable stew for dinner. Then I can re-heat that for other dinners and lunches next week, too," Angela said.

She got the ingredients out of the refrigerator and washed the vegetables. Then she chopped the vegetables into smaller pieces. While chopping them, Angela looked out the window above the kitchen sink, staring into the backyard.

"That damn gate," Angela said.

There it was. The gate in the fence line swung open. Angela sighed and went back to chopping her vegetables. She planned to shut the door later. The doorbell rang around 5:30 in the evening, shattering the silence in her home. Angela set down the kitchen knife next to the vegetables she was chopping on the counter, rinsed her hands off in the sink and answered the door.

"Hi Angela, how are you doing today? Are you okay?" Jennifer asked.

"I am, I'm okay, come on in."

Jennifer walked into the house and set her purse on the coffee table. She reached into her purse to take her cell phone out and put it into her back pocket.

"I'm just making dinner," Angela said.

"Good, I can help you out. What do you need me to do?" Jenn asked.

"Well, you could boil the noodles for me."

"Great, where are they?"

"In that cupboard." Angela said and pointed to the cupboard above the stove top.

Jennifer found the noodles and got a pot from under the sink. She filled the pot with water and set it on the stove, turning the knob to high.

"So, did you bury Lilly yet, Angie?"

"I did. Well, Edgar helped me. She's buried just behind the fence line in the backyard, close by the door in the fence."

"Who's Edgar?" Jennifer asked.

"Edgar was the guy that came out and fixed the doorknob in the spare bedroom upstairs. He did a good job too. Would you believe he had to drill through the knob in the door just to get the damn thing opened?"

"Oh." Jennifer looked outside in the backyard. "Angela, why is your back gate open?"

"Damn that door!" Angela yelled. "I don't know why it keeps coming unlatched. I knew it was open just a little bit ago. I've been too lazy to go out and shut it again."

"Well, I'll go back there and shut it for you."

"Thank you, Jennifer. This has been such a long day."

"I'm sorry, Angie, we'll relax tonight and take it easy. I'll be right back. In the meantime, figure out if we're going to have Riesling, Moscato, or Pinot Griot wine with our dinner."

Jennifer walked outside into the backyard to shut the gate. It was still light out in the day, with a pleasant breeze that bent the blades of grass as it blew in from behind the fence. Jennifer reached the opened gate and admired the land behind the fence. She watched the wind bend the tall standing grass and weeds until something caught her eye. Hidden in the grass, she could see a pair of eyes. Yellow eyes, looking back at her. Watching her. They weren't more than a foot off the ground.

"Hmm. A cat, maybe?" Jennifer asked. It was odd that she couldn't its pupils, though, so maybe the cat was born with a weird genetic difference. Maybe it was born blind?

"Poor thing," Jennifer.

Jenn grabbed the side of the gate and turned to look one more time into the grass field to see the set of yellow eyes again, but they were gone. Thinking nothing more about it, Jennifer pushed the gate door closed and locked it before walking back into the house.

Jennifer noticed the pot of water boiling on the stove, so she grabbed a package of noodles and dropped them into the pot. Then she set the timer on the stove for ten minutes while Angela finished chopping potatoes, carrots, celery, as well as a small onion.

Angela took the cut vegetables and dropped them into a pot of slow bubbling broth next to the boiling noodles.

"Thanks for your help, Jenn."

"It's no problem," Jennifer replied. "How are your feelings?"

Angela paused for a moment and then said, "Jenn, can I tell you something?"

"Of course. What is it?"

"Yesterday morning when I went outside looking for Lilly, I noticed the back gate was opened again. I thought she may have gone out that way into that back field where the creek is. So I went behind the fence line and found a small trail that led down to the creek that Mr. McGuire was talking about. I walked down this trail and at the end of it was an old well. I looked in the well and I couldn't see the bottom, so I took this white rock, and I dropped it into the well and I waited to hear a splash sound, or the sound of it hitting the ground. I waited, and I waited. And I didn't hear the rock hit the ground, or water, or anything."

"Well, I'm sure it had to have. You just didn't hear it is all. Maybe the wind was blowing in your ear, or you just missed hearing the impact."

Angela walked over to the counter and picked up the rock. "Jennifer, this is the rock that I dropped in the well yesterday morning. I found it in a ventilation hole in the wall in the spare bedroom that was locked since I moved in, coincidentally where I found my dog lying dead and torn apart in five different pieces."

"Angie, it's impossible that it's the same rock. It makes no sense. White rocks like that are all around this area. You even have some in your garden out front, which, by the way, looks amazing."

"No Jenn, this rock I remember. See this small crack here? This is the same rock I dropped in the well. Why was it in that room, too? How did it get there?"

"Let's try not to think about it too much Angie, right now we should decide on what kind of wine to have with our stew. Maybe it's just a rock that looks like the other rock you dropped in the well?"

Angela still pondered how the rock made its way into the room upstairs as she fondled it in her hand. Jennifer opened the fridge door and grabbed a bottle of pink-colored wine.

"Pink zinfandel. I love this kind," Jenn said.

Angela looked up and said, "Yes. Yes, that will be good with the stew."

"Did you remember to call your cable company for the TV?" Jenn asked.

Shit, Angela thought. She needed to call the cable company to come out and figure out what was wrong with the connection to her TV. Angela didn't normally watch too much TV, but she enjoyed watching a couple of different shows together with Jennifer.

"No, I'll do that after dinner. Thanks for reminding me," she said.

Angela set the rock back down on the countertop and grabbed two glasses from the cupboard. Before giving a glass to Jennifer, she looked out the back window and noticed that the gate was open again.

"That's it," Angela exclaimed as she set her glasses down with such force that they nearly shattered. "You know what I'm going to do, Jenn?"

"What's that?" Jennifer asked jadedly.

"I'm going to nail that damn door shut. Then I'm going to get a security video camera, I'm going to hook it up in the backyard, and I'm going to see if I can catch what is unlatching that gate. I'm betting it's the neighborhood kids coming around and playing around with it and the creek out back."

"Yeah, I suppose you could do that," Jennifer said as she removed the freshly boiled noodles from the stove, pouring them into a strainer in the sink.

"I am. Monday morning I'm going to call a security company that sells that equipment. I'll have them come out and set up a camera in the backyard and I'm going to see who keeps messing around with that gate. Lilly was barking at something on the other side of that gate while she was here. It's probably the neighborhood kids."

"It's a good idea, Angela. Want me to run out and close it again?"

"No, let's just get dinner ready and try to relax a little tonight. I've had enough going on these last couple of days. I'm not going to worry about anything more. Thank you, though Jenn."

After draining the water from the noodles, Jennifer placed them into the broth. Angela went back to cooking a flank steak in a skillet on the countertop. After finished cooking, Angela cut it up into pieces and placed the steak pieces into the pot with the broth as well. She mixed the broth and let it cook for a little longer. Dinner was finally ready.

Angela poured two glasses of pink wine as Jennifer brought over the pot of stew to set on the table. Angela went back and grabbed the ladle from a counter drawer, as well as a couple of bowls from the cupboard and brought them over to the table and filled them with stew. Together, they sat down and enjoyed a nice dinner. The flavor of the stew was excellent. Angela had an old stew recipe from her grandmother that she learned when she was watching her grandmother cook in the kitchen.

"Angela, this is really good," Jennifer said. "The broth has an amazing flavor to it."

"Thanks Jenn. The idea is boiling this kind of broth right away, then bring it down to a low simmer and let it simmer at a warm temperature for a couple of hours. My grandma taught me how to cook this stew when I was just barely a teenager. I learned a lot about cooking from her by spending some time in the kitchen. If it wasn't for her, I'd be lost on what to do for Thanksgiving dinners, too."

"So, what's on TV tonight?" Jennifer asked.

"What is tonight, Saturday? I'm not sure. We could probably find a movie on the internet, I'm sure."

"That sounds fun. We could even make some drinks after dinner and just relax and watch a movie."

"Well, now that sounds like a relaxing night in. Maybe I will get to bed early tonight too. Like I said, Jenn, these last couple days have been hell. Absolutely tiring."

A relaxing night in is exactly what Angela needed. Between the long day that she had, and the death of her dog yesterday, going out and being social wasn't in her mind that evening. However, Angela still couldn't get past how the day transpired. Mainly how her dog Lilly ended up behind the door of that locked room, as well as what happened to her. And how did the rock she drop into the well end up in the ventilation opening?

Angela didn't want to think about these questions anymore, so she simply sipped her wine, slowly blew the steam off her stew, and ate. The two girls finished their meal, then took their bowls and cleaned them in the kitchen sink. Jennifer reached down into the corner cupboard and retrieved a large Tupperware container. Angela thought it was funny that Jennifer knew where the Tupperware was, almost like she was living here too.

Jenn took the stew and transferred it into a large Tupperware container. Jennifer handed the pot to Angela, who cleaned it out in the sink as well. After all the dishes were cleaned off and placed in the dishwasher, they retreated to the living room, each with their own full glass of wine.

Angela grabbed the remote and powered the TV on, while Jennifer turned off the lights and sat down at the end of the couch. Angela sat down in her favorite recliner and reached for her grandmother's blanket that provided her with comfort and security.

She wrapped herself up and began flipping through the internet movie channels, ultimately finding a movie that they'd both enjoy. Thirty minutes into the movie, however, Jennifer heard gentle footsteps along with a clinking noise, as if a cat with claws was skittering across the kitchen.

"I didn't know you had a cat," Jenn said.

"I don't. What are you talking about, Jenn?"

"You didn't hear that sound?"

"What sound?"

"It sounded like you have a cat walking around in the kitchen. Sounded like nails on a tile floor."

"No, I don't have a cat. And I didn't hear anything from the kitchen either. You must be hearing things from the movie, Jenn. This is why we don't watch scary movies together," Angela laughed.

Jenn wasn't laughing, though; she was certain that she had heard something peculiar coming from the kitchen. She could tell what she heard hadn't come from the TV. The sound came in the opposite direction of the living room, too. Nevertheless, Jennifer let the sound from the kitchen slip from her thoughts and allowed herself to go back to the plot of the movie.

Five minutes went by when until Jennifer heard a rapid sequence of clinking, as if a ghost cat was running across the tile floor of the kitchen. Jennifer snapped her head towards the sound in the kitchen, nearly spilling her wine all over her lap.

"Angela! Now tell me you heard it this time?" Jennifer asked.

"What are you talking about?"

"I know. I heard something run across the kitchen floor just now."

"Jenn, I didn't hear anything."

Angela got up and flipped the light switch on as Jennifer got up from the couch. They walked slowly into the kitchen and Angie blindly felt for the light switch until she found it. The kitchen came to life with the quiet hum of the overhead fluorescent tube lights. There was nothing to be found. No animal, no sound, but only the hum of the fluorescent light and the running refrigerator.

"There's nothing in here Jenn, what did you say you heard?" Angela asked.

"It sounded like gentle footsteps. That made a clinking sound as it moved, like a small animal with claws. That's why I thought it was a cat."

"Are you sure it wasn't on the TV?"

"Yes, it wasn't on the TV. It was coming from this room."

Jennifer started investigating the kitchen more thoroughly, opening the cabinets and pantry doors, looking for the source of the strange sound. But the search turned up nothing.

"I guess I must be imagining it or something," Jennifer admitted.

"It's alright. Don't worry about it. We both had long night's last night. Long days today. Let's just finish watching this movie."

Angela flipped the lights off, leaving the kitchen in darkness besides the nightlight in the hallway and the blipping light on the toaster. They retreated to the living room, turned off the lights and continued watching their movie with no more unusual sounds emanating from the kitchen again.

After the movie, Angela invited Jennifer to stay the night with her again, to which Jenn agreed. Angela yawned, turned the TV off after the movie was over and they walked upstairs together to the bedroom.

Angela closed the door behind her and locked it as she always did before she turned the light on.

Jennifer quickly got ready for bed while Angela was in the bathroom. Jennifer always kept a pair of pajamas at Angela's house as she stayed the night with her these days at least once a week. Angela got ready for bed in the bathroom, brushing her teeth and washing her face. Before heading to bed, Angela glanced out the window before drawing the curtains shut and noticed the back gate was still open.

What difference did it make if it was open or not? Angela drew the curtains closed. Then she peered through the crack in the curtains and watched the gate for a minute. She noticed the area around the gate appeared to be significantly darker than usual. The rest of the backyard was well lit by the light of a full moon. But an ominous black shadow seemed to engulf the entrance to the gate, making it impossible to see beyond it.

Angela pulled the curtains shut and climbed into her king-sized bed, where Jennifer was already half asleep. It didn't take long for Angela to slip into a deep slumber herself.

* * * *

Sunday morning was dark and cloudy. A storm system moved into the area late into the night and early morning and the dark gray clouds still hung heavy, dampening the daylight.

Angela slept in until nearly 8:30 a.m. She used to go to church with her now ex-husband. But now she was too upset and embarrassed to show her face at church. What kind of person did they think she was? That her own husband would leave her for someone else half his age? For this reason, Angela didn't feel comfortable attending.

Jennifer, on the other hand, never believed in church or organized religion. In fact, Angela thought about inviting Jenn to church with her, however, she knew she wouldn't go. Organized religion wasn't Jennifer's thing.

Angela lay in bed until nearly 9 a.m. when she heard a loud crash and glass breaking downstairs. She got up, threw her robe on while Jennifer stirred around in bed and walked out of the bedroom. Looking over the banister down to the living room, Angela noticed a broken wineglass on the floor.

She sighed as she headed downstairs. As she walked down a few steps, she noticed something between the banister in the corner of her eye. There was a small set of dirt stained footprints near the third bedroom door. Angela backpedaled to get a closer look as she saw what appeared to be three sets of small footprints that resembled narrow cat tracks.

The footprints looked as if they led into the third bedroom, so Angela opened the door only to find the room clean. Again, all that was in the room was a large rug in the center, along with a closet and a window with the blinds closed shut.

Angela looked around the room but discovered no more of the small footprints that she saw leading into the room.

"Shit. There must be a small cat coming and going from this house," Angela said.

She thought that a small cat must have got into the house and made the tracks upstairs. She had the back door open a lot yesterday; it was possible that one of the neighbor's cats got in and either left or was still somewhere in the house.

Angela gave it no more thought as she left the room and closed the door behind her. She decided she'd clean up the mess later. Instead, she walked downstairs and examined the broken glass on the living room floor. The glass must have been too close to the edge of the table or something, she thought as she picked up its pieces.

"Did you see the tiny footprints upstairs on the carpet, Angela?" Jennifer asked as she came downstairs.

"Yeah, I did." Angela said. "Maybe a cat must have gotten in yesterday or something. I had the back door in the kitchen open a lot yesterday. It must have snuck in while I was in and out or something."

"I bet you that's what I was hearing last night in the kitchen, remember? Do you think it's still here?"

"It could be, but I don't think so. I mean, if it was, I would imagine I could hear it, or would have seen it by now. It probably snuck out during the night."

"So, what's for breakfast?"

"I was thinking some sliced fruit and an English muffin," Angela said.

"Sounds great. Do you have any honey?"

"Yeah, it's up in the cupboard."

Jennifer loved honey on nearly everything. Except for her meats like steaks and chicken, then she liked honey glazed barbecue sauce. Angela walked into the kitchen with the broken glass.

"Did a glass break?"

"It did yes," Angela said. "I was thinking it must have been close to the edge of the coffee table and must have just tipped over. It's no big deal. I've got a bunch of them, so it won't be missed."

After throwing away the broken glass, Angela grabbed her cell phone off the counter charger and made a phone call to her cable television company. They had an automated 24 hours a day, 7 days a week system where Angela could still set up an appointment and the next working day a cable company provider would be out to either hook the cable up or fix whatever problem was going on. After making the appointment for tomorrow morning, Angela turned her phone off and went back to slicing fruit for breakfast.

Angela grabbed a small watermelon and cantaloupe from the fridge and set them on the counter. She grabbed a knife from the drawer and cut the cantaloupe first. Glancing up, she saw and remembered that the gate to the back fence was opened again. Angela was really tiring of this gate constantly opening throughout the day and night hours.

"I can't wait to have a camera mounted outside this week on that damn gate. I'm betting I catch the neighborhood kids opening it," she said.

"Did you put a lock on the gate?" Jennifer asked.

"I did, but it keeps opening. I think the kids reach over the top to pull the lever to the lockup and then open it. I'm going to head out there and close the gate again. I'll be right back."

Angela set the knife down on the counter next to the freshly sliced cantaloupe and opened the screen door. She walked outside toward the gate. Overnight rain had created puddles and some muddy spots in her yard that she noticed on her way to the gate. When she reached the back gate, she locked it for what seemed like the hundredth time since she had moved into Suntides. On the ground, Angela noticed a small set of footprints in the mud.

They were small and nearly identical to that of a cat, but a little narrower. Angela realized that these were the same footprints that she had seen on the carpet upstairs in the hallway in front of the third bedroom.

Angela tried to think that it was a coincidence. It was probably the cat's way of getting in and out of her yard.

"That must be it," she said.

It was nice to solve that mystery. Angela turned around and walked back into the house. Jennifer was finished slicing the English muffins and was about to put them in the toaster. Jenn also started the coffeemaker, which was about halfway through brewing a full pot of coffee. Angela picked the knife up off the counter and went back to cutting the fruits.

"So, what do you have planned for today, Angie?"

"Not too much. I'm going to take some time cleaning the house today. Probably look around for a home security company who will come out and install a camera for me tomorrow, too. I just called the cable company to come out tomorrow morning to install the cable for the TV. They can do that while I'm at work. What are your plans?"

"Jeff and I are going to go out to dinner tonight. We're going to try out a Thai restaurant we've never been to that's on the east side of Portland in a town called Clackamas. Would you like to join us?"

"It's okay Jenn," Angela replied. "I don't want to be a third wheel for you guys. You guys should have a good time together."

"Are you sure, Angie? He doesn't mind when you come along with us, and you know I surely don't either."

"Yeah, it's okay. You guys have a good time. I have things to do around the house, anyway."

Angela finished cutting the fruit while Jenn toasted the last of the English muffins. The coffeemaker hissed with steam and finally spit into the pot, and went silent. Jennifer poured two cups, and the girls sat down and had a nice, quiet breakfast together.

"This is good fruit. Where did you get it, Angie?"

"There's a fruit stand down the road I always go to. The watermelon always seems in season there. I think they transfer them from Hermiston," Angela replied.

After breakfast was over, Jennifer went upstairs and changed into her clothes she wore over last night. She gave Angie a hug goodbye, and opened the front door and saw Mr. Butler, the elderly neighbor standing as if he was about to knock.

"Oh! Howdy ma'am!" Mr. Butler exclaimed.

Jennifer gasped a little, surprised to see Mr. Butler standing in front of the door.

"Hello, I'm sorry. You just startled me a little. You must be Mr. Butler from across the road," Jennifer replied.

"Yes ma'am, yes, I am. But please now, call me Tom," he said with a smile on his face.

"It's a pleasure to meet you Tom. I'm Jennifer, Angela's friend."

"Oh, hello Mr. Butler. How are you this morning?" Angela asked as she walked to the front door.

"Angie, I'll call you later. Let me know if you change your mind about tonight. It was a pleasure meeting you, Tom. I'm sure we'll see each other soon again," Jennifer said.

"The pleasures been all mine it has," Mr. Butler said as Jennifer left. "Angela, I gone heard about your puppy dog there, and just wanted to say I'm sorry. Are y'all doin okay now?"

"Thanks Tom, I am. It's sad what happened to her, but it'll be okay."

"Well, I gone brought ya the paper again. It's Sunday's paper, so them be some advertisements for some stores in there. I don't really drive around too much these days now, but I gone figure you can use them more than me."

"Thank you, Tom. At this point, I don't even know if I'll need to get a newspaper subscription," Angela said.

The two shared a laugh before Mr. Butler continued, "Well, Angela, I gone better be goin home now. If you need anything, you give me a call here?"

"Yes Tom, thank you. I will."

Angela closed the door, locked it, and sat down in her recliner. As she flipped through the newspaper, she saw some of the grocery advertisements that Mr. Butler was talking about. They looked like pretty good deals. You can't beat boxes of cereal for only $1.50 a box! Aside from the ads, perhaps she would run down on her day off before going back to work to restock on groceries. It's not every day you can even find two gallons of milk for five dollars, too.

After looking through the ads, Angela poured herself another coffee in the kitchen and did the dishes. While doing dishes, Angela glanced out the kitchen window above the sink and stared out into the backyard.

The gate was opened, yet again.

"I don't believe this," Angela said as she shut off the faucet. Frustrated, she swung the sliding backdoor open with such force that the door bounced around in its track. She walked through her backyard to the gate, looked around behind the fence, and listened. But she didn't see or hear anything but old fallen leaves from the trees around that were left over from last fall that shuffled along the ground from the wind. Angela couldn't see any footprints anywhere, nor did she see any other sign of life. It was as if no one had been behind that fence for years.

"I'm getting tired of this shit!" Angela yelled. "I want this gate shut, and I swear if I catch the person who keeps opening it, I'm going to castrate them!"

Silence. She heard nothing but the sound of the wind whistling between the tall blades of grass and whisking the dead leaves along the ground. Angela listened harder, but she could only hear the wind. Angela turned and walked back through the gate, closing it behind her and locking it again. It started to rain again as Angela walked back to the house.

After finishing the dishes, she walked back upstairs and saw the small cat-like footprints on the carpet again. She noted to herself that she needed to get some carpet cleaner to clean the tracks the ghost cat left off the carpet in the hallway. Entering her bedroom, Angela took her robe off, as well as her pajamas, and got into the shower. After her shower, Angela got dressed and ready to run some errands. She had found some good deals in the advertisements that enticed her. Before leaving her room, Angela opened the blinds and cracked the window a little to get some fresh air. Looking outside to the backyard, Angela seemed surprised that the gate was still shut and locked too. Maybe yelling into the nothingness did some good.

Angela left her room, walked downstairs, and grabbed her purse and keys. She left her house and locked the front door, got into her car and drove to the store.

*   *   *   *

Angela was gone for almost two hours. She spent most of those two hours driving from one store to another. And she made a quick stop to pick up a twenty-dollar gift card at a Rocco's Pizza for a friend whose daughter had graduated high school and was preparing to leave to go to college to Oregon State University in Corvallis. Angela liked the Corvallis area a lot and knew that her friend's daughter would as well, since she wanted to major in their marine biology program. Her friend's daughter was always good at biology, and she wanted to challenge herself in marine life. It would be a good challenge, Angela thought.

Angela drove back home and parked her car in the driveway. The rain was still coming down, harder than it was earlier. It seemed like it wasn't going to let up all day. It was times like this where Angela had wished she had a garage to park in. Angela quickly gathered her groceries into her hands and got her keys ready to enter the house as quickly as she could. Upon opening the door to the car, the handle broke from one bag, spilling oranges into the driveway. Angela thought it was fine. She would just run into the house quick and grab the umbrella and come back out and get them.

Abandoning the fruit in the driveway, she continued to make her way to the door, but dropped her keys on the sidewalk and kicked them underneath a bush by accident. Angela said a few choice words while the rain poured down even harder. She dropped to her knees and searched for the keys under the bush. Finally, she found them, got up and fumbled for the right key to unlock the front door. Angela finally found the right key and unlocked the door, walked into the house and placed the groceries on the ground. Angela thought she was going to have a garage built for her house soon.

Angela grabbed an umbrella from her closet and retrieved her oranges from the driveway. All six of them. After collecting the oranges, four of them, which had rolled down the driveway's slope and into the road, she walked back into the house, picked up her groceries and carried them into the kitchen.

Angela finished putting her groceries away after she washed the mud and dirt from the oranges. The carpet cleaner machine was still in the trunk of her car, so she went back out for the rental machine and hoped that the rain had subsided just a little. It hadn't. Angela retrieved the carpet cleaner from the trunk of her car and carried it back into the house. She then grabbed a can of carpet cleaner and walked upstairs with the machine. Shaking the can vigorously, Angela sprayed the carpet and used the machine to draw the mud and dirt from the carpet. After cleaning up the footprints, Angela walked back downstairs and put the can of cleaner under the kitchen sink and set the machine next to the door.

She planned to take the machine back tomorrow morning. Maybe by then the rain would be finished, and she could just drop it off at the store before going to work. Angela finished the rest of the chores she had planned for the day. Angela wanted to mow the front and back lawn too, however the rain changed her plans. Instead, she stayed inside all day, cleaning the living room, and vacuuming the carpets. She cleaned the kitchen, wiped down and disinfected the countertops. Angela even had time to go out back and sweep some old cut grass and leaves from the covered patio. She considered using the grill to make herself dinner. She saved her stew for her work lunches for the week. It was already four in the afternoon now and Angela was getting a little hungry, but not too hungry.

Nevertheless, she chose a chicken breast from a bag in the freezer to thaw out and marinated it in honey glazed barbeque sauce. Then she thought that she'd cook some green beans to go along with it, making it a good meal for one.

After preparing her dinner to be barbecued, Angela got onto the internet and searched for security system services. She searched for what felt like hours before she finally found a company named Ackley's Security Systems and Surveillance. The prices seemed reasonable, so Angela emailed the company to enquire about setting up a camera in her backyard.

After emailing the company, Angela got up and tended to the grill outside. The chicken was still slightly frozen, but Angela barbecued it, anyway. Putting the green beans in a bowl and microwaving them, Angela made herself a meal for one that was simple but still tasty.

After dinner, she did the dishes and went into the living room. As she sat down in her recliner and flipped the TV on, she reached over and grabbed her favorite blanket. Snuggling into the recliner with the blanket, Angela watched a movie streamed through the internet on her television for what felt like hours. No good movies were on. Angela continued to peruse through a catalog of movies and ultimately found a film she remembered watching when she was just a young child with her grandmother. The film brought back memories and reminded her how much she missed her grandmother.

She missed her encouraging words, her strong support, and consistent presence in her life right up to her death. After the movie ended, Angela slowly fell asleep. Without getting up, she curled up in her blanket in the recliner and drifted off. The glow from the television set provided the only light in the house. Angela rested peacefully throughout the night in her recliner with her grandmother's blanket clutched tightly to her chest.

CHAPTER 7

The sound of an alarm slowly caused Angela to stir in her recliner. Rubbing her eyes, Angela looked at the time on her cell phone and noticed that the alarm was going off at 6 a.m. It was time to get up and get ready for work.

Angela would have to hurry if she wanted to make it to work on time. She usually liked to wake up at 5:30 in the morning, but she must have slept through her alarm for the past 30 minutes. Angela quickly got up, folded her grandmother's blanket, and set it nicely on the headrest of the recliner.

Angela walked up the stairs and into her bedroom. As Angela walked down the 2nd level hallway to her room, she could feel a cold draft coming from the old, third bedroom that had been locked. She paused for a moment before she sauntered into the room, like she was sneaking in on someone.

The door creaked open, revealing an empty room with a small hole in the wall, which she assumed was the source of cold air. She thought she needed to get the hole fixed. Maybe she could call someone to have it fixed later in the week. Angela shut the door and went to her bedroom.

She set her phone down on her bed, slowly undressed, put on a robe and got ready to take a shower. Just as she was turning the shower on, bells chimed from her bedroom. Someone was calling her phone. Angela closed her robe and walked out of the bathroom and grabbed her phone. An unknown number was calling her.

"Hello," Angela said as she answered the phone.

"Good morning, ma'am. My name is Max, and I'm with Direct Resources, LLC. Your cable provider. I was wondering if it would be alright if I could come out this morning, and work on your cable TV?"

"Hi Max, I'm getting ready to go to work this morning. You caught me just before I got in the shower. I won't be home today until later this evening when I'm home from work."

"You know, ma'am, that will be okay. The work I need to do so far is outside of the house. We need to trace where the cable comes into your home. So why don't I do this? How about I come out this evening and by the time I'm done doing work outside, you should be getting home from work at say 5 p..m.? Then I can make sure your connections to your TV are working fine and we can get you set up with cable by this evening. How does that sound?"

"That sounds fine to me, Max. Now, if you'll excuse me, I hate to end our conversation, but I really need to get ready and go to work."

"That's no problem, ma'am. I will swing out your way between 2 p.m. and 4 p.m. and start working on the outside portion of the cable line."

"Sounds good to me. Thank you, Max."

"Thank you, ma'am."

Angela ended her call and set the phone back down on her bed. Going back into the bathroom, Angela disrobed and jumped into the shower. After her shower was finished, she got ready for work, grabbed a banana from the kitchen for a quick breakfast on the go, and left the house.

*   *   *   *

An older white van pulled onto Suntides Blvd. off the main road. Tools and cable lines clanked around the inside of the van with each turn the driver made. The van slowly pulled into the driveway of 60 Suntides Blvd., the newly purchased home of Angela Brown.

The driver's side door of the van opened, and a middle-aged man jumped out. He was no taller than five and a half feet tall and his weight was proportionate to his body type. On his shirt was the company name Direct Resources, LLC and, as true to his word, he had arrived at 3:30 p.m.

Max stretched his arms out to his sides, tilting his head back and extending his chest. He yawned and slowly walked around to the back of his van. Opening the back doors to the van, Max reached inside and grabbed a tool belt, along with some digital tools to test the cable in Angela's home. Max clipped on his tool belt, grabbed the other instruments, and shut the door. Max yawned again as he walked to the side of the house. It was a long day for the cable repairman. It was his fourth job of the day, and the second job where Max had to install an internet cable that ran the entire length of the 2400 square foot home. Needless to say, he hoped to get the work done quick. He whistled to himself while walking around the side of the house, where he found the cable line running from the power pole near Angela's driveway.

"Well, this must be where the line is going," he said, talking aloud as if someone was with him.

The line came down the side of the wall and was painted over by whomever the previous tenants were. It trailed down towards the bottom wood panel that ran just above the home's stone foundation.

"Interesting," Max said.

He followed the line from the side of the home to the back. The cable line eventually went down into a small plastic pipe in the ground.

"Shit," Max said. "This line is running under the house."

He sighed heavily, knowing that he needed to crawl under the house to continue to follow the line towards where it came up through the floor of the home. Max quickly found the covered opening that led underneath the home. He lifted the large metal covering and pulled it to the side, exposing the opening underneath the home. A freezing draft blew up into Max's face. The draft didn't bother him. It wasn't the first time he had to wedge himself into a crawlspace to trace a cable wire. Unfortunately, many homes in the area were designed similarly. Max hated it, but the past couldn't be changed. He just had to live with it.

Max grasped the lip of the metal that secured the covering under the home, then jumped in, bracing and balancing himself by holding the metal fixture. Once through the opening, Max bent down and crawled in. The crawl space was unbelievably cold, Max thought. Colder than most crawl spaces he had crawled under before. There was black plastic on the ground that covered the dirt ground. Which was normal for homes built during that time period. Max turned on his back, examined the crawl space, and quickly located the television cable that was wired through the cement foundation of the home.

"Stupid," Max said. "Just a stupid way of getting a cable wire into a home."

He followed the cable line towards the corner of the crawlspace. It was directly underneath the living room, where he found the cable went up through the floor. It seemed as if he had crawled for at least ten minutes tracing the cable. Max didn't see any flaws with the cable, other than how old it looked. Thinking it may need to be replaced while he was at the home anyway, Max turned himself around in the crawlspace and made his way back towards the entrance when he another blast of frigid air swept in from behind. The cold air sent a chill down his spine and caused every hair on the back of his neck to stand upright. He stopped moving and turned to look at the source of the cold air.

"Holy shit. There's a hole in this home's foundation," he said.

Max looked at the hole and noticed that some cobwebs at the top of the were blowing toward him. He crawled toward the hole, curious to see how deep it went into the side of the earth.

"Hello?" Max yelled into the hole. He figured the hole must have been long and went for some distance underground. It was as if an animal of sorts had burrowed its way underground and had eventually dug through the concrete. However, what animal was strong enough to claw its way through a home's concrete foundation?

He didn't want to come face to face with the animal that did that. Max continued to crawl toward the large opening and shined his flashlight into it. But there was nothing but darkness and silence. It was as if the darkness was devouring the beam of his flashlight.

He turned his flashlight off crawled back towards the exit when he heard a noise coming from behind him. A strange noise that emanated from the opening.

"What the hell was that?" Max whispered.

It sounded like a high-pitched squeal, but Max thought he could hear chattering words being spoken in a high frequency. He shone his flashlight down the hole again and saw three sets of yellow eyes reflected in the light. It was a steady gaze, and maybe less than two feet off the ground. Max looked at the six yellow glowing orbs at the end of the hole for what seemed like an eternity.

"What the hell is that?" Max said, squinting to get a better look. "Hello?"

Whatever it was let out a low, muffled scream. Then a second scream came from the hole, and finally a third. Three different screams and the eyes started moving towards Max.

"Holy shit!" Max yelled as he spun around on his belly and crawled toward the exit. He moved as fast as he could when he heard the small footsteps closing in on him.

"What kind of animal is this?" he wondered.

Max was about three quarters of the way to the opening of the crawl space when he heard small footsteps on the plastic. Whatever they were, they were now out of the hole and under the house. With him.

Max kept crawling as quickly as he could, the sounds of the small footsteps drawing closer and closer to him as he rushed toward the exit. Finally, he saw the light of day and crawled through the opening. The small footsteps were now closer than ever before. Maybe 10 feet away from him.

Max grasped the metal lip of the opening and pulled himself up and out of the hole. He swiftly rolled over onto his knees and grabbed the large metal cover to close the exposed opening. As Max slid the metal covering over the opening, a small hand with three fingers appeared along the edge. Claws, for Christ's sakes, the creature had claws. Max finished shutting the heavy metal cover and at the last moment, the small, clawed hand had retracted back into the icy darkness of the crawlspace.

Another scream exploded from under the home. Max fell backwards, panting, but never taking his eyes off the metal covering. He feared that whatever had chased him would be able to move the cover and continue its pursuit. Max quickly got back onto his feet and ran back towards his van. Opening the van door, he threw his tool belt and digital equipment inside, cracking the screen on a digital testing device. Max locked the door and fumbled for his van keys in his pocket. The tires squealed as he sped out of the driveway. Max drove straight back to Direct Resources, where he walked up to the front desk and dropped his keys off without an explanation.

"I won't be coming back to work tomorrow," he said to the receptionist.

After being under the home of Angela Brown, Max had no intention of going back to that house ever again.

*   *   *   *

Angela left work early for the day. It was her goal to get home to make sure that she didn't leave the cable man waiting any longer than he had to. Fighting through the Portland traffic, Angela made it home in decent time. It only took her 25 minutes. Pulling into her driveway, though, there was no cable repairman patiently awaiting her arrival. In fact, all that she saw were black tire marks that obviously weren't in her paved driveway when she left earlier this morning.

Angela got out of her car, grabbed her purse, and walked into her home. Setting her purse down on the coffee table, she grabbed the TV remote and turned the TV on. No cable. Nothing but static fuzz. Angela set the remote down on the coffee table and looked through her purse. Finding her cell phone, she called Direct Resources. The receptionist answered.

"Direct Resources, this is Emily. How may I help you?"

"Hi, this is Angela Brown, over at 60 Suntides Blvd. There was a cable repairman that was supposed to come out this afternoon, but I don't think he has. I just got home, and he's not here and the cable still isn't working." Said Angela.

"Well, he was there," Emily said. "But he came back shortly after being dispatched to your home, turned in his keys and said he wasn't going to be coming back to work again after today. I asked him why, but he wouldn't say. He just looked white as a ghost. It's not good too, because he was one of our best workers. He's been with our company for 13 years."

"That's weird. Well, I hope everything is okay. It's weird that he wouldn't tell you why."

"Yeah, that's what we thought, too."

"So, are you going to send someone else over?"

"Yes, yes, we can. Are you going to be home for the evening, Angela?"

"Yes, I will be."

"Good. I will dispatch someone out to you this evening and we'll get this taken care of for you. I'm sorry that Max didn't get the job done. Like I said, it's very peculiar that he didn't finish the job and quit the way he did. Maybe our supervisor can talk to him and find out more about what is going on."

"Alright, sounds good. I hope he will be okay. I'll wait until this person comes out. What's his name?"

"Matt."

"Okay, I will wait for Matt to come out this evening. Thank you, Emily."

"Thank you for calling Direct Resources of Portland. You have a wonderful evening, Angela."

"Thank you, I will. You, too."

With that, Angela hung up the phone. She thought maybe Max just got sick or burned out. After all, the receptionist said that he had been working diligently for their company for the past 13 years. Burnouts happened. Only an hour went by when Angela heard the front doorbell chime. She peered out the window and saw a white van with the Direct Resources logo on the side. She opened the door and a middle-aged man stood at the front door. He was clean cut, with a tool belt and testing device in hand.

"Hello, Ms. Brown?"

"Yes, that's me. You must be Matt," Angela replied.

"Yes, my name is Matt and I'm with Direct Resources here to check and fix your cable TV. May I come in?"

"Yes, come on in. Can I get you a glass of water or something?"

"No, ma'am but thank you. Is the living room where you're trying to get your cable TV hooked up in?"

"Yes, just over there."

Angela pointed toward the TV in the living room. Matt walked over and began working on the back of the TV, checking the connection. Angela went back to the kitchen to reheat the stew she made a few nights prior. After putting some stew in a microwaveable bowl and turning it on, Angela turned around, startled by Matt, who was standing in the hallway.

"I'm sorry, ma'am. I certainly didn't mean to startle you. Just letting you know I got it fixed for you. Turns out it was this small connection piece." Matt held out his hand and revealed a small copper TV adapter. "The cable you are running out here doesn't need this adapter. In fact, this adapter breaks the line from the cable line to the back of your TV. So, it was just a matter of taking this small piece off, directly hooking up the cable to the back of the tv, and now you have cable."

"Of course, it would be that simple, huh?"

Matt chuckled. "Yes, but how would you know?"

"True," Angela replied. "Are you sure I can't pour a glass of water for you?"

"Oh no, I'm fine. Thank you, Ms. Brown." Matt picked up his tools and walked towards the door. "I need to get going. Need to shut down the shop and call it an evening. A couple of the crewmembers are waiting for me to get back."

"Well, thank you for coming out. I appreciate you coming this evening to fix my cable."

"It's my pleasure, Ms. Brown. Have a good evening."

"You as well."

Angela shut the door behind Matt, walked over to the coffee table, grabbed the remote and started flipping through the cable channels. She laughed that something so simple was causing her a significant headache with her cable TV, but either way, it was fixed now. Angela set the remote back down on the table and heard the microwave ding. Her stew was finished heating.

She walked back to the kitchen and grabbed a glass from the pantry. Filling it with ice water, she turned and opened the microwave door to grab her bowl of heated stew. Angela then went to the living room and sat down in her chair, and enjoyed her stew as she watched TV late into the evening hours.

It was the first time she had had cable television since she left her previous home. After Angela finished her stew, she set the bowl down on the coffee table, drank her water, grabbed her grandmother's blanket, and curled up in her recliner.

Upstairs, looking through the posts of the second floor banister, a pair of small yellow eyes watched as Angela drifted off to sleep.

CHAPTER 8

Morning sunlight crept through the dining-room window, hitting Angela squarely in the face. Once again, she spent the night in her recliner; however, she was fine with that. Sometimes she almost preferred it that way since most of the time she felt lonely sleeping in an empty bed by herself.

Angela got up and noticed it was 5:55 a.m., which wasn't bad. It gave her a couple hours to get ready and have a cup of coffee before she had to fight early morning Portland traffic to make it to work by 8 a.m.

Angela stood up from the recliner and folded her grandmother's quilt. She set it down nicely on the back of the recliner and headed into the kitchen to make some coffee. After starting the coffeemaker, Angela went upstairs to shower and get ready for work. Upon walking upstairs and down the hallway, Angela looked down at the carpet and saw again a set of small footprints. They looked like the ones she cleaned off the carpet yesterday. Angela was stunned as the small set of prints looked as if they were tracked into the third bedroom, just like yesterday. Impossible. The door had been shut since she looked in the room yesterday morning.

Angela opened the door to the bedroom and looked around, only to see that old area rug carpet staring right back at her. Nothing was out of place. The closet door was still closed and the blinds to the window remained shut. Even the board covering the small opening in the wall in the room was still in its place.

"Where do these footprints keep coming from?" Angela asked herself.

She didn't have time to deal with it now, anyway. It was probably a neighborhood cat or something that kept finding its way in and out of her home. Angela shut the door to the bedroom and walked into her own room and into the bathroom. She jumped into the shower, cleaned up, and got ready for work. Remembering that she had opened her bedroom window just a crack yesterday, Angela walked over to the window to close it.

She peered out through the blinds only to notice that the gate in the back had opened itself again.

"Again?" she asked.

After she had finished getting ready, Angela went downstairs and poured herself a cup of coffee, not even giving any thought to the open gate again. She didn't have time to go shut the gate. After getting the creamer from the refrigerator, Angela turned around and poured some into her coffee. Stirring it with a spoon, she watched as the gate briefly moved back and forth in the morning breeze.

"Soon I'll figure out who keeps opening you," she said, as if she was addressing the gate itself.

Angela decided it was important to close the gate, so she walked outside with her coffee, shut the gate and locked it again. Turning around to walk back inside, Angela could hear her phone ringing in the distance. She ran back inside and, without closing the door, ran to her purse and grabbed her phone and answered it.

"Hello?"

"Good morning, Angela, this is Mark from Ackley's Security and Surveillance."

"Hello, Mark. Thank you for calling."

"Do you have a few minutes to talk?"

"Yes, I do," Angela replied.

"Good, good. I'm doing good. I got your email this morning and would like to schedule a time to come out and conduct an estimate on your property. Maybe even install it if you are ready for a security system?"

"Great, thank you. I get off work today at 4 p.m., so after that you can come out to my place, and we can talk, and I'll show you what I want done."

"Okay, I can make that work. From your email, it looks self-explanatory. You're looking for only one camera that's going to focus on your…backyard, but specifically on a gate in the backyard, is what I gather?"

"Yes, especially the gate in the backyard. I keep finding the gate opened throughout the night and I'm thinking the neighborhood kids are playing around with it. So, I want to catch them in the act."

"Sounds good. Well, I recommend getting a digital camera setup. It's wireless, and it runs through a software program called I-Axis, that allows you to view live and recorded video from your laptop or computer. And if you download an app, you can even watch a live video from your phone, too."

"Oh, that's neat. I have an older flip phone that doesn't use apps, but I have a laptop that I can watch the video from."

"That'll work just fine. I can have everything installed, and the software downloaded and formatted to your computer for, about, I'd say, two hundred and forty dollars."

"That sounds good, thank you."

"But that's just a rough estimate Angela, I could run into a problem that may need to utilize a different camera, different lens, and God forbid wires to plug everything in. As of right now, the only wire I need to plug in is a wire to power the camera, which isn't too bad and is included in the price quote I just gave you."

"That's fine Mark, it all sounds good to me. So, will you be out this evening?"

"Yes Angela, I have a software update job I need to do for the software program at another client's business, however what's great about the I-Axis Program is that you run it and a large update takes only about twenty minutes at the most, with most updates lasting about two to three minutes in all. It's a quick program and very state-of-the art as well."

"Great, so what time will you be out this evening?"

"Well, let's say 5 p.m. I don't envision myself being there for more than an hour, tops, if it's just one camera you're hooking up."

"It is just one camera; I'll see you at five this evening then. Thank you, Mark."

"Thank you, Angela. We'll see you later this evening."

Angela flipped her phone off and noticed that it was 7:15 a.m. She panicked and turned the coffeemaker off and quickly grabbed her purse and keys and left the house. Fighting the early morning Portland traffic, Angela barely made it to work on time at 8 a.m.

But when she got there, she realized she really didn't need to rush all that much. It appeared as if everyone was running late and she was the first one in the office. About ten minutes after Angela got to work, Jennifer walked in, looking as if she had a long night of very little rest.

"Jenn, what happened last night? You look like you didn't sleep at all."

"I didn't."

Jennifer shot her a look of satisfaction. Angela had seen that look before and it was clear now why Jeff wasn't at the first-floor coffee stand. At about 8:30 a.m., Mr. Marshall came in with a box of donuts for the girls. Mr. Marshall always seemed to take care of the girls up at the front desk, just like they were his kids. Less could be said for Mr. Stone, who walked into the office at 8:40 a.m. and gave an excuse that he was meeting with a client briefly before coming to work, but the girls knew better.

"So, I got a call this morning from a security company before work. After work today, they're going to come out and install a digital camera in the backyard to record the gate."

"That's cool," Jenn said. "Still trying to catch the kids, huh?"

"Yes. Who else could it be but the neighborhood kids playing around with it? So, how was your date with Jeff last night?"

Jennifer blushed and cracked a smile on her face.

"Well, we went to dinner at the Thai restaurant that we were talking about. Then afterwards we went back to his place. He has a nice apartment overlooking this park with a pond out back. We snuggled for a little while watching a movie, and well, one thing led to another…"

Both girls snickered a little as Angela took a bite from her maple bar. Mr. Marshall walked out of his office and over to the front desk.

"Ladies, I have a client coming in this morning around 10 a.m.," Mr. Marshall said. "Her name is Deloris Huntzinger, and it's regarding her divorce."

"Okay," they said as they went back to talking about Jennifer's night.

10 a.m. came by slowly as both Jennifer and Angela answered three phone calls a piece. The front door to the office opened an elderly woman entered the office. She was maybe in her late 70's with a handkerchief in one hand, dabbing away tears. She gingerly walked to the front desk and introduced herself.

"Hello. I'm Mrs. Huntzinger," she said through sobs. "I have an appointment with Mr. Marshall this morning at 10 a.m. to discuss divorcing my husband."

Angela was shocked that an elderly woman desired a divorce at her age. However, she escorted Mrs. Huntzinger to Mr. Marshall.

Mr. Marshall shut the door behind Angela and consoled Mrs. Huntzinger who was obviously having a difficult time thinking about divorcing her husband of nearly 40 years. She cited that the two of them had grown apart over the years, well, at least he did.

Listening to the cries of Mrs. Huntzinger, Jennifer cried bit too.

"That poor old woman. What is she going to do now? That's not how life should be for someone when they are older," Jenn said.

"Yeah. It's not something enjoyable to go through with Jenn. I hope you never have to go through it."

"I won't. I was thinking about it, and I don't think I'm ever going to get married."

Angela thought for a moment, and then replied, "You know Jenn, sometimes things happen for a reason. They're beyond our control. However, you can never give up on hope and never give up on love. Especially with the people you care most about. There's nothing wrong with marriage, I guess. I mean, look at me, I had fourteen years of a great marriage, then things just happened the way they did."

"I suppose. I'm just scared of getting hurt like that," Jennifer said.

"Everyone fears getting hurt, Jenn, but you can't let it stop you from living life to its fullest. The idea is not to get scared and rely on your friends and family."

Mrs. Huntzinger was in Mr. Marshall's office for nearly an hour before leaving.

"Ladies, I'm going to walk Mrs. Huntzinger to her taxi downstairs. I'll be right back," Mr. Marshall said.

"Okay, Mr. Marshall," Angela replied.

Jennifer was on the phone with a client, but gave Angela a sad look.

*   *   *   *

The day went by fast after lunch came and went. Angela and Jennifer went to eat a salad around the corner of the building at the place they routinely got their lunch at. On the way back to work, Jennifer stopped by the coffee stand and ordered a coffee from Jeff, who carried a sheepish smile on his face while he conversed with Jennifer.

Angela recognized the smile on Jeff's face, too. After getting Jennifer's coffee, they went back upstairs and worked until Angela left at 4 p.m. She retrieved her car from the garage and commuted home. Traffic was close to getting bad as it was close to rush hour, but Angela seemed to have missed most of the traffic by leaving work an hour early.

She pulled into her driveway at 60 Suntides Blvd. around 4:45 p.m. She had made great time despite the traffic. Angela parked her car and walked up to the front door, unlocked it, and went inside.

She dropped her purse on the coffee table and turned to close the door. Then she walked into the kitchen, retrieved a glass, and poured herself a glass of water. Looking outback Angela noticed the gate was still closed.

"For once, that gate's shut," she said. As she sat down at the table, she couldn't help but remember poor Mrs. Huntzinger and how desperate she looked. Angela hoped that she had children who could watch out for her and help her someday. But being her age, she was worried that maybe that wasn't a possibility anymore.

Angela sat quietly, pondering what to make for dinner. A bowl of noodles and fried vegetables, white rice and a piece of chicken sounded good to her. Maybe heating some stew up from the other night would be good.

Angela got up from the table and walked upstairs, past the small footprints in front of the door to the third bedroom. She needed to clean that area of the carpet again. Changing out of her work clothes and into a pair of jeans and a t-shirt, Angela walked back downstairs and retrieved the carpet cleaner from under the sink. She walked back upstairs and cleaned the carpet again.

After cleaning the footprints off the floor, Angela walked back downstairs to work on dinner. While getting vegetables out of the refrigerator, she received a phone call.

Angela flipped her phone open and said, "Hello".

"Hi, Angela, this is Mark calling from Ackley's Security. I'm on my way over right now. Is that okay?"

"Yes Mark, I am home, so stop on by. I'll be here."

"Thank you, Angela. I'll start heading over here in a minute. I shouldn't be too long. I'm maybe about five to ten minutes away."

Angela shut her phone, set it back down on the counter and went back to chopping the vegetables for her stir-fry dinner. After she had finished chopping the vegetables, Angela boiled some white rice and poured the vegetables into a wok on the stovetop. About ten minutes went by and her dinner was ready, which she served with a glass of white wine. After dinner, she got up and cleaned her dishes. After she had put the dishes in the dishwasher and started the dishwasher, the front doorbell rang. Perfect timing, Angela thought as she walked to the front door and opened it.

Outside stood a tall, thin man in his mid-30's, wearing a blue and white striped button up long sleeve shirt, with a pair of heavy-duty black pants. In his possession, he carried a cardboard box under one arm and a bag of tools in the other.

"Good evening, Angela, I'm Mark, I'm here to install your camera out back," he said.

"Hi Mark, thanks for coming over as quickly as you did. I'd really like to get this camera set up tonight."

"I think I can do that, and you still wanted just this one camera, right?"

"Yes, just the one."

"Perfect. Why don't you show me where you would like it mounted and we'll go from there?"

Angela guided Mark through the house and out through the sliding back door, where she pointed towards the corner of the house. "I would like for it to go there. Pointing and zoomed onto the gate along the fence line."

Mark pondered the location for a moment, looked across the yard, then back up to the corner where Angela was showing she would like the camera to be installed. Mark cracked a smile on his face and said, "That's no problem, Angela. I'll have this done and hooked up to your computer in less than an hour. Where's your computer you want the software downloaded? I'll get started on that first, so while the software is downloading, I can hook up the hardware outside."

"It's my laptop back in the house."

"Great," Mark said. "Why don't you make sure it's hooked up with a full charge? I'll start the software download onto your laptop and when that starts, I'll get to installing the hardware outside."

"Okay, I'll be back inside. Let me know if you need anything more from me."

Mark went around the house to retrieve his ladder from his work truck as Angela went back inside the house.

Angela grabbed her laptop from the coffee table to make sure it had a full charge, which it did. Meanwhile, Mark returned to the corner of the house with a ladder to install the camera.

Mark took the laptop and installed the software. Once the software installation begun, Mark worked on installing the camera on the underside of the eve of the house. It was after the last screw on the camera mount was installed that Mark looked up into the backyard and watched the back gate slowly open. Stopping for a minute, Mark watched as the gate swung completely open as far as it could open, then a few seconds later, it slammed itself shut.

Startled, Mark nearly fell off the third rung of his ladder before catching himself on the outside wall of the home. His eyes were glued to the gate, amazed at what he had just seen. Did he just see the gate unhitch and open, then slam itself shut? There was a slight breeze in the suburbs of Portland, but was it strong enough to do something like that? Perhaps it was?

Mark didn't think about it anymore and ignored what he witnessed, going back to work on installing the camera. After the camera was installed and adjusted to watch the gate, Mark hooked the camera up to an electrical power source around the house. After adjusting the focus on the camera, Mark folded his ladder and took it back to his truck. Mark then went back into the house. Angela was inside waiting for him with the computer, which had just finished downloading the software program to run the camera.

Angela noticed that something seemed off about Mark when he returned.

"Are you alright, Mark?"

But he was deep in thought, thinking about what he had seen minutes ago. He rubbed his eyes and said, "Yes, Angela. I'm fine, thank you. Just a long day of work. You got your laptop ready to go?"

"Yes, I do."

"That's good, Angela."

Mark took the laptop and ran a search for the software. After finding the software program, Mark searched for the camera name, which took about a minute to find.

"Okay, we found the camera, so what would you like to name the camera in your system?"

"Um, can we name it Backyard?" she asked.

"Okay, Backyard," he replied.

Once Mark named the camera, the camera video displayed a live feed of the backyard in color.

"Okay, at night, obviously, the camera won't work very well in color mode. You can click this link here and it'll switch the camera lens to a night vision mode that will illuminate your screen to see what is going on back there at night, too. Here is your video archive button. It's naturally set to record and file videos for a two-week period, where after that video will just continue to re-record over the oldest video first. If you must reset it, you can reset the system and the camera by just clicking this link here."

"Sounds easy enough," Angela said.

"Now, if you have any problems with the software or the camera. You've done a manual reset, and it's still giving you a hard time; call us and we can always come back out and look into the problem."

"Alright I will, thank you Mark. How much will it be?"

"Oh, let's make it $200 dollars."

Angela wrote Mark a check for $200 dollars. $40 less than what she was quoted before. What a deal! She handed them the check and shook his hand. Mark acknowledged Angela, but he still seemed nervous for some reason.

Mark left the house a little before 7 p.m. And afterward Angela decided to go for a walk at dusk, which took about an hour to stroll around the neighborhood saying hello to the neighbors that were out in their yards, or on their front porches or in their flower gardens enjoying a nice sunset evening.

When Angela got back home, she went upstairs and took a shower and cleaned up. Angela prepared a load of laundry, too. She wasn't going to stay up all night getting it done, either. It was just long enough to take the load from the wash to the dryer, turn the dryer on, and go to bed. Putting her pajamas on when she got out of the shower, Angela walked a clothing hamper of laundry back downstairs and started a load of laundry.

Afterwards, Angela sat down in her recliner to watch TV. After she turned the TV set on, Angela checked her new camera outback for a live feed to see if anything had happened while she was gone. The live video was too dark to see in just plain color. Since Angela got out of the shower, it had gotten dark out.

Angela remembered Mark telling her how to switch from the color setting to the night vision setting on the camera to see better at night. She switched over to the night vision setting and could see clearly that the gate in the backyard was swinging wide open again.

"Yes! Finally!" she said, ready to catch the culprits red-handed.

Angela thought that maybe these kids were wandering into her backyard to peep in on her, which made her uncomfortable to think about. She rewound the archived video to where she noticed the gate was closed, and then she hit play. About three minutes after Angela had rewound the recorded video and hit play, she watched the gate unhitch itself and slowly swing open. This was the moment she knew she had the kids dead to rights. Or did she?

Angela watched the video and instead of seeing the local neighborhood kids opening the gate and wandering into her back yard like she was expecting, she watched a small claw like hand grab the side of the fence post, maybe about a foot high off the ground. Around the corner of the post, Angela watched a tiny bald head with yellow glowing eyes look around the corner of the opening in the fence line before it ducked back behind the fence.

A few seconds passed and a small animal stepped out from behind the fence and into the opening of the fence line. It was small, maybe a foot tall, with long arms and hands that nearly dragged along the ground. Attached to those small hands were claws, three claws it looked like.

"My God the face," she whispered.

A smile that revealed rows of pointed teeth accompanied its yellow eyes. Its legs bent at its knee joints unnatural way and its skin matched the color of the pale full moon. Shortly after this one animal stepped into the yard, and then two more of these small animal-like creatures walked through the gate from behind the fence line with the first. Once in the backyard, all three animals walked toward her home, disappearing as they staggered under the camera and out of view.

Angela was terrified. What did she just see on video? What were these three small creatures? And most importantly, where did they go? Not to mention, she wondered how long these things had been around her home? Angela looked down at the time stamp on the camera and noticed it said 7:35 p.m. It was now 8:05 p.m.

Angela paused the security video on her laptop just in time to hear small feet running along the hardwood floor in front of the staircase. On the hardwood floor, the sound seemed to make a clicking noise like it had claws on its feet, too. Like a cat.

Angela froze and looked at the staircase leading up to the second floor. She heard small thumping sounds as if something small and lightweight was walking on the carpet upstairs. Then she heard a door open upstairs, and then it quietly closing, as the doorknob clicked shut.

She heard the clicking again. Whatever it was headed into the spare bedroom. The bedroom that used to be locked. The bedroom where her dog was found dead. Yes, whatever it was went into the only room upstairs in the house that had a hardwood floor. The third spare bedroom.

Angela stood up from the recliner and turned the TV off. Pausing for a moment, she swore she could hear the clicking sounds from the upstairs third bedroom, along with small voices chattering. She took a step back and leaned up on her tiptoes to see if she could see anything on the 2nd level hallway. Were these small beings in her house right now? Were they watching her, but she couldn't see them? Angela stepped back a few more feet to see if she could see anything upstairs moving around, but still, she couldn't.

She walked closer to the staircase, placing a hand on the newel post at the bottom of the stairs. She looked up the stairs and listened intently and heard the same noise of small clicking feet quickly running across a hardwood floor in her kitchen.

Angela gasped as she twisted around and took a step back onto the first set of stairs. She stood silent in the darkness, waiting for something to happen. Waiting for something to jump out of the darkness of the kitchen to get her. Angela's pounded in her chest. Beads of sweat ran down her forehead, dripping onto her face. She stood there on the first step, peering into the darkness of the kitchen. As hard as she tried to inspect the kitchen to see something, she couldn't. The only light coming from the kitchen was the small glow of luminescent green coming from the timer on her microwave. She watched that light intently, waiting for something to walk by it, expecting to see a shadow cover the only light source in the kitchen, but nothing happened.

Angela stepped off the first step of the stairs and walked over to the living room light switch. The feeling that she was being watched was stronger than ever. She quickly flipped the light on to the living room and in a sudden moment, light filled the room. The light drew the house in an ominous silence. Nothing moved. She only heard a grandfather clock in the room's corner as it ticked seconds away.

Angela took a deep breath, feeling relief that she could see some of the kitchen now. Gathering up her nerves, she walked towards the kitchen. The silence in the home was eerie. It was as if everything had stopped moving to watch what was going on. Angela couldn't hear the clicking noise or the noise of chattering voices. She only heard her own footsteps on the wooden floor planks.

Angela approached the corner of the kitchen and turned the light on, revealing only a cleanly kept space. Standing quietly in the kitchen, Angela heard the motor of the refrigerator. She looked underneath the dining table and, in the pantry, and slowly opened each cupboard, making as little sound as possible, but she found nothing out of place.

Angela thought she was losing her mind. Like she had some kind of cabin fever. Maybe what she saw was just in her imagination. Maybe she just needed to get out more and relax?

But then she heard a small bang and the sound of something sliding across the floor upstairs. Angela gasped again and pivoted around to investigate the living room. The house went completely silent again as Angela walked back towards the living room and to the staircase, leaving all the lights on downstairs.

Looking up the flight of stairs, Angela braced herself as she prepared to investigate the new sound. Slowly, she took the steps up the stairs and tried to look around the banister without rushing into something. Though she wasn't sure what to expect. Finally, Angela reached the top of the stairs and looked down the hallway. From underneath the door in the third spare bedroom, Angela noticed an iridescent blue light shining from underneath its crack.

Her heart jumped into her throat as she knew there shouldn't have been a nightlight coming from the room. There was no night light, and the blinds were closed. Angela's heart pounded against her chest as she looked down at the carpet and saw more of the same small footprints entering back into the room. Angela walked up to the door. As she got closer, she heard voices, as if someone was holding a conversation with someone else. But the voices were raspy, as if the source was losing their voice.

Angela faced the door, nervous. The blue light still glowed from under the door. Angela slowly placed her hand on the doorknob and turned it. The door squeaked open as Angela walked in. She turned the light switch on next to the door in the room and noticed that the blue light she had seen under the door was gone. The large area rug, along with the closet door, was still in its place, and the blinds to the windows were still closed. Finally, Angela looked against the wall where she discovered that the opening to the air-conditioned duct work was uncovered, the loud bang sound that she had heard when she was in the kitchen downstairs must have been the sound of the sheet plywood falling down. Why was this moved out of the hole? And most of all, what moved it off the wall? And still, where did these small creatures go? Did they come into her home? Are they responsible for leaving the small footprints on the carpet and making the clicking sounds in the kitchen? Angela felt more confused than she ever was before.

She turned the light off in the room and shut the door. She walked back downstairs and turned on all the lights in the home and called her best friend.

"Hello?" a muffled voice answered.

"Jenn? Hey, are you awake?"

"I was just getting ready for bed, Angie. What's up?"

"Listen, would you, umm, would you please come over and spend the night with me?"

"What? Why? What's going on?"

"I umm, I think I had a prowler around the house, and I'd like it if you could come over and just stay the night with me. I'd feel safer."

"Okay Angie, okay. Are you doing, okay?"

"Yeah, I'm fine. I just would like to not sleep alone tonight."

"Sure, I'll come over. I can be there in like 20 minutes."

"Okay, please hurry."

"Okay, I'm on my way."

"Thanks, Jenn. See you soon."

Angela shut her phone and set it on the coffee table. She then saved the video showing the three small creatures walking in through the gate and toward the direction of her house. After she had saved the video onto her computer, Angela continued watching the video, never seeing the small creatures show up again after that. It was around 11 p.m. when the doorbell rang. Angela got up and ran over to the front door, opened it and let Jennifer in. Angela was still in a panic and frightened by what she saw earlier.

"Angie, what's going on? Are you okay? And why are you acting this way?"

"I uh, okay, look. I need you to watch something."

"Did you catch those kids on video or something peeping in on you like we talked about?"

"Just watch this video," Angela replied.

Angela pulled up the archived video from her computer and hit play. Jennifer watched as the gate in the back fence opened. "Oh, you got them," she said.

Jennifer was expecting to see a group of neighborhood kids, probably wearing all black and sneaking into Angela's yard to get a peek at her. Instead, she watched as a small claw-like hand grabbed the side of the fence near the corner of the gate opening. When the small creature popped its head around the corner of the opening, Jennifer gasped. "What is that?"

Jennifer watched in horror as the small creature walked out from the corner of the opening, followed closely by two similar creatures with yellow glowing eyes. The three creatures walked towards Angela's home and then completely disappeared from camera's view. They stood only a foot, or a foot and a half in height. It was hard to see the exact details from the video. They appeared to have yellow eyes that were illuminated by the camera's lens, along with long arms and claws on their hands. They were bald; the video didn't seem to show if they had hair or not, and their teeth. My God, the teeth. They were pointed, long, and protruded from the animal's mouths.

After the recorded video ended playing, Jennifer sat back on the couch and pondered what she had just seen. Half confused, and yet half afraid, Angela was calming down but was still felt a high level of anxiety.

"Maybe they were cats?" Jennifer asked.

"Jenn, I have never seen a cat that would walk on its hind legs like that, and you and I both know those things weren't cats!"

"Oh my God, what were those things?" Jenn asked, shocked.

"I don't know. I've never seen something like that before. I don't even know who to talk to about it."

"Where are they now?"

"I don't know Jenn. I don't know if they've left or if they're still around here. If they're inside the house or outside? Just before I called you, I went upstairs because I heard clicking sounds, like tiny footsteps on the wood floor in the third bedroom. When I got close to the door, I could see blue glowing light from underneath the door, too. Jenn, there is no light in that room. No night light, no socket in the center of the room for a light bulb. The only thing in there are two windows, and the blinds were shut too, and it's dark out. Then I could hear voices. Like someone holding a conversation with someone else, but in a raspy, low tone. Like someone who had lost their voice and was still trying to talk, ya know?" Angela said, her voice quivering. " I walked into the room and there and it was empty. The only thing that was out of place was the small piece of plywood that was covering the hole to the air conditioning air duct that's running to that room."

"Why was it moved?"

"I don't know Jenn. It just was. I don't know what to do. Who should I talk to about this?"

"Let's just think about this for a minute. What could they have been? Maybe like a couple cats? Or maybe a fox? Foxes are around this area, too."

"They weren't cats or foxes, Jenn. Those are creatures I have seen before. These things I have never seen in my life."

"Well, we can show Jeff. Jeff will know what to do."

"What can he do, Jenn?"

"I don't know, Angie, but I'll be honest with you. I don't know what the hell those things were. Maybe Jeff might? Angie, do you remember a couple of nights ago when we were watching movies here in the living room?"

"Yeah, I remember."

"I heard clicking sounds from the kitchen. Like a cat with its claws out, walking on the hardwood floor planks."

"Oh God, Jenn. You're right. You said you heard that, didn't you?"

Hearing that from Jenn only made her more nervous. Angie had already spent a couple of nights with some kind of wild animals that had come into her home without her knowledge. Angela really didn't think Jeff would know much about what was on the video and potentially in her house, but she was willing to hear his opinion.

Jennifer called Jeff over to Angela's house. She gave him directions and thirty minutes later; he showed up and watched the video. Jeff didn't know what the small creatures were, either. Angela didn't know what to do.

"I don't want to stay here tonight."

"That's fine Angela, you can come stay with me at my place."

"Thanks."

"Is there anything that I can do to help Jenn?" Jeff asked.

"No Jeff, I'm just going to take her back home to my place."

"Okay, I'm going to leave then. I'll walk you guys out."

"Okay, come on Angie. We'll head upstairs and get your things for tomorrow first."

Angela and Jennifer walked upstairs, while Jeff waited downstairs. Jenn helped Angela gather some things for the night and for work tomorrow. Angela was still in shock. Why was this happening to her? Why didn't she have any answers? It was now nearly 1 in the morning, and it was getting later by the minute.

"You have your keys, Angie?"

"Yeah, I do, and my purse and phone, too. I'm taking my laptop, too. It has the security video recorded on it."

Together, the three of them left the house after Angela locked the door behind them. Jenn drove Angela back to her house for the night, while Jeff went home to his apartment.

Neither of the girls slept a wink all night. Angela couldn't get the image of the small creatures out of her mind. What were they and why were they there, but most of all, where did they go? Did they get into her house? If so, how long have they been coming in? So many questions ran through her mind.

For the first time since her ex-husband Todd left her, Angela felt vulnerable. Very vulnerable. She had told herself that she would never feel that way again, and now here she was. She was less than a few months into her fresh start and an unknown being had threatened her opportunity to begin anew. But Angela didn't know who to turn to for help. She rolled over in bed to look at the time on the alarm clock on the bedstand, which read 3:44 a.m. in bold red digits.

Angela slowly closed her eyes and tried to relax and get some rest. However, each small sound in Jenn's house reminded her of the clicking noises she had heard earlier in the evening.

CHAPTER 9

The alarm clock on Jennifer's phone sounded loud at 6 a.m. Angela slowly opened one eye in the dark room to look at the clock on the nightstand. She figured she only got an hours' worth of sleep.

Her mind was still heavy about her experience from the night before. Angela opened both eyes and stared at the ceiling while Jennifer woke up.

"Mm, it's too early. Angela, are you okay? Did you sleep alright?"

"No, I slept maybe an hour all night."

"You brought your laptop, didn't you?"

"Yes, I did."

"You should bring it to work with us today. Maybe you could show the video to Mr. Marshall. He might know what you should do."

"Yeah, I guess I could."

Angela sat on the edge of the bed and slowly cried into her hands when Jenn got up to make coffee. The feeling of a fresh start in life was all but gone. She sniffled, gathered herself, and stood up from the bed. Angela walked into the bathroom and jumped into the shower. While in the shower, Angela cried again. Her nerves were worn down, but the stress and anxiety of not knowing what to do or who to turn to bothered her. The lack of sleep didn't help her much either.

Jennifer walked back into the room and heard Angela in the shower.

"Angie, things will be alright. We'll figure this out together. Try not to think about it and we'll figure out what to do today."

"I don't know what to do, Jenn," she said. "I don't even know who I should call. Pest control? Were those even pests?"

"What about Mr. McGuire? Maybe he might know something. It wouldn't hurt to ask him."

"The realtor? I suppose. I can call him when I get to the office this morning."

Angela finished washing the shampoo from her brown hair. Shutting off the shower, she got out, grabbed her robe, and tied the waistband around her waist. Angela left the bathroom, so Jenn could get her shower in and get ready to go to work.

Angela didn't feel much like working. Her mind was still heavy on what happened at her home the night before. Maybe contacting the realtor, Mr. McGuire, would be a good idea after all. He always mentioned if there was anything more that he could do to call him. It was worth a shot because Angela was running out of ideas. In fact, Angela had no idea what to do.

She got ready for work while Jenn finished in the shower. Angela left the bedroom and went to the kitchen to get a cup of coffee while Jennifer got out of the shower and got herself dressed and ready for work. After getting ready, Jennifer joined Angela in the kitchen.

"Is your laptop charged, Angie?"

"It is. Are you ready to go?"

"I am. Let me just grab a coffee for the road. You want a mug of coffee for the road, too?"

"Yes Jenn, thank you."

Jennifer got Angela and herself a mug of coffee to take some with them to work. Both girls left Jennifer's place and went to work. Angela forgot how much she hated riding with Jenn through the early morning traffic in Portland, especially when she didn't have her mind focused on the task at hand. A normal drive from Jenn's place to work usually took about half an hour through rush hour. Jenn usually made it in half the time it took Angie by the way she drove. It was a nice sunny day in Portland. No breeze or rain, but it was rather cool and sunny.

The girls arrived at work and Jenn parking her car in her parking stall in the covered parking lot. The girls both got out of the car and walked to the building. Walking past Jeff at the coffee stand, Jeff came out from behind the stand and said, "Hey, are you two alright this morning?"

"Yeah, we didn't sleep much last night," Jennifer said.

"Is that your laptop you have with you, Angie?" Jeff asked.

"It is. I'm going to show Mr. Marshall the video and maybe he'll know what to do."

Jeff hugged Angela. It was the first time Angela felt that Jeff was sincere about hugging her rather than trying to have a one-night fling with her. Jenn hugged Jeff goodbye, and the girls proceeded to the elevator, got in, and went up to the fourth floor.

It was 8:50 in the morning. Mr. Marshall wouldn't be in the office for another half an hour, but Angela hoped he was earlier than usual. She needed answers. Badly.

Angela and Jennifer sat down at their desks, and Angela set her laptop down on the counter by her side. Mr. Marshall came in at his usual time of 9:10 in the morning. Before Mr. Marshall could walk past the front desk, he could tell something was wrong with the girls just by the way they were looking at him.

"Ladies, I know. I didn't have time to get a shave this morning. I have my electric razor in the office, and I'll just shave in my office to save some time. With the door shut this time, of course."

"Mr. Marshall, can I talk with you for a minute?" Angela asked.

Mr. Marshall could tell something was wrong. The last time she asked to talk like that was about her divorcing Todd. "I don't think this is about my face. What is the matter, Angela? Is everything alright?"

"I need you to look at something. Can you look at a video for me on my computer?"

"Of course, is everything alright? Is your ex-husband giving you a rough time?"

"No, it's nothing to do with him. Just watch."

Angela opened her laptop and played the saved archived video from the computer. Mr. Marshall watched as the gate to Angela's fence line opened and saw the three small creatures with yellow glowing eyes and what appeared to be fangs, long arms, and moon colored skin walk through the gate, towards Angela's home.

Mr. Marshall paused the video and sat back at his desk to ponder what he had just watched.

"Have you ever seen anything like that, Mr. Marshall?"

"Angie, I'm not going to lie to you. What I just saw isn't an animal I have ever seen before. Not around Portland, or any of its suburbs, for that matter. Could you tell where they went?"

"I think in my home, but they walked under the camera and after that I couldn't see where they went."

"Where did you move to again?"

"60 Suntides Blvd."

"Well, here, let's look it up online and see what comes up," Mr. Marshall said.

Mr. Marshall opened his internet browser and searched the property history, however, didn't find much more information about the property rather than it was up to date in taxes paid and its property value had depreciated over the course of the last five years, but that's normally given the poor housing economy in Portland right now.

"Angela, who did you purchase the home through?"

"McGuire Realty."

"Well, how about we call the agency? Maybe they might have some more information about the house or area? Maybe it was just a glitch in your camera, and it might have been some sort of animal. I mean, they might know since they studied the neighborhood to sell a piece of property in it."

"Okay, Jenn and I were talking about that this morning. I'll call Mr. McGuire and ask him. I'm sorry, Mr. Marshall, I just don't know what to do. If I knew what these animals were..."

"It's fine Angela, keep me posted on what he says, and we can go from there, okay? I could always see if I could get in touch with fish and wildlife, too. They might recognize it. I'll work on that, okay?"

Mr. Marshall always seemed to care a lot for the girls. He was a good man, a loving husband and a father of three. He had two daughters and a son, and always treated both Angela and Jennifer like family, much more than Mr. Stone did anyway. So, to see Mr. Marshall take an interest in Angela's well-being wasn't a surprise, but she welcomed it either way.

Angela closed her laptop and told Mr. Marshall that she was going to go down to the realtor's office during her lunch break. Turning to leave, Mr. Marshall said to her, "Let me know what he says, Angie."

Angela nodded and closed the door to his office, set her laptop down, and got back to work.

11 a.m. came by slowly. Angela plugged her laptop into the outlet under her desk to get a full charge. She left her laptop open while she worked, that way she could watch the surveillance video in her backyard. The gate door remained open, but nothing came through the gate or out the gate into the tall grass behind the fence. Angela even had time to watch the recorded, archived video again. After she grew tired of looking in the backyard, Angela pushed her computer to the side of her desk.

"I can't believe this is happening to me, Jenn."

"Oh, don't jump to conclusions too fast Angie, I mean, it could be something easily explained?"

"Were those creatures what killed my dog? Did they take her body up to that third room and rip her apart?"

"I don't know, Angie, and remember not to jump to conclusions. Maybe it's some animals from the area. Who knows at this point?"

"Well, whatever it is, I'm not letting it stop me from starting over. I'm staying at my house tonight and if I must, I'm going to figure out what they are myself."

"Well, I support you, Angie. If you need me there, let me know."

"I will, but I'm going to do this on my own. It's almost time for lunch Jenn, I'm going to head down to the realtor's office. Did you want to come along with?"

"No, I told Jeff that we could go for lunch. If you would like, you're welcome to come along after you meet with the realtor. We aren't leaving for lunch for like another 30 or 40 minutes."

"If I get finished early, I'll call you and meet up with you."

"Okay, let me know what Mr. McGuire says too."

"I will."

Angela grabbed her laptop and purse and left the office before she realized her car wasn't at the office. It was still back home because Jenn had given her a ride.

"Shit," Angela said and walked back to the office.

She walked into Mr. Marshall's office and asked to borrow his car, to which he obliged, and handed her the keys. All that Mr. Marshall asked for in return was that Angela kept him informed about what was going on And asked her to pick up a Caesar salad from Dixon's Café down by where McGuire's Realty was. Dixon's always made the best Caesar salads. The secret was in the dressing. Angela finally cracked a small smile and thanked Mr. Marshall. Turning to leave, Mr. Marshall wished Angie well.

Angela took the elevator to the first floor. The doors opened and Jeff was still at the coffee stand making drinks for a group of businessmen who looked as if they were at the building for a meeting. As soon as the doors opened, Angie jumped out, and the doors slammed shut with a loud clank! The businessmen looked over, startled by the sound of the elevator doors made.

"You guys should probably take the stairs," Angela said to them. They nodded in agreement.

Jeff waved at Angela, and Angela acknowledged him with a wave back. Angela was just accepting Jeff. At first, she thought Jeff was only a man who wanted to get his jollies off in a one-night stand and then disappear to never be heard from again. However, that seemed to not be the case with him.

Angela walked out of the building and towards Mr. Marshall's black BMW. She unlocked the car, got in and backed out of the parking garage. Sheproceeded to drive to McGuire Realtor's Service. There wasn't much traffic during lunch, but Angela left the office early enough to miss most of it as she went downtown to the realtor's office.

After parking in front of the realty building, Angela got out and grabbed her laptop and walked in. A bell above the door chimed as she opened it and Angela heard footsteps walking towards her that made a hollow thump with every step. Finally, from around the corner, Mr. McGuire appeared.

"Why, Angela sweetheart! What a nice surprise. Did my guy ever come out and fix that lock to the third bedroom for you?"

"Yes, he did. But I'm not here for that."

"Well, what can I do for you, darling?"

"Well, I need you to look at a security video I have on my laptop. I need your help to explain what I'm looking at."

Puzzled, Mr. McGuire acknowledged Angela's request and escorted her back into his office where they sat down and she opened her laptop.

"Okay, for the past few weeks, I've been having a hard time keeping the gate to the back fence closed. I've locked it, latched it, and for whatever reason, it keeps opening on its own. At first, I thought it might be the neighborhood kids coming back in and playing around behind the fence or even in my backyard."

"There are neighborhood kids around that area. It wouldn't surprise me if that was the case, Angela."

"Well, that's what I thought, too. So, I set up a surveillance camera outback thanks to a local security company. And the very first night I caught this."

Angela hit play on her laptop and Mr. McGuire watched the footage of the small humanoids entering her backyard through the gate.

"Oh my God," he said. "What are those things?"

"Well, I was hoping you might know. I really can't explain what I'm looking at either. Have you heard of any weird animals around this neighborhood that they might be?"

Mr. McGuire sat back in his chair. "I haven't heard of any strange animals in this area. I mean, you do have the creek behind the fence line. So, things like racoons, squirrels maybe and cats sure. But no animal like that, ma'am."

Angela sighed, not knowing what to say. Mr. McGuire paused briefly, as he went into a deep train of thought. Looking back up at Angela and seeing that she was nearly in tears of confusion, he swallowed loudly. He then got up from behind his desk and shut the door to his office, and walked back to his desk.

"Angela, I'm going to tell you something, and if you believe me or not, it's up to you."

Angela thought his response was strange considering the question she asked.

"Angela, the house that is next door to you. Back in the mid 60's there was a woman who lived there by herself. A younger woman who never married, nor did she have any children. However, and this is where it gets weird, and this is something that I don't believe in by any means myself, but she practiced witchcraft. Regularly in that house, as well as divination and satanic worship. She was a wicked woman, Angela. She even practiced satanic animal sacrifices, too. What was most interesting was that she would always drain the bodies of their blood. After draining the blood to sacrifice to whatever deity she sacrificed to, she would cut the animal's body into pieces and lay them on the ground in a certain pattern. Then she'd set fire to the pattern to burn the body."

Angela sat back, stunned in her chair, pondering what she had just heard.

"Now like I said, Angie. She was a weird woman. Very weird. And it was such a long time ago when she lived in that neighborhood that she isn't there anymore. In fact, I'm certain that she's probably not even living anymore."

"Why didn't you tell me that before I purchased the home?"

"Angie darling, it's not a proven fact that anything comes from witchcraft, practice, or divination. It's all in what you make of it. It doesn't affect the sale of a home or a piece of property. And the simple fact was, this didn't happen in your home. It had nothing to do with your home," he said.

"So, what are you saying, Mr. McGuire?"

"Well, these small creatures Angie, I've seen nothing like them in my life. I don't know what they are and they sure as hell don't look like any animal I have ever seen before."

"So, you're saying?"

"What I'm saying, Angela, is maybe they are a product of something that woman from next door in the 60's did?"

"So, what should I do?"

"Well, I tell you what. Do you go to church, Angie?"

"What the hell does that have to do with anything?"

"It's just a simple question, darling. Do you go to church?"

"I don't right now, no."

"Well, I do. Let me talk to my pastor from my church and I'll see what he says. Can you copy and email this video to me, and I'll take it to him to show him? We'll see what he says, okay?"

"Sure." Angela said. However, she was skeptical that would do any good at all. What good would a priest do?

Angela hadn't been to church since her divorce, and she really had no intentions of going back either. Mr. McGuire apologized to Angela for what was going on and asked her to call him if she needed anything else.

Before leaving the office, Angela asked one more question.

"Mr. McGuire, I went behind the fence line one day and found a small trail that led down to the creek you were talking about. But while I was down by the creek, I walked a little further to where this small trail ended, and I found an old well. It was behind some rough growth, like plants and vegetation. But I managed to work my way back to it. I dropped this white stone into this well and I waited to hear the stone hit the ground or water, but I never heard the stone hit anything. Did you know that there was a well there?"

"Yes, it is an ancient well, Angela. But it hasn't been used for the longest time now. Probably not since the area was first populated back in the, oh jeez, the 1830's I believe? When the first settlers came to Oregon. The well is dry though, Angela. I'm kind of surprised to hear that it even exists still."

"I see. Well, it is a very old well. The stone used to build it looks like it's been there forever. Well, thank you Mr. McGuire. If I have any further question for you, I'll call you."

"Remember, send me that video, Angela. I'll take it to my pastor and let him watch it and see what he says."

Angela said, "Okay."

She left the realty office with her laptop in hand and stopped by Dixon's to pick up a Caesar salad for her boss. She still had time to meet with Jenn and Jeff for lunch, however, she decided to skip going to lunch that day and just went back to the office. When she got back to the fourth floor, she saw Mr. Marshall was still in the office.

"Angela, bless you dear, you got me my salad."

"I did. Here are your keys back. Thanks for letting me use your car," she said.

"It's my pleasure. Come in and sit down. Let me know what he said."

"Well, I showed him the video, and he didn't know what they were. Then he told me about the neighbor from the 60's."

"The neighbor? From the 60's?"

"Yes. Apparently next door to the house I'm living in now, at 50 Suntides Blvd., lived a woman who practiced this is weird, well, who practiced divination basically. Things like occult worship and witchcraft."

"Oh. That's strange."

"It is. He never told me that when I bought the house."

"Well, I suppose he wouldn't have to. I mean, it's something that never happened in your own house. And that's something that you choose to believe in or not. Either way, is he able to do anything for you?"

"He said he wants to show the video to his minister from church."

"So, he thinks that these small animals are something that resulted in the practice of this neighbor witch from the 60's?"

"That sounds like the case, Mr. Marshall."

Mr. Marshall shook his head and said, "Angie, this is the craziest thing I've ever heard of." He set his glasses on his desktop and rubbed the bridge of his nose with his thumb and index finger.

"Okay, so are you going to show this minister the security video?"

"I don't know what else to do, Mr. Marshall, so I suppose I will."

"Well Angela, you must do what you must do. So, if I can help you out, let me know."

Mr. Marshall and Angela got up and Mr. Marshall gave her a hug and told her that things would all be okay.

"Angela, would you like a place to stay until you get things figured out?" he asked.

"No, but thank you, Mr. Marshall," she said. "I plan on confronting whatever this is. I just went through a shitty divorce, and I'm not going to let something like this run me from my home or stop me from starting a new life for myself."

Angela thanked Mr. Marshall and left his office. She was determined to outlast whatever those animals were, but she was more confused now than ever before. Was this the right thing to do? To let a pastor watch this video? And would he know what these creatures were? And even if he did, what could he even do about it?

Angela went back to her desk and opened her laptop. Linking her laptop to the wireless internet connection of the building, Angela emailed the video to Mr. McGuire. Angela then called Mr. McGuire to let him know she had just emailed the video to him. Mr. McGuire opened his email and told Angela that he had it and that he was going to forward it to his pastor and then give him a call too.

Angela thanked Mr. McGuire for his help and hung up the phone just as Jennifer came back from her lunch with Jeff. Jenn sat down next to Angela in her seat and asked Angela how things went with Mr. McGuire.

"Things went alright. I guess," she said. "He watched the video, and he didn't know what they were. Then he told me something that I'm not sure if I believe or not."

"What did he say?"

"He told me that back in the 60's a woman lived next door by herself next to my place and she practiced in witchcraft and even dabbled in satanic occult practices."

"You don't believe in that, do you Angie?" Jenn asked. "What happened to this woman?"

"I don't really know. I didn't ask Mr. McGuire, but I want to know now."

Angela grabbed her phone and called Mr. McGuire. The phone rang twice before it was answered.

"This is McGuire. How can I help you?"

"Hi Mr. McGuire, this is Angela."

"Hi Angie, I haven't heard from my minister yet."

"Oh, that's not what I'm calling about. I was wondering what happened to the woman who lived next door from the 60's."

"Oh! Well Angela, that's the weird thing. No one really knows what happened to her. Neighbors in the area didn't really converse with her, nor did they go to that home. In fact, they avoided her at all costs."

"So, no one knows what happened to her."

"That's right Angie. No one knows. One day she was living in the home and the next day she was gone. Like she disappeared into thin air. The neighbors in the area thought that she had just abandoned the home late at night when everyone was sleeping, but no one really knows what happened to her for sure."

"Alright, thank you Mr. McGuire. I'll call you later to see if you heard from your pastor."

"Alright Angie, if you need anything else, give me a call."

"Thank you."

Angela hung up the phone and relayed the newfound information to her friend.

"So, are you going back to the house tonight?"

"Yes, I am. I have to Jenn. That's my home. And what these things want with my home, I don't understand, but I'm not going to let them take it from me."

"You want me to come over tonight?"

"No, it's alright. I'll call you if I change my mind, but I'll be okay."

Angela and Jennifer went back to work, answering calls for Mr. Stone, who had walked into his office at 9:30 in the morning and shut the door and wasn't heard from thereafter. Mr. Marshall always kept his office door open unless he was with a client. He always respected client and co-worker privacy, but if it was just him alone in his office, his door was always open.

5 p.m. came fast. Angela caught up on some filing work that needed to be caught up on, as did Jennifer, too.

"Jenn, it's 5. Can you take me back to my place?"

"Sure, are you sure you want to go back tonight, Angela?"

"I am," Angela said.

Jennifer filed one last file for the day and the girls grabbed their purses from under their desks, and Angela picked up her laptop from the counter. Before leaving, she checked the security camera out back and noticed that the fence gate was still closed for the day. Thank God, because it meant those things weren't roaming around her home, or so she thought.

They stopped by Mr. Marshall's office and told him they were leaving for the day, and he wished them a good evening, telling Angela to call him if she needed help. Angela thanked him.

The girls left the office around 5:10 p.m., stopping by the coffee stand on the first floor to say hello to Jeff. They walked out of the building around 5:15 p.m. and got into Jennifer's car. Jenn as she had in the past, drove like the first woman to ever enter a car race. Angela was more afraid of not making it home alive than staying the night in her home alone, however after about thirty minutes on the road, Jennifer had Angela back home.

"Angie, are you sure you don't want me to stay with you tonight?"

"Yes, it's fine Jenn. I'll give you a call if I need help again. Thank you."

Angela shut the door to Jenn's car. Jennifer pulled out of the driveway and left the house, while Angela turned around to look at the front of her home. Truth be told, she was scared to death to go inside.

What if those things were already in there? Waiting for her to come back?

Angela walked up to her front door and unlocked it, walked in and closing the door behind her. She looked around the living room, then the kitchen. Then she checked the rooms upstairs, but everything seemed fine. Angela walked back downstairs and looked out back, noticing the gate was still shut. She went outside and walked out to the gate. Checking the lock on the hitch, she turned around and headed back to the house. Before walking back in, Angela glanced over at the camera and saw that it was still operating just fine, with a small red light emitting off its side.

Angela walked back inside the house, closed the sliding kitchen door behind her, and walked into her living room. She set the laptop down on the coffee table and turned the TV on while she sat down in her recliner and wrapped herself in the comfort of the quilt her grandmother had made her.

It was about 7 p.m. when Angela remembered she hadn't had dinner yet and it was getting late. Wanting to make something quick and simple, Angela took a frozen dinner from the freezer and threw it in the microwave to cook. While her dinner cooked in the microwave, Angela looked out in the backyard and noticed the wind was blowing a little as fresh leaves in the trees behind the fence flickered in the breeze. Spring was in full force in the Pacific Northwest, given another month and the entire area would experience summer.

The microwave dinged and Angela grabbed a fork from the kitchen drawer and took a plate from the pantry, and set the hot dish from the microwave onto the plate. Walking back into the living room, Angela sat down in her recliner and watched TV. After two bites into her dinner, her cell phone rang. Angela set her food down on the coffee table and answered her phone.

"Hello?" Angela asked, as she cleared her voice.

On the other end of the phone, a deep voice spoke, "Hello Angela, my name is Marlin Teske. I'm the pastor of St. Matthew Lutheran Church. I'm Greg McGuire's pastor. How are you tonight?"

"Hi, it's nice to hear from you. Thank you for calling. I'm doing as best I can. I'm nervous about what I saw around here last night, though."

"I understand Angela. Greg emailed me this security video of your home and told me what you said. I was wondering if you have some time to meet with me tomorrow? If you can, I'd like to talk to you about this video."

"That would be great. If you have any information or can help me, then I'd certainly welcome it at this time."

"We can talk more about it tomorrow. Would you be able to meet?"

"Of course, I'm home all day tomorrow."

"That's great, my dear. I can come to your home. Where do you live?"

Angela gave the pastor her home address. The pastor told Angela that he would stop by her home in the afternoon and they could talk more about the video. Angela thanked him for his time and hung up the phone.

She set the phone down on the coffee table and continued eating her dinner. A couple of hours went by with no incidents. Angela considered sleeping in her recliner tonight with her quilt blanket but decided not to and went upstairs. She felt that the safest place for her was behind a locked door, and she could lock her bedroom door. Angela turned the television set off and folded her blanket up, setting it on the headrest of the recliner where she had kept it for the longest time. Angela grabbed her laptop. It seemed as if she carried it with her everywhere she went, like a second set of eyes.

Upon walking upstairs, Angela looked in the spare bedrooms and noticed that everything was quiet. Nothing appeared to be out of the ordinary. The only sound in the house was the grandfather clock ticking the seconds away downstairs.

Angela walked into her bedroom, turned the light on, shut the bedroom door and locked it behind her. Angela stripped her clothes off and put on her pajamas. She then walked into the bathroom and brushed her teeth and washed her face. After she had finished using the bathroom, Angela walked to the window to close the blinds. Looking out back, she noticed the gate in the fence was still closed.

Angela cracked the window to let in some fresh air and drew the blinds closed. She then walked over and turned the light off in the room and crawled into bed. Angela thought how nice it was to have the house so quiet and prayed that it would stay that way so that she could get through the night without incident. She slowly closed her eyes and rolled her body over to face the alarm clock on her bed stand. It was 10:37 p.m.

*   *   *   *

A loud banging sound woke Angela in the middle of the night. She opened each eye individually as she looked over towards the clock radio on her bed stand. It was 3:02 a.m.

Angela rubbed her eyes and pulled off her covers as she got out of bed. She could tell the loud noise that woke her from a deep slumber certainly came from outside. Standing up from the bed, Angela walked over to the bedroom window and peered through a crack in the blinds. She looked out the bedroom window just in time to see four small creatures, the same ones that she had seen the other night, walking towards her home. They walked with a strange limp, as if they were born that way.

Angela instantly gasped, her heart pounding again against the side of her chest as she watched the small beings walk towards her home and disappear under the eaves of the home. It was then that Angela heard the glass slider door open, followed by small, tiny footsteps clinking around on the floor of the kitchen. She held her breath, listening intently and thanking God that she had locked her bedroom door. Did she lock the sliding glass door in the kitchen, though? She couldn't remember. And if she did, then these beings could certainly unlock the glass door and slide it open on their own accord.

She listened intently to the sound of small footsteps walking across the carpet. Either the creatures were on the carpet of the stairs or down the hallway from her bedroom. Between heavy breaths, sweat ran down the sides of her head. Tiny running footsteps skittered outside her bedroom door.

Angela held her mouth with her hand, trying to make as little noise as possible. Maybe the creatures didn't think she was in her bedroom. If she could stay quiet, maybe they would leave. She trudged to the bedroom door to listen more closely. Underneath the door's crack, she saw small shadows running past down the hallway. The night light in the hallway exposed the shadows of the creatures as they quickly darted back and forth in front of her door.

Each of their tiny steps made a quiet clinking noise on the hardwood floor. Angela panicked, not knowing exactly what to do. She could have called Jennifer, but then she realized she had left her cell phone down on the coffee table in the living room. She pressed her ear against the door and heard a high-pitched whisper, "She's listening."

Angela gasped. She took a step back. Shit. They knew she was in the bedroom. Things instantly became quiet in the home as Angela continued to try to listen for any other sound. The blue hallway light yielded no more shadows moving around in front of her bedroom door. For what seemed like hours going by, Angela listened intently to try to hear anything. Finally, Angela heard a distinct sound coming from downstairs. Something she had never heard before. A sound much heavier than the small clicking footsteps in the kitchen or on the carpet.

It sounded like a horse galloping through the first floor. Accompanied by the impact of each hoof was a loud thud that followed.

Angela unlocked the door and cracked it open just enough to look out the bedroom and into the long hallway. She saw a blue light in the hallway and assumed it was coming from underneath the third bedroom again. Against the wall at the top of the stairs, Angela saw a gigantic shadow. A shadow that belonged to something standing at the bottom of the staircase. The large body cast a shadow of bullhorns over its head as it walked upstairs. With every step, its hooves caused the stairs to creak beneath its massive weight.

The head of the creature turned its back to her. It was large and hairy, with horns that protruded from the top of its head, just above the ears. Angela was scared to death. She quietly shut the door and locked it as she could still hear the footprints getting louder and louder as this creature walked upstairs. Angela backed away from the door and curled up on the floor in the room's corner where she could still see the door.

Her breathing grew deeper and heavier as fear devoured her body. The large footsteps kept getting closer and closer to her bedroom door until she could see a large shadow block out the light from underneath it.

The shadow lingered for a moment, and then walked back towards the stairs and the spare bedrooms. Angela crawled on her hands and knees into the bathroom. She shut the door quietly and locked it. She turned around and pressed her ear up against the shower wall to listen in on the spare bedroom.

In the spare bedroom, Angela could hear quiet murmuring, but she couldn't tell what was being said. It was almost as if the voices in the room were speaking in an unfamiliar language. Without a doubt, though, she knew that something was in that third bedroom. Angela continued to listen against the wall when suddenly, everything got quiet again.

But then she heard a voice talking through the wall. The voice didn't sound human, nor was it talking in a language that she could recognize. The voice kept getting louder and louder. Angela continued to breathe more heavily, as she didn't know what to do. She was trapped in her bedroom at the mercy of these creatures. What are they doing in that third bedroom? What was that large creature that walked up the stairs? And what were they saying?

The voices turned into a dark Gregorian demonic chant. She could hear them laughing through the walls. There was so much noise coming from the spare bedroom, and then it suddenly ceased. The voices and chanting were gone, and the house went quiet.

Angela didn't want to move; she was afraid to leave the safety of the bathroom. With her head pressed against the shower wall, all she could hear was her own breathing. She could swear she could hear the beating of her own heart, too. The bathroom was a small room, but she felt safe.

Angela sat in the bathtub and strained to listen against the wall, but the third bedroom was dead quiet. By calming her breathing and winding her nerves down, she mustered up the strength to leave the bathroom. Cracking the door, she peered around the corner into her bedroom. Everything seemed quiet. A light breeze blew the curtains gracefully by the window like a flag on a flagpole.

The only thing she saw in the room was the alarm clock on the nightstand that read 3:02 a.m. What? That was the time she had woken up. There's no way that everything that had happened could have all taken place within a minute. Angela checked the alarm clock and saw that it was still plugged into an outlet on the wall. She stared at the clock for a few seconds as it turned to 3:03 a.m.

Angela couldn't believe it. She approached the bedroom door and pressed her ear up against it. But she couldn't hear anything on the other side. The house was still and silent, like nothing had ever happened. Had it just been a nightmare? Was any of it real? Angela gathered up her nerves, took a deep breath, and unlocked the door. Turning the doorknob and slowly pulling the door open, she peered out through the crack in the door before opening it all the way when she saw the coast was clear.

The only sound in the entire house was the ticking of the second hand on the grandfather clock downstairs. Angela opened the door wider, holding her breath to hear the slightest of sounds as she walked out into the hallway. The blue light was gone from under the spare third bedroom door. Angela shook a little as her nerves got the better of her for a moment. But then she gathered herself together and took a deep breath and walked down the hallway towards the spare bedroom.

Small footprints joined a set of large hoof prints that looked like they belonged to a horse or bull, staining the floor. Angela looked back up at the door and grabbed the doorknob. The knob slowly creaked when a loud, deep, and demonic voice from behind the door yelled, "STAY OUT OR DIE, BITCH!!"

The blue light instantly illuminated from underneath the door again and Angela heard soft voices chattering on the other side. Angela turned and dashed to the staircase and ran downstairs. She grabbed her phone and purse from the coffee table. As she turned to run towards the front door, the spare bedroom door opened and the glowing blue light illuminated the entire house. Angela bolted out the front door and ran to her car without even shutting the door. She jumped into her car, revved the engine, and shot out of the driveway.

Looking back in the rearview mirror, she saw the front door to her home slam shut on its own. Once the door shut, she couldn't see the blue light anymore. Angela cried as she drove, not knowing where to go from here. Reality set in as she pulled into an all-night gas station about five miles from her home. She sat in the driver's seat and crossed her hands on the top of the steering wheel. Eventually, she brought her hands to her face to wipe away her tears when she heard a tapping sound on the window. Angela looked up to see the attendant of the gas station, an older heavy-set man with a gray and white beard.

"Are you alright?" the attendant asked.

"I just needed a minute to think," Angela said.

The attendant offered to help her with directions if she needed, but Angela knew he couldn't help her with her real problem. It was clear tonight that something seriously wrong was happening in her home.

CHAPTER 10

It gently rained in the morning. Jennifer had gone to bed at a decent time last night, around 11 p.m. She was worried about her best friend Angela. She drew a lot of support and encouragement from her. Angela was a role model to her, and to see how she was at work shook Jennifer deep in her core. Nevertheless, she was able to get to sleep and slept well. It was nearly 430 a.m. when Jennifer heard her phone ring on her bedside stand. Slowly waking up, and looking at the clock, she wiped her face. Rubbing her eyes, she reached for her phone and answered it on the fifth ring.

"Hello?" Jennifer answered with a groggy voice.

"Jenn, I need your help."

"Angela?"

Through the cries and sniffles, Angela answered, "Yes, it's me."

"Angie, where are you? It's 430 in the morning."

"I'm at a gas station, near my house. Can I come over?"

"Yes, of course, did something happen?"

"I'll explain when I come over. I just need to leave and come over."

"Okay, okay. Come over."

Jennifer hung up the phone and turned the light on by the bed stand while she waited for Angela to arrive. It was nearly 5 a.m. when Angela finally arrived at Jennifer's home. She pulled into the driveway, raced out of the car, and rapidly knocked on the front door.

"Angie, come in. What happened?"

"Jenn, there's something wrong with that house. I woke up around 3 a.m. and saw more of those small things walking through the backyard. Once they disappeared under the eaves of my house, I could hear them in the kitchen, then the living room, and the stairs, and finally the hallway outside my bedroom door. I listened closely, and I heard one of them say that 'she's listening,'" Angela said in hysterics. "They know I'm there Jenn. They know I'm there!"

"Oh, my God. Angie, what happened after that?"

"After that, I heard something else in the house. So, I cracked the door to my room to look into the hallway, and I saw some enormous creature walking up the stairs. I could see its silhouette against the night lights, and it looked like a hairy bull walking on two legs. The creatures went into the spare bedroom where I found my dog's body. I could hear them chanting, talking and laughing with each other, and then the house went dead silent. So, I looked out my bedroom door again, and it was quiet like nothing was there anymore, so I went to the spare bedroom and opened the door."

Angie stopped and covered her mouth to catch her breath and try to relax.

"Go on," Jenn said as she wrapped her arm around Angela's shoulder. "What did you see in the room?"

"I didn't see anything. When I turned the doorknob, I heard a loud demonic voice say, 'Stay out or die, bitch.' Then I saw the blue light from under the door and heard quiet footsteps rush up to it from the other side. So, I ran. I ran downstairs and grabbed my purse and cell phone and when I turned to run outside, that bedroom door opened and the entire house was glowing in that blue light. I didn't bother to look behind me. I just went to the front door, threw it open, and left. When I was driving away, I saw the front door slam shut on its own, in the rearview mirror."

"Oh my gosh Angie, I'm sorry. You can stay here for as long as you need to. You want some coffee? Or can you lay back and relax for a little and just rest?"

"I don't know Jennifer. I don't know what to do. I just need to sit for a minute."

"Let me go make a pot of coffee. I'll be right back," Jennifer said.

As Jennifer stepped out of the room, Angie broke down crying. She had never felt this helpless before. Even when she went through her divorce with Todd, she was able to turn to Mr. Marshall, who helped her through the divorce process and guided her through the entire ordeal. But now there was no one to turn to, other than Pastor Teske.

Maybe he could help. He'd have to because she was running out of ideas. For God's sake, he wasn't even someone she had ever met before. Why would he even try to help? And what if the pastor couldn't do anything about it? If he couldn't help her, then what else could she do? Especially with how hostile the creatures acted toward her. Would she leave her new home? The place where she was planning to have a fresh start? And what if she did? Where would she go from there? Dozens of what if scenarios cycled through her head while Jennifer walked into the living room with two cups of coffee.

"I'll get some creamer. Just wait here for a minute."

"Thank you, Jenn."

Jennifer disappeared into the kitchen again while Angela picked up her cup of coffee. Jenn always made the blackest of black coffee, so creamer was a necessity if she planned to actually drink Jenn's homebrew. The cup warmed Angela's shaky hands, slightly calming her as Jenn returned with a bottle of creamer in hand.

"All I have is hazelnut Angie, is that okay?"

"That's fine," she said.

Angela poured the creamer into her coffee, mesmerized as the white cream swirled into the black coffee. With a quick stir, Angie took a sip and finally relaxed.

"It's good that it's Saturday, so you won't have to go to work without sleeping again. Do you want to take a nap here?"

"No, it's alright. I want to go back to the house. Maybe it's much quieter during the day."

"Angie, are you sure you want to go back there? It's not a problem if you want to lay down in the bedroom."

"Thanks Jenn, but it's fine. I want to go back to the house."

"Want me to come with you?"

"No, it's alright. I'm sorry I bothered you, Jenn. I just didn't know where else to go."

"Why don't you call that pastor? Maybe he can come over and help? Did you say he was coming over today, anyway?"

"Yeah, he said he would come over in the afternoon. Maybe I could call him back and ask him to come earlier."

"You should Angie."

"Well, I think I'll just wait for him to come in the afternoon. I'm sleepy and just going to go back and take a nap in my chair."

"Angie, I don't think that's a good idea. Can I at least come over to be with you this morning until this pastor comes out to your house?"

"No. Jenn, I love you. You're my best friend, but for all my life, I have depended on other people. Other people have had to carry me through life, and I'm done with that. I want to do this on my own."

"Angie, you can. I just want to make sure you're safe."

"I'll be fine. I just want to go back home. The sun is up. Maybe the house has calmed down now."

With that, Angela finished her coffee and set her cup down. Jennifer walked her to the front door and gave her a hug goodbye. It was nearly 6 a.m. and the sun rose in the morning sky; the darkness giving way to daylight.

"Angie, are you sure you don't want me to come over with you? I don't mind, really."

"Damn it, Jenn! Yes, I'll be okay. I'll deal with this!"

Jenn turned away from Angela, hurt by her response.

"Jenn, I'm sorry, I'm just overwhelmed and I'm scared and all that I know is that I don't want to give in to whatever is going on. I'll give you a call if I need help."

"It's okay, Angela. Please call if you need anything."

Jennifer closed the door behind her. Angela slowly rubbed her face with her hands, feeling awful for snapping at Jenn the way she did. It wasn't her fault, anyway. She was just making sure that she was okay.

Angela got back into her car and killed time by driving around the town until the sun peaked over the top of the hillside. She thought her home would be safe during the daytime, but worried about what night would bring. As the sun came up over the hillside, Angela drove home. Her stomach turned in knots as she got closer to her residence. Parking in her driveway, she got out of her car and walked up to the front door. As she slowly turned the doorknob, she had the feeling she was being watched.

She felt like something was on the other side of the door, waiting to jump out and grab her the moment she opened it. Slowly, she opened the front door and saw nothing out of place or missing. The carpets seemed cleaner and the wooden floor planks seemed glossier. After shutting the door behind her and locking it, Angela paused for a moment to listen intently. But she only heard the ticking of the grandfather clock in the corner of her living room. She dropped her purse and keys off on the coffee table and opened the blinds to let the sunlight in before she sat down in her recliner. She snuggled up with her grandmother's quilt and quickly fell asleep. The last thing Angela saw before slipping into a deep sleep was the grandfather clock saying 6:50 p.m.

*　　　*　　　*　　　*

It was dark throughout the house. Angela opened her eyes to find herself in her own home, in her bedroom. The warmth and comfort of her bed offered her a sense of security. The alarm clock on her nightstand read 3:02 a.m.

Angela flung the covers to the side of the bed and got up. She stood in the center of her bedroom for a moment and glanced around the room. She then walked over to her robe, that was hanging up on the bathroom door. She slipped into her robe and left the bedroom. Guided by the blue light of the hallway night light, Angela walked down the long upstairs hallway until she turned the corner of the newel post by the top of the stairs. Looking down the flight of stairs, she saw nothing but darkness in the living room. All she could hear was the ticking of the grandfather clock.

Angela walked down the steps slowly, guided by the dim nightlight in the second-floor hallway until the light did her no good. At the bottom of the steps, she turned and walked into the kitchen and opened the sliding door. Gazing through the open door, Angela watched a light mist form over the grass in the backyard. The backyard was lit by the light of a full moon, which cast an iridescent glow on the ground.

Angela walked out into the backyard. The dew wet her legs as she headed to the back gate. From a distance Angela could see that the gate was open, leading to the small trail she had discovered a short while back.

She passed through the gate and walked down to the small dirt trail leading to the creek. The trail cut into the tall aspen trees and many of the local bushes. Moonlight bled through the treetops, lighting the path she walked. Old leaves from autumn crunched underneath her feet with every step. A small dim light flickered through the trees in the distance.

Finally, she walked into a small clearing and recognized the silhouette of the ancient well in front of her. She parted a couple of bushes to the side and approached the well, brushing herself off. She noticed the dim light she saw was a lit candle, flickering from a light breeze through the heavily wooded area. Water trickled down the creek in the distance. Oddly, she didn't see any other houses. It was as if her home was the only home in the area.

Angela stood by the well for a moment, watching the light flicker in the breeze when she heard leaves crunch behind her. Someone had followed her and was approaching the well. Angela turned around and saw a woman walk through the bushes and into the clearing. She had never seen the woman before. The woman wore a black robe that contrasted with her ghostly white skin. She appeared very malnourished, with dark sunken eyes and a chiseled chin. Her hands resembled claws covered in pasty white skin.

The woman in the black garb sauntered next to Angela and raised her clammy white hands to the warmth of the candlelight. She cupped the light with her hands, concealing the small flame. The color of the light changed from a glowing yellow to a darkened red color. The woman turned and looked at Angela with her bright yellow eyes.

"Hello, Angela," the woman said.

Angela noticed that the woman's voice sounded distant, with a slight echo even though she was standing right next to her.

"Who are you?" Angela asked.

"I'm the woman who used to reside at this house. This was my home. I built it on this land, and I blessed this land. I am Esther."

There was a moment of silence between the two.

"Why are you here?"

"Because this is my land. This is my home. I blessed it. This house is alive, and it is alive with my spirit. I've been living here for over a century. I've been worshiping here for over a century. This well… This well is where I offer my sacrifices," Esther said.

"Are you a witch?"

Esther laughed at the thought of being called a witch.

"A witch I am not. In my life, I worshipped the true god of this world. I opened my home to his will and what he wanted. My home became a place of worship, a sanctuary for him."

"Who is he?" Angela asked.

"Why Lucifer, the one true lord, who else?"

"You allowed Satan into my home?"

"My dear, it's not your home. It's his. And he can do what he pleases with it. I committed the ultimate sacrifice and not only gave him my home, but myself, too. The door into this world for him and his followers is this well. You have no idea what the well represents. It is greater than you will ever know. The light of the candle is lit to call him. He comes to the red flame. When he sees the light of blood, he will come for his sacrifice."

Muffled screams and wails emanated out of the well's tunnel as the red light engulfed Angela.

"Leave my home and never come back. I want a normal life. I can't deal with this, and I won't deal with this," Angela shouted.

Esther smiled with delight. "My dear, this is not your choice. The holy man of Christ you're bringing over is not going to help you. He will only make things worse. Eventually this house, and the dark lord, will claim you as his own too."

Angela backpedaled, watching as Esther stared at her with her yellow eyes. Esther kneeled, cupping the red flame, and smiled at Angela as she retreated up the trail.

Esther uncovered the light that shifted into an awful bright red color. The screaming and wailing grew louder as Angela ran back toward her house. She pushed her way through the brush, afraid to turn around as she heard dead leaves crunch behind her. No matter how hard Angela ran, the footsteps gained on her.

Angela reached the gate along the back fence of her home and stopped. The sounds of rushing footsteps ceased, as well as did the faint screaming behind her. The mist in Angela's backyard lifted and the light from the full moon disappeared in the sky, shrouding the backyard in darkness. With no choice, she walked through the gate toward her house. It was as if she had entered a black void. A mass of darkness without an end. Her home was gone. The fence line was gone. Everything was just a black mass.

Esther whispered in the darkness, "He's coming for you."

CHAPTER 11

Angela's living room was dimly lit by the sun peering through the blinds on the sliding glass door in the kitchen. A low hum emanated from the heating unit in the laundry room, while the only other sound from the home came from the ticking grandfather clock in the corner of the living room. Covered in sweat and breathing heavily, Angela woke from her dream. She rubbed her eyes and pulled the blanket off her chest; she looked up at the grandfather clock. It was 10:47 a.m.

Sitting up, Angela folded her grandmother's blanket and set it down as she always did before, on the headrest of the chair as she mulled over the weird dream. Who was Esther? Where did she come from? She had mentioned that she has always lived here. What did that mean?

Angela stood up and walked to the kitchen to make a pot of coffee when she heard four knocks at the front door. The dream had brought even more questions and confusion about what she was going to do. She wondered how long ago Esther had lived there. Her only clue was "over a century". Angela peered out the blinds, and saw a tall lanky old man, wearing a black sports jacket and black slacks, with a white button-up shirt under his jacket. He was clean shaven, with salt and pepper colored hair. She guessed he was nearly 70 years old. Angela let go of the shades to the window and walked to the front door, unlocking it and opening the door revealing the man.

"Good evening, ma'am. My name is Reverend Marlin Teske. I'm sorry if I'm too early. I just finished some work at the church and decided to come over."

"No, it's perfectly fine," Angela said. "Please come in."

The pastor walked into the home and removed his coat.

"Would you like me to hang up your jacket, pastor?"

"Yes, thank you Angela," he replied.

Angela took his coat and hung it up in the small closet by the door.

"Please have a seat on the couch. Would you like a cup of coffee, pastor? It was just freshly made."

"Yes Angela, that would be wonderful. Thank you. No cream and no sugar."

No cream and no sugar? How could anyone drink coffee like that? Angela poured a cup for herself with creamer and then poured a cup of black coffee for the pastor. She carried both cups into the living room where she saw the pastor admiring the grandfather clock in the corner.

"This is a wonderful clock, Angela. It reminds me of a grandfather clock my father owned and kept in his wood shop. He was very skilled with his hands. He crafted a large portion of the furniture that we owned when I was still living at home with them as a child."

"Thank you. My grandparents owned it. It's very old, yet it still works well too. Just needs to be dusted off a bit, is all."

The old pastor grinned as the clock chimed eleven times for 11 o'clock. Angela set her cup down on the coffee table, walked over to the pastor, and handed him his cup of coffee.

"Thank you, Angela. So, explain to me, have you ever been to church?"

Angela paused for a moment before answering the minister's question. "I was married for 14 years before I went through a divorce. My husband, I mean my ex-husband now, found someone else to be with. During our marriage, we went to a church from time to time, you know, for holidays and special events. Not really on a regular basis. When I lived at home, before marriage, I frequently went with my parents. After I went to college, I didn't attend much but would still go from time to time. I was very busy in college. Double majoring in business law and marketing."

"That's fine, my dear, that's fine. I'm sorry to hear about your divorce. It sounds as if he abandoned the relationship. So, tell me about what happened after your divorce," the pastor said.

"It was a difficult period to go through. I was depressed. As soon as my ex left home, I needed to get a new start. A fresh start. So, I moved all the stuff I had, took a chance, and went out on my own and looked for a new home to start over in. Then I found this place. It turned out to be a good deal. It was a great price for the size of the home and the neighborhood was so quiet and peaceful. So I bought it, expecting to restart my life and establish myself as a self-sufficient adult. Someone who could stand on their own without the help from parents, or family, or a spouse."

"That seems very reasonable to me. Explain to me now, what is going on, Angela? Why am I here today?"

"It's something I can't explain, pastor, without sounding crazy, I suppose. I moved here just recently and in the past week some weird things began happening around the house. My new dog was gruesomely killed. At first, I thought another animal, like maybe a coyote or something did it, but I found...her body parts spread out in this weird star pattern upstairs in the spare bedroom."

"Her body parts were spread out in a star pattern?" Teske asked.

Yes, like her legs, tail, ears, head. They were arranged in the shape of a star in the upstairs spare bedroom. I hardly ever go in there for anything, so I keep the door locked. How could an animal have done that, let alone tear her apart and spread pieces of her around in a pattern like that? Especially since the last time I had seen her. She was outside in the backyard. So, I installed a home security system recently, recorded a security video of the backyard and a few nights later, I found something."

"You found something?"

"Yes, I don't know how to explain what I saw, but let me show you and maybe you'll know what they are."

Angela grabbed her laptop and played the surveillance video for the pastor. He watched the screen intensively as the creatures walked into the backyard and disappeared underneath the camera's lens.

"I've seen those things in person. There are more than just three of them, too. They are small, no taller than a foot or two. They look like small trolls," she said.

"Trolls?"

"Yes, Trolls. I've never seen an animal around this area like that and everyone else who I showed the video to said the same thing. They've never seen an animal like it before, either. Then I've seen…" Angela paused. "I've seen something else."

"What else have you seen?" the pastor asked.

"Well, two things. First, I saw a large humanoid creature. It looked like an animal. Like a bull. A bull that walked on two legs, but instead of human feet, it had hooves. It had the head of a bull, but the torso of a human. It seemed like it was the leader of the troll-like beings. They were all in the house, but I don't know how they got in. I keep all the doors and windows locked, but they still got into the spare bedroom upstairs. I've heard them through the walls late at night. I've seen them in the house. I've seen their shadows under the crack of my bedroom door as they walked by the night lights in the hallways."

"You've said you have heard them? What do they say?"

"I don't know. The smaller ones talk in a low, scratchy, and squeaky voice. One time I could hear one say, 'She's listening', the bigger, bull looking one told me to 'Get out or die.' And I've heard them speak in a weird language. Latin like maybe?"

"Latin?"

"Yes pastor, Latin. I'm not very familiar with the language, but if I were to guess, they would be old languages. Even if they were languages from this world, they're probably not used anywhere around the world today. I have also heard what I would describe as like dark old church rhythmic chanting. Almost like Gregorian chanting."

"I see. You mentioned two things you've seen. You've described the large humanoid like animal and these smaller beings that accompanied it, but what is the third thing you have seen, Angela?"

"The third thing came to me in a dream."

"It came to you?"

"It did. I was here in my home, and it was very dark. Even the light at the top of the stairs couldn't light the hallway like it usually did. It was like a fog or mist suffocated the hallway light from illuminating the room. I walked downstairs and into the backyard. The same fog as covered the Earth's surface outside. I could see from a distance that the gate in my backyard was opened again, so I went to go close it, but instead of closing it I walked through the gate and down to the well in the back along the creek."

"The well?"

"Yes, it's an old water well. I would guess the last time it was used was at the turn of the century and for what I don't know. Pulling water? I couldn't imagine anyone trudging through the plant life that's down there to gather water from the well though. I walked down an old trail that led to the well and found a lit candle resting on its ledge. I walked up to the well and placed my hand over the flame of the candle, however, the flame did not burn my skin. Then I heard a noise behind me. I turned to look and there was this woman approaching the well, too. She was dressed in black garb, wearing a hood, and her skin was pale and white. She walked up next to me and stood beside me. She reached out and placed her hands above the candle's flame too, but when she did, the flame changed color from yellow to blood red. Then she spoke to me. She told me she's lived here before, on this property. She said she's been here for over a century. Then she told me her name was Esther, and that she worshiped and sacrificed to the one true lord."

Curious, as he sipped his coffee, the pastor asked, "The one true lord?"

"Yes. According to this woman, the one true lord's name is Kushtaka."

The old pastor's eyes had widened at the mention of that name. Slowly grabbing his cup of black coffee and taking a sip again, the old pastor went on. "I see. Did she explain anything else to you?"

"She told me that the minister that was coming couldn't help me. She told me that the light of the candle was calling for him. When he would see the light of the candle, he would come soon."

The pastor set his cup of coffee down on the coffee table, making a small thump noise. The pastor then asked, "Angela, can you take me to this well out back?"

Angela was hesitant. She didn't want to go to the well again and would have preferred to pretend that it didn't even exist. She was afraid of it. Reluctantly, she finished her coffee, set the cup down and said, "Alright. Come with me."

Angela guided the pastor through the kitchen and out the sliding backdoor into the backyard toward the gate. She was surprised to find the gate locked and shut, so she unlocked it and they both passed through. They walked into the tall grass and followed the trail, through the trees and past the thick bushes that concealed the area from the rest of the known world.

The pastor felt a sense of dread. It was as if something was watching their every footstep and didn't want them there. A light breeze blew through the thick wooded area. The wind whistled through treetops, and rustled the leaves at their feet. Every step they took was followed by the crunching of the dead leaves beneath their feet. As they got closer to the well, pastor Teske sensed the feeling of dread grow stronger than before. It was a consecutive feeling of sadness and fear.

Angela pushed her way through the last set of bushes with the pastor, leading them to the clearing where the well was. The pastor paused for a moment as he studied the clearing. It was a tree grove, with a cleared-out area that was shaded by the trees that surrounded them. For a moment, there was utter silence. It seemed as if even the wind couldn't penetrate the thick brush and the leaves in the trees didn't make a sound at all. But the pastor heard something. He cupped his hands to his ear and strained to listen. In the distance, he heard wailing, moaning, and groaning.

The pastor looked at Angela and asked, "Angela, what do you hear right now?"

"Nothing, pastor, only the sound of a light breeze. I can hear the rustling of the dead leaves on the ground around the trail and the trickle of the creek that's not too far away from us. Why do you ask? What do you hear?"

Screams and cries continued to emanate from the opening of the well.

"Nothing," he replied. "Just the sounds of the wind and the babbling brook is all."

Pastor Teske didn't want to startle Angela by what he was really hearing. The old pastor didn't even want to believe what he was hearing from the well himself. The longer Angela and pastor Teske stood there, the more the sounds of suffering grew louder in the ears of the pastor.

"Is this where you experienced your dream, Angela? Where you met this, Esther?" Pastor Teske asked.

"It is. I was standing closer to the well, but this is the area, yes. The candle was on the front lip of the well."

The pastor walked closer to the well. The sounds emanating from the well became more and more audible. Looking at the stone opening of the well, the pastor noticed something along the edge of the side of the well. Candle wax.

"Angela, you had mentioned that in your dream there was a candle lit on the edge opening of this well, yes?"

"Yes, there was," Angela said and noticed the dried wax on the side of the well's stone.

She paused and stumbled back. Could her dream possibly have been real?

"What is that candle wax doing there?" Angela asked.

"I don't know, my dear, I don't know. I find it odd that it would be here. Has anyone been down here besides us?"

"No. There's no way in here besides through my gate in the fence line. I've always suspected that the neighborhood kids were back here playing around, but these days I'm just not so sure anymore."

The pastor touched the dried candle wax and traced his fingers along the old rocks that constructed the well. The pastor felt a need to look down the well. While the pastor was investigating the wax on the side of the well, he grabbed the side of the opening with both hands and leaned over it. Peering into the hole, the pastor only saw darkness. He held his breath while listening intently. It was at this moment that a whisper came from within the darkness of the well.

"Teske…" a voice said from the well.

The pastor backpedaled from the well and said, "We should head back up to the house."

Angela nodded and led the way back. Once they both were out of the wooded aspen grove, the pastor felt a sensation that they were not only being watched but also being followed. They both briskly walked through the gate and shut it. Angela locked the latch to the gate behind her, and the two then walked back into the house and sat down at the kitchen table. She left the sliding glass door open for some fresh air while they spoke.

The pastor was visibly startled by what he had thought he heard at the well and said, "Angela, I'm going to go. Give me some time to do some research on this. I'll see if I can figure out who this Esther woman is and what a Kushtaka is, and I'll get back to you. If anything should happen, please call me. I'll come over right away, alright? And if you think of anything else to tell me, then please tell me."

"Okay, thank you, pastor. Can I get you anything before you leave?"

"It's alright my dear, I am fine. I'll get back in touch with you soon, alright?"

"Okay."

With that, Pastor Teske stood up and walked to the front door. Angela went and grabbed his jacket. The pastor let himself out of the home and Angela followed him out. Before getting in his car, the pastor reminded Angela to call him if she needed help with anything. Angela waved and acknowledged his offer and the good pastor got into his car and drove off. She watched as the gold Buick 4-door sedan drove off into the distance. The feeling of helplessness grew the further and further away the pastor got. Finally, his car turned the corner of the road and was completely gone from sight.

A feeling of despair hit Angela like a ton of bricks. Turning around, Angela walked back into the house and shut the door behind her. With how busy the day had been so far, Angela forgot to open the blinds to the living room windows. After opening the blinds, Angela decided to do some research of her own. She grabbed her laptop from the coffee table and took the saved video off the screen. She was tired of seeing those damned creatures on her saved security video.

She opened the internet web browser and typed in a search of "Esther" as well as her residence "60 Suntides Blvd". Her laptop took a few moments to load up webpages from her search. While the webpages loaded, Angela heard a knock on her front door. She got up from the couch and walked towards the front window to look outside. She immediately recognized the old man standing outside on her porch. It was her neighbor from across the street, Tom Butler. Angela opened the front door.

"Why howdy do Angela, howdy do. How you be doin today?" Tom asked.

"Oh, not too bad. I had a friend over a few minutes ago, but he left for a bit."

"I saws that, I saws that. He looked like a minister."

"Yes, he is a minister."

"I sees, I sees. I just wanted ya ta know that it's not going to matter," Tom said.

"What's not going to matter?"

"Him. He's not gonna matter one bits to this house."

"What do you mean?"

"You don't know, I've beens here a long times Angie. Long times. I've seens many diffent peoples comes and goes from this house and they all ends up leavin the same ways. Yes, they do."

"What do you mean, leaving?"

"They leaves baby girl. They can'ts handle the pressures of livin in a home like this. It's too much work."

"Mr. Butler. Have you ever heard of an Esther that's lived here before?"

When Angela asked Tom this question, fear crossed his face. Uncertain of what to say now, Tom asked, "Howds ya hear bout that woman?"

Unsure of how to answer his question without sounding crazy, Angela said, "It just came up in some draft paperwork for the mortgage and property taxes. Like she was one of the owners of the property, but from a long time ago. I just thought I'd ask."

Tom had a look of anger on his face, as if Angela asked him something very personal that offended him.

"I don't knows no Esther! I prefers it if ya didn'ts say her name agains too."

Taken back by this, Angela said, "Alright."

She'd never seen Mr. Butler like this before. The once happy-go-lucky man with a strange accent, but jovial attitude changed to fear and anger by the mere mention of the Esther's name.

Tom's demeanor changed from a look of anger to the cheery neighbor he had always been in an instant. Almost as if he'd forgotten that Angela had even asked him about Esther.

"Well, I bests be goin back home. I have some things ta do round the house today I didn't gets to all week. I figured Saturday would be as good as any days ta gets em done, ya know."

"Yes, well, feel free to stop on by anytime," Angela said.

"I wills Angie, I wills. Thanks ya for tha offa."

"Have a good day Mr. Butler."

"This house wants you next, Angie, he wants you next."

"What did you say?"

"I says have a nice rests of your days Angie, blesses!"

Confused, Angela said, "Alright Mr. Butler, thank you."

She didn't think that she had heard Mr. Butler wishing her a nice rest of her day, but she wasn't going to press the issue either way.

Angela shut the door behind Tom and locked the dead bolt. She turned and walked back to the couch only to find that her internet had crashed. Again? The neighborhood was quiet and peaceful, but the internet service constantly crashed. Getting a stable connection was like pulling teeth. Angela closed her laptop and decided that she was going to watch some TV to pass the time on. She turned on the television set and grabbed her favorite blanket from the headrest. Slowly wrapping herself up in the blanket, Angela found a show on television and slowly drifted away into a deep sleep.

CHAPTER 12

A gold Buick automobile pulled into the parking lot of St. Marcus Lutheran Church, on 814 W. Oxford Rd. It was a small and quaint protestant church located in a nice community on the west side of Portland. Driving up to an empty stall, the vehicle parked in front of the church's office building that sat adjacent to the sanctuary. It was the only car in the parking lot this evening. The church was massive, with a large steeple in the front.

At one time in the church's history, the population of the congregation was quite big. The church was built to accommodate nearly 200 people. Recently, however, the population wasn't like it used to be. Nevertheless, the pastor remained optimistic about recruiting more members to the church for the Lord. Pastor Marlin Teske stepped out of the driver's seat of his gold.

He was a very passive man, known by all his church members as a loving human being who cared for his flock just as a pastor should, as described in the good book. He had transferred from his old church as a pastor in South Dakota, where he instructed biblical anthropology at a nearby college. Prior to the one in Wisconsin, where he started his ministry nearly four decades ago. Marlin was an avid hunter, dating back to his days spent in South Dakota. He would hunt pheasant in the state and would never kill more than he was planning on taking for meat.

Now, Marlin found himself as the shepherd of a congregation no larger than 60 people spread out among families and single persons. It was a small church with a dwindling congregation, but he remained very optimistic that he could continue to grow the church back to what it once was.

The pastor walked up a set of four cement steps that led to his office door. The worn metal handrailing that was cemented into the ground eroded away from its cement fixture after years of wear and tear and from the weather and the local children who would play gymnastics on it. Pastor Marlin Teske inserted his key into the office door and opened it. He walked in and shut the door behind him.

Walking through a small hallway into his office, he set his leather briefcase down on top of his desk and sat down in his chair. He pondered for a bit, recalling what he had seen on Angela's home security video from earlier in the day. Marlin always felt a sense of comfort being in his office at the church. It was the space where he had written many sermons, practiced them and even worked on how he could recruit more members for the body of Christ to St. Marcus. But today the only thing on his mind was what he had seen on the video, what Angela had told him, and the awful sounds he heard emanating from the well.

He wondered why Angela couldn't hear what he heard, though. Screaming. Crying. Weeping. Moaning and wailing. In his opinion, he had heard hell.

Adjacent to the pastor's office lay the sanctuary of the church. With a large steeple and high ceiling, sounds could echo and resonate throughout the church effectively. Marlin had always assumed that the original builders of the church had this in mind, making it easier for the pastor to deliver sermons that could be heard by the entire congregation, as well as for the music from the choir to fill the building.

In the pastor's office, there was a large six shelf bookcase that contained many texts and Christian manuscripts from long ago, as well as classroom textbooks from the time he'd spent in seminary school back in Minnesota. However, on the fourth level of the shelf, the second book from the end to his left, sat a book that was neither from the seminary nor was it Christian in nature. Marlin never imagined there would ever be a day that he would have to open the text to search its contents for any reason, however today he would be disproven.

Slowly, the pastor pulled the crimson colored hardback book from the shelf. It was roughly 300 pages in length and was titled, "Supernatural and Satanic: What a Christian Pastor Should Do in the Event of Encountering the Dark Forces". The book was old; however, it wasn't the oldest manuscript that sat on his bookshelf by any means. Marlin set the book down on his desk, then sat back down in his chair.

The book creaked as he opened it and thumbed through the pages. Each page crinkled as they were turned. The new book smell was still prevalent, even though it was nearly 60 years old. The pastor bet that this had to have been the first time it had ever been opened. He knew for as long as he had owned the book; it was the first time he had ever opened it himself. The book was unique in the sense that it had no table of contents and lacked any publisher information, copyright, introduction or title page.

It immediately jumped into its subject material about the supernatural on page one. He thumbed through a couple pages and saw pictures of cult emblems that had existed since the 18th century in Europe, France, Ireland, Spain. Marlin continued reading through the book, slowly, so as not to miss anything of value that could explain what he had experienced at Angela's home. On his desk, the small ticking of a desk clock clicked with each passing second. As he thumbed through the pages of the book for what seemed like hours, Marlin slowly dozed off, only to be awoken by the sound of a loud bang from within the sanctuary. It sounded as if a door had been slammed on the other side of the building. The bang echoed eerily throughout the church and was clearly audible in his office.

Startled awake and looking up from his book, Marlin sat up from his chair and walked towards the door that led to the pulpit area of the sanctuary. He tried to determine what the sound was without exposing himself to the sanctuary. Was someone trying to break into the church? Had they succeeded in doing so? Oh no, it must have been Mr. Ken Schwartz. That's who it was. Mr. Schwartz had probably shown up to practice playing the organ for tomorrow's service.

Ken was a faithful man to the church. He always volunteered to play the organ every Sunday and even during special holiday events, too. The night prior to playing in a service, he would practice the hymns alone in the church to present music the next day that was always flawless. Mr. Schwartz was the source of the noise.

The pastor pressed his ear to the office door and listened to the sanctuary area. In the distance, he heard faint footsteps in the sanctuary. Marlin's heart thumped harder in his chest. Boy, he had hoped it was Mr. Schwartz. The footsteps were very faint at first, however they grew louder. Whatever was making the noise sounded as if it was walking toward his office. All that he could do was listen as the steps got closer and closer. The clopping sound of hooves galloping filled the office space until it reached outside the office's door.

Marlin remained as still and silent as he could as he listened to the other side of the door. He tried to justify that the sounds he heard belonged to Ken Schwartz coming to play the organ. The pastor waited for what seemed like hours when suddenly a loud knocking noise came from the door behind him, the door that led to the parking lot. The pastor immediately turned around and stared at the exit. Taking a deep breath, Marlin walked up to the office door. He looked through the peephole in the door and didn't see anything. When he opened the door, however, Marlin saw a younger woman whom the pastor guessed had to be in her early 20's, with blonde hair. Her skin was is smooth and her complexion was free from anomalies and blemishes. She wore a white summer dress, bamboo sandals, and kept her blonde hair tied back in a ponytail and had eyes as green as emeralds. In all honesty, the woman was beautiful.

"Pastor," she said. "I need your help."

Taken aback by her request, Marlin forgot all about the footsteps he had heard in the sanctuary and said, "Of course, come in. What can I do for you? My name is Pastor Marlin Teske."

"Pastor," the woman said. "My name is Elena. I'm here to talk to you about this neighborhood that your church is in."

"Well, what of it, my dear?" the curious pastor asked. "Please come in and sit down."

Elena took a seat and said, "This neighborhood is full of sinners. We need to have better outreach for the damned here."

Taken aback by her words, Marlin asked, "Elena, are you affiliated with another congregation in the local area? I don't remember seeing you in my church before."

"No, pastor. I've lived in the area for a long time. But I am not affiliated with a church of any kind. In fact, I've come here today to see what you have been doing in reaching out to the damned?"

"Well Elena, we are doing a lot of community outreach through youth programs, family events, and activities that reach out to everyone in the area. I feel as if we are reaching more and more non-members of the church and making great strides in recruiting for Christ."

The young woman writhed in her chair upon hearing Christ's name. She said, "Pastor, if you are doing all these things, then why the church is failing?"

"Failing my dear?"

"Yes, failing. Failing to reach out to the damned. They are going to burn alive in hell if we don't do something now."

Marlin thought for a moment about what to say next. "Elena, would you like a bottled water?"

"I would, yes."

"Alright." With that, the pastor stood up from his chair, retrieved a bottle of water from the small cube refrigerator in the corner of his office, and opened it. He handed it to the woman and sat back down.

"Alright Elena. Now I appreciate your concern for the lost souls of the neighborhood. I would like to share some notes from our last congregational meeting that took place a few weeks ago where we addressed this very issue."

"Pastor, that would be lovely," she said and took a drink of bottled water. The pastor stood up and looked through a large metal filing cabinet against the wall of his office. He couldn't find the notes from the last congregational meeting, though. He would have to walk over to the treasurer's office to retrieve the notes from the treasurer's filing cabinet.

"Well Elena, if you wait here for a moment, I will run to the filing cabinet in the church's treasury office and retrieve some data about the things our church has done for the lost in our community. Would you be so kind to wait here while I get that information?"

"Of course, pastor. I'll be around," she said as she finished the bottle of water in a single gulp.

Marlin left his office and the young woman sitting at his desk. The treasurer's office was on the other side of the building. The sanctuary separated the pastor's office and the treasurer's office. While walking towards the front of the church, Marlin thought it was funny that Mr. Schwartz wasn't here this evening to practice on the organ. Nevertheless, he wasn't obligated to practice. Perhaps he was spending time with his loving family. They were good people, too.

Marlin finally made it back to the treasurer's office and gathered the notes from the last congregational meeting to show the young woman. While walking through the sanctuary and back to his office, the pastor noted how dark the church was. The church had multiple pieces of colored stained glass that depicted pictures of the Saints from the bible throughout the building's walls. The art included Matthew, Luke, John, and Paul, just to name a few.

The sun was still shining this evening though, so its light should've cast bright colors of red, yellow, orange, blue, and even green throughout the stained glass in the church. Yet, it didn't. The sanctuary was so dark it might as well have been night outside. The pastor finally made his way back to his office. Opening the door, Marlin spoke about how the church had voted to practice a Spanish holiday that would appeal to the local Hispanic community. But when Marlin looked up, the woman was gone along with her bottle of water.

Marlin stopped talking and looked around the office, but found no trace of the woman. It was as if she had never even existed. The chair the woman was sitting in at Marlin's desk was pushed back in like no one had sat in it for years.

Strange, the pastor thought. The woman was gone. Marlin looked around his office, thinking he may have just been robbed, but nothing was missing. The pastor looked out the exit door leading to the parking lot, but he could not find the woman there either. He only saw his gold Buick 4-door sedan. It was as if she had completely disappeared.

Marlin was confused as he sat back down in his chair at his desk. Was it all in his imagination? And the book he had been reading through had been closed. Marlin swore he never closed it himself and he noticed a piece of torn paper was marking the page where he'd left off reading. Wait, the pastor thought. He had never bookmarked where he stopped reading.

The book creaked as he opened it to the section where the book was marked with the paper. The pastor was astonished to see that the page that was marked was where the book addressed the legend of the Kushtaka.

Then Marlin realized that on the back of the torn paper was a written message. The note said, "They're all fucking sinners. They're all damned. Their skin will melt in my banquet hall, and I will feast on their flesh for all eternity. They will all belong to me, forever."

As he finished reading the message, a loud bang sounded from the sanctuary again. Marlin jumped from his seat and gasped. Looking down at the note, the pastor placed the note back into the book and closed it. He heard footsteps again, heavy footsteps. With each step in the sanctuary, thuds echoed through the office. The pastor could tell that the sounds were coming from the entryway by the treasurer's office, and they were headed his way.

Marlin stood up and walked towards the door to the sanctuary. The sound of footsteps transitioned into galloping hooves. Marlin stepped back from the door and made the sign of the cross across his chest. He uttered a prayer of protection under his breath. The clopping hooves and heavy reverberating thuds drew closer and closer to his office's door. From under the crack of the door, the pastor could see a shadow approaching. Moments later, the hoof of a bull stepped in front of the crack, followed by a second hoof.

Whatever was outside his door stood there for what seemed like minutes until the hooved feet turned and walked away, back the way it came. The pastor held his breath and stayed still, listening to the steps slowly fading into the distance of the sanctuary. The pastor walked up to the office door and slowly opened it without stepping out of the office to examine the sanctuary. Marlin took a deep breath and braced himself for what he was about to see and boldly stepped out into the sanctuary. The pastor screamed at the sight of a short, balding man with brown eyes in his early 50's standing before him.

"Pastor!" the man said.

The pastor clutched at his chest to hold his heart and calm himself down. "Oh, Mr. Schwartz. You startled me."

Thankfully, it was Mr. Schwartz who arrived to practice the organ as he always did on Saturday evenings prior to the Sunday morning service.

"I'm sorry. I had no idea you were here, pastor. I was just coming to practice on the organ for tomorrow."

"Ken, it's alright. I will be okay. Ken, did you come from the front of the church, through the breezeway?"

"Yes, pastor, I did."

"Ken, did you see or hear anything before coming in?"

"No pastor, I didn't. In fact, that's why I came to check if you were here. I know you like to come in Saturday evening to work on your sermon and perfect it before the service."

"Are you certain you didn't hear anything?"

"Yes, pastor. I am certain."

"Ken, did you see a young woman around here, too? Maybe in her early 20's? Out in the parking lot? Around the building outside? In here?"

Mr. Schwartz wondered if the pastor needed a break from his sermon to go home and get some rest. "No pastor. No, I didn't."

"Okay, Ken. You probably think it's odd of me to ask so many questions," the pastor chuckled.

"Absolutely not, pastor. It's okay. I'm going to go practice on the organ."

"Very good, Ken. You always play a beautiful organ. We really appreciate the service you give to our congregation."

"Thank you, pastor."

Ken turned and walked towards the organ to practice. The pastor then turned and went back into his office, sitting at his desk with the closed book still sitting on the desk and the paper note holding its place in the book. Maybe the pastor was just hearing things. After all, there was clearly just Ken in the sanctuary, coming to do what he's done ever since he and his family became communicant members of the St. Marcus congregation nearly 20 years ago.

Marlin shut the door and sat again at his desk. A short while later, he heard the pipe organ coming to life in the sanctuary as Ken played his tunes. The melody to Be Still My Soul played beautifully.

Marlin had always enjoyed that song. He opened his book, looked at the note briefly again, and wondered where the mysterious girl had gone. Marlin just couldn't believe that she had left as fast as she had shown up, as well as leaving such a foul note in his book. He read the pages that were marked by the note about the demon called Kushtaka. The cryptic text revealed its origin from Native American folklore from Alaska out of all places. According to the local legend, the cryptid beast could shapeshift. The otter was apparently its most assimilated creature, but it was also capable of assimilating the shape of other known animals. Like goats, bulls, wild dogs, and even humans.

Marlin continued to read on about the mythical creature until he came to a paragraph that described how it captured its human prey. It demonstrated its power and intelligence through a series of events that toyed with its prey. Events that proved there was no way to combat the creature or defend oneself.

The Kushtaka also changed its victims into shortened imp like beings. Beings with pale whitish blue skin, long bony arms with three large claws attached to their hands, sharp jagged teeth, and yellow eyes. The folk-legend depicted what a changed human would look like, which resembled the creatures in Angela's security video.

Astonished at what he was reading, Marlin recognized the similarities between the details in the text and Angela's video. The book explained the creatures were bound to fulfill the Kushtaka's requests. They misguided more and more humans to join the Kushtaka's mass army of small imp like creatures. As the pastor continued to read on, he found that the creatures were called Faes.

Faes had an unnatural ability to resume their human form, however. It was a trait passed down from the Kushtaka to aid in the Faes ability to trap more and more human victims. The Kushtaka was a dangerous being that had to be treated with respect. The text said to never underestimate its intelligence and raw power. Though it also revealed the Kushtaka was afraid of the sunlight. And in its original form, it was unable to attack its victims in the light of day. It could only appear to its victims in human or animal form, rendering it incapable of attacking during the day and making the creature nocturnal.

The Kushtaka was also a being susceptible to fire. The text mentioned that the origin of the creature was once a human female. A woman that was burned alive at the stake. Local townsfolk executed her in a suburb of Portland, Oregon called Happy Valley for practicing witchcraft and devil worship. While the female burned alive, she cursed the local colony of the area for killing her and swore by the will of Satan she would come back to enact justice on the townspeople for her death. So, the internal fear of fire would never leave the Kushtaka. What was left of the witch's remains after the fire had dissipated, were thrown down into a well and then sealed off with a wooden cover. The wooden seal to the well was blessed by a local colony catholic priest named Joseph Clark. It was supposed to be sealed for all of eternity.

It was believed that the Faes in their elfish forms were also nocturnal. Faes used their original human forms during the daylight hours as it protected their bodies from the daylight like the Kushtaka. The Kushtaka loved the sacrifices the Faes made to it. Usually, the sacrifices were of animals, anything that the Faes could catch. They tore the animals apart, limb from limb, and set the body parts into the shape of a star on the ground. The Kushtaka cannot come into a home without being invited, but once it was invited, it was impossible to get rid of. The owner of the property or home needed to uninvite the Kushtaka, as well as the Faes from coming to the home and causing havoc. As a result of their deep hatred for bright daylight, the Kushtaka and the Faes always found dark places to hide. Usually, they preferred absolute darkness and settled for heavily shaded areas such as caves, forest groves with heavy canopies or even deep holes in the ground.

Marlin thought, "Deep holes in the ground... Such as a well..."

The pastor continued to read a list of general guidelines on how to exorcise the property. 1) Demand that the demon leaves the home. 2) Inform the demon that this is not their home/property, and that they are not welcomed here. 3) Should the demon confront you, demand to know the name of the demon. (In this case, you know the demon is a Kushtaka. You may not need to do this. If so, revert to step 2). 4) If it is a home, bless each room of the home. Sprinkle holy water from the river of Jordan. The waters where the Christ was baptized by John the Baptist. 5) Leave the bible that the minster uses during the exorcism of the home/property behind in the home. Leave it in a visible place, somewhere centrally located so that everything can see it and be reminded that only peace and God are welcomed in the home.

After Marlin read through the guidelines to property exorcism, he shut the book. He picked up the note off his desk that the young woman had left him, crumpled it and threw it away in a trash can under his desk. The sounds of the pipe organ were still playing in the sanctuary as Marlin decided it was getting late and time for him to leave.

He believed that he may have figured out what had been going on in the home at 60 Suntides Blvd. The pastor gathered his brown leather briefcase and slid the old book he read from into it. He planned to visit with Angela tomorrow after his church service to talk about what the information he uncovered.

Rather than going out the office door to his car, Marlin walked back to the treasurer's office to put the congregational notes away from the last congregation meeting that they had. Marlin turned the lights off to his office and walked out into the sanctuary. Walking past the pulpit, he saw Ken at the pipe organ, playing the tune of "Onward Christian Soldier". It was the theme of tomorrow's sermon. Marlin paused for a moment and admired how well Ken played the organ. Ken looked up from his music sheet and Marlin smiled and waved at him.

Ken's face looked different. He had a wide grin on his face, a smile that seemed larger than normal. His eyes looked different, too. They weren't the normal brown color they had always been. The iris of Ken's eyes seemed nearly black. The pastor shook his head and thought nothing of it. It was late, and he was tired. He had a sermon to deliver tomorrow, so with a wave goodbye, he left the pulpit and walked down the center aisle back to the treasurer's office.

Ken watched as the pastor left the sanctuary. Marlin opened the door to the treasurer's office and slipped the paperwork into a manila folder that had a tab labeled "church meetings" on it. Placing the folder back in the metal filing cabinet, he turned and left the office as he shut the door behind him.

Marlin walked to the front door of the church and looked over at the pamphlets on a nearby folding table, ensuring everything was clean looking for tomorrow. Afterward, Marlin walked out of the church foyer and exited the building. On his way to the parking lot, a tall red truck drove into the parking lot and parked next to the pastor's gold colored Buick sedan.

"Where have I seen this truck before?" the pastor thought.

The door to the red truck opened, and out of the driver's seat jumped a short, balding man with brown eyes, in his 50's. Marlin froze in his tracks, his mouth hung wide open at what he was looking at.

"Good evening, Pastor," Mr. Ken Schwartz said. "Sorry I'm late. We were having a family dinner. You didn't lock up the church for the night, did you?"

Marlin didn't know what to say. He was looking at Ken Schwartz. If this was Ken, then who was the man that was playing the organ in the church? Without saying a word to Ken, Marlin turned around and rushed back up to the front doors of the church. He opened the doors and strode in to look into the sanctuary. But Marlin saw no one. Nothing. No lights on. No organ playing. No sign of human life. Nothing. Ken walked into the church behind the pastor.

"Pastor, is something the matter?" Ken asked.

The pastor looked around the church to see if anything had moved. Looking down the main aisle of the church, near the pulpit laying on the floor was what looked like a crumpled piece of paper. Marlin walked over to it, bent down and picked up the balled-up piece of paper. He unraveled it in his hands and the note read, "They're all fucking sinners. They're all damned. Their skin will melt in my banquet hall, and I will feast on their flesh for all eternity. They all will belong to me, forever."

It was the note he had thrown away in his office. Marlin then remembered what the book said about how the Kushtaka was able to assimilate the shape of living animals, even humans, to trick other humans. There was no doubt in the pastor's mind now that what he was up against in Angela's home was a Kushtaka.

CHAPTER 13

Sunday morning came as any other morning would in the spring season in the Portland area. It was cloudy, with a little wind from the northwest and a lot of rain. It rained everywhere, seemingly biblical in proportion. The rain was so intense that Angela woke up from the heavy patter of raindrops on her roof.

She was surprised to have slept through the night with no problems. The constant fear of something potentially happening during the night was wearing on her. She was afraid that she would wake up and one of those small creatures would be sitting along the edge of the bed. Or the large creature would be standing at the foot of her bed, watching her, waiting for her to wake up before it jumped on her. Of course, she slept in her room with the bedroom door locked. Being in her recliner downstairs in the living room made her feel vulnerable. Even in her bedroom with the door locked, though the anxiety of something happening weighed heavily on her mind.

For the first time in a long time, she had brought her grandmother's blanket from her recliner chair downstairs, up to her bedroom. She hadn't kept the blanket on her bed since her days in college. The blanket brought her a sense of comfort as a family heirloom. She received a strong sense of protection from the blanket. More protection than any weapon like a mace or a gun could offer her. She sought comfort in knowing that her grandmother made this blanket specifically for her. The blanket had brought her comfort during her divorce and when she moved here. And at least for the night last night, it brought a small peace of mind knowing that maybe the watchful eye of her grandmother was watching over her, too.

Angela continued to lie in bed, enjoying the silence throughout her room. Stretching her arms out to the sides and rubbing her face with her hands, she threw the covers back and got out of bed. She threw her robe on and walked to the bathroom, where she splashed her face with water from theb sink and brushed her teeth.

For a moment, she considered going to church, though she ultimately decided against it. After brushing her teeth, she got in the shower. The shower was refreshed her and helped wake her up. After her shower, she threw her robe back on and went downstairs and walked into the kitchen.

As Angela started to get the milk out of the refrigerator, she again had the feeling that she should try to attend church this morning. She paused for a minute and put the milk back in the refrigerator. Closing the refrigerator door, Angela turned around to look out the kitchen window that was just above the sink into the backyard. From the kitchen, she could see that the back gate was open again.

"Good God," she thought. Did those things come back? Did she just not wake up this time and see or hear them? Could they have been in her bedroom without her knowing it, or were they still there? Could they be in the spare bedroom? Hiding in her bedroom closet? Or even around the corner of the sofa in the living room? She knew she had locked the gate in the fence the day before, and she could only think of one culprit behind it, those things.

Instead of going out to close the fence again or sitting at the dining room table and having a bowl of cereal like she had planned on, Angela walked back upstairs. She walked into her room and got dressed. Angela decided she was going to attend church. But what church should she go to? She didn't feel comfortable going back to her old church, where she and her ex-husband attended for nearly 16 years. It was the church where they had met one another, then a couple of years later were married in the very church they had started their relationship in. If she went back now, how would people look at her? As a failure? Someone who wasn't capable of being married or raising and managing a family?

Angela feared failure more so than anything else. She had always had that fear. In school she came home her freshman year of college in tears and told her parents that she was going to drop out over the A- she got in her business math class. Angela never settled for mediocrity and the thought of giving up, or quitting, was not in her plans now either. Especially not after her marriage had failed. She didn't want to have the feeling of running away, quitting, or giving up be associated with her life ever again.

Pastor Teske, Angela remembered, suddenly aware of where she needed to go. Looking at the digital alarm clock on the bedstand, Angela started her laptop and looked online to see what time St. Marcus Lutheran Church started. Service started at 9:30 a.m. Angela knew she had plenty of time to make there before it started. So, she stripped off her robe, got dressed and left to make the drive to St. Marcus Lutheran church.

The church was on Oxford Rd, on the other side of the Portland Metro. Angela hadn't been to that part of Portland for quite some time. She didn't know many people on the west side, nor did she know all that many establishments. The last time she was out west was when she shopped at an outlet center bookstore to find a book on law for her husband at the time. God, that was nearly ten years ago. But she knew St. Marcus now, and she knew Marlin Teske.

Angela couldn't believe how hard it was raining on her drive to the west side of Portland. It was clearly a spring day in Portland, Oregon. The drive took twenty minutes. Driving on Sunday mornings in town was simple, especially on the highways. It seemed like there weren't any cars to be found anywhere on the road. It was almost like a large ghost town. A lot of small businesses were closed, and the gas station attendants sat in their small buildings reading the newspaper. Though she'd see the occasional jogger or someone walking their dog along the sidewalk, but overall it was a quiet morning.

As Angela drew closer to Oxford Rd. she spotted the steeple of the church off in the distance. It was a beautiful square cylinder with a large bronze cross atop the structure. Just below the bronze cross was a large church bell. It was worn by the wet weather of the northwest and looked as if it had been there for over a century. The bell added to the nostalgia of the church.

She drove into the church's parking lot. She was still early and all but two spaces were empty. For a moment she thought that perhaps the church was closed and not in business until she saw the gold Buick sedan parked by what she thought must have been the door to the pastor's office. Angela got out of her car, locked it, and walked up to the church's front doors. They were large, heavy wooden doors with a crucifix symbol on the front and red stained glass bricks in the middle. The door creaked as she pulled it open, hearing the sound echo loudly in the large foyer. In the entrance foyer was a tan colored carpet, with a set of stairs to the left that lead down to what Angela thought must have been a basement or second level. A large black leather couch sat along the other side of the foyer, and next to the couch were grayish white folding tables with different pamphlets, devotional magazines and fliers for St. Marcus Lutheran church and its events and activities for its congregation and community.

That was nice to see. Angela's old church hardly ever did anything together as a congregation. They would go to church and visit with people in the church, but as far as getting together outside the building, it never happened. She saw they held many planned events, music, golf trips, Saturday morning men's breakfast at Denny's, women's bible study on Tuesday evenings, wine and art events, and more. She even saw a planned hiking event in a month up at Mt. Hood.

Angela was astonished by all the different activities that the church had planned outside the building. After looking through the fliers, she picked up a pamphlet to an activity to read more about it when she heard a familiar voice speaking to her from behind.

"Angela?" the voice asked.

Angela turned to see Pastor Teske. Marlin stood in front of her in a long white robe, with a green stole that draped over each shoulder and led down his chest that depicted a golden dove on the left and the cross of Christ on the right. The pastor wore a gold chain with a large wooden cross suspended just over his heart. He clutched a bible in his left hand that appeared to be old. There was no doubt it was his own personal bible, worn from over the many years of his teaching and leading of the church.

"Pastor," Angela said with a smile. She nodded her head and shook his hand.

"Angela, it is a delight to see you here. Did you come for the service?"

"I did, yes."

Marlin vigorously shook Angela's hand and escorted her into the church. Angela walked from the foyer to the nave of the church. She couldn't help but notice how tall the ceilings of the nave were. Angela guessed they must have been at least 80, 90, maybe even 100 feet tall! The side aisles were heavily decorated with stained glass bricks mixed with regular bricks to make up the church's walls. On the walls were also stained-glass portraits of the Christian Saints, John, Matthew, Luke and even the apostle Paul. A red carpet lined the main aisle that led up to the transept and the sanctuary of the church, and dark brown glossy tiles rested underneath the long wooden pews.

The front sanctuary was decorated with banners to celebrate Easter that faced the congregation. A blue banner reading "He has risen, Christ has risen indeed," as well as another purple banner that read, "He has died so that you might live." Also in front of the church were Easter lilies. Large lilies with beautiful white bells opened on them. They seemed to cover the sanctuary all throughout the front of the church and around the pulpit.

"You have the pick of where you would like to sit this morning, Angela," Marlin said. "I would remind you, however, that we are Lutheran's, and we have some families who have been sitting in the same pew since before the church even existed. A very normal Lutheran trait," the pastor said and chuckled.

Angela smiled and laughed. "Alright," she said. "I wouldn't want to intrude. Where would it be okay for me to sit then, pastor?"

"The third pew up on the left side will be as good as any. In front of you will sit the Lennon family, and behind you will sit the Mackie family," Marlin said. "Believe you me, Lennon will come in first, followed by Mackie a few minutes after the service starts. It has been that way each Sunday since before I can remember, unless the families go on a summer vacation."

"Alright, I will sit in the third pew up on the left, then."

"That will be fine, Angela."

Angela thanked the pastor and walked towards the front of the church when Marlin stopped her.

"Angela. After today's service, would you be willing to visit me in my office for just a bit? We need to talk about what I came to visit with you about yesterday. I have some more information about what is going on that may be beneficial to you," the pastor said.

"Of course, I would like that," Angela said, relieved he might have the information needed to help her.

Angela turned and walked towards the front of the church while Marlin walked back to the foyer. She took her seat in the 3rd pew up on the left side, sitting closest to the red carpeted main aisle of the church. She watched as a small balding man walked down the side aisle and took a seat on a bench in front of the pipe organ. He cracked his knuckles and played familiar hymns that Angela remembered from her time at her Baptist church.

The pastor knew his congregation very well as people piled into the church one by one. True to the pastor's word, a family consisting of a husband and wife who looked to be in their mid to late 40's entered the church, along with three boys whom Angela would have guessed to be in their teenage years, sat in the pew in front of her. It was the Lennon family, no less.

A church usher walked up to Angela and handed her a service bulletin with the order of worship for the morning. Angela thanked the usher as he smiled and continued to hand out bulletins to the other members of the church. She watched as the usher set down five bulletins on the pew behind her. The small bald man continued to play different songs on the organ, songs that Angela continued to recognize as hymns from her old church, too. But he also played some new songs that she didn't recognize too. Either way, each song was unique and pretty and led to the start of the church service.

After the last song subsided, Angela heard church bells chime from the steeple outside. Marlin appeared from his office and walked out into the sanctuary. He began the order of worship by welcoming the members of St. Marcus Lutheran Church to the morning's service. After delivering his welcome to the members and guests, the pastor sat down in a small pew next to the pulpit and the first hymn was played. Halfway through the first hymn, a family sat down behind her, coming in a few minutes late to the service. It was the Mackie family, no less. A husband and wife again, both appearing to be in their early 40's, accompanied by two boys and a girl, all three who looked to be just shy of their teenage years.

The service went without a hitch. The order of worship with the opening hymn led to a confession of sins. After the confession of sins, the service went into an absolution and a prayer of the day. The pastor gave a short epistle reading from the book of second Corinthians from the bible. Angela recognized the biblical story that the pastor was referencing. After the epistle was read to the congregation, the pastor followed the reading with a special devotional for the children. After the devotional for the children, the holy gospel was read.

The gospel came from the book of Mark from the bible. After the gospel was read, they sang a hymn of the day. After the hymn the pastor then delivered the sermon about trusting and finding faith in God to overcome your earthly fears, worries and temptations. It was a sermon that spoke about nothing being beyond the capability of God to handle.

After the sermon, the congregation collected their offerings to the church and went into a prayer of the church, followed by a confession of faith and a recital of the apostle's creed. The pastor then read the benediction and the blessing to the church members. The service concluded with a closing hymn sung by the choir and finally a dismissal and a blessing from Marlin.

Angela really enjoyed the service and was glad she went. The sermon meant a lot to her, and she was very impressed in how Marlin delivered a short devotional specifically for the children of the church that was related to the sermon's subject matter. She had never experienced that at her old church. At the conclusion of the service, the organist played a song on the organ and the church ushers dismissed the rows and Angela got up and walked out of the nave, back to the foyer of the church where she met some people who introduced themselves to her and asked her questions to get to know her better.

Angela felt good about talking to the members of the church and meeting new people. She hadn't had the opportunity to get out in such a long time and meeting new people at church who were so welcoming made her feel at ease with the world. After visiting with a nice older couple, Angela felt the tap of another hand on her right shoulder. She turned around to see that it was Marlin. He gestured with his hand for Angela to come with him. Marlin led Angela back into the nave of the church and to his office at the front of the church.

"You'll have to forgive me for pulling you away from the members like that. They are good people. Very welcoming. I'm not sure if that was too much for you on your first day of church here with us," Marlin said.

"No. Not at all. In fact, it's nice to visit with people like that," Angela replied.

The pastor smiled and said, "Good. You're welcome back anytime, Angela."

Entering the pastor's office, Angela sat down in the chair in front of Marlin Teske's desk. Marlin sat behind his desk. Angela found the pastor's office to be rather cluttered, with maps of the promised land and books laying all about.

"You must forgive the mess, Angela. Prior to being just a pastor, I was also an instructor of biblical archaeology back in South Dakota for years. I have always enjoyed a passion for anthropology, especially of the biblical kind."

"It's alright," Angela said. "It's good to have an interest in human history like that."

"Indeed," the pastor replied. "Angela, I'm glad you came to the church today. But I am very glad that you came to my office to visit with me for a bit. I do need to speak to you about what we had talked about yesterday."

"I understand. Thank you for spending the time with me, pastor."

"It is my pleasure. Now, Angela, what I am about to explain to you may seem shocking at first. You may not believe in such matters and to be entirely honest, prior to a day ago, I didn't believe in such things myself, either. But after seeing your situation firsthand, it has caused me to re-think my own philosophy on the supernatural. Even what I had experienced here in my own church yesterday evening."

Angela sat in silence, listening to every word the pastor had to say.

"Yesterday, after we had met at your home, I came back to the church to start doing some research into what you have been experiencing in your home and on your property."

Marlin looked down at the book on his desk.

"Angela, this book is titled 'Supernatural and Satanic: What a Christian Pastor Should Do in the Event of Encountering the Dark Forces'. To be honest with you, I've never looked at this book for as long as I've been in the seminary until now. This book explains supernatural entities that we, as clergy, may encounter at some point in our tenure in the ministry. After reading through this book, I believe what you are experiencing in your home is something called a Kushtaka. Along with these smaller beings, which the books mention, are Faes."

Marlin explained the history of the Kushtaka, dating all the way back to ancient Native Alaskan tribes, such as the Tlingit tribe. The pastor explained what a Fae is. What they look like, but more importantly, what they were before they became Faes. Angela was shocked and frightened.

"Pastor," Angela said respectfully. "I'm not going to lie to you. I don't know what to do. I know that I'm not going to be giving up my home so easily to anything. I'm going to fight for what I have if I must. I was married to my ex for 14 years when he decided that he didn't want to be with me anymore. He left me for someone who was at least 25 years younger than I was, but when I think about it more, I realize that I was truly under his control. He never hit me or abused me or forced me to do things that I didn't want to do. But we always seemed to do things the way he wanted them. I didn't have much of a say in anything. Whether you believe that is abuse or not, I certainly do. My freedom and my right of choice was taken away from me the moment I said, 'I do.' When I left that home, I gained a level of independence back, and I'm not going to give that up without a fight."

"Angela, I am glad to hear you say that," the pastor replied. "You are a strong-willed woman and with the power of God, nothing is impossible. I will help you in any way I can. Now, this book goes on to say that you need to tell the entity to leave the home. To not come back. Under no circumstances will it be invited back into your home. Do you understand, Angela?"

Angela paused for a moment and finally said, "Yes, pastor. Yes, I do. I don't know if I can do that on my own, though. I really appreciate your help."

Angela couldn't believe that she needed help from someone else again. It was difficult for her to admit to herself that maybe she couldn't do this on her own, and that she would still need the help of someone else. Even if that someone else was Marlin Teske.

Marlin closed the book, marking the pages that spoke about The Kushtaka with a blank piece of paper. He handed the book to Angela and told her to read more about The Kushtaka. The pastor told Angela that when she is spiritually and emotionally ready to let him know and he will come to assist Angela in telling the spirit to leave the home. Angela took the book from the hand of the minister and thanked him. She got up and began to leave the pastor's office when Marlin stopped her.

"Angela," Marlin said.

Angela turned back around and said, "Yes?"

"Keep in the back of your mind that it is your home, Angela. Your home. You are buying it. You are taking care of it. You clean it. You live in it. You sleep in it. You eat in it. This is your shelter. Your life is put into this home. Don't let evil take that from you," Marlin said.

With that, Angela turned to leave the office. Before she left, Angela said, "Pastor. You mentioned that something had happened to you yesterday evening. Here at the church? What was it? What happened?"

Marlin looked with a blank stare at Angela, not knowing exactly how to explain what he had experienced. However, not wanting to cause Angela to worry, the pastor's blank expression melted into a smile. "The overactive imagination of an old man, Angela. Nothing more than that, I'm afraid."

Angela smiled and thanked the pastor, and left his office. With the book in hand, she walked back towards the front of the church and said goodbye to some church members that had approached her and talked with her. Angela thanked them for their hospitality. The church members smiled and thanked Angela for coming and invited her to come back to their church. One person had even invited her to come along for the hiking trip the members had planned. Angela thanked them for that and left the church. In the parking lot Angela walked to her car and while she was inserting the key in to unlock the car, she heard a voice over her shoulder.

"You'll be coming back, right?" the voice asked.

Angela turned to see an older man standing next to the driver's side of an older red 4-door car. His hair was white as snow with a full beard that matched. He was a taller man. Well over 6 feet, she imagined. Brown eyes and an average build for what looked to be like a 70-year-old man. His ears, however, were pointed and Angela thought they looked abnormal.

In the front passenger seat of the red car, sat a woman. She looked younger compared to the older man. She was maybe in her early 40's. Angela couldn't get past how bright white her skin tone was. Nearly pale. Her ear was also pointed and protruding through her long, black hair. Angela noticed that this woman had a blank expression on her face while she lifelessly stared forward towards the church. She sat so still that at one point Angela thought she must be a mannequin.

"Yes. Yes, I do plan on coming back," Angela replied with a smile.

The man stood there by his car, smiled back, and said, "You know he won't be able to help you."

Angela paused for a moment, questioning what the man meant. "I beg your pardon? What did you say?"

"The minister. He won't be able to help you."

Angela didn't want anyone to know about her problem at home. Or the reason why she had met Marlin to begin with, so Angela played coy and asked, "Help me with what?"

The man continued to stand by the driver's side door. The woman sat still and silent in the passenger seat.

"You're Angela Brown, right?" the man asked.

"Yes, I am. I'm sorry, have we met?" Angela asked, thinking that she didn't meet this man in the church, so how did he know her name?

"We have, but not in the sense that you think. I am familiar with the home you live in. I have seen many people come and go from it. The home is cursed. There is no hope for it. It's destined to be a house of horror. A house of pain, sadness. Its history is ripe with innocent blood spilled on the grounds. It has been this way for years, Angela. Long before you were born. Long before that minister was born. And long before anyone was born. It should be burned to the ground and sent back to hell," the man said.

"What is your name, sir?"

The man ignored her question and said, "The longer you stay in that home, the more time it will have to slowly consume you. It will consume your life. It will consume your soul. You will be stuck there for eternity, along with all its inhabitants."

"How do you know that?" Angela asked.

The man then smiled. His smile, though, seemed to be wider than a normal human smile. It seemed to take up most of his face, spreading from ear to ear, while his eyes slightly squinted. His stare towards Angela gave her a sense of unease. It was frightening. She instantly felt vulnerable, even there in the church parking lot.

The man finally broke the silence and, with the sound of a cocky, arrogant tone in his voice, said to Angela, "I just know. Personally. So. How about that sermon today? Hmm. Trusting in God to overcome your fears and worries."

Angela was starting to get nervous around him. And the woman in the passenger seat made her feel uneasy as well. She just continued to stare towards the front of the church, as if she was watching everyone leaving the building one by one.

"Yes, I thought it was a good sermon," Angela replied. "It was very reassuring to me. Made me feel good. Safe. Secure."

"A crock of bullshit is what it was," the man quickly replied. "To think God cares that much about everyone? How can he care about everyone in this world? Do you know how many people are in this world, Angela? Seven and a half billion people. How in the fuck is God going to have enough time for seven and a half billion people, hmm? Someone must be on the outside looking in. I'm betting that there are a lot of people, much like yourself, Angela, who are on the outside looking in. Let me ask you something, Angela. How did God work for your marriage? Was God there to save that? Or did he just go and let your ex run off with some twenty-one-year-old, fresh out of college, perky tit young bitch who still doesn't know how to pay her own phone bill, hmm? Still trying to learn how to shove a tampon into herself. Where was God for you then, Angela?"

Angela was very nervous now, shocked and caught off guard by what she was hearing from this man. All she could do was stand there and watch the man talk. Watch the man smile. Fear gripped her stronger than ever before. Angela fought to find the words to say to this man.

"I'm sorry. I really don't know how you know me or who you are. Are you a church member here?" Angela asked.

The man chuckled, his white beard bouncing with each hearty laugh. Turning his attention towards the church, the man said, "No, Angela. I wouldn't waste my time on this load of horse shit if it meant inheriting the world. Which I pretty much already own, anyway. I can do what I want and when I want, Angela. You can't do that when you go to a church. You must live by his rules. His guidelines. Why anyone would subject themselves to that is beyond me. And I'll tell you, Angela, God certainly wasn't there for you when your ex was banging the college kid, and he certainly won't be there for you now either. There's nothing that fuckin minister can say or do to help you. There's nothing that you can do, Angela. Nothing but allow yourself to be just another inhabitant of the house. Either that or you can give up and run away. The choice will always be yours to make, Angela. Just remember, no one can help you." The man pointed up to the skies and said, "Not even him."

He must be crazy, Angela thought. He must have something mentally wrong with him. But she thought to herself, how does he know so much about her?

"Alright, well, I've got to get going. I have a lot to do this afternoon," Angela said.

"Like what? Go home?" the man asked. With a small laugh and a smile, he said, "If you're going home, then I'll be seeing you later, Angela. Soon you'll be mine too." The man pointed to the woman in the car and said, "Just like her."

"Good luck, Angela," he said.

The man opened his driver's side door and sat in the car.

With a devilish smile, the man said, "I'll be seeing you later, Angela."

He started the car, and Angela could hear the gears of the car shifting. The woman in the front seat finally broke her lifeless gaze towards the church and looked at Angela. Angela could clearly see her face now. The woman waved to Angela as the car pulled out of the parking lot and out onto the street. The woman's eyes were bright yellow, and they were missing pupils. There was no iris in her eyes. The woman then smiled, which revealed a row of sharp teeth coming to a point. Her smile was unearthly. Her smile also took up her entire face from ear to ear.

What did Angela just see? Maybe it was just her nerves of talking to this bizarre man that was getting the better of her. Maybe it was the lack of sleep she had had the last couple of nights. Maybe it was the fact that she wasn't eating much lately, or she had so much on her mind that she had just thought she had seen what she just saw. Or maybe, maybe she saw something that was all too familiar over the last few days in her home. Maybe she saw the thing she had seen from the other night. It had left her home. It had followed her to the church.

If it was that, then did it follow her into the church? No. There's no way. Angela took two deep breaths and sat down in her car. She turned her car on and turned the air conditioning on. Maybe she was too hot and experiencing a slight hallucination. She had done that once before when her ex and she went to Arizona to visit his parents. She had got too hot one time and thought she had seen a car accident in the front yard by the road. All of it turned out to be a poorly misshapen cactus. Todd laughed at her for days after that. Angela didn't think it was too funny at the time. So, she thought to herself that maybe she was experiencing the same thing again. She sat in the parking lot for a few minutes, with the motor running and the air conditioning on. Her hands grasping the wheel while she stared forward. Angela then heard a small knocking on the window of the car door.

Startled, she whipped her head towards the window and saw Marlin, the church minister, standing there. Angela rolled the window down.

"Angela, my dear. Are you doing alright? Are you having car troubles?" Marlin asked.

"Oh, thank you, pastor. I am doing fine. Just thinking a little to myself before I leave," Angela replied.

"Oh, alright then. I will see you soon, Angela."

"Thank you, pastor."

Marlin walked away while Angela rolled her window up. After her window was closed, she put her car into drive and pulled out of the parking lot. Some families were leaving at the same time and waved goodbye. Angela waved back to them, and she drove to the parking lot exit. Stopping to look both ways, she slowly pulled onto the road while it was clear and began her drive across Portland to get back home.

CHAPTER 14

It was a lazy Sunday afternoon, no less. Angela always hated Sunday afternoons. It seemed like these days all her ex would do was sit in the recliner chair, with a bag of popcorn and a couple of mixed drinks and watch football all day. Angela would sit around and do nothing. And after football season ended, sure enough, baseball season started, and the cycle would continue. For as long as she knew, Angela was bored with Sundays, and this Sunday was no different.

She found herself back in her home with nothing to do. When she got home from church, she carefully checked the whole house to make sure everything was safe and, these days, that everything was normal. It was.

Angela set the book the minister had given her down on the coffee table when she walked into the home. She thought maybe she could do some gardening today. Or mow the lawn? But she knew the one place she didn't want to be was by that gate in the fence line out back. The gate was swinging wide open, revealing the tall grass from the other side of the fence line. Angela could see the tall blades of grass swaying in the wind from the safety of her kitchen window. She strained to look deep into the long grass to try to see something, if anything. She could not.

She turned around and walked back into the living room, sitting down in her recliner. She gazed at the red hardback book sitting on her coffee table. She asked herself if she really wanted to open it or not. Of course she did. She wanted her home to be normal. Why couldn't she have a normal life, anyway? Why did something always have to keep pulling her down? Restricting her freedom of choice? Freedom of peace? And her freedom of living life?

"Oh grandma, how could my life come to this?" Angela asked, shaking her head and looking towards the floor.

She felt like a failure. Sure, she got good grades in college, but what had she ever done with her life since then that wasn't an uttermost screwup? Her marriage was a screwup. Her life was a screwup. Even her own mother felt that she was a screwup.

A few years ago, she and her mother got into a big argument on Christmas as to why Angela hadn't had any children yet. It was also the first time Angela had sworn at her mother. She hadn't talked to her since. Angela always thought about what it would be like to have children. Birthing, raising, and watching them grow into teenagers and adults. Her ex, though, never cared for children much.

"Children are too expensive! Plus, they usually turn out to be little assholes anyway, no matter how you raise em." Angela never forgot those words, and with an ex who again made the decisions for her, she went with it.

Perhaps when her mom pointed that out in the argument, she was right, even though at that time Angela didn't want to believe it. She hoped someday that she could reconcile with her mom. Maybe someday.

The ticking of the grandfather clock in the corner of the room was the only sound in the house. Sometimes it felt like the grandfather clock could be heard all throughout the home. Angela reached for the book on the coffee table but stopped just before picking it up. Jennifer. She hadn't talked to Jennifer in a while and Angela wondered what she's up to.

Angela tapped the top of the hardbound book and sat up. Walking to the dining room table, she grabbed her phone, flipped it open, and called Jennifer. The phone rang twice when Jennifer answered the phone.

"Hey stranger!" Jennifer said.

"Hi Jenn, how are you doing?" Angela asked.

"I'm good, just having a lazy Sunday. What's up?"

"Not much. I just thought maybe you'd like to come over and hang out for a bit."

"I'd love to! What time are you thinking?"

"Anytime, Jenn. It's just me here. I went to church this morning."

"You did? How was it?"

"It was good! Something weird happened to me in the parking lot, but I can tell you more about it when you get here."

"Okay, I'll be on my way in half an hour. I need to finish cleaning my living room and when I'm done, I'll head on over."

"That sounds good, Jenn. Thanks. I'll leave the front door unlocked for you."

"Okay, sounds good. I'll see you soon!"

"See you soon, Jenn."

Jennifer hung up and Angela flipped her phone closed and looked back out towards the opened gate in the backyard. Angela thought about going out to close it, but to be honest, she didn't want to walk to the gate alone. She'd wait until Jennifer was here. While looking at the gate, she could have sworn she saw something small run across the opening from one side of the gate to the other on the other side of the fence. A neighborhood cat, no less. That's what it was.

Angela turned and walked out of the kitchen and back into the living room. The house was still quiet and relaxed. It seemed very much like a normal house, although lately it was as abnormal as a house could get. Angela sat down in her recliner chair and stared at the book on the table. The ticking of the clock in the corner of the room was still the only sound emanating from the home.

Angela reached out and grabbed the minister's book. She opened the first few pages of the book, with the paper sheet still marking the section that applied to her situation. She briefly skimmed through the introduction of the book. The book was written by an old Irish catholic priest named Danny Murphy during the 17th century when the Druids practiced in Ireland.

Danny wrote in the introduction that the stories that were in the pages of the book were written by firsthand accounts from other Druids around all of Ireland. Those who practiced divination, as well as those who would practiced exorcisms. The original title of the book after it was written in 1690 was "The Testimony of the Irish Druids", although when the Lutheran church gained access to the book in 1872 the title was changed to its present title of, "Supernatural and Satanic: What a Christian Pastor Should Do in the Event of Encountering the Dark Forces."

Angela thought it was interesting that the title of the book changed from what it was originally to what it was today. She wondered if the Lutheran church used it as an instruction tool for pastors within the Lutheran church, so rather than going by its old title they changed it to a more Lutheran friendly name? Angela wasn't sure and didn't question it much further than that.

Angela flipped through the first half of the book. Skimming through chapters dedicated to spirits, ghosts, poltergeists, demons, astrology and even aliens. Finally, Angela flipped to the page marker of the chapter that pertained to her situation at home. The section that talked about The Kushtaka. Angela was about to read the section when suddenly there was a loud thump at the front door. Startled, Angela dropped the book off her lap and spun to look at the front door. Angela stood up, expecting the worst, when she could hear a voice from the other side of the door.

"Angela, I thought you said you were going to unlock the door?" the voice asked.

Jenn. Angela forgot to unlock the door when she got off the phone. Breathing in a sigh of relief, Angela bent over and picked up the book. After setting the book back down on the coffee table, she walked to the front door and opened it. Jenn was standing on the doorstep, rubbing the side of her arm and shoulder.

"I really walked hard into that door," Jenn said.

"I'm sorry Jenn," Angela said. "When I got off the phone with you, I just went right back to the living room, sat in the recliner and started reading this book that the minister gave me."

Angela walked back to her recliner while Jenn stopped rubbing her arm and shoulder. Jenn sat down on the couch and set her purse down on the coffee table next to the book.

"What is that?" Jenn asked.

"Well, it's an old book from what I gathered so far. I read the introduction before you got here. It was written by an old Irish catholic priest. It contains a collection of testimonies from ancient Druids of Ireland," Angela said.

"What's a Druid?"

"The introduction explained that a Druid was an ancient Celtic person. They served educational roles in society, such as being a philosopher or a teacher. They taught communal wisdom about the natural world and the traditions of the people, and they were mediators between humans and God. They lived in the forests of Ireland and people valued their high class in society."

"Oh. Weird."

"Yeah, really. But the pastor that came to my house yesterday, I went to his church this morning and he met with me and gave me this book to read. He says that what I'm experiencing around here could be attributed to this thing called a Kushtaka."

"A what?"

"A Kushtaka. Some sort of shapeshifting demon thing from Alaska is what it sounded like."

"From Alaska? What the hell is something like that doing here in Oregon, then, Angie?"

"I don't know. But I was about to read the chapter about it. The pastor bookmarked it in the text. Jenn, you want a cup of coffee or something to drink?"

"You got any wine?"

"Yeah. I've got Riesling and merlot. What would you like?"

"Ugh, merlot. So bitter. I'll take a glass of Riesling, Angie."

Angela got up and walked to the kitchen, while Jennifer sat on the couch looking at the book. Angela grabbed a couple wineglasses out of the cupboard and filled each glass with wine. She walked back to the living room with the glasses in hand to see Jennifer flipping through the pages of the book.

"Poltergeists, Angela?" Jennifer laughed.

"A strange book no less, but with everything that is going on around here, I figure maybe this minister may know what he's talking about," Angela replied.

Setting the glasses down on the table, Jennifer grabbed her glass and took a sip.

"Mmm… that's good wine. What brand is that?" Jennifer asked.

"Silverlake."

"Well, it's good."

Angela positioned the book on the coffee table at an angle so that both Jennifer and Angela could read from the book. She opened it to the bookmarked section that talked about The Kushtaka. Angela read out loud about The Kushtaka.

"According to Native and local legend from the Alaskan people, the cryptid beast can change shapes and assimilate known creatures. The otter was apparently the most assimilated creature, but it could also assimilate the shape of other known animals. Goats. Bulls. Wild dogs. Even humans."

"That's creepy as shit," Jennifer said.

Angela glanced over at Jenn, then back down at the book. She flipped to the next page.

"It demonstrated its power and intelligence through a series of events that toyed with its prey. Events that proved there was no way to combat the creature or defend oneself. The Kushtaka also changed its victims into shortened imp like beings. Beings with pale whitish blue skin, long bony arms with three large claws attached to their hands, sharp jagged teeth, and yellow eyes. It amassed these beings into its army."

"Those must be the Faes he was talking about," Angela said.

"Faes?" Jenn asked.

"Yes, Faes. You remember the security video that I have on my laptop from the other night? The pastor thinks those things are Faes. And it makes sense now too."

Angela continued to read on and out loud about how the Faes were what was left after The Kushtaka transformed them from humans. Faes had an unnatural ability to resume their human shapes, however. A trait passed down from The Kushtaka to help in aiding the Faes into trapping more and more human victims. The Kushtaka is a dangerous being and should be treated with respect.

"Angela, this is serious. You're in danger living in this home," Jennifer said.

"This is pretty serious," Angela said. "If the pastor said that he didn't think he could help me, I'd probably have to move out."

"Angie. You're serious, you're going to stay here? Knowing all this that's going on now?"

"Yes. Jenn, I've been a weak person for far too long. Now that I have my place and show a shred of strength in myself, I'm not about to let something like this take over my life."

"Take over your life? Angie, it sounds like this thing can and will, eventually. Are you sure you don't want to come stay with me for a little bit?"

"No, Jenn. Thank you for the offer, though."

"Well, then I'm going to stay the night tonight. I'll just borrow some of your clothes for work tomorrow."

"Jenn, you don't need to do that."

"No, I want to. We're going to take this thing on together."

Angela felt some relief that she had such a supportive friend as Jenn.

"Alright, let's keep reading," Angela said.

Never underestimate the intelligence and raw power of The Kushtaka. The Kushtaka is afraid of bright light, such as the light of the sun. In its original form, The Kushtaka cannot attack its victims in the light of day. It can only appear to you in human or animal form, rendering it incapable of attacking during the day, making the creature nocturnal. The Kushtaka is also a being that is susceptible to fire. The origins of the creature were once a human female. The Kushtaka, while it was still human, was burned alive at a stake. Executed by local townsfolk in a suburb of Portland, Oregon called Happy Valley for practicing witchcraft and devil worship. While the human woman was burning alive, she had cursed the local colony of the area for killing her and swore that by the will of Satan she would come back to enact justice for her death on the townspeople of the area. So, the internal fear of fire will never leave The Kushtaka.

The witch's remains, after the fire had dissipated, were thrown down into a well and then sealed off with a wooden cover. The wooden seal to the well was blessed by a local colony catholic priest named Joseph Clark to keep it sealed for all of eternity.

It is believed that the Faes in their elfish forms are the same, nocturnal. Faes use their original human shapes during the daylight hours as it protects their bodies from the light of the daytime sun, like The Kushtaka. The Kushtaka loved sacrifices that were made to it by the Faes. Usually, these sacrifices were animals of any kind. Anything that the Faes could catch. They tore the animals apart, limb from limb, and set the body parts into the shape of a star on the ground.

"Angie. Remember your dog?" Jennifer asked.

"I'd like to not think about that, Jenn."

The Kushtaka cannot come into your home without being invited, but once it is invited into your home, it is nearly impossible to get it to leave.

"Angela, you never invited these things into your home," Jennifer said.

"You're right, I never did, but the old woman who lived here before me years ago did. And it's been coming here ever since," Angela said.

The owner of the property or home needs to uninvite both The Kushtaka, and the Faes from coming and rousing havoc in the home. As a result of their deep hatred for bright daylight, The Kushtaka and the Faes find dark places to hide. Usually preferring absolute darkness, they will settle for heavily shaded areas such as caves, wooden forest groves with heavy tree canopy or even deep holes in the ground.

"That makes sense. Because out back you have all those trees and the tall grass, and that well that you said seems to go on forever," Jennifer said. "So, can't you seal the well? Have a tree cutting company come in and remove the trees in the grove?"

"I don't think it's that easy, Jenn. The things already have a free invitation into the home. They're going to come whether we seal the well or remove every living vegetation from behind that fence."

"So, what can you do?" Jenn asked.

"I don't know," Angela said, hanging her head while looking at the floor. "All I can do is hope that this minister has the answer."

"I hope he does, Angie. I really do. You don't need this going on in your life right now. So, tell me about this old woman you were talking about. The one that invited the things into the house in the first place."

Angela took a sip of wine, setting her glass back down on the coffee table, and said, "Well, I don't really know all that much about her other than what the realtor told me. Did I tell you I had a weird dream a few nights back, and I saw her? I was out by that stupid well, and she was there. Told me her name was Esther."

"Esther?"

"Yeah, Esther. But that was just a dream, Jenn. Who knows if that's really her name or not," Angela replied.

"Have you tried looking it up on the internet?"

"No, it was just a dream, Jenn."

"I think you should try, anyway."

"Well, what could it hurt? I guess."

Both girls took a sip of wine. Angela set her glass down on the coffee table and opened the internet browser on her laptop. Typing in her address and name into a search engine, Angela was hesitant at first. Thinking that there was no reason she should be doing this, and it wouldn't give her any answers or solve her problems, until the search came back.

"See! I knew there'd be something about it," Jennifer said.

Angela sat silent while she clicked on a link that opened the historic archives to the Portland Journal.

"Article dated June 4th, 1858, from the Oregon Spectator," Angela said.

"That's an old article. What does it say?"

Angela read the article aloud.

"Townsfolk around the Happy Valley area were discouraged to find that a neighbor in the town has been confirmed as a practicing witch. On June 2nd, 1858, 65-year-old Esther James was convicted in front of the courthouse along Main Street of practicing witchcraft when she was observed by the Tanner boys in the forest grove just south of the township. Among lit torches in the outdoor court, the trial lasted approximately 17 minutes before a guilty verdict was entered. Esther James was taken to the forest grove south of the township where she was hung from a tree until she died for practicing witchcraft. It took approximately 2 minutes for Esther to suffocate and die. Her body was disposed of down a nearby well where the Tanner boys indicated they had witnessed Esther dancing around and chanting in rhythm. Once the body of Esther James was disposed of into the well, the well was sealed with a large stone and Reverend Joseph Clark from the church blessed the stone and the well to seal the evil that it now contained. The last words from Esther just before the rope lifted her off the ground were, "He's here from the north. He's here to punish. He's here to kill. He's here to rule."

"Wow, what a story," Jennifer said.

"That is. What's scary about it is that the old township was supposed to be located out here somewhere," Angela said. "I can't remember what the realtor said before, but I vaguely remember him saying something like that."

"You don't think that well out in the back has something to do with the story, do you, Angela?"

"You know what? Maybe it does. But I don't remember seeing a large rock around there. Large enough to seal the well's opening."

"Let's go look," Jennifer said.

"You know what? I'd rather not," Angela replied.

"Come on. It's daylight out, and you just read that these things don't like daylight. It's safe until it gets dark."

Angela was hesitant, but she knew Jennifer was right. She just read that, and if the book was truthful, then they would be okay during the day. The creatures were in hiding at this time of the day.

Angela finished drinking her wine and said, "Okay. Let's go."

"Should we take a weapon or something? Knife, gun?" Jennifer asked.

"Jenn, you just convinced me that we're going to be okay during the day. And now you want to take a weapon?"

"Yes, you're right. We'll be okay."

Jennifer finished her glass of wine and both the girls stood up and walked to the glass sliding door. Angela slid it open and walked out first, followed by Jenn. It was dusk now. The light of the sun set over the hillside. Shadows of the pine trees in the neighboring vicinity cast ominous shadows in the backyard. The gate was still swung wide open from earlier.

"Jenn, it's too dark now. By the time we get down to that well the sun will have fully set, and we'll be in the middle of that forest grove in darkness," Angela said.

"You're right, Angie. Should we shut the gate at least?" Jennifer asked.

"I'm going to," Angela replied.

Angela walked towards the gate while Jenn walked out into the grass and stopped to watch Angela. A cold shiver went up Jennifer's back, causing the small hairs on her arms to stand on end. Angela walked up to the gate, but before closing it, poked her head out the opening to look down at the trail leading to the forest grove. Darkness. The trail led down through the tall grass and directly into the heavily wooded area. It seemed to Angela that a shroud of darkness hid what was behind the opening of the forest grove leading to the well.

Angela looked hard, trying to look past the darkness of the grove to try to see something. Anything. But there was nothing but blackness. The trees and the bushes in the grove faded to black.

Angela brought her head back in and shut the gate, locking it and pulling on the gate to make sure that the latch stayed shut. She walked back to the house to find Jennifer had walked back to the patio and was waiting for her by the sliding glass door.

"That should hold. I made sure that the latch to the gate locked it for good," Angela said.

"Good. Let's go back inside. Maybe we can watch a movie. I'm gonna stay the night here with you, Angie."

"Jenn, you don't need to do that. You can go home if you want to."

"No, I insist. I want to stay the night here with you. I'll feel better knowing that we're together rather than you stay alone here in the house."

"Well, thank you, Jenn. You're welcome to stay. You can sleep with me in my room. If you're gonna stay the night, I'd rather have you stay the night with me in the same room."

"Sounds good to me."

Jennifer walked back into the house, followed by Angela. Angela slid the glass door shut, locking it with the latch. Jennifer walked back to the living room and picked up both empty wine glasses. She paused for a moment, looking at the minister's book. Breathing out a sigh, she turned and walked the glasses back to the kitchen. Angela grabbed the glasses from Jennifer and thanked her for bringing the glasses to her.

"Thank you, Jenn. Why don't you try to find something fun to watch on TV?"

"That's a good idea. I need a good laugh," Jennifer said.

Angela took the glasses to the sink and washed them. Jennifer walked back to the living room, turned the tv on and flipped through the channels. Angela finished washing the glasses out and put them in the dishwasher. She turned the faucet off and walked into the living room.

"Golden Girls?" Angela asked, smiling.

"Yup, Golden Girls," Jennifer replied. "This show always makes me smile and laugh when I need a good smile and laugh."

Angela sat down in her recliner while Jenn was on the couch. Both girls had a good laugh from the episode. Hardly giving any thought to what was going on in the backyard and behind the fence line. The grandfather clock in the corner of the room chimed eleven times.

"11 o'clock," Angela said.

Yawning, Jennifer replied, "Yeah, we should probably get to bed."

"We should. Do you have clothes for work tomorrow?" Angela asked.

"I do. I have a set of clothes I left here the last time I stayed the night."

"Okay."

Angela turned the tv off and set the remote control down on the coffee table. Both girls got up and walked upstairs to the bedroom. Angela walked in first, followed by Jennifer. Before going into Angela's bedroom, Jennifer placed the side of her head on the door of the spare bedroom, trying to hear something. Anything. If she heard something, though, what would she have done?

However, she could not hear anything. Jennifer didn't spend much time trying to listen before she gave up. Angela was in the bathroom brushing her teeth while Jennifer found a pair of pajamas from Angela's dresser drawer.

"Angie, can I wear these tonight?"

Angela popped her head around the corner of the bathroom door and nodded her head up and down, indicating that she could. Jennifer got dressed into the pajamas while Angela finished brushing her teeth. When Angela left the bathroom, Jennifer went in and washed her face, brushing her teeth too while Angela got ready for bed herself. When she finished brushing her teeth, Jennifer shut the light off in the bathroom and walked over to shut the bedroom light off, too. She then crawled into bed. Angela finished dressing in her pajamas and shut the dresser drawer. Angela walked over to the bedroom window, slowly pulling the window blinds out of the way to investigate the backyard.

"Son of a bitch," Angela said.

Jennifer turned over to look at her. "What?" Jennifer asked.

"The gate is wide open again."

CHAPTER 15

Knock... Knock...

Jennifer woke to the sound of two small knocks in the backyard. She had always been a light sleeper throughout her life. The smallest of sounds would wake her up in the apartments she lived in in downtown Portland. Even when she was a small child, the smallest of sounds emanating from her parents' bedroom made for an awkward and embarrassing situation for her parents. In her adult years, anything from emergency vehicle sirens off in the distance to the sounds of the neighbor's toilet flushing at 2 in the morning could wake her up from a deep slumber. This time, however, the culprit was two small knocks coming from the backyard that caused her to wake up.

The wind, no less. Probably slamming the opened gate back and forth on the fence post, thought Jennifer. She turned over in bed to see the alarm clock on the bed stand on Angela's side, rising up slightly in bed to look over Angela sleeping.

3:00 a.m.

Angela was still fast asleep, her back to Jennifer and already facing the alarm clock. Jennifer fell back in bed, sighed, rubbing her face with her hands when she heard knocking in the backyard again.

Jennifer was more alert now and thought, it must be the gate swaying against the fence in the wind. Jennifer pulled the covers back and sat up in bed. She paused briefly, feet dangling close to the floor, but not quite touching.

I'm thirsty, Jenn thought. She breathed a heavy sigh again and stood up from the bed. Walking over to the bedroom door, Jennifer looked back at Angela. She was still asleep in the bed. Jennifer swore at one point she had heard Angela snoring. That was the first thing she thought. Out of all the nights she stayed with Angela, she never knew she was a snorer.

Jennifer turned back to the door, reached out, and grabbed the knob. Turning the bedroom doorknob, she opened the door and walked out into the hallway. Turning around, she quietly closed the bedroom door behind her. She stepped out into the hallway, the nightlight in the hallway lighting her way. It was eerily quiet in the house besides the ticking grandfather clock in the living room.

Jennifer, living in the bigger city of Portland, wasn't used to the quiet of Angela's home in the suburb. Jennifer walked down the hallway and paused for a moment by the spare bedroom door. The spare bedroom, too, was quiet.

Good, Jennifer thought to herself. Maybe nothing weird will happen tonight. Especially to her. She turned the corner of the banister and walked to the top of the staircase and then started descending the stairs.

Knock… knock… Jennifer could still hear the knocking of the gate against the fence outside while she descended the flight of stairs. Finally reaching the bottom of the stairs, she covered what seemed to her to be the longest yawn of her life. Jennifer paused for a moment at the bottom of the stairs and looked around the living room, the kitchen, down the first level hallway that led to the utilities room and a small office that Angela hardly ever used let alone even went into other than for storage. Everything was so quiet, she thought.

Knock… knock….

"Damn, that gate is loud," Jennifer said as she walked towards the kitchen. When she reached the kitchen, Jennifer opened a cupboard near the stove and got a glass of water. She walked over to the kitchen sink and filled the glass with cold water from the faucet. The flavor of well water was so good for her.

Jennifer remembered the time she grew up on the farm, playing with her friends in the dead of summer months and coming inside on a warm summer day for a glass of cold ice well water. That was the best. It could only be topped by her mom's homemade lemonade. Her dad loved it, too. Jennifer stood at the sink for a moment with her eyes closed, admiring the fresh flavor of the water. She finished the first glass and went to re-fill her second glass when she heard knocking again. Jennifer looked up and out the kitchen window.

Jennifer expected to see the gate swinging against the fence, causing the knocking noise, but it wasn't the gate. Jennifer saw a woman in the back corner of the yard.

Startled, Jennifer set her glass down and with wide-open eyes said, "What the hell? Who is that?"

Jennifer watched from the kitchen as the woman in the backyard had her back turned to her. The woman in the backyard drew her arms and shoulders back and swung down, causing a knocking noise. Jennifer paused for a moment and thought about going upstairs to get Angela to see this, but she couldn't help but continue watching what the woman was doing in Angela's backyard.

From the kitchen, Jennifer could tell that this woman was dressed in what looked like old Victorian clothing. A bonnet covered her head. A white and tan sundress of sorts, worn as if she had been working outdoors all day with dirt and some sweat stain on her back. Jennifer watched as the woman continued to draw her arms and shoulders back and swing down, causing the knocking noise that woke her from her sleep in the first place.

As Jennifer continued to watch, she realized that this woman was chopping wood. The woman was near the fence line, so Jennifer couldn't make out too much detail other than that her figure was slender. Slowly, Jennifer walked towards the sliding door in the kitchen. A pair of Angela's slippers rested by the sliding glass door. Jennifer slipped them on and reaching out, she grabbed the latch, unlocked the door, and slowly slid the sliding glass door open. Taking a step out of the house and onto the patio, she realized the cement patio was gone. She stepped onto dirt.

Jennifer walked out to where the edge of the cement patio should have been. She noticed the barbecue grill, table, chairs, patio covering, and even the wooden picket fence were gone. All gone. Nothing but dirt, rocks, and an old stump where a tree must have stood years ago. Jennifer turned to look at the house, which was still there. The sliding glass door was still open. She could still see into the kitchen and even read the time on the LCD screen on the microwave. The green numbers on the microwave control panel read 3:00 a.m.

How is that possible? I've been up for almost a full five minutes. The time on the display screen of the microwave must be slow by five minutes, she thought. Jennifer turned around to look back at the woman in the yard. She was still in the corner of the yard, chopping wood. The sound of wood being chopped was more predominant now that she was outside of the house. It wasn't just knocking anymore, but a knocking along with the clanking of falling wood into a freshly cut wood pile.

A mist hung heavy over the landscape, and the leaf trees around the land were changing to bright brilliant colors of red and orange. There was a crisp cold in the atmosphere, feeling very much like the fall months of the year. Each exhale in Jennifer's breath caused a plume of white mist to puff out into the air.

Jennifer continued to walk up towards the woman while she continued to work the axe and cut wood. Jennifer couldn't believe what she was seeing. Perhaps this was a dream? Maybe none of this was real? This new backyard certainly wasn't real. The landscape looked rugged. Tall grass was all around her. The well-manicured backyard was all but traded for weeds, unkept grass and bald dirt spots everywhere. If it wasn't for the house still being where it was, then Jennifer would have sworn she traveled back in time to the old rugged Pacific Northwest, in the days of fur traders and explorers from the eastern coast of the United States. Jennifer continued walking towards the woman. She walked through tall grass, pushing some taller weeds aside and walking through the bald dirt spots. Jennifer drew closer and closer to the woman. The sounds of chopping wood grew louder and louder until, finally, Jennifer was about ten feet away from the woman.

"Shit, what do I say now?" Jennifer asked herself.

Her breathing got heavier and heavier as it finally dawned on her that she was very vulnerable. Here she was wearing pajamas with slippers. Not even real shoes and in the landscape she was in, she thought it would have been wise to be wearing actual shoes with some foot protection. The woman with her back turned to Jennifer didn't know that she was there. She only continued in her work of woodcutting. Finally, Jennifer drew up enough courage and broke her silence.

"Hello?" Jennifer asked.

The woman continued cutting wood, as if she didn't even hear Jennifer, or perhaps just ignored her.

"Hey," Jennifer said a second time with a little more assertiveness. "It's 3 in the morning, and this isn't even your house. What the hell are you doing here?" Jennifer asked.

The woman brought her axe up and down with force, continuing to chop wood. Jennifer didn't understand what was going on. Was she ignoring her? Was she high on some kind of drug or drunk? And furthermore, what the hell happened to the backyard? Where was the BBQ, the patio, and the picnic table?

Jennifer doing anything to control the situation then said, "What did you do to the backyard? Where is everything? The BBQ, the table, the patio? I'm going to go back inside and call the cops if you don't start talking to me, you crazy bitch!"

No response from the woman.

Jennifer didn't know what to say or do. It was the strangest thing she had ever seen. Jennifer walked up to the woman and around to the front of her. Jennifer could then see the face of a younger woman. She was maybe in her early 20's with black curly hair, white, and pale skin. She was breathing heavily from her work of chopping wood and her dress was dirty and loose fitting. Sweat poured down her face from her brow, down her neck and to her chest, causing sweat stains on the front of a dirt covered white and tan sundress. Along the side of her face, Jennifer could see a small, thin scar cross from her right eye down to her jawbone. It was very hard to see unless you got up close to her.

Jennifer was out of ideas. She didn't know what else to say or do other than say, "Hello?" but with less assertiveness this time.

Again, there was no response from the woman. She just continued to breathe heavily, set wood on the top of a chopping block, and swing the axe down to cut it in two. It was like Jennifer wasn't even there. She never existed or wasn't supposed to be there.

Jennifer watched the woman continue cutting wood. She took a step back from her and felt that she needed to walk back towards the house. She took two steps back towards Angela's house when Jennifer heard noises coming from behind her, in the tall grass down by the creek. Jennifer turned and looked down at the old dirt trail that was still in its place where she remembered it, but now the dirt trail was wider, almost like a road. It surprised her because the trail was now wide enough to get a large car up and down with relative ease if she wanted to. In the distance, she could see light dancing through the thick trees and the tall grass. It was coming in her direction. It looked like fire.

Jennifer walked two steps backwards towards the house but stopped where she first talked to the woman chopping wood, maybe ten feet behind her. She wanted to see what the source of the light was. It was still coming her way. Eventually, down the dirt trail, she clearly saw a large group of men and women carrying clubs and rifles, with lit torches lighting their way through the night. Everyone was wearing old clothing, the same as the wood chopping woman. Some men wore hats made of straw and string, while others wore old, worn leather hats. The women wore bonnets, like the wood chopping woman. Jennifer could hear random chatter among the group as they drew closer and closer. The crowd appeared to be led by a man dressed in a black garb at the front of the crowd. He carried a lone lit torch, but no weapon like the members of the crowd did. The crowd continued to draw closer to the woman, who saw the crowd approaching her. She stopped her work and set the head of the axe on the ground while she leaned on the wooden handle to rest.

As the crowd drew closer to her, they stopped. They must have been maybe 20 feet away from the woman, Jennifer thought. The man in black walked closer towards the woman, distinguishing himself from the rest of the crowd.

"Esther Ann James!" the man in black shouted.

"I am she," the woman chopping wood said, finally breaking her silence.

"I am Reverend Joseph Clark!" exclaimed the man in black. "We are here to take you into custody under the charges of witchcraft and sorcery as reported to us by the Tanner boys, Seth and Matthew Tanner."

"Burn the bitch!" someone in the large crow said.

"No," the reverend said. "You will be given a fair trial under the charges brought forth tonight and we will determine whether you are practicing in enchantment or not!"

Two men from the crowd walked up to Esther. They grabbed her by each arm, and Esther resisted. One of the men drew back and slapped Esther in the face with the back of an opened hand.

"Fucking witch," he said as he stood over Esther, holding her arm.

The axe fell flat against the ground with a thud. Esther fell back, but just before her back hit the ground, she was violently yanked back up to a standing position by both men. Pain flowed through her face and her arms and shoulders. The men dragged Esther towards the crowd, who were yelling and screaming curses at Esther. The minister led the two men, who were followed by the crowd, down the trail and away from where Jennifer was standing. An eerie silence fell around Jennifer as she watched the lights of the torch fire dance back through the trees and disappear into the darkness.

In that moment, the fog in the area grew dense. It covered the trail and thick wooded trees, slowly creeping towards Jennifer. The fog then swirled around her legs, moving up her body and eventually covering her torso, chest, and then her face. She gasped and took a step back, but the fog completely covered her. She couldn't see even a foot in front of her face. Jennifer stood in a cloud of fog. Turning all around her to see where she was and who or what could be around her. As soon as the fog had come, it had disappeared.

When the fog completely subsided, Jennifer was standing in a dirt street looking towards a large white building. Had she wandered towards the dirt road while she was turning around? Trying to find her way out of the fog? Jennifer was now standing behind the large crowd, with the minister up on an elevated wooden platform. The platform was uneven, an attempt by a carpenter to make the platform as even as he or she could without the best of wooden boards to use. The woman who was chopping wood was now standing on the corner of the platform for all to see.

The crowd continued to hurl curses and insults towards Esther. Jennifer even saw one man throw a burned-out wooden torch at the woman, just barely missing Esther's face and chest. Jennifer turned around and looked back behind her and saw Angela's house, still with the sliding glass door open just the way she had left it. Although this time Jennifer was quite a distance away from the home. Did she really wander this far away from the house while she was briefly engulfed in the fog? Jennifer turned back around to look at the crowd. The man dressed in black, Reverend Marcus Smith, stepped onto the stage, turned to face the crowd, and began speaking.

"Ladies and gentlemen. Here before you stand Esther Ann James, accused of witchcraft, as witnessed by both Seth and Matthew Tanner, children of James and Mary Tanner. Seth and Matthew Tanner, who both hereby testify that they had witnessed the accused, slitting the throat of three sheep, and boiling the blood from the bodies in a cauldron over the fire. Along with this, Seth and Matthew Tanner also reported they witness the accused speaking in Latin and recall the name

Lucifer being repeated at the beginning of each Latin sentence. Therefore, Esther Ann James, you are hereby found guilty of witchcraft, and it has been voted unanimously by the Happy Valley colony. The book of Leviticus, chapter 20, verse 27 says, 'A man also or woman that hath a familiar spirit, or that is a wizard, shall surely be put to death: they shall stone them with stones: their blood shall be upon them.' Esther, because of your guilty verdict of witchcraft, you are not given the opportunity to represent yourself under the laws of the constitution of the new free colonies and, more importantly, under the laws of God. You are hereby condemned to death by the laws of both the land and the holy book of God. You are, however, hereby given the opportunity to say your last words so that the township can record your final words in our town journal and can hear the repentance of a witch."

"I will repent not but issue you this warning," Esther said. "I was happy to leave you people alone. Live on the outskirts of the land. By myself. For myself. For my god. Now one who is truly more powerful than I or your unmerciful God will surely avenge me. He whom I have dedicated my life to."

The crowd fell silent, listening to the words of Esther.

"The one true master of this world, and the afterlife. This land will forever be cursed. A testament of the wrongdoing that was done this day. Forever, the Happy Valley will be anything but happy. Forever, the townsfolk will suffer and burn in agony. They will lose their identity and become minions of the one true master of this world. For each stone cast this day may a hundred more be cast upon them. May your God have mercy on my soul? No, my god has brought me into his paradise on this day. On this day, I meet my Lucifer. May the God you worship have mercy on your own souls."

At this, the townsfolk grew angry. They stooped down and picked up rocks from the streets, many running to the sides of the dirt road to find jagged rocks the size of baseballs. Children run into the weeds and tall grass to find their own rocks. The minister placed the noose of the hangman's rope around Esther's neck. The ball of the noose nuzzled against the back of Esther's neck, right against her spine. It was done this was so that her fall from the stage wouldn't break her neck. She would rather suffocate and choke to death while the people stoned her. The townsfolk grew restless, each man, woman, and child now with a rock in hand.

The stage lit with the fires of burning torches. When each member of the town had their rocks collected, the minister shoved Esther off the corner of the stage. There, Esther dangled from the crude makeshift gallows by the neck. Gagging and gasping for air with her hands tied behind her back, still alive. The minister left the stage and walked down the wooden steps to the front of the townsfolk. A man in the front row handed the minister a stone and the first stone that was thrown was from the minister's hand.

"Back to hell and back to your master you go. There is no place for you in this godly world!" the minister exclaimed, throwing his stone and striking Esther in the left side of the face.

Esther's face immediately split from the jagged edge of the rock, causing a small streak of blood to run down her cheek. Pain radiated from the wound on her face. The minister disappeared into the crowd and the rest of the townsfolk screamed and yelled and threw their stones at the defenseless hanging woman. Rocks struck her all over her body, in her chest, torso, legs, and face. Some rocks missed Esther, and hit the wooden stage and rolled off the backside of the stage, but many found their mark.

Eventually, one man threw his stone, striking Esther on the left side of her forehead. A sickening crack was heard, much like the sound of a cracking egg. Blood instantly poured down Esther's face onto her chest, staining the front of her sundress a crimson red. Finally, Esther stopped, gasping for air. Her body went limp and stopped swaying back and forth. In that moment, Esther died.

Jennifer wasn't certain if it was the hanging or the rock that the man threw that split Esther's skull open, but nevertheless, Jennifer was shocked. Covering her mouth with her hands, she held her breath in utter shock. She watched the lifeless body of Esther, hung by the neck and slowly swaying in the late-night breeze. Silence overtook the area. There was only the sound of the wind in the trees, falling yellow and orange leaves around Jennifer, the crackling of the fire on the torches, and the moaning of the wooden gallows under the weight of Esther's lifeless body. Jennifer looked around at the crowd. Men and women wore satisfied smiles on their faces for the good they had thought they had done.

Something different happened now, though. While Jennifer was glancing over the crowd, she came across a small child standing in the corner of the crowd with what looked to be his mother. A young boy, only 5-6 years old, but he looked right at Jennifer. Rather than looking into the bright blue or brown eyes of a young child, she was looking into two bright yellow orbs for eyes. Void of pupils or irises.

"Where were the eyes of this child?" Jennifer thought.

Jennifer watched the child tug on the dress of his mother, as if he was trying to grab her attention. The boy never broke his gaze from Jennifer. Jennifer then glanced to the right of the child. She now saw that the woman who was standing next to the child was turned around, looking at her too. Her eyes too were large, yellow, and glowing. One by one, each member of the town turned and looked at Jennifer and one by one, each man, woman, and child stared at Jennifer with bright yellow glowing orbs for eyes. The last person who looked up towards Jennifer was Esther, who was still hanging from the rope. Her bright yellow orbs for eyes glowed in the darkness. A smile crept onto the dead woman's face.

Through the blood, Jennifer could see a row of sharp teeth that came to a point in the woman's mouth, revealed by a large inhuman smile that ran the length of her face, from ear to ear. The townsfolk all smiled this way at Jennifer now too, with the same sharp rows of teeth that came to a point. They somehow knew now that Jennifer was there, watching. Jennifer was terrified. She took a step back and gasped at what she was seeing.

This group was only 50 feet away from her. The boy who she first saw took a step towards her. The townsfolk followed suit. Jennifer's heart jumped into her throat. Jennifer took a couple of steps backward, only to watch the townsfolk run towards her, silently, making no noise in their pursuit. Jennifer turned and began running back towards Angela's home. It was so far in the distance, but Jennifer ran, nonetheless.

Jennifer pushed her way through tall grass and weeds, back to the dirt road leading back to the house. Halfway back to the house, Jennifer could hear feet beating on the dirt road behind her. She could feel that the group was getting closer. The fog closed the area in, as if even the fog was trying to snare Jennifer. She was getting closer to the house and could see that the sliding glass door in the back was still slid open. She drew closer when she heard the chattering of the townsfolk behind her. Inhuman chattering, more devilish and a squeakier high pitched.

Jennifer turned to look at her pursuers to see how far behind they were and, to her shock, the townsfolk weren't humans chasing her anymore. They were small 2 to 3-foot-tall creatures. Each with bright yellow orbs for eyes that glowed in the night along the trail. Each with long claws on their hands with long arms. Each ran sluggishly, but were still capable of catching up to Jennifer. Each with a row of sharp, pointed teeth revealed in a devilish smile.

Jennifer turned back around and continued to run as hard as she could. She was back in the yard now. She ran past the chopped wood pile and the axe that Esther was using earlier. The sounds of the creatures were getting closer. For a moment, Jennifer thought she might not make it. The tall grass and overgrown weeds only slowed her down long enough for at least one creature to jump on her back, knock her to the ground and allow the others to catch her and to do God knows what to her.

Jennifer didn't want to turn around and look at the creatures again. She knew what they were; she continued to run as hard as she could. Finally, Jennifer came to within ten feet of the house. Breathing heavily, she pushed the last weed aside and was shocked to hear that the same weed she pushed aside was instantly pushed aside again behind her.

They were right on her heels.

With a final effort, Jennifer dove through the open glass door and back into Angela's home. She fell onto the tile floor of the kitchen, wheezing. She rolled onto her back and leaned up, using both elbows to brace herself and see out the glass door. She looked up to see the glass door was still open. Looking into the backyard to see her pursuers, she noticed that the backyard looked normal again. Freshly cut grass with a nice wooden picket fence line. The damn gate opened and swayed in the cool Oregon night breeze. The glass Jennifer used for water, still on the kitchen counter by the sliding glass door. Jennifer was astounded. She picked herself up off the kitchen floor and took a step outside of the house. She stepped down onto a concrete patio. With a barbecue grill to her right and a picnic table to her left. She touched the barbecue, and it was real. She walked out into the backyard, taking a step off the concrete patio into well-manicured, soft, green grass.

Jennifer looked around the yard and apart from the gate being opened along the fence line, everything was normal. There was no wood pile that was chopped, there was no axe, there were no overgrown weeds in the yard, nothing was out of place.

"Jennifer?" a voice said behind her.

Jennifer shrieked, startled by the sound of an unexpected voice. Was it one of the creatures that had chased her back to the house?

It was Angela.

"Jennifer, what are you doing out here?"

"I, umm… I thought I heard something out here."

"Jenn, it's 3 in the morning. You should be in bed. It's late," Angela said.

Impossible, Jennifer thought. She woke up at 3 in the morning. There was no way. Not after everything she had experienced. Jennifer walked back into the house and looked at the time on the microwave, which now read 3:01 a.m. No. How can this be? Time stood still during her experience. Was it a dream? Did she sleepwalk downstairs and outside to the grass?

"Angela, I don't know what happened."

"Well, you woke up and came downstairs. I remember hearing you get up and out of bed. It's when you opened the sliding glass door, and I heard a loud bang downstairs in the kitchen that woke me up. So, I got out of bed and came down to see if you were okay. You must have been sleepwalking or something? Did you fall into the kitchen? What was that loud bang down here?"

Jennifer didn't know how to answer Angela's question. She didn't even know how to explain how an event that seemed like it took longer than just a minute really didn't. Jennifer grew nervous, realizing she had her own supernatural experience at Angela's house.

"Angie, can we go back inside and talk at the kitchen table?"

Both the girls left the backyard and walked back inside Angela's home. Closing the sliding glass door behind her. In the distance of the yard, two yellow eyes glowed, watching the girls through the opened gate in the fence line.

CHAPTER 16

"Jenn, do you want to go back to bed? Or do you want me to make you a cup of coffee?" Angela asked.

Jennifer sat herself down at the kitchen table, holding onto herself in the early morning hours. Slightly chilled from the night air but frightened by the experience she had. She shook slightly, not because she was just cold, but because she was afraid of how to explain what she had just experienced firsthand to Angela.

"I don't think I can go back to sleep, Angie."

"Okay, I'll make us some coffee then."

Jennifer braced herself at the table and readjusted in her chair, not sure what to say but knowing she had to say something. "Angela, I need to tell you something, but I don't know how to say it without scaring you, too."

"Jenn, you can tell me anything you want to tell me. You always have and being here in this house now doesn't mean that will change. What is it?"

Angela had the feeling that something had happened to Jennifer. She experienced something. Angela got the coffee grounds from the pantry. She filled the coffeemaker with the grounds and poured water in the maker's reservoir. She flipped the switch on to brew and walked over to sit by Jennifer at the dining room table.

"Angie, something did happen to me, and I don't know if it was real or if it was something that I just dreamed up."

Jennifer started by explaining that a knocking noise from the backyard had woken her up, then she spent the next ten minutes telling Angela that the backyard had changed, she found an angry mob of people, watched a public hanging, and was chased back to Angela's home by some kind of yellow-eyed short creatures.

Angela sat in utter silence, listening to what Jennifer had to say. The sounds of the coffeemaker were the only sounds in the room while Jennifer talked. Finally, she ended her story. Which explained the loud thump that had woken Angela up from her sleep. Angela leaned over and gave Jennifer a hug, who was in tears and afraid to be left alone in the home.

For as long as she lived, Jennifer would never forget those bright yellow eyes, chasing her through the night, along the dirt trail, through the woods, through the tall grass. She could still vividly hear the sounds they made as they chased her. Clear as crystal, as if the sounds were a part of her psyche now. The sounds of chattering and tiny footsteps slapping the dirt trail. The coffeemaker had stopped brewing minutes ago, and Angela got up from the table to grab a couple of mugs from the kitchen pantry. She turned to walk towards the refrigerator and got the coffee creamer out when she stopped in mid step to the refrigerator. With a hand on the handle of the door, Angela spoke with confidence.

"Jenn, this upcoming weekend I'm calling the pastor and inviting him out to help rid the house of these things."

Wiping her face with the back of her hand, Jennifer said, "Angie, can you really wait that long? That's 3 more days."

"I can. I mean, if it gets worse, I can always get a hotel room for a couple of days. It's not a big deal."

"You don't have to do that; you can stay with me if you want."

Angela opened the refrigerator door, leaning in, she grabbed the creamer from the side of the door and said, "I appreciate that, Jenn. I'm not going to let whatever this is beat me, though. It will not win. I've let too many things best me in this life to get to this point. You know how things happen for a reason, Jenn? Five years ago, I didn't think I would ever in the world have to deal with something like this. Five years ago, I never thought my husband would run off with some early 20's college graduate intern. I always thought I would have a happy marriage, with a couple kids by now. It's what my mom always wanted for me and now that things have happened the way they have, it had to happen for a reason, you know? I really feel like I've let my grandmother down. What would she say to me if she were alive now?"

Angela shut the refrigerator door, turned, and walked back to the counter. Pouring some creamer in each coffee mug and then pouring the coffee in. It was satisfying to Angela to watch the coffee blend in with the creamer and change from a bright white to a cream, tan color in the mug right before her eyes.

"She'd probably say look, Angela, your husband left because you didn't do a good enough job around the home. You took him for granted. Didn't make him happy."

Jennifer sat in silence, listening to Angela talk.

"Look Jenn, all I'm saying is that there has to be a reason for my being here."

"For you being terrorized here?"

"No. I'm lost, Jenn. After he left me, I realized that the life I wanted would never happen. I fell in love with the wrong man. Who knows, maybe I didn't do a great job of being a wife? Maybe I drove my husband into the arms of a 20-year-old? Either way, though, now I'm trapped in this hell, and I've got to find a way to get myself out of it. Everyone else has always held my hand through all the difficult times, and now it's time that I confront whatever this is and fight back. For myself."

"Angie, I get it. But at what cost? This is too strong for you. This is too strong for anyone. Can an old minister really help you rid your home of whatever this thing is?"

Angela walked back to the kitchen table with two coffee mugs, one in each hand. She set one mug down in front of Jennifer and the other she kept for herself.

Sitting down at the table, Angela said, "Jenn, at this point, it's not even about this house anymore. It's just another... fuckin thing that has come up in my life to keep knocking me down. I've never learned to stand up on my own and maybe this is God's way of giving me that one last chance to stand up for myself. If I don't accomplish anything else in my life, Jenn. If I never get married again, never have kids, never progress anywhere in my job, at the very least if I knew that I took a stand for myself and fought back for myself, with no one there to hold my hand along the way then I'll know I've really accomplished something."

Jenn grabbed her mug with both hands. The warmth of the sides of the mug was refreshing to her.

"Angie, I support you no matter what. No, I more than support you. I look up to you like you're my role model. I always have. I admire your courage and standing up for this, but Angie, at what cost? What if something gets a hold of you here? It could kill you."

Angela took a sip of hazelnut flavored coffee. She looked at Jennifer and said, "Jenn if that happens, then it's almost worth it to stand up against something that is trying to ruin my life, anyway."

Jenn knew that. Jenn had known Angela for quite some time now to know that she's right. Apart from marriage and graduating college, Angela hadn't done much with her life up to this point. There were no children in her life, no family now, and no big career moves. She hadn't written a book, or achieved a lifetime achievement award, or even conquered a hike along a popular nature trail. She was just Angie. Very predictable. Monday through Friday, and housewife on the weekends. Cooking dinners on weekday nights. She had never done anything to establish herself as an independent woman before. Maybe this was God's way of giving Angie a second chance at her independence. Crude, but a way, nonetheless. The sun was now peaking over the hillside. Morning had come while both girls were talking with one another. Jennifer looked over at the time clock on the microwave, which now read 5:44 a.m.

"Angie, I'm gonna head home to get ready for work. Are you gonna be okay?"

"Yeah, Jenn," Angela said with a smile on her face. "Will you?"

"Yeah, I will be." Jennifer forced a smile to convince Angela that she would be okay.

Jenn drank the rest of her coffee in her mug and got up from the table. She walked over to the kitchen sink and washed the mug out with water from the faucet. Jenn looked up into the backyard, now illuminated by the morning sun. The backyard was fresh and green, with grass with dewdrops on their tips, which cast a rainbow of colors from the sunlight. A clean picket fence line with the gate in the backyard opened, revealing the tall grass behind the fence line and the small dirt trail which led to the grove with the well in it. It was where she was no more than a few hours ago, seemingly running for her life.

Jennifer tucked her head down quickly, as if to avoid making eye contact with anything that could be out there. She set the washed-out mug down on the countertop and walked back over to the kitchen table. Angela sat up from the table and walked Jennifer to the front door.

"Jenn, you got your purse?" Angela asked.

"Yes, it's here on the coffee table," Jennifer replied.

Jennifer swooped down and picked up her purse. Angela opened the door for Jenn and gave her a hug goodbye. Jennifer walked out of the house and out to her car. She unlocked the car, got in, and started it. Putting her car in gear, she backed up and drove onto Suntides Blvd., and out of view from Angela.

Angela was alone now. Or so she thought. Angela saw her newspaper at the end of the driveway, walking out to the end of her driveway she bent down to pick it up when she heard a voice speak to her from across the road.

"This house intraduce its-self to ya friend, did it?" the voice said.

Startled, Angela quickly stood up and looked around. Tom Butler. The little old neighbor from across the street was slowly walking his way across the street to where Angela was standing. Angela heard what Mr. Butler said but didn't want to allude to the strange happenings of what was going on in her home to Mr. Butler.

"Oh, no," Angela said. "My friend just had to go home to get ready for work this morning. In fact, I should start to get ready soon myself."

"How ya enjoy dat house so far, Angie? Ya havin a good time in there are ya?" Mr. Butler asked.

"Oh, it's a beautiful home. I very much enjoy it." Angela paused for just a minute, seeing a weird look on his face. No less, he was a strange little old man. Not strange, but different. Angela paused for a moment and said, "Mr. Butler, I know we've talked briefly about this before, but what all do you know about this house?"

"Oh, it's quite a house it is, with quite a history at that," Mr. Butler said, laughing to himself. "Eventually, dat house will getcha it will."

"Get me?"

"Getcha! Ya know, like fall in love wit it!"

"Oh. Well, I need to get going, Mr. Butler. I hope you have a nice day today."

"Oh, thank ya, Angie. Thank ya indeed. Y'all have a good day at work there!"

With that, Mr. Butler turned and strolled back across the street. Angela watched as the small old man slowly shuffled across the road and down his driveway back to his home. Angela opened the newspaper at the end of the driveway. The Portland Journal. A front-page article told the story of a small business, picketing for better health care benefits in downtown Portland. It always seemed to be the topic of conversation in the business world these days, she thought.

Angela folded the newspaper in half and turned to walk back towards her home. Admiring the small landscaping project that she had done with the flowers in her front yard. How could things get so crazy so fast for her? Everything at one point was so simple. She had finally moved into this beautiful home, cleaned it, planted flowers in the front, and took care of the backyard. A sense of pride that only came from owning a home, and she had felt it for the first time being out on her own.

Walking back into the house, Angela shut the door behind her, locked it and walked towards the kitchen. She set the newspaper down and picked up the coffee mugs to wash them out in the sink. Angela looked up and out the kitchen window as she had done many times before to admire the beautiful green grass in the backyard. The gate. The gate was wide open again. Angela sighed. She cast her eyes down from the window and finished washing out the coffee mugs. Setting the mugs down in the drying rack on the counter next to the sink, Angela turned the water off. She squeezed the water out of the sponge and set it down next to the sink and walked towards the sliding glass door.

Angela slipped into a warm pair of black fuzzy slippers and took a step out through the open glass door and onto the patio. She noticed how considerably cold it was, even for this time of the year. It was quiet and everything was still. The sounds of freeway traffic were not even noticeable this morning. Maybe because it was still too early for people to be driving.

Angela walked out onto the edge of her patio, stopping for a moment before stepping onto the green grass. Droplets of dew hung on the tips of each blade of grass. Angela took a step out into the yard and began walking towards the opened gate in the fence line. From where she was, she could clearly see the trail that led down to the creek and the old well in the back behind the fence. The tips of Angela's slippers were soon soaked with cold dew from the grass.

As she drew closer to the gate, she peeked her head out through the opening and looked around. Tall blades of grass and weeds were standing still behind the fence. Standing to attention. Angela listened quietly, only to hear a babbling brook from the creek off in the distance. Everything was, for once, normal, it seemed. Angela thought nothing more of it and brought her head back to her side of the fence line and shut the gate. Locking it with the latch and hearing the latch click meant the gate was locked. Angela turned and walked back towards her house. Her slippers were completely soaking wet now. Cold, not warm like they were before she left the house.

Halfway back through the yard, Angela had the feeling she was being watched. By a neighbor, maybe? She stopped halfway through the yard and looked to her left. Then to her right. Her neighbors weren't out. The blinds and shades to their home's windows were all closed. Angela then looked behind her. The gate still latched shut, and nothing was out of place.

Angela then decided to look up at her home. In a second level window, the blinds were pulled down, revealing the face of a man in the window. It was in her bedroom. Angela gasped and at that moment, the man let go of the blinds, closing them shut. Angela could see the blinds moving as if someone was behind them. She thought she had an intruder in her home. She quickly ran back through the grass to the sliding glass door. She knew she had her cell phone on the kitchen table. If she could get to it in time, she could quickly grab it, get back out of the house, and call the police.

Once she got to the patio door, she paused again and listened intently. She crept into the house slowly, not to make any sound to announce that she was back in the home. Maybe the man thought that she didn't see him. Maybe he was waiting for her up in her bedroom. It would be a great opportunity to grab her cell phone from the kitchen table. However, her cell phone was not on the kitchen table.

"Shit!" Angela said. "Where is it?" she quietly muttered under her breath.

Angela looked around the kitchen and did not see her phone. She looked towards the living room and saw her phone on the coffee table. Angela thought maybe she shouldn't try walking that far for it. She should go to a neighbor's house to call the police. But were any of her neighbors still home? She wasn't so sure if her neighbors were or not, and Mr. Butler from across the street… who hadn't even owned a landline for years. The bottom line was, there was no one else. She needed her cell phone to call for help.

Angela began the treacherous slow walk through the dining room and kitchen to the living room coffee table. She did her best not to make a sound while she walked, frightened. She could feel her heart beating in her throat. She figured as soon as she took a step past the staircase that whoever it was would be standing right there at the bottom of the stairs, waiting to grab her.

Angela stopped and backtracked toward the kitchen, never breaking her eyesight from the living room. She backtracked to a drawer in the kitchen, slowly opened it, and grabbed a large butcher's knife. She didn't bother closing the drawer, but instead began walking back towards the living room. She braced herself as she got closer to the staircase and the bottom of the stairs. She raised the knife up to the side of her face so that all she would have to do if the man jumped out from the corner was to drop her arm down into him.

She slowly crept to the corner of the kitchen where she could peek out into the living room without revealing all her body. She slowly drew her face around the corner of the wall and looked up the stairs. Nothing. No one was standing there. A slight sigh of relief came over Angela. At least whoever this was, wasn't standing right there at the corner waiting for her. Angela still had to make it to the coffee table. And it was a good ten feet away.

Angela gripped the handle of the knife tightly as she started walking slowly towards the coffee table. The feeling of something watching her had started again as she entered the living room and drew closer and closer to her cell phone.

Angela thought to herself, what if she doesn't make it? What happens if this person comes downstairs and grabs her before she gets out? Would they kill her? Small beads of sweat dropped from Angela's brow. Her hands were wet, clammy, and shaking from fear with the knife in hand. She was maybe a couple feet from her cell phone now, but completely exposed in the living room. She reached out with her left hand and leaned to grab her cell phone off the coffee table.

A loud creak came from the hallway upstairs, near the banister of the hallway that overlooked the living room. Angela turned around and saw a man standing there, looking at her. His eyes were completely yellow, and he wore a straw hat with old-fashioned farmer clothing on. His worn pants were held up with suspenders wrapped around his shoulders and back. He had beard stubble on his face, and his smile was abnormally large. He stood there watching with his yellow eyes and a crooked large smile that seemed to run from ear to ear on his face.

Angela shrieked and ran back outside the home, through the kitchen door and into the backyard. Her hands fidgeted with her cell phone, trying to find the numbers to dial for help. Finally, she did, and she called the local sheriff's department.

"Multnomah County Sherriff's office, what's your emergency?" the operator asked.

"Hello! Yes! There's someone in my house," Angela whispered.

"You think there's someone in your house, ma'am?"

"Yes. I saw him upstairs looking out the window while I was in the backyard, and I went inside to get my phone to call for help and I saw him in the upstairs hallway looking over the banister at me!"

"He was looking at you, ma'am?"

"Yes, I saw him. He was wearing a straw hat! With a dirty white button up long sleeve shirt, and gray overalls with suspenders that looked dingy and dirty. He was a white man, with some beard stubble like he hadn't shaved in a couple days, and, and his eyes were yellow!"

"His eyes were yellow, ma'am?"

"Yes, his eyes were yellow! I couldn't even see the whites of his eyes; all I could see was a reflective yellow! I know that sounds weird, but you must believe me when I say his eyes were yellow."

"A reflective yellow?"

"Yes! They were yellow!"

"All our eyes look like that, ma'am."

Taken aback, Angela said, "What?"

"All our eyes look like that."

Surprised, Angela said, "What do you mean?"

"Once you become one of us, you're going to have yellow eyes, too."

Angela closed the phone shut and dropped it on the grass. She couldn't believe what she had just heard. Why would the operator say that?

Angela bent over and picked her phone up from the grass. She looked back towards the house, and it sounded quiet from where she was standing in the backyard. Angela took a couple more steps back towards the house and stepped up onto the patio. Walking up to the sliding glass door, she poked her head inside the parted door. She looked around the kitchen and the dining room and from where she was, she could see her purse on the coffee table still too.

She knew she had her keys to her car in the purse. Angela listened and didn't hear any sound coming from inside the home besides the ticking of the grandfather clock in the living room. Angela took a couple of steps into the home. The house was still quiet. Maybe the man was still upstairs and waiting to see her walk into the living room again, slowly Angela walked towards the staircase and looked around the corner of the staircase with the knife poised in her hand, ready to attack the intruder.

She was careful not to make a sound and gave away her position in the home. Angela looked around the corner of the wall and didn't see anyone on the staircase. Maybe now, if she made a break for it, she could quickly grab her purse from the coffee table and run for the front door. Angela took a deep breath, braced herself, and ran. Her feet thudded harshly on the first level living room floor. Angela made it to the coffee table. She reached down to pick up her purse when she was grabbed on the shoulder from behind. The grab was strong and hard, causing a rush of pain throughout her body and she was violently thrown across the living room towards the wall next to the TV. Her body crashed into the wall... which caused her to wake up.

Angela found herself on the floor of her bedroom. She was soaked in sweat and breathing heavily. She looked up at the alarm clock on her bedstand, which read the time of 3:01 a.m. Angela picked herself up off the floor, stood up, turned around and sat on the bed. She was still breathing heavily, wiping the sweat from her brow with the back of her hand. It was all a dream. She looked over to where Jennifer was, to find her resting quietly on the bed. A slight snore came from her, but it was nothing out of the ordinary.

It had been a dream. Angela couldn't believe how real it felt. She sat on the edge of the bed, trying to gather her thoughts. In the dream when the man threw her, that must have been the moment she was falling out of bed, and obviously her hitting the wall was her hitting the floor. It made sense. The dream was so real that she must have flung herself from her own bed and onto the floor.

Angela rubbed her face with her hands and rubbed her eyes with her knuckles and fingers. She took a deep breath and got up from the bed. She began walking towards the bathroom when she felt a blast of cold air. Angela turned around to see the window in her bedroom was slightly open, causing a cool night breeze to blow into the room. Angela walked over to the window and shut it. Being soaked in sweat and feeling that cold breeze chilled Angela. She turned back to walk towards the bathroom. Jennifer was still sleeping soundly. Angela walked into the bathroom and shut the door behind her. She turned the light on in the bathroom and then turned the water on in the bathroom sink. She gave her eyes a minute to adjust to the bright light of the bathroom.

Angela scooped warm water from the sink onto her face. She then looked up into the mirror and saw a bruise that she didn't remember going to bed with. It was a bruise on her shoulder, in the shape of four long fingers, as if someone grabbed her hard. Angela turned her back to the mirror and saw a large thumbprint on her shoulder blade. Sure enough, it appeared to be a handprint on her shoulder. She remembered that in her dream she was grabbed by the shoulder and thrown across her living room. Was it really all just a dream?

CHAPTER 17

Jennifer woke up when the alarm went off in Angela's bedroom. Opening her eyes, she stretched in bed and rolled over to look at the clock. The time read 6:00 a.m. on the bedstand alarm clock. Jennifer rubbed her eyes with her hands and breathed a deep sigh of relief for waking up this morning. She had one of the worst nightmares last night. She had dreamed about being in Angela's backyard, confronting a woman who was cutting wood. Then an angry mob came and took the woman. They hung her after a makeshift trial and her dream finally ended with her being chased back to Angela's home by small creatures with yellow eyes. She had woken up just in time before one of the small creatures had reached out to grab the back of her leg just before she dove back into Angela's home through the open sliding glass door in the kitchen. Thank God it was just a dream. It felt so real to her. Too real.

After rubbing her eyes, Jennifer looked over to see if the alarm clock had woken Angela up too. Angela wasn't in bed, though. Jennifer sat up in bed and touched Angela's side of the bed, expecting to feel her body there, hidden under the covers and comforter, but it wasn't. Jennifer looked around the bedroom. Everything looked normal. The bedroom door was shut. Where was Angela?

"Angie?" Jennifer said. No response.

Jennifer threw the bedcovers off herself and swung her legs out of bed. Getting up from the bed, Jennifer reached to the ceiling, stretching her back out. She walked to the bedroom door and opened it. Walking out into the hallway, Jennifer said, "Angie?"

She walked down the second level hallway towards the staircase to see light from the kitchen illuminating the living room. Jennifer turned around the corner of the staircase and descended the flight of stairs down to the first level. After reaching the living room, Jennifer walked around the corner and into the kitchen to see Angela sitting at the table, drinking a cup of coffee.

"Angie, there you are. Did you not sleep well last night?" Jennifer asked.

Angela looked up at Jennifer and said, "No. No, I really didn't."

"Why? What happened?"

Angela took a sip of coffee, swallowed, and set the cup down on the table. Exhaling deeply, Angela said, "Well, I had a dream where I had woken up, and you had a nightmare yourself. You were down here in the kitchen, and I made some coffee and we talked about your dream you had."

Jennifer sat down at the table next to Angela, listening intently. Angela continued explaining her dream, "You left to go home and get ready for work in the morning, and I went back to close the gate in the backyard. When I looked up at my house in the backyard, I saw a man looking at me from my bedroom window. So, I called 911 and was trying to get help to come out, but it wasn't 911. Like it wasn't the operator who I was talking to. So, I decided to grab my purse and get out of the house and when I grabbed my purse I was grabbed on the shoulder from behind and thrown into the wall. Then I woke up on the bedroom floor at three this morning. I got up off the floor and walked to the bathroom to splash some warm water on my face when I turned on the light to the bathroom and noticed this bruise on my shoulder. It looked like four finger marks, so I looked at my back and found one finger mark bruise on my back too."

Angela pulled her robe open around her shoulder just enough to expose the four long finger shaped bruises on her shoulder, and the thumbprint on her back. Jennifer was startled.

"Oh my gosh, Angie. Does it hurt?"

"Yeah, it's sore to the touch. Like a burning sensation. Not really like a normal aching you get from a bruise, ya know?"

Jennifer thought for a moment and said, "Angie, you said that I had a dream in your dream too, right?"

"Yes, you did."

"Did I explain to you my dream in your dream?"

"Yes, you did. You had mentioned to me you were woken up by a knocking noise from the backyard and that there was a woman chopping wood in the back. Then an angry mob of people came and took the woman. They publicly hung her in the night for witchcraft, and then you were chased back to the house by some of those yellow eyed, short creatures."

Jennifer was shocked at what Angela had just told her. How could she know that? "Angie, that's the dream that I had last night. It was more of a nightmare. It was so real. But how would you know that in your dream? Like I would have had to have told you that for you to know that?"

Jennifer was right, Angela thought to herself. There should be no way that she would know what Jenn had dreamed about last night, unless Jenn had told her. She couldn't have told her. Angela thought she shouldn't have known that. How did she know what Jennifer had dreamed about from her own dream?

Angela finished her cup of coffee. Getting up from the table, Angela said, "I'm calling that minister this weekend to come over to take care of all this with me."

"Angie, it's Wednesday. Saturday is 3 full days away. Are you sure you don't want to call him out here sooner than that? What about tonight? Or tomorrow night?"

"No, I'll be fine to wait until the weekend, Jenn. But I can't handle this anymore. It's affecting my sleep. Making me anxious. It's disrupting my life. I need to do something about it."

"I understand, Angie," Jennifer said. "You know what, Angie. I support whatever decision you decide to make and just know that I'll be there for you whenever you need me to be. We're in this together."

Angela leaned over and hugged Jenn. For the first time in a while now, Angela finally didn't feel completely alone. She felt that she had a real friend in Jennifer and that's what had been missing in her life lately. Someone she could trust. Someone who would be there for her.

After they finished hugging, Jennifer said, "Angie, I'm going to go home quick to get ready for work. Are you gonna come in to work this morning?"

"I plan on it, yes."

"Okay." Jennifer smiled. "Things will be okay. You have the right attitude. When the minister comes this weekend, I want to be there to support you."

"Thank you, Jenn." Angela smiled.

With that, Jennifer got up from the dining room table, walked to the living room, and grabbed her purse from the coffee table. She reached in her purse for her keys while Angela got up from the table and walked towards the living room door. Opening it for her, Jennifer found her keys and walked out of the home.

"I'll see you in a couple hours, Angie."

"Okay, see you in a couple hours."

Angela closed the door while Jennifer was walking to her car. She turned around and took a deep breath, stepping into the living room. She thought what if she saw that man she saw in her dreams, standing on the second level hallway overlooking the living room over the hallway railing, staring at her? Angela looked up at the second level of her home. He wasn't there. Three more days. Could she really make it three more days? Or will these things get her before the minister could come? Would The Kushtaka get her before then? In fact, would the minister even come this soon?

Angela hoped he would, trying not to think much more about it. She walked to the kitchen and grabbed her coffee cup from the kitchen table. Walking it over to the kitchen sink, she washed it out and put it in the drying rack; she turned and walked towards the staircase in the living room.

Honestly, she still expected someone to be upstairs waiting for her, but there was no one. Before walking up the stairs, Angela eased her way around the corner of the staircase to see if someone was standing at the top, looking down at her. Again, there wasn't anyone there.

Angela breathed a sigh of relief, walking up the stairs to get back to her bedroom to get ready for work this morning. Angela walked past the spare bedroom door, pausing for a moment as she stood in front of the door, facing the door. An uneasy feeling crept over Angela. She expected something was in there. She just didn't want to know what. She stepped to her left while still facing the bedroom door, then turned and continued to walk into her bedroom to start getting ready for work.

Angela chose a nice black skirt that reached down to her ankles, along with a professional button-up white women's blouse which seemed like a good choice for her today. She could wear her black heels with the skirt, too. After picking out her clothes, Angela walked to the bathroom and got herself ready to take a shower. Getting in the shower and turning the water on hot felt so good on her skin. Except for the bruise on her shoulder. The heat of the water caused the bruise to feel like it was burning, more painful than it already was. Angela finished her shower, turned the water off, and got out. Drying off, she wrapped a towel around her chest and brushed her teeth at the bathroom sink. Shortly followed by getting dressed in her bedroom and slipping on her new black heels, she had recently got on a shopping trip with Jennifer. Jenn thought the heels would look good on Angela, and Angela agreed. They did look good on her.

Angela walked back to the bathroom to straighten and comb her hair when she heard the faint sounds of creaking. Angela paused for a moment to listen. What did she just hear? With the water in the bathroom sink off, and the sound of her hair being brushed stopped, Angela could tell the creaking sounded was closer than she thought. Not necessarily downstairs, but upstairs. Was it the sound of someone walking up the stairs? Or down the hallway? No, no. It was like the creaking from the sounds of an old rocking chair, with a repetitive rocking back-and-forth motion.

Angela set her hairbrush down on the bathroom counter and trudged out into her bedroom, careful not to make a sound. The creaking sound was getting louder now that she was out of the bathroom and in her bedroom. The bedroom door was open, and Angela was exposed to whatever was making the noise in the hallway. The noise was in her second level hallway, for sure. But that was impossible. There was nothing in the hallway that could be making a rocking, creaking noise like what she was hearing.

Angela walked to the bedroom door and slowly poked her head out of the doorway to look in the hallway. The sounds of rocking and creaking got louder in the hallway, but nothing was there. Angela stepped out into the hallway to listen and heard the creaking sound become even more apparent. She walked down the hallway towards the staircase. Maybe the sound was coming from the living room. The sounds got louder and louder as Angela walked towards the banister of the top floor, but the sound wasn't coming from her living room. It was coming from the room behind her. The spare bedroom.

With her back now towards the door, Angela felt a sense of worry and fear overcome her. There was something in that spare bedroom. Whatever it was, it was making a rocking, creaking noise. She had to open the door. She had to see what it was. Maybe she should call Jennifer quick and wait for someone she could trust to come over and be there with her just in case something bad happened. Or maybe she should call the sheriff. What would she say to them, though?

Jennifer was trying to get ready for work herself. What would she have her friend do? Drive back across the city of Portland to come back to her home because she was hearing creaking and rocking sounds coming from the spare bedroom? Or what would the sheriff do? Come out to investigate a creaking noise? No. Only she could find out what was making that noise.

Angela wanted to confront whatever it was on her own. It was another opportunity to stand on her own. Confront something on her own. Be her own independent woman. She gave herself a sense of strength. A sense that she could confront anything and beat it. Angela took a deep breath in and exhaled. She took another deep breath and braced herself as she reached out for the doorknob with her hand. Grabbing the doorknob, she slowly turned the knob. A slight creaking came from the hinges of the knob as the door opened.

A chill rushed out of the room and hit Angela in the face, slightly blowing her hair back. The door slowly squeaked open, and Angela looked in the room before stepping foot into it. What she saw shocked her. The room was decorated from an old-fashioned time, with a decent sized chandelier in the center of the room. The room was now had a hardwood floor with a large, blue circular area rug in the center of the room. In the corner of the room was an old piano, with two candelabras on top of it. A large bookshelf also sat in the other corner of the room. Angela gasped as she held her hands to her mouth and stared at what was making the rocking, creaking noise that was by the window.

In the other corner of the room by the window sat an old woman in a rocking chair, knitting a blanket with multiple colors of red, orange, yellow, and purple threads. And the color she was stitching into the blanket was blue. She knitted intently, rocking while her hands fidgeted with the knitting needles, knitting a beautiful rich blue color into the blanket. The old woman had white hair that looked as if it was recently permed into curls. She was an old woman with beautiful blue eyes and wrinkled skin that was clean and without blemishes or scars. She wore a long blue sundress with white polka dots and tan slippers. Around her neck hung a necklace with a Black Hill's gold rose pendant. She hummed the tune of Fur Elise by Beethoven to herself while she stared out the window, rocking in her rocking chair, and knitting with her hands.

Angela was utterly shocked. Her eyes were wide open at the sight she was looking at. Her legs grew weak. Angela reached out for the doorjamb to hold on and brace herself from falling. She recognized the blanket that the old woman was knitting. Angela turned to look over the banister in the living room and noticed that her favorite blanket, her grandmother knitted for her, was gone from the back of her recliner. Angela turned around and looked back at the old woman. She recognized her. The old woman she was looking at was her grandmother, and she was working on knitting her favorite blanket. The blanket that brought her comfort and peace through all the hard times and all the years that overwhelmed Angela.

"Oh my God..." Angela said. "Grandma?"

The old woman stopped knitting in that moment and looked up. A smile crept onto her face and her blue eyes made contact with Angela's. "Angie, baby," the old woman said.

Angela smiled and laughed. She walked into the spare bedroom towards the old woman. "Grandma, what are you doing here?"

"Well, I'm crocheting your blanket, my dear. I know you've always liked more than just one color. Do you remember that sweater that I knit for you at the Christmas program when you were 6?"

Angela smiled and laughed again; a small tear dropped from the corner of her eye down the side of her cheek. Angela dropped to her knees and kneeled at the side of the old woman in her rocking chair. "Yes, Nana. I do remember. I sang the solo of Silent Night. You were so proud."

"Yes, I was," the old woman said, smiling and looking down at the blanket she was knitting. "I was always proud of you." The old woman looked back up at Angela. "Do you remember when your dad set fire to the turkey in the oven during the Thanksgiving of 1989?"

Angela laughed out loud. "Yes, and momma had to get the fire extinguisher from the washroom and put the fire out in the oven. I remember that Thanksgiving we had chicken. Thank goodness daddy always kept spare chicken in the freezer."

"Yes, he did. Angie, my dear, I know you've had a rough life. I'm so proud of you and how you've overcome so much."

Angela gave the situation some thought, though. Her grandmother had been dead for quite some time now. So, what was she now doing in her spare bedroom?

"Grandma, what are you doing here? You passed away when I was 19 years old."

"I did," the old woman said with a smile. "And do you know why I did?"

"Momma said it was because you just got old. My heart was broken when you died. I miss you so much. You meant so much to me, Nana."

"Oh really? Meant so much that you would leave your old nanna and move away?" the old woman forcefully asked.

"Grandma?"

"You abandoned me, Angela. You moved away." The old woman's voice went from a sweet and comforting tone to a raspy, deep sound. "You left me for school and broke my heart. I made you this blanket because it was the best thing I could give you, and you fuckin left me!"

Angela was shocked. Her grandmother would never talk to her like this.

"Grandma, I went away to school to educate myself. To make myself a better person. Most of all, to make you proud of me."

"Better yourself, my ass. What have you done with your life?" the old woman barked. "All you ever did was get a piss poor education, and you married a man you had no business of marrying! You married him because you couldn't support yourself! You were too stupid to even live through life on your own that you had to give it up to any man that would come by and give you the time of day! You fuckin killed me! You broke my heart, and I died from that! Your momma just didn't give a shit enough to tell you the truth!"

Angela was crushed. Was it true? Was it really her fault that the one person she felt the most love for in her entire life died because she left home? To simply go to college? Angela felt a sense of greed. That she never put her family and what was most important in life first. Angela then realized something was wrong. Her grandmother wouldn't say this. Her grandmother would be proud of her. Even after all the times she screwed up when she was a little girl around the home, her grandmother was there to pick her up, support her, and show her love.

"No," Angela said, standing up and taking a step back away from the rocking chair.

"What did you say to me?" the old woman asked.

"I said no. You're wrong. I've always loved you. You were the only support in my life. I worked so hard in school for you. Everything that I did after I left home, I did to show you I was worth a damn. You aren't my grandmother. My grandmother would have more respect than you."

"You spoiled little bitch. I am so disappointed in the woman you've become! You could barely get through school, and you couldn't even manage your own relationship with your husband! Your husband always hated you. That's why he fucked a 20-year-old and ran off to marry her, over half his age younger! You couldn't even have children yourself. That's why the family hates you. You turned out to be worthless to them. You failed everyone and most of all, you failed me, Angela!" The old woman threw her knitting needles onto the floor. The needles made a clanking sound from the impact on the hardwood floor. Angela took another step back towards the bedroom door.

"And you know what the worse thing is about it all, you whore? Is that I wish I never made this fuckin blanket for you. You don't deserve anything, especially from me! You are going to die in this house! This house deserves to have you here for all eternity! I hope you rot in hell because you are a worthless child, and you do nothing but continually disappoint me and this family time and time again!" the old woman yelled.

Angela shook her head slowly, with tears streaking down her face. "You're wrong," Angela said. "You're wrong... You aren't my grandmother. My grandmother did nothing but love and admire all the hard work I did when I was a child, and I made her proud by standing on my own and going away to school. I never killed her."

"Can you be so sure you didn't kill me? You bitch."

"I NEVER KILLED YOU!" Angela screamed. "You aren't my fuckin grandmother!"

The old woman smiled at Angela. But the old woman's smile consumed her face, the corners of her mouth reaching from one ear to the other. The old woman opened her mouth and revealed a row of sharp, jagged teeth. Angela took another step back. She knew for sure she wasn't talking to her grandmother at all.

"Don't fight it, Angela," the old woman said. "There's no hope for you. The old minister you're going to call, he won't stop me. You won't stop me. Your time is coming soon, and I will have you and you will live here for all eternity with me in the well and in this home. For all eternity, you will serve me. Soon, you will be mine."

As the old woman was speaking, Angela walked backwards to the opening of the door.

"Where are you going, Angela? Perhaps the old minister will know what to do," the old woman said, laughing a deep and bellowed laugh.

"You're wrong. I am not giving up. And you are not going to win. I am going to beat you, and I am going to live a long and productive life," Angela said.

The old woman stopped laughing. She stared at Angela with fire in her black eyes and said, "Soon Angela, soon…"

With that, the old woman vanished in front of Angela. The rocking chair dissolved into the atmosphere. The blanket disappeared and the knitting supplies and threading were gone, along with the chandelier, the piano, and everything. The room was empty, as it always had been. Quiet. The only sound in the home came from the grandfather clock downstairs. Angela stepped out of the room and slammed the door shut. She fell to the floor in the hallway and sat up against the wall and cried into her hands. The words that the being she was speaking to in her spare bedroom echoed in her mind.

She had killed her grandmother. She let her family down. She was a failure in life. It was difficult to come to terms with. Jennifer had always offered her support and encouragement, but beyond that, there was no one else that would tell her she was doing a good job. That she was doing things right. There was no one that would tell her that they were proud of the woman she was today. This thought replayed over and over in Angela's mind.

Furthermore, it was all her fault. Could that be true? Was it really all her fault? Angela was away at college when her grandmother became ill and died before Angela could get back home, before she could say goodbye. Before she could give her one last hug and one last kiss on the cheek. Angela couldn't stop crying. Her heart was broken. And the creature had worn her down again. Angela wiped the tears from her face and slowly got up off the ground. A sickening feeling came over her, like she was going to vomit, but only dry heaved. It felt like she was punched in the gut.

Angela slowly walked back to her bedroom down the hallway. She walked into her bedroom and looked at the bed. There at the foot of her bed was her grandmother's quilt. Knitted in fabulous bright colors of red, orange, yellow, purple, and bright, brilliant blue. Angela's heart sunk deep into her stomach. She took her heels off and walked to the foot of her bed. She sat down next to her grandmother's blanket and picked it up in her hands. Clutching the fabric to her chest, she fell back onto the bed and continued to cry. A broken woman.

CHAPTER 18

It was the chiming sounds of a cell phone ringing from somewhere in the house that caused Angela to stir from her brief slumber.

Angela swore she heard her phone going off, but she was too comfortable on the top of her bed to care much about it. It didn't dawn on her until a few seconds later that she had fallen asleep on the foot of her bed, clutching her grandmother's quilt to her chest.

"Oh, shit!" Angela said. It was 9:25 a.m. Angela had cried herself back to sleep after she had seen her "grandmother" in the spare bedroom. Angela quickly swung the quilt off her chest and got up from the bed. The cell phone finished ringing once she got out of the bed. She ran out of her room, past the spare bedroom and down the stairs. Where was her phone? Where did she leave it?

Angela looked in the kitchen first, at the dining room table and on the kitchen countertops. Her phone was nowhere to be found. She knew it was in the house. She heard it clear as day from her bedroom upstairs. She turned and looked back in the living room and saw her phone there on the coffee table. How she had run right by her phone was beyond her, but with all that was on her mind these recently, it made sense. She ran back into the living room and to the coffee table and picked up her phone. Nine missed calls, all from Jennifer. She quickly called Jennifer back to let her know she was okay.

"Angie? Where are you? Are you okay?" Jennifer asked.

"Yes, I, uh, I laid down on my bed and fell back to sleep. I can't believe I did that!" Angela said. Angela didn't want to really reveal the real reason she was late to work and what she had seen in the spare bedroom. It would only worry Jennifer more than she already was.

"Well, I covered for you with Mr. Marshall. He just wants to know if you're okay and if you're coming in to work this morning. If you need to take the day off, he understands. And it's not really all that busy, Angie. Maybe you could call that minister back and take care of the house today?"

"No, Jenn. I'm okay. I can wait until the weekend to call the minister back. Let Mr. Marshall know I'm on my way," Angela said, walking back up the stairs to straighten her hair up and gather her things.

"Okay, I'll let him know. Are you sure you're okay, Angie?"

"Yes, Jenn. I'll be fine. I'm on my way in."

"Okay, thanks for calling me back. See you soon."

"See you soon, Jenn."

With that, Angela hung up the phone. She walked into her bedroom and went back to the bathroom. Brushing her hair out and cleaning herself up a little bit, she gathered her belongings and left for work. Of course, traffic was an issue again. It was always in Portland. Especially in the morning. Angela felt like she was really rushing, too. She was never late for work. This was the second time she could remember this happening to her in her 16-year career with Marshall and Stone Family Law. The first time she was so sick in the morning, she woke up and ended up being a half hour late. Mr. Marshall had turned her away and given her the day off, telling her to go to the doctor. Even back in school, Angela preferred to be on time for her classes, never tardy for a lecture or meetings with her high school or college supervisors.

After fighting through downtown Portland traffic, Angela finally made it to work. It took her nearly a half an hour to get through the thick Portland traffic. She parked in her spot in the garage, right next to Jennifer, and got out. She ran up to the Ed Hock Business Building. She opened the front door and ran right past the coffee shop.

"Hey Angie," a voice said from her left.

Angela turned around to see Jeff, the barista, at the coffee stand in the corner of the first floor of the building.

"Oh, hi Jeff. How's it going this morning?" Angela replied while walking briskly towards the elevator.

"Running late this morning?" Jeff asked.

"Yes, I got stuck in some pretty thick traffic out there," Angela said.

"Oh. Hey, you and Jennifer want your usual coffee this morning? I can bring it to you guys if you'd like?"

"Oh, that would be nice. Would you be able to bring it up to us?" Angela asked while she pushed the button for the elevator to come down.

"Not a problem," Jeff said. " I'll bring them up to you guys here in a bit when I get caught up with orders."

The elevator door slowly opened once it reached the ground floor.

"That's great, thanks Jeff!" Angela said while she jumped inside the elevator quickly just before the doors slammed shut on her. She pressed the number four on the elevator door and the elevator ascended to the fourth floor.

"I wish they'd fix this elevator," Angela said under her breath. The elevator dinged when it passed the second floor. Until it got to the third floor. The elevator stopped abruptly. Angela pressed the number four button repeatedly, but the elevator would not move. Not even budge.

"God, can this really be happening?" Angela said out loud and frustrated. The third floor belonged to a variety of different small businesses and independent clinical counselors that all carried memberships to either the American Psychological Association or the National Association of Social Workers. Social workers and clinical psychiatrists had offices on this floor and called it their business location. Regardless of who was on the floor, though, the elevator was stuck. Angela wasn't going anywhere.

Giving up on thinking the elevator would move on its own ever again, Angela pulled her phone out of her purse to call Jenn at the front desk to let her know what was going on. Jenn could call someone to come help her, too. She tried turning her phone on, but the battery was dead. Interesting, Angela thought. She had just charged the phone's battery earlier. It shouldn't be even close to dead yet, not at least until the late afternoon. Angela felt the temperature in the elevator fall. It was late spring in Portland, but the Ed Hock building was running the thermostat. Which was always set to 72 degrees all throughout the building. Even in the elevator.

Why was it getting cold in the elevator? Cold enough for Angela to see her breath when she exhaled. Finally, the elevator doors opened. Slowly, with their usual creaking noise, but rather than slamming shut when the door opened, the doors stayed open.

"Thank God," Angela said. At least she could get out now and just take the stairs up to the fourth floor. Angela watched as the elevator doors opened slowly, but they opened to a floor that Angela didn't recognize as the third floor. She knew the third floor. It was a large hallway with office doors on each side of each individual business and counselor, but the floor the elevator doors opened at appeared to be more of like a storage floor for the building. Almost like a basement. Cold, dark, and dreary. Boxes and clutter littered the entire floor, with old dirty blankets covering nearly everything in the room. Dust and spider webs hung from the ceiling that looked like it was a good 30 feet high.

It appeared as if no one had been on this floor for years. The floor was dark. The only light came from the elevator door as it illuminated some boxes and clutter directly in front of her. Angela struggled to stare into the darkness to see windows or any other light coming from the room, but there was none. Just darkness. Angela noticed that for some reason, the elevator door was still not slamming shut. No matter how many times she pushed the button for the fourth floor, the door would not shut. The doors stayed open, exposing her to the darkness of the room.

"What the hell is this?" Angela asked. She checked her phone again, and it was still dead. Angela poked her head out the elevator doors to look around the room. It looked as if the room continued for a way. Angela peered into the dark room and thought she could see the light of a red exit sign in the distance on the other side of the floor. She would have to try to go for it, because apparently the elevator decided that today was the day that it was going to stop working. Out of all the days, the one day in a long time, she was late to work. Maybe now the maintenance crew would do something about it and fix it.

Angela slowly stepped out of the elevator and onto the floor, looking all around her. After taking a couple of steps onto the floor, the elevator slammed shut. Angela jumped and turned around to look at the elevator. She could hear the elevator come back to life and go down to the first floor. The sound of the humming elevator was the only sound in the room until it finally stopped at its destination, and the room was utterly silent.

Angela walked back to the elevator and pressed the button on the wall, but the elevator didn't come back up for her. Angela, with her back pressed against the closed doors, turned and investigated the room. She was looking into pure darkness. After her eyes adjusted to the darkness, she was certain that she could see a red exit sign off in the distance in front of her. The room was cold. Bitter cold. She had to be in the basement, but she knew that the basement of the building wasn't this large, nor was it used for storage. It was used for generators, water tanks, and electrical panels.

In that moment, Angela remembered something. She quickly rummaged through the pockets of her purse. She remembered that she had a small hand-held flashlight in her purse that she got one year for Christmas. A stocking stuffer gift from her ex-husband Todd. At this point, Angela didn't even know if the flashlight worked or not. She prayed that it did and that the batteries weren't dead or that the flashlight even had batteries. Thank God it worked.

Angela clicked the flashlight on and flashed the light into the large room. Angela saw an endless number of wooden crate boxes, stacked one on top of the other, dust, clutter of smaller boxes of papers and junk. Dust and spider webs hung off the ceilings and off the large boxes. Old dirty blankets laid on top of some of the wooden crates. Angela walked into the room and up to a box. The wooden crates were stacked 4 to 5 crates high.

Angela continued to pan the light around the room when she saw an opening in the wooden crates. She walked towards the opening with the assistance of the light and flashed the light into the opening. It was a path that led towards the center of the room, towards what Angela assumed must be the red glowing exit sign that hopefully led to a door out of the dark abyss. The path led deep into the room, and the light hit the end of the path, which turned left.

"Great, now I have to wander through a damn maze in darkness because of that damn elevator," Angela said.

Frustrated, yet feeling quite uneasy about the idea of wandering into the maze of crates, Angela had no choice. She prayed that her flashlight didn't die on her. She had to enter the maze of wooden boxes and crates to get to the exit light. She had to take the chance of going in to get out.

Before she started walking along the path into the wooden crates, Angela turned to look one more time at the elevator door. Dead. Not even a light illuminated the elevator's panel to indicate that it was even turned on. With no other choice, Angela walked into the maze of crates. She couldn't believe how many turns and corners she had to make. It was as if it really was a maze. Angela just continued to pray that the flashlight wouldn't die on her halfway through the floor. She wouldn't know what to do if it did. The room was cold. Like the room was exposed to the dead of night in the winter. Angela could see her breath in her flashlight's beam, exhaling blooms of carbon dioxide in front of her as she walked on.

She couldn't believe how quiet the room was, too. There wasn't even the sound of running electricity through the room. Angela reached a path that led to a dead end. Wooden crates seemingly blocked her passage through, stacked four crates high. There was no way she would even be able to climb over it.

"Damn it," Angela said, sighing. She turned around and look down the long path she had just walked down and started walking back from where she came to try a different path when she heard a strange noise. Angela paused for a moment in the darkness and listened. In the distance, from the direction she had started in about ten minutes ago, Angela heard a clopping sound. It was as if there was a horse walking on the cement floor of the room. It sounded just like hooves walking in the room with her, but not the sound of a set of four hooves hitting the floor, but only two. Angela turned her flashlight off. She could feel her heart pounding inside her chest, her breathing getting heavier. It sounded as if something was in this room with her.

Angela had to turn her light back on, though. The room was pitch black if she had it off. She couldn't see where she was going. Even if the light exposed where she was, she had to have it on. Angela slipped her heels off her feet. That way, she wouldn't make any noise while she walked in the room.

Probably wouldn't help her much, she thought, because the light had to be on still, but at least she wouldn't be clicking with her heels with each step. She turned the light on and tried her best to hide the light with her hand, cupping the light from going up above the boxes and deflecting it down towards the path. Angela ran back barefoot to where the pathway had split and turned down a different path. Thank God the path continued to go through the maze of crates, but whatever was in the room with her was trailing through the maze behind her. Hooves clopped on the cement floor and echoed through the room, followed by a vicious, deep growl. It was demonic in nature, and the sounds she was hearing were getting closer and closer to her.

Angela felt panic settle over her. She started running through the endless maze of crates. The sounds of her feet patted against the cement floor. All the while, she could hear heavy breathing and clopping sounds drawing closer and closer to her. Angela turned the corner of the path she chose and ran into a dead end.

"Shit," Angela whispered.

She was trapped. She turned to quickly run back in the direction she came from, but whatever was making the clopping noise was behind her. Angela could hear the snarling and grunting noises of the creature. It caught up to her. Angela quickly looked around the dead end. Could she climb out and over the crates? She couldn't. There was no way she could safely scale four crates tall in time.

Whatever was behind her was closing in, growling and snarling. With each step, there came a loud hoof clopping sound that echoed into the darkness and back into Angela's ears. With her hand covering the light of her flashlight and directing it to the floor, Angela kept looking around her and noticed that a wooden crate to the right of the dead end was slightly opened.

Angela ran to it and pulled on the wooden panel with everything she had. It opened with a loud clank as the panel hit the floor. Quickly she got into the wooden crate and saw a knothole in the wood of the crate panel. She reached down with her hand, stuck two fingers through the knothole and pulled the panel back up, shutting herself into the wooden crate. Angela turned her flashlight off and did her best to control her breathing. Her heart was pounding against her chest.

She prayed that whatever was coming towards her wouldn't be wise enough to look in the crates. Angela did her best to be careful not to inhale or exhale too loudly to give away her position in the maze. The sounds of hooves clopping behind her and the growling drew closer and closer to her. Whatever it was, it was directly on the other side of the crates on the path she needed to go back down that would lead to another path. It was loud. Very noticeable and, whatever was making the noise, sounded very large.

Angela could hear the snarling and growling coming closer and closer toward the dead end of the path. It was almost fifteen feet from Angela now, who was still hiding in the wooden crate near the dead end. The creature took one step at a time into the dead end, snarling and growling the whole time.

Angela thought it sounded like a bull. Its snarls and growls unnerved her. She didn't want to be caught by whatever that thing was. She looked as hard as she could out through the knothole in the wooden panel. Dark shadows crossed in front of the knothole. A hoof stepped, stopping directly in front of the crate she was hiding in.

Angela could see deep, dark red hair hanging from the shadow in front of her crate. The shadow was in the shape of an inhuman leg. A leg that bent at the knee in an unnatural direction. The creature snarled and growled directly outside of her crate. Angela controlled her breathing, careful not to move and make a sound. With a little luck, maybe the thing would turn around and go back, thinking that she had gone down a different path. Seconds later, the creature bellowed a loud cry, the intense sound of a bull. The bellow echoed through the room, and Angela gasped, quickly covering her mouth with both her hands.

After the creature finished its scream and loud bellowing, it turned and began walking back in the direction it had come. The sounds of hooves and heavy thuds against the cement floor echoed through the room. Angela could tell by the sounds of the creature moving that it had walked out of the dead end and around the corner of the crates, back down the path it had come. As soon as the loud thuds of the creature's hoof steps faded in the distance, Angela slowly opened the wooden crate panel and carefully peeked outside. Everything seemed quiet, but she wasn't sure what she was doing. She couldn't see anything, so peeking out the crack of the crate's opening was simply just wasting time for her to get away. All she could do was pray that she was certain that she heard the beast go back in the direction it had come. She couldn't hear the hoof thuds where she was anymore.

Angela slowly lowered the crate's wooden panel to the floor, careful not to drop it and make a loud sound to draw the creature back to the dead end she was stuck in. She was careful not to turn her flashlight on yet either, fearful that the light would draw the creature back to her location as well.

She climbed out of the crate and stood up, not even bothering to replace the panel and close the crate. She slipped her wrist through the small rope on the end of her flashlight, careful not to drop her only means of light that may eventually help get her out of the maze alive. Carefully she felt her way with her hands against the other crates until she walked herself around the corner of the dead end, and back on the path that led her to the dead end.

Angela prayed that the creature had just stopped in the pathway and waited for her to make the first move. Angela couldn't see anything. She was completely engulfed in darkness. For all she knew, the creature was right in front of her. She didn't dare turn her flashlight on yet, but she prayed to God as she felt the side of the crates down the path, hoping the creature was far enough away to make a break for the exit. But it still felt like the exit was such a long way away.

Finally, Angela felt her way back down the path she had come, towards the section where the path split off into another direction. Angela stopped for a moment in the middle of the pathway to listen. She could still hear the faint sound of clopping hoof steps on the cold cement floor off in the distance, back in the direction she had come. It was at that moment that Angela heard another loud bull's bellow coming from a distance away. It sounded as if the creature was in pain, but she knew whatever it was, it wasn't in pain. Angela knew this would be her only chance to make a break for the exit she had seen earlier.

Angela shut her eyes for a moment, whispered to herself, "Christ, please help me."

She reached for her flashlight that was tied to her wrist and took it in her hand. Angela opened her eyes and took a deep breath, and, in that moment, she turned the light on and ran for the path she had not yet taken. The moment her light turned on, she ran. She heard the creature bellow loudly as it sprinted after her. The creature knew now where she was. This was it, Angela thought. She either navigated her way correctly through the maze of crates this time, or she didn't, and the creature would get her.

Quickly Angela ran, taking corner after corner, guessing which direction to go. She heard the creature behind her. Its hooves clanked loudly on the cement floor, grunting and snarling along its way. Angela came across another crossroad of crates. She could either go left or go right. Angela paused for only a moment to decide, when she heard the bellow of the creature from behind her again, gaining ground. The wooden crates rattled on top of one another.

Angela went right. She ran down the long pathway, her flashlight illuminating her way. Angela turned left, around another set of crates, and then turned right again. Thank God she had made the right choice in the direction she had gone. She found the exit of the wooden crate maze and found the red illuminated exit sign against the wall. She ran ahead, flashing her light ahead of her to expose a large exit door. Angela ran up to the door and pushed on the exit door's handles. The door refused to open. It felt like it was locked from the other side.

Angela gasped again, turning to look behind her and shining the light on where she had exited the large maze of crates. She could hear the creature closing in on her. The sounds of hooves and growling drew closer.

Angela pounded her fists on the exit door, yelling for someone to help her. Praying that someone would open the door from the other side. Angela could hear the creature getting closer and closer through the maze. In a matter of moments, the being would run out of the maze's exit and get her.

Angela threw her body up against the door, but it wouldn't budge. It bellowed loudly, directly behind her. The creature was within a few steps of exiting the maze of crates. Wooden crates vibrated so loudly that a couple on the very tallest of the stacks fell and burst open on the floor, revealing old dry human bones.

Angela watched in horror as the wooden crates burst open upon impact on the cement floor. More crates fell from the vibrations of the creature's hefty stride. Angela watched as, one by one, each crate burst open with human remains. Some bones were small, compared to that of a young child's while others were more mature adult bones in size. With one last ditch effort, Angela threw all her weight against the exit door, with all her might, and the door burst open. It wasn't the weight or the force of the impact that caused the door to open, though. Angela collapsed onto the other side of the floor, covered her head with her hands and curled into a fetal position. Angela slowly looked up and on the other side of the door, a man in a maintenance suit stood over her. The door handle was in his left hand, and his right hand was in his pocket.

The maintenance man recognized Angela and said, "Jesus, Angela. What the hell is going on?"

It was Mark, one of the maintenance men of the Ed Hock building. Angela looked up to see Mark standing above her. She slowly took her hand down from her eyes and her face, her voice crackled when she spoke back to him, "I uh, I."

Angela turned to investigate the room of crates, only to see the third-floor hallway of the Ed Hock building just as how she remembered it. There were no wooden crates or spider webs hanging from the ceiling. Nor were there any crates filled with human remains. Most of all, there was no sign of the creature either. Fluorescent tube lights hummed overhead, illuminating the hallway. A window at the end of the hallway cast sunlight into the foyer.

Angela looked around her and realized that she was now on the staircase of the Ed Hock building, with Mark looking down at her. Some people on the third floor opened their office doors to look out into the hallway to see what all the commotion was.

"Angela, what is going on?" Mark asked.

"I, uh, I was stuck in the elevator and eventually the door opened. Where is the floor with all the wooden crates?" Angela asked as she sat up.

"The wooden crates?" Mark asked with a curious look on his face.

"Yes, the wooden crates. It looked like the basement, but the elevator stopped on the 3rd floor and there were wooden crates everywhere. It looked like a large storage area." Angela didn't want to say what was in the wooden crates, though. She was fearful of coming off as crazy. Nor did she want to say anything about her experience. Only validating that there was a floor with wooden crates in it was good enough for her to know she wasn't losing her mind.

"Angela, we don't have anything like that here in this building. You know that. The basement is just a large equipment room. I mean, it's dark down there, sure, but it's a basement. You're on the third floor. There's not much here other than the offices."

Angela stood up in the stairwell, shocked. What did she just experience? Her problem from home followed her to work. It was clearly The Kushtaka, invading her life, trying to take control through its fear inducing tactics. Angela gathered her wits and dusted herself off. Dust and spiderwebs covered her black dress.

"Look!" Angela said. "Dust and spiderwebs on my black dress. That certainly didn't come from this floor."

"Angela, you fell on the floor of the staircase. Hardly anyone uses the staircase. It gets dust and dirty and sure, there are cobwebs here too," Mark replied.

Unconvinced, Angela said, "Thank you for opening the door for me, Mark."

"Are you going to be alright, Angela?"

"Yeah, I'll be fine. I'm just going to take the stairs up to the fourth floor." Angela started walking up the staircase, while Mark looked down the third-floor hallway again.

People went back to work and shut their office doors. Mark slowly closed the door to the stairway. The door banged closed behind him, while Mark descended the staircase down to the first floor. The moment Mark closed the door, though, the room changed back to a large dark floor, without lights or windows. The room was filled with cobwebs, dust, wooden crates stacked one on top of the other. Some wooden crates burst open on the cold concrete floor, revealing dried human bones. The Kushtaka stood there in front of the exit door, brightly illuminated by a glowing red exit sign. The creature's eyes glowed with a fierce bright red color, growling, and breathing deeply. It knew it almost had her.

Angela reached the top of the fourth-floor exit door to the staircase. She reached out, hoping to God that she didn't end up back in the dark room with the wooden crates and the creature again. She grabbed the door handle with her right hand and she gently pulled the door open and looked out into the hallway. At the end of the brightly lit hallway, she noticed the elevator in proper working order. As properly working as it could be. Jose, the janitor for the building, was running the vacuum cleaner in the hallway, as he usually did around 10 a.m. every weekday morning. Angela saw her office door ajar, and from where she was standing in the doorway to the staircase, she spotted Jennifer talking on the phone at the front desk.

Angela breathed a sigh of relief and stepped out into the hallway, ignorant of the fact that a single red glowing eye was peering through a small opening in the door from the third floor. As soon as Angela stepped out onto the fourth floor and the door shut, the door shut to the third floor.

Angela didn't know what she was going to say to Jenn this time. She took her time walking to the office, taking deep breaths. Jose smiled and nodded his head to say hello. Angela wasn't sure if Jose spoke English or not. She had never heard the man speak English. But she wasn't going to speculate if he did or not. Angela acknowledged Jose and said, "Good morning, Jose."

Jose nodded his head up and down and smiled as he said, "Morning."

Angela walked into the office of Marshall and Stone Family Law Firm. Jennifer looked up and saw Angela. She instantly knew from the look on her face that something had happened. Again. Angela walked around the corner of the front desk, sat in her chair, and tucked her purse under her desk. It was already 10:25 a.m.

Jennifer finished speaking with her client, from the sounds of it Angela guessed it was a husband inquiring about divorce after he had found out his wife was involved in a local orgy club in downtown Portland. Jennifer hung the phone up and looked over to Angela.

"Angie, are you okay? You don't look good," Jennifer said.

"No, Jenn. I don't feel too good either."

"What happened? Did something happen after I left the house this morning?"

"Oh yeah. Something sure did."

"Mr. Marshall said that he would just use your sick time to make up for the hours you missed this morning," Jennifer said.

"Okay, that's fine by me."

"So, what happened, Angie?"

Once the phones were quiet for long enough for Angela relayed her experience to Jennifer. She started by explaining the rocking sounds coming from the spare bedroom upstairs, and seeing her grandmother, or what she thought was her grandmother. All the way to laying back down on her bed with her grandmother's quilt and falling back to sleep. And finally, Angela talked about her experience in the Ed Hock Building on the 3rd floor. The fact of the matter was that things were getting worse, and the frequency of events were occurring more frequently.

Jennifer shook her head and said, "Angela, you need to go see the minister. If things continue to get worse, then something bad may happen to you."

Angela paused and said, "Jenn, you're right. I'll see him on my lunch break."

The next two hours seemed to take forever to pass by. Maybe it was because Angela was worried about her situation, her mind focused on figuring out what to do next. What was the right decision to make? Obviously, Jennifer was right. Things seemed to happen more often now, and things were getting worse. True to his word, Jeff came about 20 minutes after Angela sat down with the girl's favorite coffees. Jenn smiled and thanked Jeff, while Angela was talking on the phone, smiling, and mouthing the word thank you to Jeff, while she listened to her client.

Angela handled a couple of phone calls at her desk, setting up appointments for divorce consultations. One was with Mr. Stone and the other was with Mr. Marshall. She gave Mr. Stone the more difficult case assignment. Mr. Stone was always rude to the girls, anyway. He was even rude to his business partner, Mr. Marshall. So, Angela gave him the consult of the woman calling in and claiming that her husband was participating in a gay men's chat room behind her back, and she couldn't live with knowing that her husband was having nearly daily affairs with other men while she worked full time to support their family. His wife had found out because one of the men had come to the couple's home during the evening hours while she was home from work, asking for a private one on one personal session with her husband. The man had thought that she was her husband's secretary.

Soon enough, it was time for lunch at 12:10 p.m. Jenn elected to stay behind and have a late lunch so that Angela could see the minister. Angela thanked her for covering the desk while she went to see the pastor. Angela picked her purse up from the ground and left the office. She walked towards the elevator and thought twice about taking it again. What if the damn thing stopped on the third floor again, and she relived that hell from this morning? Rather than taking the elevator, Angela elected to take the stairs.

She walked towards the staircase exit and opened the door. Stepping onto the staircase, Angela descended the flight of stairs. As she was passing the third floor, she stopped for a moment by the door. She could feel a cold draft blowing from the crack beneath the door and through its frame. She reached her hand out and placed it on the handle of the door. It was ice cold. She squeezed the handle to open it, but an internal instinct told her not to open the door. It was a clear warning to leave the door shut.

Angela placed her other hand flat against the door, and it too was ice cold. Angela released her grip on the handle. She backed up from the door and walked down the flights of stairs down to the first level, never stopping to look behind her and at the door that led to the third floor. She opened the first-floor door with relative ease and walked out into the entryway. She walked towards the entrance of the Ed Hock building and, while leaving, thanked Jeff for bringing her and Jenn their coffee to their desks. Jeff smiled and waved back. Angela walked out of the building and to the parking garage. Getting in her car, she started the ignition and pulled out of her parking space and started her drive to St. Marcus Lutheran Church. It was about a 15-minute drive from where Angela worked, even with traffic. Not bad, considering it was downtown Portland traffic, too.

Angela arrived at the church and was grateful to see the pastor's gold Buick parked in front of the church office at 814 W. Oxford Rd. She pulled her car up next to the pastor's and got out of her vehicle. From where she stood in the parking lot, she could see the old pastor sitting at his desk, with his head down, as he wrote something on a piece of paper.

Angela was grateful that the old man was here today. She walked up to the front door of the pastor's office and knocked. The pastor looked up from his desk and acknowledged Angela with a smile. He got up from behind his desk and walked to the office door. The door opened with an old moan.

"Good afternoon, Angela. What brings you back to me?" the pastor asked.

"Pastor, I'm ready."

"Are you ready?"

"Yes, I am ready to confront The Kushtaka."

CHAPTER 19

It was a cloudy day in the Portland area. There was no rain, some wind, but it was overcast, dark and dreary. The weather report had called for some breaks of sunlight throughout the day, but whatever promises made by the local weathermen had thus far failed to come to fruition.

Angela sat in the pastor's office across from Pastor Teske, separated by an old wooden oak desk. The room was a comfortable temperature, but Angela found herself sweating in places she didn't know she could even sweat. She was nervous. She knew that she had to confront the evil that was in her home, but could she do it alone? She most certainly couldn't. She needed the pastor's help. She needed Jenn's help. The creature was too strong for her. It overwhelmed her emotionally, mentally, and even lately from her dreams, physically.

The small creatures that The Kushtaka commanded also overwhelmed her. Just the sight of the small creatures sent chills up her spine. But here she sat in the minister's office, with no one else to turn to for help. Who else would she call out to for help? The police? What could they do? Would they even believe her? Most certainly they would not. They would think she was a crazed, drunken lunatic for even calling for help for such a thing. Yes, clearly this old pastor was her last hope in ridding her life of this curse. The minister rummaged through a drawer in his desk, pulled out an old silver cross, and set it down on top of the oak desk.

"Angela, I want you to do me a favor."

"Okay, what is it?"

"Do you see that silver cross on the top of this desk, Angela?"

"Yes."

"I want you to pick it up and hold it in your hands."

Angela was dumbfounded by his request, but she obliged. She reached out with her right hand and grabbed the silver cross. Bringing it close to her chest, she grasped the cross with her left hand with relative ease. The minister smiled.

"Angela, you may set down the cross."

"Why did I have to do that?"

"Angela, I needed to make sure. The Kushtaka is a very strong creature and can assimilate into the shape of anything it wants. Even humans. To know I'm talking to the real Angela, I needed to be sure. The Kushtaka can't encounter Christian religious artifacts or relics. For me to know that I'm talking to the real Angela, I needed to test you."

"Oh, well, it's the real me," Angela said, annoyed.

"I'm sorry, my dear. Believe me, it's for your own protection that I just make sure."

"Alright."

"Angela, I'm happy to help you and I'm glad that you came to me today. The longer that you wait to address this problem and rid yourself of it, the harder it is to get rid of The Kushtaka. The longer you wait, the more it comes to control your life."

Angela broke down in tears. As usual, she was scared, worried, and nervous about what the future would hold for her. She remembered a time when she wasn't so scared. So many years ago, on her wedding day. The day that she thought that this was what it meant to be a woman. To be cared for and comforted for. To depend on her husband through thick and thin. To rely on that steadfast rock. But when that rock drifted away from her, she felt fear and wondered what she had done with her life. Just recently, in buying her home, Angela felt what it was like to be an independent woman. She could do it, but now, after all that had happened, she was as certain as she once was before. Covering her face from the pastor, Angela cried tears not of sadness, but of despair. Tears of fear and uncertainty.

"I understand, pastor. Believe me, I want to rid myself of this creature. I want my life back. I need my life back."

"And I will help you, my dear, but you and I need to be on the same page when we work together about this."

"What do you mean?"

"Angela, this is going to require a full commitment on your part. I need to make sure that you are fully vested in this."

"Oh, believe me, pastor, I'm fully vested. You have no idea what I've been experiencing lately. First subtle little instances in my home, then outside of my home. I had an experience at work this morning. It's hard to explain, but things have even been following me to my work." Angela hung her head down, her eyes downcast towards the floor between her chair and the desk. "Things are getting worse, and I'm scared."

"Everyone is scared, Angela. Some for different reasons than others. The first thing you need to do for yourself is to admit that it's okay to be scared. Being scared can potentially save your life. All that you need to do is know in your heart that this is what you are ready for. From the sounds of it, not a moment later either."

"Yes, I am ready for this, pastor."

With that, the old minister stood up from behind his desk and walked over to his library. He pulled out a book from the middle shelf. The color of the book was faded, yet another old book from an old minister. Angela was certain this book had seen better days. The pastor turned around and walked back to his desk, setting the book down on the desktop with a thud. The old man sat in his chair that creaked under his body weight. Scooting the chair forward, the minister opened the book. The binding of the book cracked under the pressure of being opened after so many years spent closed on the shelf. Pastor Teske flipped through the pages of the book, careful not to miss a paragraph from skimming over the text. The old minister found the pages he was looking for, a quarter of the way into the book.

"Yes, this is it."

"What's that?" Angela asked.

"This is what we will need to do. To rid the home of evil, we need to go through each room of the house, blessing the room in the name of the Father, and of the Son, and of the Holy Spirit. We need to bless the rooms and instruct the evil that in the name of God that evil is not welcomed there. We need to do this around the property, and room by room."

Angela knew that this would be a difficult task. The home she was sure was fine, but the spare bedroom upstairs… The room where everything seemed to emanate from. There was something about the room that set the house off. Nevertheless, Angela believed that it would work.

"Alright, let's do it," Angela said.

The minister stood up from his desk again, walked over to the bookshelf, but this time he removed an old wooden jewelry chest. Opening the box, the minister pulled out a silver crucifix cross pendent attached to a silver chain.

"Angela, for your protection while we do this, I've noticed you aren't wearing any signs of the Christian faith. For your safety, I want you to wear this cross, knowing that Christ is your savior, and God will protect you from all harm that could potentially come your way. Will you wear the cross?"

Out of options, Angela said, "Yes, pastor. I'll wear it."

The pastor set the box down on his desk. Taking the necklace with the pendant attached, he draped the chain around her neck. The silver crucifix was only the size of a half dollar and landed peacefully on her chest.

"Thank you for your help, pastor." Breaking out in tears, Angela said, "I don't know what else to do."

The pastor kneeled next to Angela, placed his hand on her shoulder, and said, "Angela, it's not by our own works, that we can get ourselves out of the worldly problems that we encounter, but it is by the works of God. Our trust and faith in him are what support us on this earth. You need to remember this when we work on ridding your home of this creature."

Wiping the tears from her face with the back of her hand, Angela said, "I'll try."

Satisfied, the pastor stood up and sat back down in his chair at the desk.

"Angela, we can do this together whenever you are ready for it."

"I want to do this on Saturday."

Astonished, the minister asked, "Angela, wouldn't you like this sooner rather than later?"

"Yes, I would, but I can't, pastor. I would love to go home and take care of this right now, but I must work today. I already let my boss down by showing up late. Just not coming back to work would be the end of my time there, I'm sure."

"Angela, when you are ready then I will be too."

"Alright, then Saturday in the afternoon, if that's okay."

"That's fine, but Angela, do me a favor and do not stay in the home tonight. Do you have a friend whom you can stay with for the night?

"Yes, I do. Jenn. She's invited me over a couple of times already because of the problems with that house."

"Then stay there. Be careful, Angela. Hold this cross tight to yourself. The power of God will help to protect you, but we need to take care of this sooner rather than later, before it becomes too strong of an influence in your life. Hold this cross tight to yourself and place your faith in God. He will protect you."

"I understand, pastor. Thank you."

The pastor stood up and walked around the corner of his desk. Angela stood up and gave the old minister a hug. She wiped the tears from her face with the back of her hand, sniffling. She turned to leave the minister's office.

"Angela."

Angela turned to face the minister again, who was standing by the old oak desk.

"Angela, have faith in God that he will make all things right. He will use you as an instrument to fight the forces of evil. You are special, Angela. You are a child of God. He won't disappoint you."

Angela smiled, thanked the pastor and walked out the office door. It closed with a thud behind her. She walked back to her car and went back to work. The traffic was getting heavy at the end of her lunch hour. She hit the rush of traffic of other commuters trying to get back to work after their lunch. The onset of traffic caused Angela to be a little late getting back to work herself.

After parking her car in her parking spot at the office, Angela walked into the Ed Hock building and took the stairs again, avoiding the elevator. Angela rushed up the stairs, reaching the fourth-floor landing. She reached out and opened the door, when she heard a door on the third-floor slam shut.

Startled, Angela stopped in her tracks. Taking her hand off the handle of the fourth-floor door, she looked behind her where she saw the third level door below her. The sound of the slamming door was close, Angela knew this hadn't been an echo from downstairs, the sound of the door was directly behind her.

Angela stood at the top of the stairs and watched the third level door for a moment. Instinctively waiting to hear a bellowing growl from an angry bull, or even see the door crack open slightly, to reveal a set of glowing eyes looking back at her. The door, however, never opened. And the sounds of she expected never came. All she heard were the sounds of businesses that faintly echoed up and down the staircase. Angela turned back around and opened the fourth level door and walked into the hallway. The door shut behind her.

In the hallway, Angela walked up to her station. She thought she was about 10 minutes late, but then remembered that she had left late for lunch, anyway. She wasn't late at all. Jennifer saw her coming in and grabbed her purse from under the desk.

"Hey Angie, did you see the minister?"

"Yes, I did. He's going to come out tomorrow to work on cleansing the home."

"Good!"

"Jenn, I know you're going to lunch, but I need a favor from you that I can talk to you about when you get back."

"Oh, just ask me now. I don't like the anticipation of waiting, Angie."

"Well, since the minister is coming tomorrow, would it be alright if I stayed at your place tonight? The minister said it might be a good idea after I had told him all that's been happening to me lately."

"Yes, that's fine!" Jennifer said happily. "You're always welcome in my home, Angie."

"Jenn, thank you so much. You've been such a good friend to me. I love you."

"I love you too, Angie. But I'm going to head to lunch. I'm starving. I'm going down to El Rincon to try their new taco salad that they have on their menu. Want me to bring you back something?"

"That would be sweet. I didn't have time to pick something up. Just get me whatever you're getting, and I'll pay you when you get back."

"Okay, I will."

Jennifer clutched her purse to her side, swinging the shoulder strap over her shoulder. Jenn walked out of the office, leaving Angela alone at the front desk. Angela started her computer back up when she heard a sound of a filing cabinet behind her. It was Mr. Marshall.

"Hi, Angela."

"Hi, Mr. Marshall."

"Listen, I'm heading out to do a field meeting this morning with a client, and Mr. Stone is in court this afternoon. He left while you were out of the office, so can you and Jennifer run the place while we're both gone this afternoon?"

"That's what you hired us to do." Angela smiled.

Mr. Marshall laughed. "Yes, we did. And you two do a great job. Believe me, I don't know where Mr. Stone or I would be without your guys' help. You both do great."

"Thank you, Mr. Marshall."

"Well, I need to be on my way soon. Angie, if there's an emergency and a client needs to get ahold of me immediately give my cell phone a call, otherwise just schedule face-to-face meetings like you normally would."

"Will do, Mr. Marshall."

Mr. Marshall grabbed some files from an old gray metal filing cabinet behind her desk. Mr. Marshall and Mr. Stone kept the files up front for the girls to access when they needed them to schedule appointments and meetings appropriately. For nearly the last 20 years, that plan worked out perfectly, too. Mr. Marshall went back to his desk and set his files down. He quickly threw his overcoat on, took the files, and stuffed them into a brown leather satchel. Mr. Marshall always carried his files in his satchel when he went out to visit clients in the field. After that, Mr. Marshall walked out of his office, shut the door behind him and left, saying goodbye to Angela on the way out.

Angela was alone again. The office was eerily silent. A ticking clock emanated from Mr. Stone's office. It was peculiar because it seemed like everyone these days was clamoring for legal advice to divorce their partners. Angela sat at the desk, clicking through emails and wasting time when the phone rang. Angela looked at the caller ID on the phone's handset. It read unknown.

"Marshall and Stone Family Law, this is Angela. How can I help you?"

Silence lingered on the other end of the phone.

"Hello?" Angela said.

"Hello?" a woman replied.

"Hi, this is Angela with Marshall and Stone Family Law. Can I help you?"

"Yes, you may," the voice said.

"What can I do for you?"

"I need to divorce my husband," the voice said quietly.

"Why? What's the nature of the problem?"

"He's cheating on me," the woman said.

It sounded all too familiar to Angela. Even she had been in this poor woman's shoes before.

"What is he doing?" Angela asked as she was typing notes on her computer.

"Well, he's seeing someone younger than me. He works in an office, and I found out that he's seeing this girl that just recently graduated from school."

Ironic. That's exactly what happened to Angela too.

"Okay, so you would like legal advice for filing for divorce with your husband?"

"Yes."

"Okay, what is your name?"

"Angela."

Angela stopped for a moment. Nevertheless, she couldn't be the only woman in the Portland area that shared her name.

"Okay, well what's your address?"

"1487 Evans Dr.," the woman replied.

Hearing her old address shocked Angela. Was this a joke? Or did someone move there with the same name and the same problem that she experienced?

"Umm, what's your husband's name?" Angela asked in a reserved manner.

"His name is Todd Kennedy."

"Is this a joke?" Angela asked. "Because if this is a joke, this is bullshit!"

"No, ma'am, this is no joke," the woman replied. "My husband and I have lived here for years. We would always spend Saturday evenings snuggling on the couch and watching a movie together. Or, during the holidays, we'd always decorate the home together for Christmas. We'd put the tree by the window with the lights on so that people could see it as they drove by. We'd always go up into the mountains to get our fresh tree with our friends too. But those days are long gone. Never coming back. There's no hope for me. Nothing that I can do. I can't subtract my age by 20 years, and I can't grow a set of perky breasts that he likes or lose weight like he likes."

Angela realized that what this woman was saying to her over the phone, word for word, clearly mirrored her own life and feelings.

The woman continued, "The bottom line will be that I'm never going to be good enough. Never for him. Never for anyone. I would disappoint all my friends if I had any friends. I disappointed my parents and now I'm stuck in this clerical job answering the phone for a law firm. Look at that, I have a fuckin college degree and all I'm doing with the thing is answering phones."

The woman laughed on the other end of the phone, but the laugh didn't seem like it came from the woman. The laugh was deep, harsh, and dark. Angela sat in her desk chair, no longer asking questions to gather information about this client to schedule an appointment. She was not listening, as if she was under the speaker's control.

"Anyway, so now I'm living in this home that I have no control over. Beautiful as it may be, I don't own a home. Something else does. And on top of this all, there is nothing I can do to save myself from this home. From what lives on this property. I'm helpless. I can't do it on my own. Eventually the home is going to consume me too because I'm too weak to do things for myself, and I deserve to be a part of this hell for all eternity. And I think the thing that hurts the most is that I know for a fact that my grandmother is disappointed in the person I've become. I know she hates me. She died while I was in college, and I didn't even care. She made me this quilt, a multi-colored quilt, and it's all that I have left of her. But she hates me too."

Angela slammed the phone down, ending the call. In tears, Angela knew the caller wasn't a real client looking for legal advice. It was the same thing that had been harassing her since she moved. The pastor even said that the forces that were following her would only get stronger and stronger, to drive her deeper and deeper into sadness and depression before it finally just came and took her. The phone rang again. Angela looked at the caller ID and discovered another unknown number.

Angela's heart was in her throat. Was this force calling her back to continue to harass her and bring her down even more than she already was? Angela drifted her hand over the receiver, questioning whether she was going to answer the phone again. With each ring of the phone, the phone grew louder, and Angela grew more hesitant to answer. Angela slowly placed her hand on the receiver and was about to pick it up when she heard a loud thump right next to her. It was Jennifer, coming back from lunch with two taco salads in hand.

"Angie, are you going to answer that?"

Angela looked at Jennifer with a blank stare in her eye.

"I uh. Actually, can you get in Jenn? I'm sorry. I need to go use the restroom."

"Umm, sure," Jennifer said.

Angela quickly stood up from the front desk and walked into the bathroom and shut the door behind her. She walked over to the sink, breathing heavily as she placed both hands on the edge of the sink, bracing some of her body weight with her arms and hands. Cool water poured out of the faucet as Angela pulled some paper towels from the dispenser. She wet the towels with the cool water and dabbed her face and forehead. Angela couldn't believe what she had heard. Was that a real call? Was that a joke someone was pulling on her? Or was it something else?

The way things were going lately for Angela, she leaned towards the latter option. Whatever this creature was, its force was undeniable. It was boldly putting itself deeper and deeper into Angela's life. And the scary thing is that Angela knew it. Tomorrow couldn't arrive fast enough. Angela had the fear that she may not make it to tomorrow. Lost, and with nowhere else to turn, Angela lowered herself onto her knees, crying into the cool towel as she began to pray. She prayed to God right there in the bathroom for strength, but also for help and safety. She knew that The Kushtaka was strong, and above all else, it wanted her.

After she finished praying, Angela stood up at the sink, using it to pull herself up from the floor. She threw the paper towels away and grabbed another handful of towels. She wet those with cool water and again washed her face with them, taking some makeup off with it. Taking some deep breaths and regaining her composure, she walked out of the bathroom and back into the office. Jennifer could tell that there was something wrong instantly, no matter how much Angela tried to hide it.

"Angie, what's wrong?"

"Nothing. Thanks for grabbing that call."

"It was no problem."

"Who was it?" Angela asked.

"Oh, it was weird," Jennifer replied. "I answered the phone, and no one was on the other end. It was completely dead. I've been waiting for whoever it was to call back, but they haven't yet. Are you sure you're, okay? You look anxious."

"Yes, Jenn. I'm fine. Thank you for asking."

Angela sat down in her chair at her desk and continued to work the rest of the afternoon with her partner and friend. They both ate their taco salads from El Rincon Mexican restaurant. It was a little spicy for Angela, but she made do with a glass of water. Jennifer had always enjoyed spicy foods, so she never gave any thought to asking the restaurant to make one salad a little milder than the other.

Mr. Marshall returned to the office later in the afternoon, greeting both girls on the way back in and reminded them as he always did of how much he appreciated them and what they did for the firm. Shortly after Mr. Marshall came back to the office, Mr. Stone came back. He walked briskly by the girls at the front desk, not even acknowledging them.

Mr. Stone had always been that way, so even so much as a hello from him would have been out of character for him. He went straight to his office and shut the door behind him, just like usual. 5 p.m. came quickly and eventually it was time to close up business for the day, and ultimately the weekend.

This weekend would change Angela's life. This was the weekend that she would get back to a normal life. As normal as it could be, with the help of an old minister. The phones were dead silent for the last hour of the day. Angela and Jennifer got lost in conversation about the newest issue of Cosmo. They discussed a new color of mascara that Jenn was thinking about trying for herself, and a clearance sale at a local clothing shop that the girls were planning to visit in the next couple of weeks. It was the first time in a long time that Angela lost herself in normal conversation. It was nice for a change to not talk about the supernatural and all the strange occurrences in her life for once.

"Angie, it's 5 p.m. Already. This afternoon went by fast!" Jennifer said.

"Yes, it did. Jenn, thanks again for letting me stay with you this evening."

"Hey, I'm happy to have you! We can continue talking about clothes when we get back to my place for the evening. You think you might want to go out tonight, too?"

"No, I just want to rest and relax before tomorrow. I want to be physically and mentally prepared for this. I know if I go out tonight, that won't happen. I just want as normal of a night as I can get."

"Okay, no problem, Angie. Hey, we should order pizza tonight and watch a movie then!"

"Okay." Angela laughed. "I will meet you halfway on that one. We can order pizza and watch a movie."

"Great! Sounds fun!" Jennifer smiled.

Jennifer was so full of life and energy, Angela thought. A little part of Angela wanted to go out. After talking with Jennifer in the afternoon about normal things, going out seemed to be something that Angela was missing in her life. Her life over the past few months had been completely focused on the happenings going on in her own home. It was disheartening, but soon she would be rid of the problem in her life, and she could finally get to living life the way she wanted to. All with the help of this minister, she could get her life back. As 5 p.m. came and went on a Friday evening, so did Angela and Jennifer.

They picked up their purses and set them on the front desk. They placed their phones on auto-answer for the weekend and grabbed their purses and walked out the doors of the building, wishing Mr. Marshall a good weekend while they walked by his office. Mr. Marshall looked up, smiled and wished the girls a happy weekend as well.

"You girls have a good weekend, too! Angie, if there's anything that you need, give me a call, okay?" Mr. Marshall said.

Angela smiled and said, "Thank you, Mr. Marshall. I appreciate that."

The girls walked by the office of the salty Mr. Stone. His door was shut and they could barely see through the blinds where Mr. Stone had his head tilted down at his desk, signing papers to file with the courts. Angela and Jennifer left the office and while in the hallway, Angela turned to look back at her office, knowing that the next time she saw the office and that desk she worked at, her life was going to be normal again. The sooner the better, too.

The girls both took the stairs down to the first floor. Angela was still hesitant to take the elevator. Once on the first floor the girls walked to the exit, waving goodbye to Jeff the barista as they went by. Jeff waved back as he was cleaning up his coffee stand and preparing to leave soon as well.

"You can follow me back to my place," Jennifer said.

"Okay, but don't go so fast, Jenn. Your apartment isn't going anywhere," Angela said.

"Please, I don't drive that fast," Jennifer replied.

Angela got into her car first and started it up before Jenn got in hers. In no time, Jennifer had her car started and moved out of the parking garage and towards the exit of the parking lot. Angela sped to keep up with her the whole way back to her apartment.

CHAPTER 20

"I thought I told you not to speed on your way home?" Angela asked.

"I didn't, you just can't keep up with me." Jennifer smiled.

The girls parked their cars at Jennifer's apartment. It was a nice three level apartment complex. Jennifer found herself on the top floor, with a beautiful view of the river from her balcony. It was a nice one bedroom, one bathroom, and the building was newly built. It was a very modern apartment.

Both girls grabbed their purses from their cars, locked their cars, and walked up the stairs to Jennifer's apartment. Jennifer talked the whole way up the stairs about what movies they could find on the internet to watch. Before they knew it, they were both upstairs and outside her apartment's front door. Jennifer rummaged through her purse for her keys. She found them, brought them out of her purse, but instantly dropped them on the ground.

"Damn," Jennifer said. "I always drop my keys every time I try to find them to get into my apartment."

"Well, if you didn't have so many keys on your key chain, you wouldn't fumble with them so much," Angela replied.

"Well, I need all these keys. This key is for my parent's house, then this one for their garage. This one is for…"

Angela cut off Jennifer mid-sentence, "Jenn, just open the door."

"Oh, right."

Finding the right key to her apartment, Jennifer unlocked the front door and opened it. They walked into the small apartment, one bedroom, third-level apartment of a three-level complex, but it wasn't uncomfortably small. There was still plenty of space to roam around, even if two people lived there. A decent sized living room occupied most of the square footage, along with a decent sized bathroom, and kitchen with a small nook that contained a small dining room table for two. There was a small hallway that led to a bathroom on the right, and to the left, opposite the bathroom, was the bedroom.

A large four-sided wall stood right in the middle of the apartment, separating the living room from the kitchen and the front door. Almost like a pillar, as they could still walk around the structure in the apartment. Why it was there? Jennifer never knew. Unless it was to add another wall to the living room, but beyond that, the large pillar was simply in the way. Jennifer did her best to make use of it. On the living room side, she added a nice picture of Klamath Falls, and on the kitchen side of the wall she added a nice wall hanger to hang all her kitchen utensils. The apartment was spotless, though. Everything was organized and in proper order. Nothing seemed to be out of place. Jennifer even had a couple of plants in the living room.

"Angie, do you want to go back to your place really quick to get some clothes for tonight, or would you like to just use the clothes you have here?" Jennifer asked.

"To be honest, Jenn, I'd rather just use what clothing I have here. I really don't want to go back to that home without the pastor there with me. The next time I go home, he and I are going to rid it of whatever those creatures are," Angela replied.

"Alright. You want to go shopping? Or just want to order a pizza and a movie?"

Angela set her purse down on the coffee table and sat down on the living room couch.

"Let's just order pizza and find a movie to watch." Said Angela.

"Okay." Said Jennifer.

Jennifer went into her bedroom and set her purse down on the vanity in her room. Jenn's bedroom was quite large compared to the rest of the apartment. She was able to squeeze a king-sized bed into the room. When Angela stayed the night with Jenn after a long day of shopping, or just hanging out, she always thought that Jennifer's bed was far more comfortable than her own, too. After setting her purse down in her bedroom, Jennifer quickly got undressed and changed into a pair of pajamas early. After Jennifer was in her pajamas, she left the bedroom.

Angela stood up and took her purse to Jennifer's bedroom and looked through the bottom vanity drawer. She found herself a set of pajamas that she had kept at Jennifer's place, just for such an evening. It was easier for Angela to keep some clothes at Jenn's place. That way, she wouldn't have to drive back and forth to her house and then back to Jenn's place. Angela changed into the set of pajamas she had found and walked back out into the living room.

"Angie, what kind of pizza do you want to order?" Jennifer asked as she sat back in a leather recliner.

Angela sat back down on the couch and said, "Oh, I'm okay with anything that has pineapple on it. And order some cheese bread too. That sounds good."

"Oh, that does sound good. Okay, so how about a pepperoni, pineapple, and jalapeno pizza, with cheese bread sticks?" Jennifer asked.

"Yes, that sounds good. Like sweet and spicy."

"Okay."

Angela got up and walked to the kitchen to get herself a glass of water while Jennifer got her phone. Angela could hear Jennifer dialing the number to a local pizzeria, and placing an order for a large pineapple, pepperoni, and jalapeno pizza.

"Don't forget the cheese bread sticks!" Angela yelled from the kitchen.

"Oh, and cheese bread sticks," Jennifer said over the phone. "Angie, with what kind of dip?"

"Blue cheese and marinara," Angela replied.

"With blue cheese and marinara," Jennifer said. "Okay, $21.87. How long will it be before it gets here this evening?"

Angela stood in silence in the living room with her glass of water.

"30-35 minutes," Jennifer said. "Alright, we will see you in half an hour. Thank you!"

Jennifer hung up the phone and looked at Angela. "Well, I guess now we gotta find a movie to watch. Do you want to find a movie on television, or order one from online?"

"Either or, Jenn. I'm okay with whatever. Do you want to look online first and see if there's something that looks interesting?"

"Sure! I'll try to find something to watch."

Jennifer turned her TV on and began flipping through the online movie channels. Angela walked back into the kitchen, finished her glass of water and set her glass on the counter next to the sink. Angela paused for a moment, placing her hands on the counter, and looked into the sink's drain. She stared into the deep, dark hole. She couldn't see the bottom of the drain, reminding her of the well behind the fence. Angela was mesmerized for a moment, staring into the dark abyss of the drain. Then she had heard her name being called. For a moment, Angela thought it sounded as if her name was being called from within the drain. Her name was called again, and Angela snapped out of her daze. Turning around in the kitchen, she saw Jennifer standing behind her.

"You, okay?" Jennifer asked.

Angela took a deep breath, turned back around to grab her glass from the counter.

"Yes, I was just getting some more water," Angela replied.

"Oh, okay. Hey, I found a movie on one of the internet channels. It's one that we've talked about going to see in the theaters a little while back, but I found it on one of the movie channels. Want to watch?"

"Yes, I'll be right there."

Angela refilled her glass with cold water, walked into the living room, and sat down on the couch. Jennifer was right, Angela saw that the movie she found was a sappy romantic comedy, but it was a movie that they had wanted to see in the movie theater, but just never got around to. Ever since she knew her, Jennifer always had access to movie channels on the internet that streamed to her TV that may not have been "legally" obtained. Angela never asked questions though, and Jennifer never talked about how she got these channels and internet links. She just got them.

The pizza, sure as promised, arrived half an hour after Jennifer placed the order. Angela got some money out of her wallet, and Jennifer covered the rest of the bill. The girls ate their pizza and watched their movie, like life was normal, like how things had always been before. A time when Angela could simply be a girl and enjoy her evenings without having to worry about what was lurking in the dark corners of her own home. Not having to worry about a spare bedroom, or what was behind her fence on her property, was liberating. For once, Angela could relax and have fun with her friend. After the movie, the girls talked and laughed until it was late in the evening.

"Goodness, it's 11 p.m.!" Jennifer said.

"It is late. I have a big day tomorrow too. Want to head to bed? In the morning, I'll give the minister a call and figure out what time he wants to go out to the house," Angela said.

"That sounds good. I'm happy for you, Angie."

"Why is that?"

"Well, tomorrow you finally get your life back. You should have got it back when you bought that house to begin with, but now you're going to get it back for sure. I'm happy for you."

Angela smiled and said, "Thank you."

Jennifer returned the smile and gave Angela a hug.

"I'm going to turn things off. You want to head to the bedroom? I'll be there in a minute."

Jennifer began shutting the lights and the TV off, while Angela walked down the hallway to the bedroom. Before going into the bedroom, Angela turned and walked into the bathroom. She had a toothbrush that she kept over at Jennifer's place as well, just how Jennifer had personal effects at her house and in her bathroom as well.

Angela brushed her teeth while Jennifer walked into the bathroom to brush her teeth as well. After Angela finished, she left Jennifer in the bathroom and walked into the bedroom. The king-sized bed she knew was so comfortable, warm, and roomy. One day Angela was going to get her own king-sized bed, too. She sat in her corner of the bed, closer to the window than the bedroom's door. Sitting there, Angela felt nervous about what tomorrow might bring.

In her entire life, Angela never thought that she would be a part of anything like this. It was quite overwhelming for her, and as much as she loved Jennifer, she knew that she wouldn't be able to really share her feelings about what needed to be done tomorrow. She wouldn't understand. She never lived in a home that had such an ill-fated past, with a negative atmosphere strengthened by death and sadness. Angela stood up from the mattress, pushed the sheets back and crawled into bed. Just when she laid her head down on the pillow, Jennifer walked into the bedroom. Shutting the door behind her, she flipped the lights off and walked over to her side of the bed. Crawling in under the cover, Jennifer's head hit the pillow, and she was out like a light.

Angela never knew how she could fall asleep so fast. Maybe she could fall asleep so fast because she wasn't experiencing so much stress or anxiety in her life from really anything. Maybe after tomorrow Angela could feel the same way, too. Maybe. Angela turned her back towards Jennifer in the bed and faced the window of the room. Slowly Angela relaxed her body and drifted away to sleep, quickly praying that tomorrow would be the beginning of a new day for her.

*   *   *   *

Jennifer's eyes opened, facing the alarm clock on her bedstand on the side of her bed. The time on the clock read 3:02 a.m. in bright, bold red numbers. Jennifer looked over to her right and saw that Angela was still fast asleep in the bed, facing towards her. Jennifer looked up at the ceiling. Moving the covers to the middle of the bed, Jennifer swung her legs off the mattress and sat on the corner of the bed. She took her hands, rubbed her eyes a little, and then her face.

Taking a deep breath, Jennifer stood up. Her feet were standing comfortably on the soft carpet. She walked to the bedroom door and opened it. Stepping out into the hallway, Jennifer walked to the kitchen to get a glass of water. There was a low humming noise coming from the refrigerator. A small blue night light in the kitchen's corner illuminated the front entryway, as well as the kitchen. Jennifer opened the cupboard where she kept her drinking glasses and grabbed a glass. Turning the faucet onto cold, she placed the glass under the running water and filled her glass. Turning the faucet off, she drank her water while standing at the sink in the kitchen. After finishing her water, she set the glass down on the countertop and walked back to the bedroom when she heard something coming from behind her. The sound wasn't coming from the kitchen, more so from the front door.

"What is that sound?" Jennifer asked herself.

She walked back through the kitchen, turning the corner of the kitchen and looked towards the front door. Jennifer stopped to listen when she heard the sound again. Looking at the door, Jennifer began to panic when she saw it was the doorknob. Someone was messing with it from the other side of the door. Jennifer's eyes grew large, and she felt her heart thumping in her chest. Panic set in, and Jennifer didn't know what to do. She knew that the door was locked. The deadbolt and the doorknob itself. She walked towards the front door, careful not to make any sound while she moved. A small light from the outside of the apartment gleamed through the door's peephole. Jennifer stepped up to the entryway and placed her hands on the door. She braced herself as she prepared to look through the peephole. Closing her left eye, she looked out the peephole with her right eye.

She saw nothing. No one was there. How could that be? Jennifer knew what she heard and even thought she saw the doorknob moving. Was it possible that she had just imagined all that? Jennifer took a step back from the door, gathered herself, and began walking back to her bedroom. She had to have just imagined it. It was in that moment, though, that the front door of the apartment unlatched and slowly opened. Jennifer panicked. She darted behind the wall and faced the hallway to her open bedroom, where Angela was sound asleep. Jennifer's eyes opened wide. She didn't know what to do but brace her back against the side of the wall and wait to hear what was going to happen.

The front door slowly squeaked open, and a blast of chilly night air flooded the apartment. Jennifer had to force herself to control her breathing. She couldn't let whoever was ther know where she was in the apartment. The squeaking stopped, and a chill ran up Jennifer's spine as she heard the sound of heavy footsteps enter her apartment. Dense clopping steps bounded off the hardwood floor.

Jennifer stood frozen in fear and silence. The hoof steps sounded from the opposite side of the pillar she was standing behind. Whatever was outside the door that she couldn't see before was clearly in the apartment. She wanted to yell out for Angela, but worried it would clearly give away her position. Could she run back to the bedroom, shut, and lock the bedroom door? Even if she could make it, what would she do then? She could call for help. Her cell phone was back in the bedroom, but would this intruder break the door down and get her and a sleeping Angela by the time she called out for help?

Jennifer truly felt helpless as she saw the intruder's shadow cast across the kitchen's wall in front of her. A blue silhouette of a tall being with thick legs that bent awkwardly at the knee, with a large chest and long arms that hung below its waistline, moved across the wall. Jennifer stared at the shadow, terror-stricken. Long appendages that resembled horns curved out of the intruder's head.

The intruder moved in Jennifer's direction. The shadow grew against the kitchen's wall. Jennifer clung to the wall facing the hallway. As the intruder drew closer to her, she heard heavy breathing. Breathing that sounded inhumanely deep, like a bull. The intruder was right around the corner of the wall. Warm breath grazed her face. She knew she needed to work her way around the corner of the pillar in silence. Slowly Jennifer moved towards the living room, careful not to make any noise as she clutched the pillar.

She heard the utensils on the other side of the pillar moving. She knew the intruder was right around that corner. Soon it would be in clear view of her if she didn't get around the corner of the pillar in time. Jennifer clutched the wall, easing herself around the corner of the pillar as the intruder walked out from the kitchen and into the dining room nook. Jennifer turned the corner of the pillar and, just as she was drawing her second leg from around the corner, the floor squeaked beneath her feet, revealing her position.

The intruder stopped and stood still in the dining room nook and growled as it turned to look at the wall where Jennifer was just moments ago. On the other side of the pillar, Jennifer stood quietly, facing the living room. The front door was wide open and cold air flowed into the apartment. Jennifer felt the chilly draft breeze across her body. Doing the best to control her breathing, she clutched the wall and continued to listen to the intruder. The intruder walked down the hallway of the apartment and towards the bedroom where Angela was fast asleep.

Jennifer saw the intruder's back as he trotted down the hallway. She was shocked and confused by what she was looking at. Was it a man? A bull? Its legs were hairy like a bull's, and it had muscular legs with hooves for feet. The intruder's arms hung low, well below its waist. The back and torso of the beast were thick and muscular. However, it was the head of the creature she would never forget. Terrifying horns protruded from its skull. The beast snarled an otherworldly growl that could freeze a human's soul. With each step from the intruder, a loud thump followed until the intruder turned the corner and walked into Jennifer's bedroom where Angela remained asleep.

"My God, Angela," Jennifer said under her breath.

What was she supposed to do? Yell for help? If she did, though, surely the beast was large enough to kill her with ease, or at the very least, seriously maim her. Jennifer had to think quick, worried about Angela's safety. Silence fell over the apartment. There were no more sounds of walking from the intruder, nor heavy thumps from its footsteps. Angela wasn't even snoring as she usually did. Sheer silence fell over the apartment.

It was the silence that scared Jennifer into action. With no other options left, she ran down the hallway towards her bedroom. Maybe if she woke Angela up, the two of them could get out of the apartment before the beast got them. Jennifer didn't know what else to do. As Jennifer neared the door to her bedroom, dread overcame her. It was very possible that the creature was standing outside of the bedroom, waiting for her to come to it. Jennifer took that chance though as she turned the corner and yelled, "Angela!"

Jennifer stood in the doorway of her bedroom, shocked, as she saw Angela sleeping soundly. But a second body was also lying in the bed. It was herself. Jennifer looked at her sleeping self lying peacefully on the bed. A gentle smile formed on sleeping Jennifer's face, and her light breathing created a slight snoring sound, barely audible to the human ear from where Jennifer stood in the doorway.

It was clear to her that she was dreaming again. But why? What was the meaning of this dream? As Jennifer was breathing deep, trying to control her breath, she heard the front door to the apartment open again. Jennifer stood in silence as she turned and peeked around the corner of the bedroom door. She watched as the front door slowly opened and two small gangly creatures walked into her apartment. Jennifer gasped. She had seen these creatures before in her dream back at Angela's home.

Their yellow eyes shined like two bright orbs in the darkness. Their bodies were only two or three feet tall at the most. Their arms hung low towards the ground, long and bony, with no meat on them that ended in a hand with long narrow fingers and claws nearly dragging on the floor. The two creatures didn't see Jennifer as she watched them both walk into the apartment. Eerie sounds of clicking and high-pitched vocal chatter came from them, as if they were communicating in a language with one another only they could understand.

They walked into the apartment and around the pillar that separated the living room from the kitchen and the front door. Careful not to make a sound, Jennifer shut the bedroom door and locked it as quietly as she could. Panic set in. She felt her heart pounding against the side of her chest. The lock to the bedroom door made a clicking noise when its mechanism was engaged to lock.

Jennifer prayed that the creatures didn't hear the sound. Sher turned and ran to the bed. She grabbed her sleeping body by the shoulders and shook her lifeless body, trying to wake her up. But it was to no avail. Jennifer took a step back from her body because she thought she had heard something. She stood frozen in the bedroom, staring down at her lifeless body.

Jennifer heard clicking coming from the hardwood floor down the hallway. It sounded like a dog with long nails walking on the hardwood floor. The two small creatures she saw enter her apartment skittered down the hallway toward the bedroom. Their unearthly chatter was faint, and the only sounds in Jennifer's ear. She knew they were drawing close to the bedroom door. Jennifer ran around the bed and grabbed Angela by the shoulders. She tried her best to shake Angela awake, but she also refused to wake up.

Jennifer quietly called Angela by her name while she shook her. Claws scratched against the bedroom door, splintering the wood as they dragged their nails down the door. Jennifer panicked. She said Angela's name louder and shook her harder and harder. She had to wake up, but she wouldn't. Jennifer turned to look at the bedroom door and spotted a tiny hand reach underneath the door. Long claws on their fingers gripped the inside of the door, digging into the wood, cutting through the door's white paint, trying to pull it open. Jennifer turned back to Angela and cried, yelling her name as she shook her violently.

"Angela, please wake up!" Jennifer screamed through fearful tears. She didn't know what else to do.

Jennifer turned once more, and the hand under the door was gone. The creatures relentlessly clawed at it from the other side, trying to tear their way through. The door creaked and moaned under the pressure applied by the creatures. Jennifer continued to scream at Angela to wake up. She was shaking Angela so hard that Angela's body was bouncing up and down on the bed.

Jennifer saw both the creatures' faces, peering through holes in the door that they had clawed out. Their yellow amber eyes glowed brightly while they stared at her. The smiles on their faces were wide and unearthly, revealing teeth that came to a point. The high-pitched chattering noise they were making to communicate with one another was accompanied by demonic laughing. Jennifer turned back to Angela and continued to shake her as she screamed for her to wake up.

The door finally gave way and the creatures burst into the room. Angela woke up violently, inhaling loudly. Her eyes were wide open, staring at the bedroom door.

The door was slightly cracked open. The way it was when she and Jennifer went to bed hours ago. Angela sat up and looked around the darkened bedroom. She turned to look at the alarm clock on the nightstand next to Jennifer's side of the bed. It read 3:02 a.m. Angela looked down at Jennifer. Her body was under the bedsheets, her face covered by a pillow. Angela nudged Jennifer to wake up, but she didn't respond.

"Jenn," Angela said. Slowly, Jennifer pushed the pillow away from her face until her eyes connected with Angela's. Tears soaked the side of the pillow that pressed up against her face.

"Oh my gosh, Jenn. What's wrong? Did you have a bad dream?" Angela asked, concerned for her friend.

Jennifer sobbed in bed. Her tears were filled with fear and worry. She hadn't cried that hard in quite some time. She clutched the bed sheets close to her chest in a tight grip.

"I did. I did Angie, I just need a minute to think," Jennifer replied.

"Do you want to talk about it?" Angela asked.

"No. I just want to lie here for a moment and think."

Angela placed her hand on Jennifer's tense hands. "You're safe, Jenn. You're okay. It was just a dream. Nothing bad is going to happen."

Jennifer pushed the covers off her body. She looked over at the alarm clock on the bedstand by her side of the bed that read 3:06 a.m.

"I need to get up and grab a glass of water," Jennifer said as she swung her legs out of the bed and stood on the soft carpet.

"I'll come with you," Angela said.

She too swung the covers off her body and got out of bed. The girls both walked to the kitchen. Once there, Jennifer got a glass from the cupboard for Angela and herself and filled their cups with cold water from the faucet. They both drank in the kitchen. All was quiet in the apartment again.

"Jenn, tell me what happened," Angela said.

"I don't know, Angie. I had another dream, and it had those creatures in it. Then a bigger creature. It was like the size of a large man, but it looked like a bull. They had broken into the apartment, and I tried to wake you up, but you wouldn't wake up. I had the creatures locked outside the bedroom door and when they finally broke through the bedroom door I woke up, and I cried, because I was afraid. I don't know what's real or what's not anymore. I don't know if I'd be dead if those creatures got me in my dreams."

Angela stood next to the kitchen counter and listened to Jennifer tell her story of what she had experienced in her dream. The way Jennifer described the large man that looked like he was a bull seemed eerily similar to what she had seen on the third floor of her office building, earlier in the day. Angela never told her about the large creature. Maybe it was because she didn't want Jennifer to worry more than she already was, but she didn't want to give the creature the satisfaction that it was getting from her and her friend. Maybe it was because Angela was getting used to such supernatural things happening to her, too. Jennifer set her glass of water down on the counter. She turned to look at Angela.

"Angie, what if these creatures are coming after me, too? You're getting help later today, but do I need help now too? They were here!" Jennifer said.

"No, you've been having dreams, Jenn." Angela hugged Jennifer in the kitchen. "All you've been doing is having dreams. They aren't real. What's been happening to me is real. The damn well in the back behind my backyard fence line, and the small creatures I caught on the security video. That's real, Jenn. Sweetheart, you have nothing to worry about. And after today, I'm going to have nothing to worry about too."

Angela let Jennifer go. Jennifer took a step back; she grabbed her glass and took a drink of water.

"I hope you're right, Angie. We never asked for this to happen, but it's going to control our lives until something is done about it."

"And something will be done about it, Jenn. You just got to have faith that it's going to be okay." Angela smiled, trying to encourage her friend.

"And what if it doesn't work?" Jennifer asked. "What if the minister can't stop it? What happens then? We spend the rest of our lives in fear of being attacked by these creatures and being afraid of them? I don't want to live my life in constant daily fear, Angie. I know you don't want to either. I just hope that this ends tomorrow."

"It will. It will end tomorrow. I have faith it will end tomorrow."

Jennifer finished the glass of water and set it down in the sink. Angela walked to the front door and checked to ensure it was locked. Jennifer walked to the front door too, watching Angela check the front door. Angela turned and walked back to the bedroom, while Jennifer stood looking at the front door. A small light shined through the peephole, Jennifer walked up to the door and leaned into it. She wasn't sure of what she was going to see, but she brought her eye up towards the small glass opening and looked out.

A brightly lit breezeway was all that she saw, along with a neighbor's front door that had apartment number A305 on the outside of the door. There was nothing there. No small yellow eyed creatures with long arms, claws and pointed teeth. No large man that looked like a bull. Everything looked normal.

Jennifer breathed a sigh of relief and backed away from the door. Checking the front door herself just to make sure it was locked, Jennifer was satisfied with its security and went back to the bedroom, where Angela had crawled back into bed, waiting for her to come back. Jennifer walked into the bedroom and shut the bedroom door.

"Angie, I love you. And no matter how hard things get, how difficult things get, I will be there for you," Jennifer said.

"I know, Jenn. I love you too." Angela smiled.

Jenn walked to her side of the bed and crawled in. Pulling the covers over the top of her body, her exhaustion got the best of her and she fell asleep. Angela lay there on her side of the bed. Her mind wandered to the thoughts of what would happen if the minister failed to exorcise the creatures. That would truly be the worst-case scenario for her. What would she do? Could she really live the rest of her life, haunted by this beast and its creatures? What would happen to her friend Jenn if the minister wasn't successful? One day, would they both become these smaller creatures and a part of whatever this beast was for all of eternity? Angela tried her best not to think about it. She rolled over, facing the window. Slowly, she shut her eyes and eventually fell into a deep slumber.

The apartment was quiet for the rest of that night. There were no more sounds coming from anywhere in the apartment, other than the bedroom where both the girls snored in their slumber. The apartment was dark, but a faint light shone through the peephole. The light cast a soft yellow glow against the wall of the apartment that led to the corner of the kitchen. But in a moment, darkness drowned the light out. Through the peephole of the door, a red glowing eye peered through. The rumble of deep, heavy breathing was clearly audible from the other side of the door. In a moment, the eye was there, looking through the peephole, and then it was gone. Never to come back to Jenn's apartment again.

CHAPTER 21

Morning came soon enough, and the light of the morning sun shone brighter than any other day of the year. It was a Saturday morning at Jennifer's apartment. Both the girls lay in bed, resting comfortably. Light from the sun broke through the small creases in the blinds of the window, adjacent to where Angela was lying in bed. Light from the sun hit Angela in the face. It started from under her chin and worked its way up to her lips. The light was bright, but apart from being just bright, it was also warm. Sunlight from the warmer summer months in the Portland area.

Angela felt the warmth of the light on her chin and stirred in bed. Finally opening her eyes, she opened and closed them tightly, and then re-opened them again. She recognized she was in Jennifer's room still, but more importantly, she recognized that today was the day she planned to rid her home of the creatures that had haunted her the whole time she had been living there. They probably haunted it well before she was ever living there, she figured.

Angela brought her hands from under the covers and raised them over her head. She clenched her hands into tight fists and stretched as far as she could. After stretching, she took her clenched fists and rubbed her eyes. After rubbing her eyes, Angela looked over and saw Jennifer resting comfortably on her side, facing away from her towards the alarm clock. Angela leaned up a little to look over Jennifer's body. The alarm clock on Jennifer's bed stand read 7:57 a.m. It was the longest Angela had slept in quite some time. Angela went to lie back in bed, contemplating maybe going back to sleep, when suddenly Jennifer woke.

Jennifer squeaked out a faint whimper while she stretched her arms. Finally, Jennifer opened her eyes and looked over towards Angela. Angela smiled while looking back. Jenn returned the smile.

"Good morning, Angie," Jennifer said.

"Good morning, Jenn. How did you sleep last night?"

Jennifer sighed in bed, then stared straight up at the ceiling. "I slept alright after the nightmare. My God, it was so vivid, so real. I just thank God it wasn't real. I'm tired of this thing. I can't wait until it's taken care of later today. I know that minister is going to be able to beat it."

"Yeah, yeah, he will beat it," Angela said.

Angela thought about what would happen if the minster wasn't able to take care of the problem. My God. What would she do then? For sure, this creature and the smaller ones that followed it would get her. They might even go after Jennifer next, too. Angela wasn't so certain that the nightmare Jennifer had last night was a dream. There was always the chance that it was real. And if it was real, it meant the being was so powerful it always knew where she was. It had been incredible to see where the beast had shown up, as things progressively got worse. It truly had been following her, haunting her. Possibly waiting for Angela to let her guard down before it took her.

But the thing that scared Angela the most wasn't this creature or the smaller ones that followed. What scared her the most was failing, again. Setting out to accomplish a task. A mission. Then feeling the repercussions of failure again. She had felt that feeling before, in so many of life's circumstances. Failure scared Angela the most. If the minister didn't get the job done, then she would fail again and lose much more than just her pride.

Angela laid back in bed, her head squarely on the pillow, facing up towards the ceiling like Jennifer.

"Well, it's almost 8. I need to get some grocery shopping done today. Hey, you want to have a quick breakfast and then help me with some shopping? What time do you need to be at the church by?" Jennifer asked.

"Well, I need to call the minister sometime this afternoon when I'm ready. I can go to the store with you," Angela said.

"Great!" Jennifer said.

Jennifer threw the bed sheets back and swung her legs out of bed. She almost bounced into a prone position as she got up and walked to the bedroom door. Jenn opened the door and walked across the hallway towards the bathroom. Jenn walked in and shut the bathroom door behind her, while Angela laid in bed. Yes. Today was going to be the day Angela finally succeeded for herself.

Angela removed the covers from her body. She swung her hips to the side of the bed and her legs followed over the edge of the bed. She leaned up, sitting on the edge of the bed. Angela yawned while the warm light of the sun hit her in the face. Angela slowly stood up from the bed and walked over to the dresser drawer where she kept some personal clothes for overnight stays. The girls always planned to have an all-girl's night at one or the other's home, so they each kept clothing and some bathroom essentials over at the other's home to be prepared for those, spur of the moment all girl's nights.

Angela found a decent set of clothing in her part of the dresser drawer and laid it out on the bed. She heard the shower turn on in the bathroom, so while she waited for Jennifer to finish in the bathroom, Angela walked out to the living room. All was quiet. There were a couple thuds from the neighbor's apartment next door, but beyond that it was a quiet Saturday morning at Jenn's apartment.

Angela turned and walked into the kitchen. She grabbed the water glass she had set in the sink during the middle of the night and filled it with cool water. She stood at the sink and took a drink. As seconds ticked by, Angela's confidence grew stronger because she knew everything was going to be alright. She hadn't felt that way in quite some time. She had always lived in a state of constant fear and worry about what was watching her from the banister of the second floor, or what was going on in the spare bedroom next to her. Or the worst, what was happening at night behind that fence line in her backyard. But now, Angela had a sense of invincibility. A sense of confidence. She had the minister on her side. Angela set the glass of water down on the kitchen counter, turned and walked to the living room and picked up her purse. Rummaging through the pockets, she found her phone. She looked through her contact list and found the saved phone number for Reverend Marlin Teske. She hit the dial command and listened to the phone ring three times until an elderly man answered.

"Good morning," he said.

"Good morning, Pastor Teske. This is Angela."

"Are you still prepared to work together today and take care of the creature?"

"Yes!" Angela said with confidence. "I was thinking this afternoon. Say 4 p.m.?"

"That will be fine, my dear. I will be prepared. We will do this together."

"Thank you, Pastor."

"You're very welcome. I will see you here at the church at 4 p.m."

"Yes, I will have my friend drop me off and we can drive out together from the church."

"Sounds good, Angela. I will see you here at 4 p.m."

"Thank you, Pastor Teske. Goodbye."

"Goodbye, Angela. See you this afternoon."

With that, the old minister hung up the phone. Angela placed her phone back in her purse and set her purse back down on the coffee table. She turned just in time to see Jennifer coming down the hallway after her shower.

"Who was that?"

"I just called the minister. I need to be at his church this afternoon at 4 p.m."

"Okay, that shouldn't be a problem. I can drop you off down there if you would like?"

"No, it's okay Jenn. I'll drive down to his church and then he can follow me back to the house."

"Okay, that works. Well, the shower is free if you want to jump in. I'm going to make a quick breakfast. You want some pancakes, Angie?"

"Yeah, sure, that sounds good. You have any maple syrup?"

"Yeah, I do."

"Okay, pancakes sound good, then!"

Angela left the living room while Jenn started working in the kitchen. She walked to the bathroom. Walking into the bathroom, she shut the door behind her and grabbed a bath towel from the cabinet. She set the bath towel down on the closed toilet seat and stripped down to get in the shower. The warm water felt so good on her skin. Angela breathed a sigh of relief, happy that even the shower felt so refreshing and so normal to her again. She finished and turned the shower off. The bathroom was filled with steam, fogging up the mirror above the sink. Angela moved the shower curtains back and stepped out of the shower. She leaned over and grabbed the bath towel off the toilet seat and dried her face off. When she moved the towel from her face, Angela saw it. There was a message in the mirror, carved in the steam in the mirror.

The minister won't work, Angie. We'll be waiting for you.

Angela stood there, water dripping off her body, staring at the message. Angela was going to ask if it was Jenn playing a joke on her, but Angela knew it wasn't Jenn. Jennifer would not do something like that. Plus, she never heard the bathroom door open. Doubts crept back into Angela's mind as the letters in the message oozed water down the mirror from the bottoms of the letters. A sense of helplessness followed the feeling of doubt. Angela dried the rest of her body off, choosing to ignore the message in the mirror. Angela knew what it was, but she wasn't going to give it the benefit of the doubt. After drying off, Angela tied the towel around her chest and walked out of the bathroom, turning the lights off behind her. In the bathroom's darkness, a small pair of glowing red eyes slowly faded away.

Angela walked into the bedroom and got dressed. From the kitchen, she could hear Jennifer yelling for her.

"Angie! Pancakes are ready," Jennifer said.

"Okay!" Angela shouted from the bathroom. She threw her shirt on, followed by her jeans. She quickly buttoned her jeans on and walked out of the bedroom to the kitchen.

"I didn't burn them this time either, Angie."

"Well, look at that. Even a blind squirrel can find an acorn, Jenn," Angela replied with a forced smile.

Jennifer laughed while she grabbed the syrup from the pantry.

"Here's the maple syrup too," Jennifer said as she passed it over.

"Mm, thank you," Angela said, with a mouthful of pancake. She had forgotten she even asked for syrup to begin with.

"So, what store do you need to go to today, Jenn?"

"Well, I need to go grocery shopping. As you know, I like to make scrambled eggs and sausage with my pancakes, but as you see, they aren't present with our meal this morning. So, grocery shopping is at the top of my list and if we have more time, maybe we could do a little clothes shopping. I need to go get a new bra today."

"Sounds fun. I'll just ride with you. Then when we get back, I can just take off and go see the minister at the church.

"Okay, sounds like a plan to me."

The girls finished their pancakes and cleaned up the dishes. Jennifer cleaned up the mess she had made cooking. Angela was in the process of throwing away the rest of the pancakes they didn't eat when she saw burned pancakes in the top of the garbage can. She knew she had smelled burnt food earlier, but she didn't say anything. Jennifer was proud that she had cooked a set of pancakes that weren't burned for once. Jenn walked back to her bedroom while Angela grabbed her purse from the couch. Checking to see that her phone was in it, she was ready to go. Jennifer came out of the bedroom with her purse.

"Okay, are you ready, Angie?"

"Yup, ready to go," Angela replied.

Both girls walked out of the apartment, and Jennifer locked the door behind her. They walked down the stairs and Jennifer talked the whole time talked about taking a weekend trip to the Oregon Coast to enjoy some beach activities in the summer. They made it to the ground floor and walked over to Jennifer's car.

"Jenn."

"Yes, I know. Don't speed," Jennifer replied.

"You're right. Don't speed."

The girls got into Jennifer's car. Jennifer started her car up and stepped firmly on the gas, pulling out of the parking space in the lot with a squeal.

"I said don't speed!"

"This isn't speeding!"

"So, what grocery store do you shop at?" Angela asked.

"I like to go to Safeway, over on Jefferson St. They always seem to have the freshest produce."

"Sounds good. I can't remember the last time I was in that Safeway."

Jennifer drove down the road until she got to Jefferson St. She cut hard enough to the left to make Angie think she was about to flip the car as they drove down Jefferson St. and finally turned into the parking lot. Both girls got out of the car when Jennifer parked it.

"Jenn, honey, every time I go anywhere with you, I always thank God that I made it there alive."

Jennifer laughed as they walked into the store. Jennifer grabbed a shopping cart, and both girls set their purses down in the child seat of the cart. Angela strapped their purses in with the child seatbelt of the cart. They both began by perusing through the produce department.

"Angie, look at these pineapples. Look how fresh they look. I don't think I've ever asked if you like pineapple?"

"I do like pineapple. I'll eat pineapple in almost everything. Turnover cake, fruit smoothies, or just by itself," Angela replied.

"Is there any fruit you don't like?"

"Yeah, I'm not a big fan of coconut. The milk flavor tasted weird, and the texture of the coconut meat is strange to me."

"Jeez, well, I hope you never get stranded on a deserted island, ever."

"Well, if it was a deserted island with pineapple, I would be fine."

The girls both laughed again. Angela felt normal again. The thought of the message in the mirror this morning completely faded from her memory. When Angela finished laughing, she looked up and saw a man standing by the deli. The man was looking right at her. He was a middle-aged man, bald, and tall. Angela guessed he was well over 6 feet tall. There was a blank expression on his face. He wore black jeans, with a black shirt and a black sweater jacket. At first Angela wondered if she knew the man from somewhere before, but she couldn't remember. Thinking nothing of it, Angela turned her attention back to Jennifer.

"Okay, now I got strawberries, pineapple, blueberries, and bananas. I need some vegetables now. I need bell peppers, broccoli, carrots, jalapenos, and an onion,"

Angela hunted down some produce, looking for the carrots and jalapenos, while Jennifer looked for the bell peppers, broccoli, and an onion. When Angela found the jalapenos, she grabbed four and bagged them up. While she was bagging them up, she looked up again and the man that was staring at her had moved. He moved to the end of the produce aisle but looked directly at her from around the corner of the aisle.

"This is creepy," Angela said to herself. But she tried not to think much of it, ignoring the man.

Maybe the man was just looking around the produce section of the store and it looked like he was looking at her. Angela's mind was jumping to conclusions before they were even a reality. Nevertheless, Angela finished bagging her peppers. She walked away and back towards the shopping cart that Jennifer was pushing.

"Oh good, you found the jalapenos. And they look fresh too!" Jennifer said.

"Oh yes, I did. Did you find the other vegetables?" Angela asked.

"I did. Now I need some toilet paper. I was running low when I checked this morning. Then I need to get some nail polish too. I'm almost out of that purple color I like to wear at work."

The girls walked on with their cart, out of the produce aisle and into the store. Angela sensed she was being followed but didn't want to turn around to find out. What if she would have seen the man in the produce section following her? What would she have done? She was in public, and Jennifer was right here. Nothing bad would happen so long as she was in a busy area.

"Down here. This is where the nail polish is," Jennifer said, turning the cart to walk nearly towards the opposite end of the aisle.

Angela followed her. Stopping by the nail polish, Jennifer began flipping through bottles. She found her purple color, shook the small bottle, and looked at it. Angela looked at the various colors of orange, red, yellow, but then turned to look behind them. She saw the man, again, dressed in all black at the end of the aisle from where they had just come, staring at her with that neutral expression on his face.

"Jenn," Angela whispered.

"Yeah?"

"Do you see that man at the end of the aisle staring at us? He's been following us ever since we were in the produce section of the store."

"What man?" Jennifer asked.

Angela turned to see the man still standing at the end of the aisle, watching them both.

"That man there. Dressed in all black. The bald man."

"Angie, there's no one there."

"Jenn, he's standing right there in the middle of the aisle. How can you not see him?"

"Because I don't see anyone there. There's no one in this aisle, well, except that lady that just walked into the aisle."

True, Angela also saw the woman pushing a stroller with a baby in the seat into the aisle, but Angela could also still see the bald man in black staring at her. Jennifer couldn't see him. Angela began to breathe heavily. If Jennifer couldn't see this man, then what was this man? Angela did her best to play it off.

"Well, maybe I was just seeing things then," Angela said.

"You okay, Angie?"

"Yeah, I'm fine. Did you find your nail polish?" Angela asked, changing the subject.

"Oh. Yes, I did. This is the purple coloring that I use for work. I like it. It's a nice color. Subtle, but stands out, ya know?"

Jennifer put the nail polish in the cart and began walking on. Angela turned while they left the aisle, only to see the bald man in black still at the end of the aisle, watching her.

"Now. Toilet paper, that's back this way."

Angela followed Jennifer to the aisle that had the toilet paper. Jennifer turned her cart down the aisle and Angela followed. She looked up towards the far end of the aisle and again; she saw the man in black. He was motionless, staring at her as she walked closer and closer towards him. His face carried no expression to it. He was cold.

"Jenn, I think I'm going to go use the restroom. I'll be back in just a bit," Angela said.

"Okay, I'm going to get toilet paper here and some milk, and then I'm going to be finished, Angie."

"Okay, I'll meet you up at the front of the store, then."

"Sounds good. I'll see you there in a bit."

Angela left the aisle, without turning around to see the man in black. Angela walked up towards the front of the store where the bathrooms were located. She walked into the women's restroom. The bathroom was a decent size for the size of the store. The women's restroom had four stalls that were kept very clean.

Angela was alone in the restroom, so she found the furthest stall away from the door and entered it. Shutting and locking the door behind her, she sat down on the toilet seat and tried to control her breathing and anxiety. Who was this man that was everywhere in the store around her? Angela placed her hand flat on her chest, attempting to control her breathing while she lifted her head up and looked at the ceiling when she heard the bathroom door open.

Another woman, Angela thought. It was just another woman shopping in the store, coming to use the bathroom. The sounds of heavy thuds entered the bathroom like someone was wearing boots. Angela noticed the temperature in the bathroom drop and heard that the footsteps close in on her stall.

She tried to slow her breathing, but the sounds of her inhaling and exhaling were still too audible. When she looked down, she saw a large black boot with black jeans step in front of her stall door. Another large black boot swung around from behind the other and stepped towards the other side of the door. Angela knew that it was the man who had been following her. He was in the women's restroom, standing in front of her bathroom stall door. And the worst part about it all was that she was alone.

Angela could see her breath in the cold air every time she exhaled. A faint scratching started at the stall door. The sounds started low and then continued to get louder and louder. Angela saw the indentation form on her side as the scratching intensified. Angela panicked. She thought, what if she tried to crawl under the walls of the stalls towards the bathroom door? But would she make it? Angela heard a guttural growl. The bathroom light went out, and the scratching at the stall door continued to get louder and louder. The bathroom door swung open, and the light turned back on.

The scratching noise stopped, and the indentation on the door disappeared. All that remained were the two feet and legs of whatever was standing outside the stall door. Angela could hear a woman walk into the bathroom and turn the faucet on. Angela thought that if she was going to get out, it had to be now, while someone else was in the bathroom with her. Boldly Angela stood up from the toilet seat and opened the door to see a woman washing her hands at the sink. Angela dared not look around the stall door towards whatever was standing there. She simply pretended that it didn't exist, while she walked out of the bathroom, leaving the woman in the room alone with whatever that thing was.

Angela walked towards the cash register where she found Jennifer paying for her groceries.

"Angie. Good timing. You, okay?" Jennifer asked.

"Yes, fine. Just had to go." Angela laughed nervously.

"Alright then. What time do we need to get you to the church by again?"

"4 p.m."

"Okay, we can stop by one more store, then we'll head back to my place, so you can pick up your car and get to the church. I don't want you to be late for a meeting with the minister."

Jenn and Angela walked towards the exit. Angela was careful not to look behind her, as she was afraid that she would see something she didn't want to see. Jennifer left the cart at the entrance of the store. They filled their arms with grocery bags and headed out into the parking lock. Together, they loaded Jennifer's car with groceries and got inside. While they were pulling out, Angela looked back towards the entrance of the store and saw the bald man in black again. He was standing at the entrance of the store, watching her.

Standing by the man's side was a woman with black hair, nearly half his height. She too was watching her, and Angela recognized the woman as the woman who was in the bathroom. Angela could see her face, with a wide inhuman smile. Her bright yellow eyes stared at her. Angela looked away as Jennifer pulled out of the parking lot and onto the street to driveway. She knew exactly what it was now.

*   *   *   *

From the grocery store, the girls went clothes shopping. Thank God Angela didn't feel like she was being stalked while shopping for clothes. Getting out and having fun with Jennifer after what happened at the grocery store helped relax her. She almost completely forgot about the man that was stalking her in the grocery store. The girls grabbed lunch at a quick fast food Mexican restaurant. They laughed while they watched people walking by the window outside, heading to the nearby outlet center to do some shopping. Afterwards, the girls finished up their clothing shopping at some small shops around the outlet mall. Angela got a few shirts that were on clearance and a nice pair of pants that fit just right.

Jennifer found herself a couple bras and a couple of button up blouses she could use for work, too. It was a successful day out shopping for both the girls, but the reality of what Angela had to do was slowly creeping into her mind. In her heart, she wished she could simply just sell the house and be rid of the abomination that the property contained, but it wasn't that simple anymore.

The creature and the beings that served it were following her in her everyday life. At work. At the store. Even in her friend's apartment. Angela looked down at the clock in Jennifer's car. Watching the minutes tick away, closer to 4 p.m. The clock in the car read 3:16 p.m. It was time to go back to Jennifer's apartment, get her car, and drive over to the church.

God, Angela wished she could just pretend the home never existed and pretend none of this was happening. Her nerves were getting the best of her. Fear caused her heart to pulse faster as they drove back to Jenn's apartment. Before she knew it, Jennifer was pulling into the parking lot of her apartment complex. It was time for Angela to leave and go to the church.

Angela did her best to stall by helping Jennifer take the groceries and shopping bags upstairs. Angela took the clothes she bought and dropped them off at Jennifer's apartment. She sat down on the couch in Jennifer's apartment, feeling frightened. Jennifer sat next to her, gave her a hug around the shoulders.

"You can do this," Jennifer said.

"I wish none of this ever existed."

"It does. It's not your fault that it does, though, but you can do this. This is your home now. This is your property. I don't care what happened there last week or a hundred years ago. You bought that property and it's yours now. I know you can do this," Jennifer said.

Angela sat on the couch, being held by Jennifer. They hugged tightly as Angela wasn't sure if it would be the last time she would ever see Jenn or not.

With a smile on her face, Angela said, "I'm going to go take back my house."

Jennifer stood up from the couch and walked Angela out to her car. Before getting in her car, Angela turned and hugged Jennifer.

"Thank you, for always being you. Jenn, you have always been there for me, and I couldn't ask for a better friend than you."

Jennifer said nothing, but hugged her back. Tears rolled down Jennifer's cheeks as she watched Angie get into her car. Starting the ignition to the car, Angela pulled out of the parking lot. She waved goodbye to Jennifer while pulling out of the parking lot and Jennifer waved back at her. It was 3:50 p.m and Angela was on her way to the church to meet with the pastor.

She was nervous, and she was kidding herself if she told herself she wasn't, but the excitement of finally taking care of the problem kept her feeling hopeful. Angela got a small taste of what a normal life would be like this afternoon over lunch, and she desperately wanted to reclaim that sense of normalcy. In her heart, after today, Angela knew she was going to get her life back. Her home would be normal again and the creatures that inhabit the land and the property and her home would be gone. She would never have to deal with them again. With confidence, Angela drove to the church, ready to reclaim her life back.

CHAPTER 22

Angela pulled her car into the parking lot of St. Marcus Lutheran Church at 4:02 p.m. There she found Pastor Teske's gold Cadillac. There were also other cars in the parking lot of the church, too. Angela parked her car near the church's entrance, near the pastor's gold Cadillac. Angela got out of her car and walked up to the church's front door. Opening it, she walked into the foyer of the church, where she could hear people singing inside. Walking into the sanctuary, she saw a group of people in the choir loft of the church singing while being led by a conductor.

Mr. Schwartz was playing at the organ of the church while the conductor of the choir led the group with his hands. There were 13 choir members in total. Five men and eight women. In the front row, an old man sat, watching the group as they practiced their melodies for the upcoming church services. Angela walked into the church and up to the pew the old man was sitting in. She entered the row and sat down next to him. The old man leaned over and gave a smile to her.

"Angela, it's so good to see you," Pastor Teske said.

"It's good to see you too, Pastor."

Both the pastor and Angela sat and watched the choir as they sang the lyrics to an old Lutheran hymn. Mr. Schwartz played the organ.

"You who dwell in the shelter of the Lord,

Who abide in his shadow for life,

Say to the Lord, 'My Refuge,

My Rock in whom I trust.'"

"I've always liked this song," the pastor said.

"What song is it?" Angela asked.

"This song is called On Eagle's Wings," the old minister replied. "When I was a young boy back in Wisconsin, my grandfather passed away, and every time I hear this song, I always think of him. This was his favorite song, and we sang it at his funeral, the last day I saw him before he was placed down in the ground."

Angela didn't say anything but simply just listened to the choir sing the song. It was beautiful and harmonious. After the choir finished singing the first stanza, the old minister stood up.

"Well Angela, I suppose we should get working on taking care of your home. Follow me, my dear," he said.

Angela stood up and followed the pastor back to his office while the choir continued to practice their song. The organ playing lightly in the background, careful not to drown out the singing of the choir. The pastor pushed open the door to his office and went in. Angela followed from behind.

"Let me gather a few things before we leave, Angela," the minister said.

"That's fine, whatever you need, pastor."

The old minister picked up an ancient copy of the Holy Bible, along with an old oil lamp.

"What is the lamp for, pastor?" Angela asked.

The pastor held and stroked the sides of the old brass lamp. It wasn't very large, maybe a foot in length at the most. Its brass was stained nearly green from the years it spent sitting on a bookshelf with no care given to it. While holding the lamp, the pastor looked up and replied, "The Kushtaka is a creature that hates fire. Fire is a destructive force in this world, and even in the world of The Kushtaka. The creature knows how destructive fire is, and because of that, it fears it. This old oil lamp is a lamp I have kept for many, many years, and I've come across many different times where I should have thrown this lamp out. It served no use. But now I can see that perhaps maybe there was a reason why I held onto this old oil lamp."

"Is there anything else that you will need, pastor? Do you need me to help you carry something?" Angela asked.

"No, I see that you are wearing your cross pendant." The pastor smiled. "That is good. Christ will protect you this day."

With that, the old minister put his hands on Angela's arms and said, "Follow my lead, I will speak, and all you have to do is follow me."

Angela nodded. The pastor picked up the old bible from his desk and said, "Lead the way, Angela."

Angela walked out of the office and through the church, followed by the pastor. The choir members were preparing to leave themselves. They were still huddled in the choir loft, gathering their coats and purses. Mr. Schwartz was preparing the list of music to play for the church service the next morning. Angela walked out of the sanctuary, through the foyer of the church and out the front doors. The pastor kept up with her pace.

"I have the little red car there. I'm going to 60 Suntides Blvd. just in case we get separated in traffic, pastor, but I'll drive slowly so I won't lose you."

The pastor waved his hand in acknowledgment and turned to walk towards his gold Cadillac. Angela got into her car. She began to panic, wishing how much she wished not to go back to her house. She knew, though, that this was her home, and was something that she needed to fight for. She needed to put forth an effort in taking back her home.

What was reassuring was that she had a pastor who knew what he was doing. He was prepared for this, and he could help get her rid her home of evil. Angela started her car and pulled out of the parking lot, followed by the pastor's gold Cadillac. She drove through town, missing nearly every red light while on her way back to her home on the other side of Portland. Angela could tell that she was back in the Happy Valley suburb of Portland, Oregon. Outside the city limits was where the small spring flowers called Johnny Jump-Ups grew only mere inches from the grass. The flowers were a bright yellow, surrounded by the bluest of blue colors, and they grew in the grass fields and home's lawns like an army. They were beautiful, and for whatever reason, they wouldn't grow anywhere else around in Portland, or any other suburb other than the Happy Valley area. Angela wasn't too far away from Suntides Blvd. Maybe only another mile. A quick drive around the block, a right turn, and then a half a block away would stand her haunted two-level home, with the well out back down by the creek.

The closer Angela got to her home, the more dread and fear crept into her heart and mind. She wanted to ignore it. Pretend it didn't exist. She wished she could go be roommates with Jennifer and still pay for the home and then try to sell it. Dump it off to whatever poor soul would buy it from her. But it wasn't that easy.

Before Angela knew it, she was driving down a long stretch of the residential neighborhood. She approached a street sign that read, "Suntides Blvd." She was here. Turning right onto Suntides Blvd., Angela drove another half a block down the road and pulled into the driveway of her home. The pastor followed in behind and parked his car along the side of the road in front of the home.

The old minister got out of his gold Cadillac and walked up to the house. Angela got out of her red car, shut the door, and looked at her home. It was quiet and dark inside. The blinds were closed, blocking out the windows. The flowers she had planted out front were dying as they craved water for life.

Marlin Teske walked up to the front door with Angela. She nervously unlocked the door and cracked it open. A blast of cold air rushed through the opening.

"I don't remember turning the air conditioner on," Angela said.

"My dear, more likely than not, that isn't air conditioning," the pastor replied.

Angela got behind him as he pushed the door open. Another rush of cold air blew into their faces, whipping Angela's hair back. Together, they entered the quiet home. The grandfather clock ticked away in the living room's corner. Angela shut the front door behind her and looked around the living room. Everything seemed to be in its proper place. Nothing was out of the ordinary. Even her favorite quilt her grandmother knitted for her was resting peacefully on the back of the recliner.

For the life of her, Angela couldn't remember if that was where she left it or if she left it upstairs. Nevertheless, it seemed safe. Angela looked towards the kitchen, which also appeared normal. She could see the glowing green numbers on the microwave tell the time of 4:34 p.m.

Angela stepped into the first level hallway towards an office room she hardly ever used for anything other than storage, as well as the laundry room with a door that led out to the backyard. The old minister looked around the living room himself. He paused for a moment to feel the room and what was going on around him.

"There certainly is something here, Angela," the minister said.

"Is it the creature?" Angela asked.

"I don't know, but I do know it is strong," he replied. "We should begin on the first floor."

Angela nodded her head in agreement. The minister walked into the first level hallway. He opened the door to the small office and walked in. A cold draft whistled through the office. The minister examined the wall and noticed a small hole, about a foot in diameter, a few inches off the ground. The minister bent over to examine

"Angela, what is this for?"

"Well, I was told that was for duct work. It was for the duct of an old heating and air conditioning unit the previous owners were going to put in, but they never got around to it. I ended up having to hire someone to put it in, and I guess they never used this hole," she said.

The minister handed the old lamp to Angela to hold as the minister retrieved a bottle of water from his robe's pocket. With the old bible in one hand, the minster walked around the room, shaking the bottle, sprinkling the floor with water. Angela watched as the minister blessed the room, reciting a passage from the bible.

"My people will live in peaceful dwelling places, in secure homes, in undisturbed places of rest."

Angela watched as the minister moved on from the small office to the laundry room in the hallway.

"The rain came down, the streams rose, and the winds blew and beat against the house; yet it did not fall, because it had its foundation on the rock."

He sprinkled water around the laundry room, repeating the passage three times. The minister moved back to the hallway, sprinkling more water as he went, continuing into the kitchen. He repeated another passage, sprinkling water on the countertops and around the dining room table. He blessed the windows with the sign of the cross, as well as the sliding glass door.

The minister finished blessing the kitchen and a bathroom before moving into the living room. He turned in circles, drizzling holy water throughout the room.

"Now be pleased to bless the house of your servant, that it may continue forever in your sight; for you, Sovereign Lord, have spoken, and with your blessing the house of your servant will be blessed forever." As soon as the minister finished reciting his passage, the wood moaned from upstairs.

The floorboards squeaked as if someone was walking around upstairs. Angela and the pastor's eyes shifted to the banister above them. Darkness shrouded the second floor, making it impossible to even see the white paint on the walls.

"We shall move on to the second level of the home," the minister said.

Angela nodded and followed the pastor up the staircase as he sprinkled more water in their wake. Together, they walked into the darkness on the second floor. Marlin Teske passed by the newel post and glanced down the hallway, but he couldn't see through the blanket of darkness.

The pastor looked to his left and tried to look down at the first level of the home, but couldn't see beyond the banister. He pressed on into the darkness, with Angela behind him.

She too couldn't see in front of her and held onto the pastor's robe so that she wouldn't get lost in the darkness. They continued down the hallway until the minister stopped outside of the spare bedroom's door. He opened the door, sprinkling water in front of him, and repeated the passage, "Unless the Lord builds the house, the builders labor in vain. Unless the Lord watches over the city, the guards stand watch in vain."

After blessing the room, the darkness vanished, and Angela could see the room clearly, spotting the clothing dresser in the room and the mirror above it. Though the room was still slightly dark without the lights on, it was no longer a pure black cloud of nothingness. Angela turned to look out the bedroom door back in the hallway. In the pitch-black darkness of the hallway, Angela saw two red eyes glowing from the corner of the door, watching her and the old minister. The eyes then slowly backed into the darkness, heading toward the staircase.

The minister finished blessing the room and then prepared to bless the rest of the second floor. Angela took hold of the minister's robe as he walked back out of the room, sprinkling water in front of him while he crossed the hallway into another bedroom. The room was covered in a blanket of black. Angela speculated that it was her bedroom from the path the minister walked. The pastor stood in the middle of the darkness and walked in circles, sprinkling water in front of him as he went.

Angela heard unholy whispering, and faint high-pitched voices talking in the darkness. While sprinkling the water in the room, the minister repeated the passage, "Whoever dwells in the shelter of the Most High will rest in the shadow of the Almighty. I will say of the Lord, He is my refuge and my fortress, my God, in whom I trust."

Angela shut her eyes in the darkness, letting the words of the minister reverberate through her mind. She opened her eyes and noticed that the heavy darkness in the room had lifted. She recognized her room now. Her bed. The closet with her clothes in it. The windows with the blinds pulled down.

The minister blessed each window in the room, as well as the master bathroom, repeating the passage and sprinkling holy water. The veil of darkness lifted, and the minster walked back out into the bedroom and looked at the door. Two small glowing yellow eyes watched him in the corner of the door, lurking in the darkness. When the minister saw the small yellow eyes, they quickly disappeared to the right, back down the hallway of the second level.

"We need to continue on, Angela," he said.

"There's only one room left, pastor," Angela whispered.

"Where is it?"

"Here on the second level. It's the other spare bedroom, next door to my bedroom."

"Then let's go."

Angela grabbed hold of the minister's robe from behind again as the old man ventured out into the darkness of the hallway. He sprinkled the water in front of him as he walked. There was a cold draft the pastor could clearly feel now. A faint wind blew stronger and stronger the closer he walked towards the spare bedroom. He must have walked right by it in the darkness because he never saw a door there looming in the hallway. Finally, the pastor reached the door in the darkness. Cold air blew from a crack beneath the door. The bottom of the pastor's robe faintly flapped in the icy breeze coming from an unknown source in the room. Angela stood behind the pastor, listening to the faint whistling of the cold air and the voices behind the door.

"I hear them," Angela whispered.

"Hear who?" the minister asked.

"Them. Their voices. They call to me," she said.

"What do they say?"

"I can't tell. I hear them whispering for me to come, but I don't know what they are saying."

The pastor placed a sign of the cross on the bedroom door before walking in. As he placed his index finger on the door and began the sign of the cross, a chill ran through his body. His hand froze, feeling as if he had just touched a solid block of ice. He knew whatever was terrorizing Angela had nowhere else to hide but this room. Slowly, the pastor grabbed the doorknob. It was ice cold to the touch. The pastor pulled away from the door, wrapped his hand in his robe, using it as a barrier between his skin to grab the doorknob.

The pastor turned the knob, and the door creaked under the pressure. Finally, the latch released the door from the frame as it slowly creaked open. A blast of cold air rushed out from the room, enveloping Angela and the minister. They could see their breath in the air as they enter the room.

Pastor Marlin Teske sprinkled water from his bottle in front of him. The room was too dark for the pastor to even see his own hand in front of his face. Holy water turned into flakes of ice that struck the floor, making small clinking sounds every time the pastor shook the bottle in front of him. The pastor cleared his throat and recited a passage from the book of Psalms, but the passage had nothing to do with the home anymore.

The pastor sprinkled his water in front of him while walking in a circle in the center of the room, repeating the passage, "The Lord is my shepherd; I shall not want. He makes me lie down in green pastures: he leadeth me beside the still waters. He restoreth my soul: he leadeth me in the paths of righteousness for his name's sake. Yea, though I walk through the valley of the shadow of death, I will fear no evil: for thou art with me; thy rod and thy staff they comfort me. Thou preparest a table before me in the presence of my enemies: thou anoint my head with oil; my cup runs over. Surely goodness and mercy shall follow me all the days of my life: and I will dwell in the house of the Lord forever."

As the pastor finished the passage in the center of the room, he heard a voice from behind him. A familiar voice that he remembered from his childhood. It was a man's voice. Deep, broad, and commanding. He recognized the voice. It was his grandfather's. The voice called out to him from the darkness.

"Marlin," it said.

"Who is that?" Asked the old pastor.

"Marlin, it's your grandfather, Marlin. Why are you here?"

"I am here to serve the will of God. Who are you? Show yourself to me. I command you in the name of Christ, our Savior, show yourself to me," the minister demanded.

A dark shadow stepped out of the darkness. The minister was able to see it, but Angela couldn't. She stood alone in the darkness while the minister watched the dark shadow walk towards him.

"Who are you?" Marlin asked.

"You know who I am. I've told you, I am your grandfather, Marlin," the shadow replied.

"You are not. My grandfather has been dead for a great deal of time. To say that you are he is a lie," the minister replied with confidence.

"You are so certain of yourself. Tell me, grandson, where does your confidence come from?"

"It comes from Christ alone," Marlin said.

"Christ? Are you so certain about that? Perhaps a little of that confidence comes from your ability as a minister? You've walked through this house and vanquished evil all throughout the home. For years, men, women, children, they all have come to you for advice. They have come to you for help. Humans who submit themselves before the higher power. You are that higher power, Marlin. You don't need anyone to tell you anything more than that, and you certainly need no God to tell you what you already know. Marlin, you are so blind. You have led so many people to God, but in truth you have been leading them to yourself. You are God. You don't need the power or the help of something that doesn't exist. You simply need yourself. You do this all on your own."

The minister peered into the darkness and saw visions of his congregation. Visions of his church. The minister saw visions of the members of his congregation praising him. They sang songs for him. The minister saw visions of members of his church erecting a lifelike color statue, made in his likeness at the altar of the church. One by one, each member of the congregation kneeled, declaring their praise for the old pastor.

"Do you see, Marlin? You've have always been God. You've never needed a God because you have always been God. You can do this on your own."

In that moment, the vision that filled the eyes of the pastor disappeared. Darkness filled the room.

"You've made a mistake, creature," Marlin said.

The shadow in the dark grunted deeply.

"I am no God. I am simply a mortal man. To think that I am God brings a life like what is surrounding in this room. Emptiness and darkness. You will not deceive me, beast. Submit yourself to God. Resist the devil, and he will flee from you," the pastor said.

"Wasn't Christ also tempted by the beast in the desert for 40 days, Marlin? He never deceived Christ. Christ could have had everything. All the power in the world. All the kingdoms would bow down before him. All the riches, the fortunes, the love of all the people. Something that you have never had in your life, Marlin. Love from a family. You've devoted your whole life to God, and for what? You have no heirs. All you have is yourself. You are now old. Well beyond the years of being a father, of being a husband. You have squandered your life away, and for nothing," the shadow said.

The old minister laughed in the darkness, and said, "You contradict yourself, beast. For what profits a man if he gains the whole world and yet loses his own soul? There is a realm beyond this earth where paradise awaits those who hold to the faith of Christ as their savior. This woman, by my side, holds Christ as her savior. I, hold Christ as my savior. You will never win, beast. You will not deceive me. You are not my grandfather. You are simply a demon, and God will triumph over you."

"You're a fucking fool!" the shadow yelled in a malevolent tone of voice. "You will die in this home, along with this stupid bitch! You will forever serve me, and you will forever be in misery and hell with me because you're a fool! Here you stand to inherit the world, and you foolishly throw it all away, and for what? A God that neglected you and made your life lonely, filled with lost love and sadness? Here you stand to regain your youth, the opportunity for riches, for love, for fame and fortune. And you throw it all away. Oh yes, you will die, minister. You and this bitch!"

"Be gone, beast!" Marlin shouted. "You are not welcome in this home! You are not welcome in the life of this woman! You are not welcome in my life! In the name of God, in the name of Christ, you will leave this home!"

The room filled with a soft light emanating from the hallway. It was from the light of the living room downstairs. The room was still dark, but the cloud of pure darkness was no longer in the room. The minister looked around the room. He found a hole in the wall, nearly a foot in diameter. In the hole, he saw a face staring back at him with evil, red, glowing eyes. A deep grunting sound came from the hole as the face withdrew down a long, dark tunnel, disappearing into the darkness.

"Angela," the minister said.

Angela looked over at the pastor. She had heard nothing, nor saw what the minister had experienced moments ago.

"This isn't over yet. Where do you think this hole in the wall goes?"

Angela didn't know exactly where the duct led. Angela thought long and hard. She recalled the white stone she had thrown down the old well behind the fence line in her backyard and how it somehow ended up in the opening to the duct.

"Pastor. It leads to the well behind the fence in the backyard," Angela said.

"We must go there now."

Angela led the way out of the home and back downstairs with the old oil lamp in hand. The pastor followed her through the kitchen and out the backdoor. Angela ran through the backyard and the minister followed closely behind. The gate in the backyard was shut. She tried to open it, but the latch refused to budge.

"I don't understand why this lock isn't opening?"

"Look out, Angela," Marlin said.

Angela stepped out of the way as the minister poured what was left of holy water onto the lock. To her amazement, Angela watched as the lock melted and dripped to the ground with the water. The gate swung open. A strong wind blew through the opening of the gate, nearly knocking the pastor and Angela to the ground.

"Let's go!" the minister shouted. "Show me the well!"

Angela led the minister down the small dirt trail, nearly overgrown with tall grass, towards the old well in the back by the creek. They moved through the thick, overgrown brush and past the tall Aspen trees. The wind whipped and howled through the wooded expanse of untouched land.

Angela pushed her way through the thick brush while the minister followed behind. Finally, Angela stepped out into a clearing with the minister. It was the small woodland grove clearing with the old well at the center of it. The moment Angela and the minister stepped out into the clearing, the wind stopped and the birds ceased to chirp in the trees. Sound died in the clearing and an eerie silence fell upon the forest grove. The grove was covered in a cloud of darkness. Angela could barely see her hand in front of her own face. The minister caught his breath, leaned forward and whispered into Angela's ear.

"Angela. Whatever happens, remember to keep your faith in God close to your heart," he said. "Lead me to the well."

Angela took a few steps towards the old well in the center of the grove and stopped. She heard her name being called from within the well. Angela and the minister walked towards the well when

Angela heard a voice speak to her from her right. The voice was familiar to her, soft like a woman's voice. Angela looked to her right and saw her friend Jennifer.

"Hey, Angie," Jennifer said.

"Jenn. What are you doing here?"

"I was going to say the same thing, Angie. It was your house that was cursed, not this well. You shouldn't be here. It's too dangerous for you."

"Jenn, I must be here. If the pastor and I don't take care of this now, then I will live with this for the rest of my life. I must be here."

"No, you don't. You've always been stupid, Angela. You buying this home was stupid. You should never have divorced your husband because you can't live without someone there in your life. Most of all, I regret the day I ever became your friend."

"Angela," the voice said.

Angela watched as Jennifer took a step back and faded into the darkness of the grove. Angela turned around and saw a man standing behind her now. A man she hadn't seen in months. Her ex-husband, Todd.

"Angela, baby," Todd said.

"Todd? What the hell are you doing here?" Angela asked.

"I came back for you. I can't live without you, Angela. I love you."

"I, I love you too."

"Look, I'm sorry for what happened. I made a mistake. I want you back. I want to go back to the way things used to be. Do you remember our Christmases, baby? How we would spend our Saturday evenings watching movies, and snuggling up on the couch?"

"I do."

"I miss you."

"I miss you too, Todd. But it's over between us."

"No."

"Yes, Todd. It is. You made your decision and moved on. You slept with that college intern behind my back. It's over, Todd. You and I will never happen again, so long as I live."

"You're a stupid bitch, Angela. You always have been. Sex with that college intern was the best fuck of my life. She's something you could never be to me. You enjoy dying a lonely life, you old bitch."

Slowly, her ex-husband backed up into the darkness and disappeared into the shadows of the darkness.

"Angela?" another voice called out to her from behind. Angela recognized this voice from her past. It was her mother.

"Mom?"

"Yes sweetheart, it's your mom," she said, stepping out from the darkness and into the grove opening.

"Mom. What are you doing here? This isn't a place where you should be."

"Baby, I've always been there to support you through the toughest of times. Do you remember that time in high school when you didn't make the cheerleading squad? You were so heartbroken about that, but I was there to lift you back up and support you then. So why not now too?"

"I love you, mom."

"I love you, too."

"But you aren't real."

"What?"

"You aren't real. You're just in my imagination. There's no reason you should be here right now, as there was no reason for Todd to be here, and no reason for Jennifer to be here. You aren't real."

"You've always been a fucking disappointment, Angela. Starting off when you were born. I wanted to get rid of you. I was willing to abort you, but your stupid, dimwitted father had to have you around. Ever since you were born, you've been a disappointment to me and the whole family. If you died today, I wouldn't miss you one bit, and then your husband. Your perfect husband left you. What the hell is wrong with you? Didn't suck his dick right or something? You're pathetic, and you deserve to die alone, you little bitch."

Slowly Angela's mom backed into the darkness and disappeared, but her words lingered in the back of Angela's mind. Angela continued to walk towards the center of the grove where she believed the well was. The old oil lamp in her hand, and the minister following closely from behind.

"Angela," the minister said. "Let me light the lamp."

Angela held the old oil lamp out and the minister took a small book of matches out of his pocket. Lighting a match, he held it to the wick of the lamp and lit the lamp with fire. The light of the lamp shined bright through the darkness. Angela held it out in front of her and the minister as they continued to search for the well in the grove.

"Angela," the voice of an older woman said. The sound of the voice came from directly in front of her. Angela kept walking towards the sound of the voice, where she saw an old woman standing in front of her.

"Grandma?"

The old woman smiled as Angela walked closer. "Yes, dear. It's me."

"Grandma." Angela smiled. "What are you here for?"

"I've always been here, Angela. I've been living in this well for a long time now."

"What do you mean?"

"Angela, if you carry through with this, you will kill me. I will never be there for you ever again."

"Grandma, you died decades ago. When I was younger and in college."

"My physical body died, yes. Spiritually, I have never left your side, my dear. I have guided you from the most difficult times in your life and if you let that minister near this well, I will die and never be there by your side again."

"Grandma, I love you. In my heart, I've always known you were there, even when I was a little girl. I love the quilt that you made for me. It reminds me so much of you. But you are not real."

The old woman let out a faint growl.

"You shouldn't be here right now. Spiritually, you may very well follow me and be my guardian angel, but you, along with mom, Todd, and Jennifer. None of you are real. Neither of you should be here. You are just a part of my imagination."

The old woman's face sneered, growling at Angela. Her face contorted, forming an evil grin with flaring teeth. Angela watched as the old woman disappeared into the darkness. Her eyes glowed red as darkness engulfed the old woman. From where the old woman was standing, Angela could see the outline of the well. She had reached the well. She wondered if the minister had seen all the apparitions that she had seen in the darkness. The minister walked around Angela, stepping up to the well.

"Angela, hold the light of the lamp close to the well," Marlin said.

The minister leaned towards the old well. A cold draft blew up from within the well. Angela walked closer to the well, holding the lit lamp in her hand. The light of the flame flickered in the cold draft.

The minister set his bible down on the edge of the well, along with his bottle of water. He placed his hands on the edge of the well and a frigid chill ran through his body, coursing into his hands.

Angela leaned over the well and peered deep into the well. She shined the lamp's light at the edge of the well. She wasn't sure of what she could see, but there appeared to be a small light from deep within the well. The bright red light flickered out of the well. Angela couldn't tell what it was. The minister, with his hands placed on the well, looked over at Angela.

"It's here. In this well. In this darkness," the minister said.

Marlin picked up his bible, and the bottle of water. Taking a step back and clutching his bible in one hand and the bottle of water in the other.

"I know. I can feel it here," Angela said.

She looked back down into the well. The small red light appeared to be closer than it was before.

"Angela, bring the lamp here."

Angela turned and walked over to where the minister was standing. She angled the light onto his bible. The minister opened the bible up and read a passage from the book of James.

"Submit yourselves, then, to God. Resist the devil, and he will flee from you," Marlin said.

The minister moved on again to the book of Psalms, reciting the passage, "The Lord is my shepherd; I shall not want. He makes me lie down in green pastures: he leadeth me beside the still waters. He restoreth my soul: he leadeth me in the paths of righteousness for his name's sake. Yea, though I walk through the valley of the shadow of death, I will fear no evil: for thou art with me; thy rod and thy staff they comfort me. Thou preparest a table before me in the presence of my enemies: thou anoint my head with oil; my cup runs over. Surely goodness and mercy shall follow me all the days of my life: and I will dwell in the house of the Lord forever."

Angela looked up towards the well. A red glowing light rose from the well, along with a faint growling noise.

The minister repeated the passage. "Submit yourselves, then, to God. Resist the devil, and he will flee from you."

The minister moved on again to the book of Psalms, reciting the passage, "The Lord is my shepherd; I shall not want. He makes me to lie down in green pastures: he leadeth me beside the still waters. He restoreth my soul: he leadeth me in the paths of righteousness for his name's sake. Yea, though I walk through the valley of the shadow of death, I will fear no evil: for thou art with me; thy rod and thy staff they comfort me. Thou preparest a table before me in the presence of my enemies: thou anoint my head with oil; my cup runs over. Surely goodness and mercy shall follow me all the days of my life: and I will dwell in the house of the Lord forever."

Angela watched the well, her eyes wide and waiting to see what would come from within the depths of the well. She watched the red-light glow brightly from near the top of the well. A deep, growling voice cursed the minister. Angela watched in fear as a large hand with claws reached out of the well, scraping against the stone. The minister now rebuked the beast as it climbed out.

"You are not welcome on these lands anymore! You are not welcome here!" Marlin yelled.

The beast in the well, now dragging a second large hand with claws out and grasping the other side of the well's ledge.

"In the name of Christ Jesus, and in the name of the Hebrew God of the Heavens and the Earth, I cast you back from the hell you were summoned from years ago! You have no purpose here on this earth! You don't belong here! In the name of Christ, leave this land! Never return!" the minster screamed.

Angela watched as the beast lifted its head up from the well. It stared at her with large horns protruding from the side of its head, its eyes glowing red with the fires of hell. Angela shut her eyes. The minster continued to repeat passages from the bible and rebuke the beast coming out of the well. The beast continued to drag its body from the well.

Laughing at the minister, the beast said, "You will not win, preacher. You will die, and on this day your flesh will melt from your bones, and you will be with me in hell!"

"Begone, beast!" the minister rebuked the beast. "The power of God will forever triumph over you! You are not welcome here anymore; you will never be welcome here anymore! In the name of God and the name of his son Christ Jesus, go back to hell! Go back to where you have come from!"

In that moment, the beast changed and appeared to the minister as his grandfather. "But Marlin, you wouldn't send you grandfather back to hell now, would you?"

"Begone, king of liars, prince of deceit! Begone in the name of Christ! Begone in the name of God! Leave!"

Angela kept her eyes shut while she heard the most God-awful screaming coming from the well. A bright light illuminated the glow with a massive blast that rocked through the woods. Wind whipped and howled through the bushes and the trees, screeching throughout the grove. The trees creaked and crack under the supernatural that filled the forest grove.

Angela felt the wind whip around her body, hearing the weeping of lost souls swirl around her. She dared not to open her eyes. She sank down to her knees, dropping the oil lamp onto the ground. Angela curled up into a fetal position on the ground by the legs of the minister. She covered her face with her hands, hiding behind her palms.

Pure silence filled the grove.

Angela heard the faint chirping of birds in the distance. She lowered her hands from her face, careful not to open her eyes. Through her eyelids, Angela could see light. She could feel a calm breeze whisk across her skin. It was absent of ice and malice.

She finally opened her eyes slowly. Sunlight shone through the Aspen treetops in the grove. Angela turned to look at the minister, who was on both hands and knees, breathing heavily. Angela dropped to her knees and crawled over to the minister, placing her hand on his shoulder. The minister looked over towards Angela and whispered, "It is finished."

Angela smiled as the minister smiled back. She gave the old man a hug on the ground next to the well. She looked up at the old well and saw a stone covering the entrance.

"Pastor. Where did that large stone come from?"

"The well is sealed, for all eternity, Angela. The stone came from God and how it got there, I do not know. Know this, though, the well is sealed. It is over."

Angela stood up from the ground and locked arms with Marlin, helping him up. The minister stood in an upright, prone position. He was exhausted and tired. Angela bent over and picked up the old bible and began helping the pastor to leave the grove.

"Angela, wait."

"What is it, Pastor?"

"The lamp."

Angela turned and saw the lamp lying on the ground by the well. When she had dropped it, the light of the lamp went out.

"Take the lamp with us. It was the guiding, protecting light. It was the instrument God used as a light to light our way when all other lights went dark," Marlin said.

Angela let go of the minister for a moment, turned and walked back towards the well. She bent over and picked up the old oil lamp from off the ground. Angela turned with the oil lamp in hand and walked back to the minister. Together, they walked back to the house. Angela guided Marlin up the dirt trail back through the gate into the backyard.

She turned to the gate in the fence line and noticed the latch returned. She locked the gate, knowing it was the last time she'd have to do so. Finally, they walked back into the house. Once inside, the minister sat at the dining room table. Angela got a glass from the cupboard and filled it with water. Without saying a word, she set the glass of water down in front of the old minister along with the oil lamp.

"Angela," he said.

"Yes?"

"This oil lamp is important to you. This will forever be a guiding light for you in darkness. When the time is right, you will know when to use this lamp again, and until then, keep this lamp close to you. Always be prepared for the darkness, always be prepared to light your way."

Angela grabbed the lamp and stroked the side of it. Its old dirty brass worn from the years of use. The minister took his glass of water and drank.

Setting the glass down on the table, the minister looked at Angela and smiled. "My work is done here. It is time for me to go."

Angela understood and knew that the minister had done it. He helped her. After all that he had been through, he had earned time to rest. The old man got up from the dining room table and thanked Angela for the glass of water. He grabbed his bible and placed his bottle of water back into his pocket. Angela walked the old man to the front door. The home was brightly lit. Darkness no longer invaded Angela's home. She opened the door and a bright evening sunset light shone through the entryway of the front door. The pastor walked out of the home and turned back to Angela.

"Remember what I said about the lamp, Angela."

"I will. I will keep it in my home."

"You will know when the time comes to use its light again. Until then, keep it close. Always be prepared to light it."

With that, the minister turned and walked away, back towards the gold Cadillac parked along the edge of the street. Angela watched as the old man sat in his car, started it and pulled away. She waved goodbye to Marlin, thankful the man had saved her and her home from the evils that infested the property for years. Angela was so grateful.

She turned back into the home and shut the front door. Breathing in a sigh of comfort for the first time since the day she moved into the home, Angela felt comfort and peace. Excitement came upon her as she ran through the home, room by room, only finding peace and quiet. Finally, she ran upstairs to the spare bedroom.

Without fear, Angela swung the door wide open. The spare bedroom was filled with light. The cold air in the room was gone. A gentle peace came over the home. Angela left the spare bedroom and shut the door behind her. She walked back downstairs to the kitchen and back outside to her car. She just remembered that she had left her purse in her car when she and the minister first got to the home. Angela walked out to her car, grabbed her purse, and walked back inside. Setting her purse down on the dining room table, she grabbed her cell phone and called Jennifer to tell her the good news about her home. While she talked on the phone with Jennifer, Angela looked out the back window of the kitchen and saw that the gate in the fence line of the backyard was still shut and she was certain that she saw it was still locked.

Angela smiled and walked back to the living room. She hung up the phone with Jennifer and sat down in her recliner. Grabbing her grandmother's blanket from the headrest of the chair, she curled up in the blanket and, for the first time in a long time, relaxed in her own home. She glanced at the dining room table, gazing at the old oil lamp. The eternal light in darkness. She remembered the words of the old minister and how important that lamp was going to be to her.

"Always be prepared for the darkness, always be prepared to light your way."

The minister's words rang through her mind. Angela took her grandmother's blanket and swung it to the side of the chair. She got up and walked back to the dining room table, picking up the old oil lamp off the table. She rummaged through a kitchen drawer until she found a small box of matches.

She shut the drawer and took the matches and the old oil lamp and walked back into the living room. Looking for a place to keep the oil lamp, Angela saw a good place on her bookshelf next to the front door. Angela set the lamp down on the shelf at about eye level with her, along with the book of matches next to the lamp, listening to the advice of the old minister.

"He got rid of her problems, so he must have some idea of what he is talking about," Angela thought.

Angela went back to her recliner, reached down to the coffee table, and grabbed the remote control for the TV. Flipping the internet TV to a channel, Angela grabbed her blanket and relaxed watching a comedy show on the internet. Angela laughed and enjoyed her time in her home. Before she knew it, it was nearly 10 p.m. She shut the TV off and placed her grandmother's blanket on the back of the recliner. For the first time, she walked upstairs and past the spare bedroom without getting a sinister feeling. She almost opened the door to walk in and look for herself, but what was the point? Everything was back to normal again.

Angela continued to her bedroom, shutting the door behind her once she walked in. She got herself ready for bed, brushing her teeth and washing her face before she finally crawled under the covers in her bed. Angela fell asleep quickly. The peacefulness of her home lulled her to sleep. Angela was so grateful for what the minister did for her. She would never forget the man or all the help that he had given her. Perhaps she would go to church tomorrow morning too.

CHAPTER 23

Clang... Clang...

Angela rose from a deep slumber.

Clang... Clang...

She heard the wind blowing outside. She rubbed her eyes with the backs of her hands and looked over at the alarm clock on her bed stand.

The alarm clock read 3:02 a.m.

Clang... Clang...

"What is that?" Angela whispered.

She peeled off the covers and hopped out of bed. It sounded like the noise was coming from outside, but Angela couldn't certain. She walked over to the window and cracked the blinds. The gate in the fence line was open. It swayed in the breeze, striking against its post.

"Blown open in the wind, no less," Angela said.

She thought the clanking noise must have been the metal lock striking the metal latch when the door would slam against the fence. It was windy outside tonight. She could hear the wind beating against the side of her home too, with loud howls and thumps. Angela thought nothing more of the gate as she lowered the blinds and crawled back into bed, facing away from the alarm clock's red light.

Angela fell asleep again when another light dimly lit the room. She noticed the light from behind her eyelids and opened her eyes again. Sitting up in bed, Angela looked over to her dresser where the light seemed to be coming from. It was her laptop, sitting on top of the dresser. It was folded shut, but somehow the screen was operating, emitting a faint light from its side. Angela swung the covers off her body again and got back out of bed. She again looked at the alarm clock on the bedstand by her bed.

The alarm clock read 3:02 a.m.

That couldn't be right, she thought. At least a minute passed when she peered out the bedroom window. Angela turned and looked back at the laptop on the top of her dresser. It was still lit, still emitting a dim light on the top of the dresser. Angela walked up to the dresser and grabbed her laptop.

Instinctively, she took her laptop back to her bed and crawled in. Once she was sitting upright back in her bed, Angela flipped it open. The security video was filming. Whatever it was filming had already come and gone through.

She thought the wind must have blown some debris by the sensor on the camera. Or maybe the camera picked up a neighbor cat walking through her backyard.

Angela went into the camera's video archive and pulled up the recorded video for that night. She hit play and watched as the camera turned on around 3:02 a.m. All that she saw were a few leaves blowing by the sensor of the camera in the wind. Angela looked over at the alarm clock on the bedstand.

The time on the alarm clock still read 3:02 a.m.

"What the hell is wrong with this alarm clock?" Angela asked. But before she could check the alarm clock, the camera Angela was watching flashed briefly. The brief flash that drew her attention back to the laptop.

"What was that?"

Angela rewound the security video and hit play. What she saw in the security video frightened her to her core.

In a moment's flash, Angela watched a couple of leaves blow by the sensor on the camera, quickly followed by a small object that resembled a small human. It came quickly up from the bottom of the camera, a foot away from the lens. The small humanoid had bright yellow eyes and a balding head with pale gray skin. It smiled into the camera, showing an inhuman smile from ear to ear and revealing a row of sharp, pointed teeth. As quickly as it was there, it was gone. The laptop went dark. Its battery died. Darkness enveloped the room. Angela, breathing heavily, recognized what she saw in the video. She knew exactly what creature that was. Angela again looked over at the alarm clock on the bedstand.

The time read 3:02 a.m.

Impossible. It had to have been nearly 10 minutes since she first got up and looked at the alarm clock. How could a minute not have even passed?

Angela then heard a loud bang and a thumping noise that came from downstairs. It sounded as if someone had tripped and fallen on the first floor. Angela got up and quickly got dressed, throwing on a pair of jeans and a shirt. Her purse. Where was her purse? She thought for a moment and realized that it was downstairs, on the dining room table with her car keys inside.

Angela put on a pair of tennis shoes, tied them up quickly, and then got up and walked to the bedroom door. She placed the side of her head against the door, and she could hear the faint sounds of glass breaking from downstairs. Angela eased the door open, only to be greeted by total darkness.

It didn't work, Angela thought as she stepped into the hallway. She couldn't see far in front of her. She placed her hands on the wall and used it to guide her toward the staircase. More glass shattered downstairs. Angela peered over the banister down toward the living room. A faint blue light moved around the center of the living room.

Angela watched the light for a moment when the light suddenly stopped moving. It held perfectly still for a moment, and then it shot toward the staircase. Angela still couldn't see the source of the light. The darkness was too strong, but Angela knew that whatever the source of the light was, it wasn't good. The light came up the stairs, shaking the ground with heavy footsteps on the staircase.

Angela spun around and rushed back toward her bedroom. If she could get there, then perhaps she could break a window and crawl out that way. It would be a jump down to the ground, but it would be worth it to avoid whatever was causing this blue light.

Angela looked over her shoulder and saw the light was already on the second floor, closing in behind her. She rushed into her bedroom, slammed the door shut, and locked it. She dropped to the floor with her back against the door. The thumping footsteps drew closer to the bedroom. Finally, whatever the blue light was, reached the other side of her bedroom door.

Angela was breathing heavily against the door. The blue light shone underneath the door's crack. She tried to control her breathing, listening to the heavy wheeze of what sounded like a bull on the other side of the door. A faint tapping sound followed.

"Angela," a deep voice whispered from the other side.

Angela didn't reply to the voice. She remained motionless, careful not to make a sound.

"Angela," the deep voice said again. "I'm here for you. Did you think that fuckin minister could really stop me from getting what is due to me?"

Angela looked around the bedroom, desperate to find something to defend herself with. But there was nothing in her room that she could use as a weapon. The only choice she had was to go through the bedroom window and jump down to the first level of the home.

"Angela, why do you choose to ignore me? This has always been your destiny to be a part of me. Do you know what happened to the previous owners of the home? They all have tried doing what you did, but here I stand. I can't be stopped, and you will come home with me."

Angela knew that she would have to go out the bedroom window. It was her only chance. Angela carefully stepped away from the bedroom door and began walking quietly towards the window.

"Angela, you're really pissin' me off! Open this fuckin door and be with me!"

Angela heard scratching on the bedroom door. She quickened her pace to the window.

"Angela, open the door!" the creature yelled. Its scratching became frantic as it attempted to claw through the door. Angela hurried towards the bedroom window and pulled the blinds up and swung a window open. Angela looked out the window and saw the moonlight lit backyard. The backyard looked clear. She saw nothing in the yard other than well-manicured grass and the fence line.

As Angela tried to crawl out of the window, a large hand grabbed her leg and yanked her back into the bedroom, throwing her across the room with an immense force. The creature stood before her in the room. It had clawed its way through the bedroom door before Angela could get out through the window. Its bullish horns nearly scraped against the ceiling as the massive beast lingered over her.

Its massive hooves and hairy legs carried its muscular torso that was thicker than a tree's trunk. Its inhumanely long arms hung at its side with large hands and razor-sharp claws. Angela recognized the creature from the description in Marlin's book. It was The Kushtaka.

Angela rolled to the side and shoved herself off the ground. She sprinted past the splintered door, out into the hallway. The Kushtaka trailed behind her, calling for her by name as she blundered through the darkness.

"You didn't think the power of God could have stopped him, did you?"

Angela looked over to her right and saw the old minister, Marlin Teske, standing next to her in the hallway. Angela knew it couldn't be him. It was The Kushtaka, assimilating the form of the minster to deceive her.

"He's too strong, Angela. I knew that. That's why I left you alone here, to save myself. There's no stopping the creature. It is going to kill you, and there is nothing that I, nor God, can do about it," the illusion said.

"You're wrong," Angela said. "God can stop you, and he can conquer you."

"Then why is it that the creature is here with you right now? After all that you and the minister did to stop me, to rid me of this world, how am I still here then?" the minister asked as he transformed back into the creature before disappearing into the darkness.

Angela reached the corner of the banister and knew that she was at the top of the stairs. Angela looked down the staircase and saw many sets of glowing yellow eyes looking back up at her from the living room.

"They're beautiful, aren't they?" a voice said behind her.

Angela turned around and saw a young woman, in her early 20s, standing behind her. She had long blonde hair and blue eyes, skin smooth to that of a younger woman.

"Who are you? What do you want?" Angela asked.

"I've already taken what you've wanted. I took your husband for myself."

Angela knew that she was talking to a manifestation of the woman that persuaded her husband to leave her, but Angela knew that it really wasn't the woman. Certainly, it was the creature, again playing a mind trick to emotionally break her down.

"Didn't you hear me, Angela? I took your husband from you. He's an amazing fuck. Gives it to me hard whenever I want it too. I certainly make sure that I take care of his needs too, of course."

"You forget one thing, creature. I don't love that man anymore. There are more important things in life than just sex. Maybe someday you'll understand that too."

With that the creature went back into the darkness and disappeared, not before giving an inhuman frown of disapproval that perhaps he couldn't break Angela much how it had done to his past victims.

Angela turned and looked back down the staircase into the living room. The bright yellow eyes were gone, but Angela knew the creatures were still in the living room, waiting for her to come down. Rather than going downstairs and risk being grabbed by the smaller creatures, Angela walked back down the hallway, towards her bedroom. But Angela knew that The Kushtaka was nearby. It was possibly even waiting for her to walk into its arms in the darkness of her bedroom.

Angela felt her way along the hallway in the dark when she felt a doorknob. It was the doorknob to the spare bedroom. With no other choice, Angela grabbed the knob, turned it, and walked into the bedroom. She shut and locked the door behind her. The room was dark, but Angela could see the window in the room. Moonlight shined through, illuminating the bedroom.

Angela headed to the window when she heard a voice coming from the darkest corner of the room. A young woman stepped out of the corner, into the moonlight.

"Jennifer! What are you doing here?" Angela asked.

"Angie, I'm here to help you. I know those things are all downstairs and they are waiting for you," Jennifer said.

"I know. I'm going to go out the window of the bedroom. I don't have any other choice. Come with me."

"You mean you come with me."

"What did you say?" Angela asked.

"Come with me, Angie. Everything will be okay where we're going. It'll all make more sense once we get there, too," Jennifer said.

Angela realized she was talking to another manifestation created by The Kushtaka.

"Tell me, friend. Why should I come with you?" Angela asked.

"Because it's your only choice. Those creatures are all over the place. They will take you tonight, regardless of what you do to save yourself. Tonight, you will die. Why die so painfully when you can just walk willingly into the darkness with me?"

"So long as there is fight left in my heart and in my soul, I will never come with you. You will not have this life," Angela said. "I am stronger than you."

Angela walked towards the window, opened it, and looked out the window. Again, she could see nothing but a well-manicured lawn in the backyard. Angela turned to look back at Jennifer. The human shape of Jennifer she had come to know was all but gone. There was nothing in the room. Darkness engulfed the room. A bright blue light was shining into the room from under the crack of the bedroom door. Angela knew that The Kushtaka was coming into the spare bedroom. Where the small creatures in the living room were now, Angela did not know. They could be anywhere.

Angela braced herself and swung both legs out the second level window. She then leaned forward and jumped out the window, landing with a heavy thud on the ground in the grass. Pain shot through both her legs and into her right ankle. Angela moaned in pain, but she was still alive and struggling to walk with a bad limp. She sprained her ankle when she landed on the ground, but at least it didn't feel like anything was broken.

Angela realized she needed the keys to her car to get out alive. She thought maybe she could just walk off the property and leave, but how far could she get with a severely sprained ankle? The keys were in her purse on the dining room table. Angela examined the home through the sliding glass door. She still couldn't see any glowing eyes from the living room, and she thought she could faintly see her purse on the dining room table.

Angela tried opening the sliding glass door, and fortunately it opened. She crept back into the home and heard a loud thud upstairs. Fear gripped her as she stood frozen, listening to the footsteps from upstairs. She took a deep breath and ignored the footsteps as she walked over and grabbed her purse from the dining room table. Angela looked through her purse and found her car keys. She took the keys out and stuck them in her pants pocket when a thought came over Angela's mind. Something the old minister had told her yesterday evening. The old oil lamp. How the lamp would be a light in dark places for her. At that moment in the dining room, the minister's words rang clearly in her mind.

"This oil lamp is important to you. This will forever be a guiding light for you in darkness. When the time is right, you will know when to use this lamp again, and until then, keep this lamp close to you. Always be prepared for the darkness, always be prepared to light your way."

Angela knew it was a long shot to try to get the lamp from the kitchen. She would have to go through the living room to the bookshelf by the front door to get to the lamp. Angela set her purse down on the table and began walked towards the living room. She hid around the corner of the ground level hallway against the wall. She peered into the living room and saw nothing but darkness. No bright yellow glowing eyes or any sign of the Faes.

Angela walked out into the living room. Another loud thud came from upstairs, along with the floor creaking underneath the creature's heavy weight. Angela paused in the living room for a moment to listen. She heard voices behind her, although she couldn't make out what they were saying. She was too petrified to turn around, so she kept moving towards the bookshelf, getting closer and closer until she saw the bookshelf by the front door.

Angela felt her way past the recliner in the living room, then towards the couch. A sharp pain shot through the back of her leg and into her calf. The pain at first burned, then felt wet running down her leg. The pain caused Angela to lose her balance and fall to the ground, where she found herself face to face with a brightly lit pair of yellow eyes. Angela felt another small hand with claws grab her by the leg and begin to drag her back into the living room. She kicked her way free from the small creature's grip and looked up to see another pair of yellow glowing eyes in the darkness.

Another claw grabbed Angela by her left arm, but she balled up her right hand and swung as hard as she could, striking the creature hard enough for it to release her. Angela crawled on her hands and knees towards the bookshelf. She reached the bookshelf when she could hear the loud footsteps of The Kushtaka up on the banister of the second level of the home. More clawed hands grabbed and scratched her. Angela reached the bookshelf and began pulled herself off the ground.

A set of claws scratched Angela across the face, causing deep cuts that instantly poured warm blood down her cheeks. Angela swung her arm in the direction the scratch came from, encountering one of the small creatures. The small creatures were all laughing around Angela as they grabbed and scratched her body. Angela finally reached out and grabbed the oil lamp. She grabbed the small box of matches from next to the oil lamp, while the creatures clawed at her legs. Angela opened the box, took a match, and struck it against the side of the matchbox. The match lit with a bright yellow flame and Angela lit the oil lamp. Instantly, the creatures stopped scratching at Angela. Light filled the room from the flickering wick of the oil lamp. Angela could see The Kushtaka from the top of the balcony, looking at her from the second floor. The creature cast an ominous shadow against the wall behind it.

"You put that fuckin lamp out, Angela," The Kushtaka said.

"I'll be damned I do."

"What do you think that lamp will do for you, Angela? You place your faith in an inanimate object?" the creature asked. "Do you finally realize that there is nothing that you can do to save yourself, so that you think this oil lamp will save you now?"

"You criticized me when I put my faith in God, my faith in the minister to get rid of you."

"And how did that work for you, Angela?" The Kushtaka asked. "Are we gone?"

The Kushtaka began walking towards the stairs of the home. The creature turned on the banister of the stairs and walked down. With each step, a loud thud rang throughout the home. Angela looked around the living room and saw dozens of the smaller creatures, all with bright yellow eyes, watching her. Angela stood by the front door and watched as the Kushtaka walked down the stairs towards the living room.

"Angela, it's time to come with me. Come with me to the well. It is finished," the creature growled.

"You're right, it is finished," Angela said. Knowing she had one option left, she remembered the words of pastor Teske while she visited with him in his office.

"The creature has an eternal fear of fire."

Angela took the oil lamp in both hands, releasing the lid of the lamp. The Kushtaka's eyes opened wide, releasing a high-pitched scream into the living room. Angela took the oil lamp and threw it at the creature. Oil splashed all around the carpet of the living room, all over the staircase, and most of all, onto The Kushtaka. The carpet caught on fire and the living room erupted into flames that swallowed the staircase and The Kushtaka.

The smaller creatures ran frantically through the living room, screaming and crying. Their small pale bodies melted into liquid under the flame's heat. The Kushtaka squirmed and writhed in pain and fear from the fire. Angela turned to run out the front door of the home but stopped and went back into the living room. She quickly grabbed the blanket her grandmother knitted for her when she was younger. Angela turned to run out the front door when she heard the Kushtaka.

"You stupid bitch!" the creature screamed. "It burns!"

"You will burn. Go back to hell where you came from!" Angela shouted.

The Kushtaka looked at Angela through the fires of the living room. The smaller creatures in the home, one by one, fell to the ground and completely melted away, dissolving into the fire. The Kushtaka bellowed a loud moan and growl. Fire engulfed the entire living room. The Kushtaka got up and ran towards Angela in its final attempt to grab her and drag her back into the uncontrollable blaze, but Angela ran out the front door, leaving the monster behind. Angela ran to her car when she heard wailing and crying coming from the street. Angela turned to look and saw Tom Butler, the old neighbor from across the street, but standing now in the street.

"Tom!" Angela yelled.

Tom stood in the street, staring at the home as it quickly engulfed in flames. He could hear the screaming of the creatures in the home, and the screaming of The Kushtaka. Tom then looked towards Angela and Angela saw his eyes. His eyes were brightly lit yellow orbs looking back at her. Angela knew now that Tom Butler was one of the creatures all along, too.

"What did you do to it, Angela!? It was beautiful!" Tom Yelled.

Angela got into her car while Tom ran towards her. Throwing her grandmother's blanket on the passenger seat, Angela stuck her keys in the ignition of her car as Tom reached the back of her vehicle. Angela threw the car into the reverse gear, slammed her foot on the gas pedal and ran Tom over in the driveway. Tom let out a high-pitched screech as the pressure of the car crushed him underneath its wheels. Angela then put her car into drive and peeled out into the street. Turning to look behind her, she saw the home where she was prepared to start her life over at in flames. It looked as if the fire had now made its way to the second level of the home. The fire reached high into the night sky and even down the block, she could hear the screaming of the small creatures and The Kushtaka as they burned inside.

Angela pulled out of Suntides Blvd without stopping at the end of the road. As she turned the corner of the road, the night sky behind her glowed in a bright orangish red color. Angela knew that it was now over, but at the highest cost. She was now homeless.

*   *   *   *

Angela drove down an old country road in the suburbs of Portland, Oregon. She had no destination to go and wasn't certain what to do now. The clock on her car radio read 4:21 a.m. It was still dark out. Angela thought maybe she should go to the hospital for her scratches, but what would she tell the nurses or the doctor? That small creatures had scratched and clawed her at home? Maybe she could go to the minister, but she didn't know where he lived. She thought maybe she could sleep in the church's parking lot, or maybe even go over to Jennifer's apartment. Angela found a 24-hour gas station that was open.

She pulled into the gas station and stopped in the parking lot near the road. It started to rain heavily in the area. Angela sat there for a moment and began crying into her hands. The reality of her home being gone now was overwhelming to her. She had lost everything. Her furniture, her possessions, her home, but most of all, her life. Of course, she didn't die in the home, but buying that home was a way for Angela to regain her life after her husband left her. To take back her independence as a strong, independent woman. All of that was gone now. She truly had nothing left. Once again, she had let someone down, but this time it was herself.

Angela sobbed into her hands when she heard a faint voice to her right.

"Angie," the voice said.

Angela wiped her eyes and her face with the backs of her hands and looked over at the passenger seat. Sitting in the passenger seat of her car was her grandmother, whom she hadn't seen since she was a teenager.

"It's alright, Angie."

Somehow Angela knew that it was alright. What she was looking at truly was her grandmother. She didn't sense a hint of malevolence.

"Angie, baby, I am so proud of you," she said.

"Grandma, I've lost everything. This has truly been a year of devastation. I've let you down in so many ways. I'm divorced grandma, I don't have any children. I have no home. I have nothing. Nothing but this car and your blanket. I'm so lost without you, Grandma. I wish you were here," Angela said.

"Angie, I've never left you. The day that I died, I stuck around, but I stuck around for you. I watched you from silent corners when you couldn't see me. I've seen the times you've been the happiest and the times you've been the saddest, but my dear, you have persevered. You're still alive today, and that is what is most important."

Angela sat motionless in her driver's seat.

"Angie, what you have in this world is irrelevant. Possessions are meaningless. What matters the most is what you do with the time that you have in this world. The lives you touch and the importance you serve. God has a purpose for everyone, my dear. Sometimes those purposes can be good or bad. The bottom line is that we all go through experiences that are both good and bad and we learn from them, and they make us stronger than we were before the experience. Angie baby, you have experienced something that no other woman has experienced and lived to talk about. There is a greater purpose in this world for you, Angela. There are others out there that experience similar fears that you have experienced before who need your help."

Angela looked up out into the street, watching the rain patter onto the pavement.

"Baby, I will always be proud of you. For everything that you've done in your life. But right now, there are people out there that need you. They need your leadership and your friendship."

"I wish you were still here, grandma. I could really use you in my life," Angela said.

Angela's grandmother smiled and said, "Sweetheart, it may feel like sometimes I'm not there, but I have always been there by your side, and will always be by your side until you come home to be with me and the rest of your family. I'm so proud of you. I love you, sweetheart."

"I love you too, Grandma."

Angela watched as her grandmother smiled back at her and slowly disappeared in front of her. Angela felt a new level of comfort knowing that her grandmother was there by her side and was going to be by her side for a long time to come. The advice of her grandmother gave her a newfound confidence in herself. Angela may have lost all her material possessions, but what she gained meant more than any possession. She had gained her independence. She stood up to something that no one had ever stood up to before, and she came out alive. She did it on her own.

Yes, the minister may have given her advice or help the day before, but that night she made a decision that affected her future and prepared her for a new life of independence. She still didn't know where she was going to go from here, but Angela knew she had become a strong, independent woman.

Angela smiled and put the car into gear. She turned the windshield wipers on and drove off out of the parking lot, back onto the road. She drove through town that night with a newfound sense of self-worth. When she finally reached Jennifer's apartment, it was a little after 5 a.m. Angela parked her car next to Jennifer's in the parking lot, got out, and went to Jennifer's apartment. Angela knocked on the door until Jennifer answered.

A groggy Jennifer opened the front door and invited Angela into her apartment and shut the door behind her. Angela knew that she could stay with Jennifer for a while until she got back on her feet. Perhaps this time she could just rent an apartment or buy a condo with the home insurance money that she was going to be receiving from the home fire. Maybe she would do things differently this time.

Or just maybe, she would do what she wanted to do this time without any fear.

EPILOGUE

"Mom! Cindy keeps licking her finger and touching me with it!" a young girl said from the backseat.

"Children, we are getting ready to move into a new house today. Can you please give it a rest for just today? Your mom and dad are both exhausted and we have a long way to go before we can stop today," the mom said from the front passenger seat.

A red minivan drove along the road in the suburbs of Portland, Oregon called Happy Valley, following a big yellow moving truck containing their property. A husband and father of two young girls sat in the driver's seat of the van, while his wife and the mother of his two daughters sat in the passenger seat. In the back, two young girls were both excited to see their new home in the suburbs, a place that was advertised in a local real estate guide as a two-level steal of a deal. The home came with three upstairs bedrooms and 2.5 bathrooms. A nice office area, or possibly a fourth bedroom downstairs next to the laundry room. There was also a spacious backyard at the back of the home, with a sliding glass door and a cement patio where the kids could go play outside. The family was very excited about their new home.

"I can't believe that we got this house for as cheap as we did," the husband said. "A two-level home, with minimum 3 bedrooms and 2.5 bathrooms, out in the Happy Valley suburbs. Jesus," the husband said, laughing and smiling.

"It seems like a dream come true," the wife said.

One of the young girls in the back spoke up and said, "Daddy! Do we get to pick what bedroom that we want?"

"Yes, baby. We will figure that out when we get there," the dad said.

"We should have stopped for lunch before coming out today. Once we unload the moving truck, I'm just going to want to get it all done at one time. You know me. I won't stop until all the work is done," the wife said.

"Babe, that's why we work out so well together. You know I'm the same way. In about 3 hours, I'd say we should be completely moved in, and it'll be around that time for dinner, anyway. Let's say we order a couple of pizzas and call that our dinner for tonight," the husband said.

"Pizza!" the girls screamed.

The husband laughed in the driver's seat. "Yup, pizza. Did I say the magic word?"

"We should get 3 pizzas!" the girls said.

"Oh, ya?" the wife asked. "Why three?"

"So, then we can have leftovers for tomorrow night, mom," the oldest said.

"You girls are pretty clever."

"Hey, we're almost at the house!" the husband said.

The husband turned the van with his family down Suntides Blvd.

"Okay... We are looking for house number... 60. Do you guys see 60 anywhere?"

The wife peered through the front windshield, shielding her eyes from the sunlight while she looked for the house number 60.

"There it is," she said.

The yellow moving van pulled into the driveway of 60 Suntides Blvd. Once the van came to a stop in the driveway, the two young girls jumped out of the van and ran around to the backyard with a small soccer ball. It was a well-manicured back yard; the grass was so green and lush on a warm summer day.

The husband got out of the driver's seat of the van, stretched, and yawned, looking at the home while he walked to the front of the van. The wife, in turn, got out and stretched as well. She walked up to the side of the husband as the two gazed at the shortly over 2200 square foot two level white colored house with forest green trim around the doors and windows. The wife also saw a chimney along the side of the home, where she imagined the living room had to be.

"What a beautiful home," the husband said.

"It really is. The pictures in the brochure don't do it justice," the wife said. "Look at the beautiful flowers planted here in the front yard."

"They are pretty."

The movers in the moving truck unloaded the big yellow truck and started moving their things into the home. The husband and wife watched the movers unloading the truck when they heard a voice from behind them.

"Well, howdie. How y'all folks do there?" the voice said from behind.

Both the husband and wife turned around to see an older man shuffling his feet across the road to meet them.

"Hello sir," the husband said.

"Oh, hello der. My name's Butler. Tom Butler. I gone done live right across the street dere in dat dere house over dere."

"Mr. Butler, it' a pleasure to meet you. This is my wife, Peggy. And my name is Andy. We have two young daughters, but they took off to the backyard already. They're both lively spirits," the husband said and laughed.

Mr. Butler laughed with them, "Oh, they be lively spirits den they be lively spirits indeed. Y'all are gonna love dis house, yes y'all will. Dis house is gonna love you too!"

In the backyard, the two young girls ran and chased each other in the grass, kicking the soccer ball around. One of the girls kicked the ball and watched it roll towards the fence in the backyard. The girl, however, did not realize that the gate in the fence line was open, and the soccer ball went through the open gate. The ball rolled down a dirt trail that led to the creek in the back, through the tall weeds and blades of grass.

The girls gave chase to the runaway ball, as it continued to roll and roll towards a thickly wooded grove. The ball came to a stop towards the end of the dirt trail. The girls could hear running water from the creek and kept walking down the trail. They both came into a clearing through the bushes and the wooded grove to see an old stone well in the middle of the clearing. The girls walked up towards the well, each holding each other's hands. They both placed their hands on the edge of the well, leaned over and peered deep into the darkness of the well.

One young girl glanced over at the other and said, "Cindy, stop breathing so hard. You're being too loud."

The other young girl looked back toward her sister and said, "I'm not the one breathing hard, Ashley."

Please feel free to leave a review on Goodreads by using the QR code listed below.

Made in the USA
Coppell, TX
28 February 2026

72589159R00150